By the same author:
Australian Melodrama, Eighty Years of Popular Theatre (1981)
Gentleman George, King of Melodrama (1980)
Sydney As It Might Have Been (1973)
Theatre Comes to Australia (1971)

Dictionary of the Australian Theatre 1788-1914

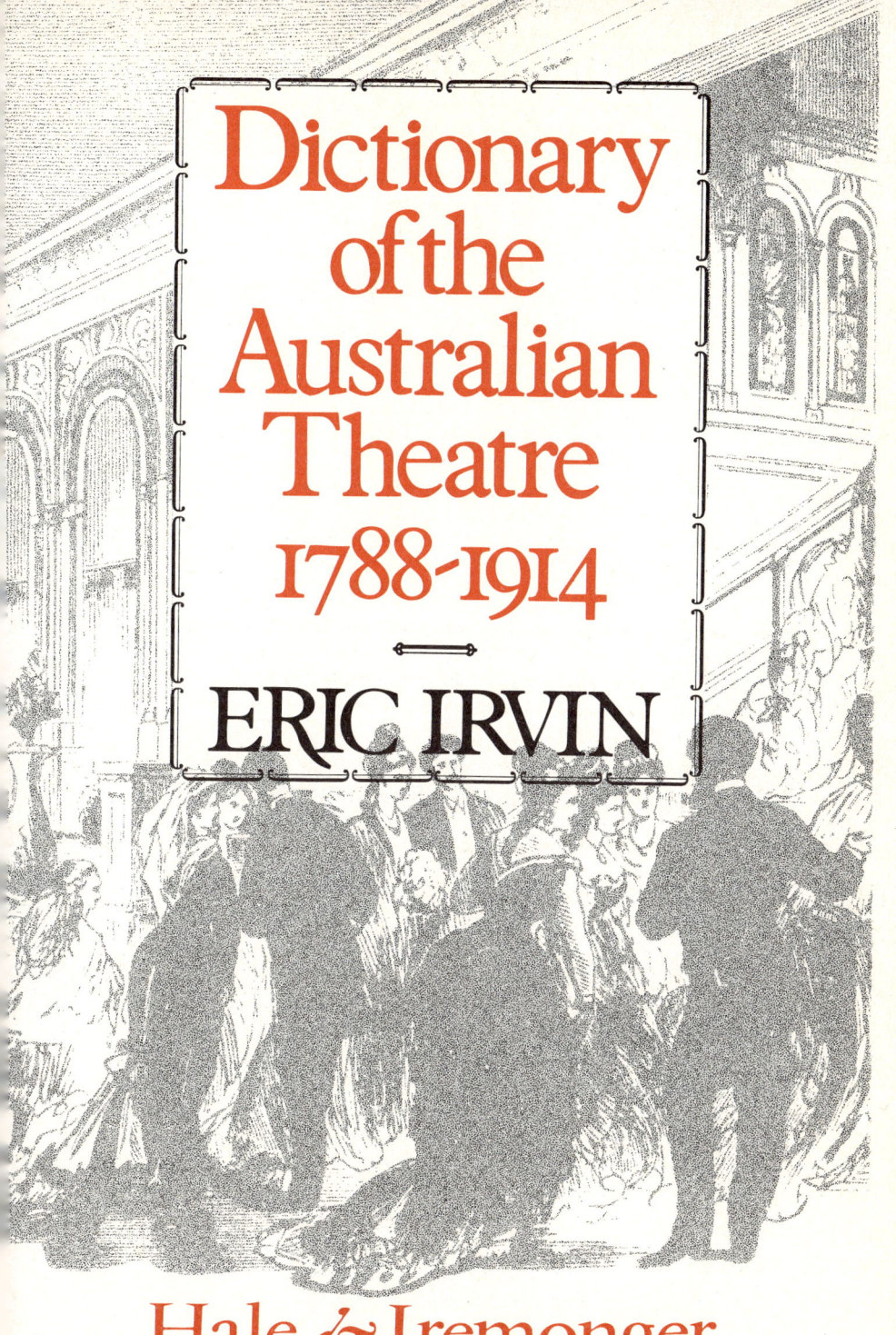

Dictionary of the Australian Theatre 1788-1914

ERIC IRVIN

Hale & Iremonger

Acknowledgements

My thanks are extended to the principals and staff of all the State Libraries in Australia, for permission to read the various colonial newspapers and magazines held in their collections, and also to the Mitchell Library and the Archives Office of NSW in Sydney, and the La Trobe Library in Melbourne.

Note

The secondary definition of the word 'dictionary' is 'book of reference on any subject with items arranged in alphabetical order.' In that sense the present work is a dictionary of the nineteenth century Australian theatre, which began at the end of the eighteenth and ended at the beginning of the twentieth century. Wherever possible, the word 'theatre' has been dropped from titles to save space, so that Globe, London means Globe Theatre, London; Royal means Theatre Royal, and so on.
The initial number of performances shown for each stage work does not include matinee performances. These, given once or twice a week, were often shortened versions of the evening performance.

© 1985 by Eric Irvin
This book is copyright. Apart from any fair dealing for the purposes of study, research, criticism, review, or as otherwise permitted under the Copyright Act, no part may be reproduced by any process without written permission. Inquiries should be made to the publisher.

Typeset, printed & bound by
Southwood Press Pty Limited
80-92 Chapel Street, Marrickville, NSW

For the publisher
Hale & Iremonger Pty Limited
GPO Box 2552, Sydney, NSW

National Library of Australia Card no. and
ISBN 0 86806 127 1

Published with the assistance of the
Literature Board of the Australia Council

Illustrations

Facade Lyceum Pitt Street Sydney 1891   *7*
Handwritten playbill for convict performance at Royal Victoria Norfolk Island 1840   *8*
Queen's Theatre Adelaide 1846   *15*
Exterior Adelaide Royal 1868   *15*
Hudson's Bijou Adelaide 1890s   *19*
Interior Adelaide Royal 1878   *19*
James R. Anderson   *27*
William Anderson 1910   *27*
Apron: typical small English provincial theatre c. 1820   *30*
Performance on board ship *Galatea* Sydney Harbour 1869   *30*
Sarah Bernhardt in her Paris studio 1890   *46*
Kyrle Bellew   *50*
Edwin Booth 1860s   *50*
Gustavus Vaughan Brooke   *50*
Billy Barlow sheet-music cover   *61*
Nellie Stewart as Camille 1905   *62*
Marcus Andrew Hislop Clarke   *80*
Anna Maria Quinn in *The Middy Ashore* 1855   *80*
General Sir Ralph Darling   *82*
Alfred Dampier   *82*
Charles Dillon as Othello   *88*
Poster for *The Double Event*   *94*
Convicts' theatre advertisement Emu Plains 1830   *99*
Scene from *Faust* Prince of Wales Sydney 1864   *100*
Scene from *La Fille de Madame Angot* Sydney Royal 1877   *100*
Playbill for *The Royal Masquer* (Geoghegan) 1845   *108*
John G. Griffiths as Iago 1854   *114*
Phillip W. Goatcher   *114*
H.M.S. Pinafore Sydney 1879   *120*
Joseph Bland Holt 1878   *123*
John Hennings 1881   *123*
Auditorium Hobart Royal 1862   *128*
Proscenium Hobart Royal 1862   *128*
Frank Howson in *Jenny Lind at Last* 1847   *137*
Punch cartoon of Coppin, Brooke, etc. 1855   *137*
Essie Jenyns 1883   *144*
John Stanley James 1882   *144*

Regentville, Sir John Jamison's country seat Penrith c. 1825 *148*
Laura Keene *150*
Mrs Charles Kean in *The Winter's Tale* *150*
Laura Keene 1854 *155*
Alice Lingard 1884 *156*
Samuel Lazar *156*
Nellie Stewart as Mam'zelle Nitouche 1894 *168*
Exterior Melbourne Royal 1855 *168*
Auditorium Melbourne Royal 1869 *178*
Exterior Melbourne Olympic 1855 *178*
Exterior Melbourne Royal 1872 *178*
Smoking room Her Majesty's Melbourne 1900 *180*
Crush-room (lounge) Her Majesty's Melbourne 1900 *180*
Auditorium Melbourne Princess's 1857 *184*
Exterior Melbourne Princess's 1857 *184*
Promenade saloon Academy of Music Melbourne 1876 *187*
Exterior Melbourne Haymarket 1862 *187*
Noted female impersonator J. F. Sheridan *195*
American female impersonator Francis Leon 1879 *195*
Auditorium Melbourne Academy of Music 1876 *204*
Interior Sydney Music Hall 1895 *204*
Scantily-clad chorus girls *208*
Dr J. E. Neild 1898 *211*
Poster for *The Naked Truth* 1883 *218*
Characters in *On Our Selection* 1912 *219*
Scene from *Othello* Sydney 1854 *219*
Pantomime transformation scene Melbourne Royal 1858 *220*
Children enjoying pantomime 1884 *220*
Exterior His Majesty's Perth 1904 *227*
Auditorium His Majesty's Perth 1904 *227*
Playbill for Levey's Saloon Sydney 1832 *236*
Scene from *Quite Colonial* 1854 *238*
George Rignold as Marc Antony 1889 *243*
George Fawcett Rowe 1863 *243*
Harry Rickards 1889 *246*
G. H. Rogers 1854 *246*
Sardanapalus London production 1834 *252*
Sardanapalus Melbourne production 1857 *252*
Built-up set for *Merchant of Venice* 1853 *257*
Set scene for *My Sweetheart* 1883 *257*
'Indian temple' stage boxes Palace Sydney 1896 *276*
Interior Prince of Wales Sydney 1855 *279*
Interior Royal Victoria Sydney 1874 *279*
Exterior Queen's Theatre Sydney 1882 *284*
Exterior Sydney Royal 1875 *284*

Exterior Victoria Hall Sydney 1881   *287*
Portion of Her Majesty's Sydney 1903 rebuilt after 1902 fire   *290*
Warehouse which housed Sydney Opera House 1882   *287*
Exterior Gaiety Sydney 1882   *290*
Exterior Criterion Sydney c. 1913   *294*
Interior Sydney Royal after 1892 fire   *299*
Stage trap   *304*
A *parallèle* used in transformation scene   *304*
'Hop' goes to *Thunderbolt* 1905   *308*
William John Wilson 1883   *318*
Garnet Walch   *318*
Nellie Stewart as Prince Charming 1901   *323*
Emma and Daniel Willmarth Waller   *326*
Drawing of proposed J. C. Williamson Memorial Theatre 1913   *326*

Facade Lyceum Pitt Street Sydney 1891

ROYAL VICTORIA THEATRE.

Norfolk Island

On Monday 25th May in honor of HER

MAJESTY'S BIRTH DAY,

Will be Performed by Permission
Two Acts of the Admired Comic Opera of the

CASTLE of ANDALUSIA.

Don Cæser	Jn° Lawrence	Sanguina	Jo° Cranston
Scipio	Geo° Rolfe	Rapino	Ja° Porter
Fernando	Ja° Walker	Calvette	Will'm Smith
Alphonsa	H° Wilton	Vasquez	R° Sanderson
Spado	Ja° King	Lorenza	Do
Pedrillo	Ja° Monds	With the usual Banditti	

After which a Musical Melange consisting of

Glee "Prithee Brothers speed to the Boat"	Wilton, Walker, Porter, Cranston, Sanderson, Smith	Song "Powder Monkey Peter"	J. Lawrence
Song "Old England for Ever"	H. Wilton	Song "Spirit of the Storm"	H. Wilton
Comic Song "Walker the twopenny Postman"	J. Monds	Song "The tight Irishman"	J. Porter
Song "Bound prentice to a Waterman"	J. Laurence	Glee "Some Love to Roam"	Wilton, Walker, Porter, Cranston, Sanderson, Smith
"The Fishermans Glee"	Wilton, Walker, Porter, Cranston, Sanderson, Smith	Song "The Old Commodore"	J. Laurence
Song "Paddy from Cork"	J. Walker	The Tent Scene in Richard 3rd	H. Wilton
Glee "Behold how Brightly"	Wilton, Walker, Porter, Cranston, Sanderson, Smith		

Naval Hornpipe — Mich° Burns. Dance Tyroleze Waltz — Tho° Barry

After which the Musical Entertainment of the

Purse or the Benevolent Tar

The Baron	J. Cranston	Will Steady	J. Laurence
Theodore	J. Ralph	Sally	J. Monds
Edmund	W. Yelverton	Page	J. Rae

After which

Paddy Carey in Character — J. Laurence   The Banner of War — J. Wilton

The Whole to conclude with the Grand National Anthem of GOD SAVE THE QUEEN.

Vivat Regina

Handwritten playbill for convict performance at Royal Victoria Norfolk Island 1840

A

Aborigines. The first mention of an Aboriginal in connection with the theatre occurred early in 1833, when it was reported in the *Sydney Herald* that 'a gentleman introduced an Aboriginal black to the theatre on Monday night.' The play being performed was W.T.Moncrieff's *Monsieur Tonson* (1821), one of those Frenchman/broken-English farces in which the English Mr Thompson becomes Monsieur Tonson. The Aboriginal was said to have been so delighted with what he saw 'that he threw himself on the floor and twisted his body into a thousand contortions in an agony of laughter.' Aborigines first appeared (always played by white men) in the drama in David Burn's *The Bushrangers* (1829), written, or partly written, it is assumed, in Australia. It was performed twice in Edinburgh, but never in Australia. This was followed in 1834 by Henry Melville's *The Bushrangers; or, Norwood Vale*. Both plays were set in Tasmania, and in both Aborigines were represented as less than human enemies of the white man, and were slaughtered unmercifully. Melville's play was produced in Hobart on 7.6.1834. The 'sympathetic' Aboriginal, in many respects more like Uncle Tom than an Australian native, first appeared in such plays as *The Bushranger; or, The Last Crime* (1854), and *The Australian Bunyips* (1857). By 1863, with the arrival of Charles Edwards's *Canowindra; or, The Darky Highwayman and the Settlers' Homesteads on the Abercrombie*, the Aboriginal had become the impersonator of the bushranger rather than his hunter. In their way all these representations of the Aboriginal were as far from reality as the Aborigines presented in Burns's play. But from the 1850s onwards, up to Randolph Bedford's *White Australia* (1909), Aborigines were usually represented in the drama as kindly, comical, helpful creatures who often saved or otherwise helped their paternalistic white masters in all kinds of misfortune. At times, especially if they were supposed to represent highly prized and useful black-trackers, they were allowed to return in kind what could be taken for insults or abuse heaped on them by their masters. But perhaps this abuse was meant to represent no more than the Australian habit of 'chiacking', or 'poking borak'.

Achurch, Janet (1864-1916). English actress notable for her performances in Ibsen's plays, and as a theatre manager. The first, in 1889, to mount matinee performances of intellectual drama in London. She produced and acted in the first Ibsen play performed in Australia. (See: *Doll's House, A*).

Act divisions. The use of act divisions in 18th and 19th century plays was derived from the drama of ancient Greece, specifically from the comedies of Aristophanes. In tragedy the usual practice was to divide the play into 5 main portions, broken by choral chants. When the choruses disappeared from these plays, the 5 divisions still remained. Horace advised the playwright to make his play of neither more nor less than 5 acts. In his book, *Play-Making* (1912) William Archer noted that 'both in theory and in practice, of late years, war has been declared in certain quarters against the division of a play into acts.' It was a practice he refused to condone, and in defence of the writer he quoted the *Oedipus*. He was writing, of course, as a man of his time, particularly when he stated his formula: 'Acts, then, mark the time-stages in the development of a given crisis; and each act ought to embody a minor crisis of its own, with a culmination and a temporary solution.'

Act drop. As its name implies, a painted cloth or drop lowered between acts to close in the proscenium opening. Usually the lowering of the act drop indicated intermission, the end of an act of the play, and also that a scene change of some kind was being made while it was lowered. The act drop was used because the front curtain was felt to have an air of finality about it once it was lowered, indicating the end of the play. Before the general adoption of the act drop changes of scenes were made in view of the audience, except for the occasional use of the front curtain. Increasingly elaborate scene changes made the use of a curtain or drop necessary. They became an ornate and artistic part of the 19th century theatre furnishings. Classical, architectural, costume, and landscape designs were among many used to create what were attractive examples of the scenepainter's art. In many instances these drops were also notable for the *trompe l'oeil* effect of the modelling of their painted drapery. Each time a theatre installed a new act drop it was greeted with applause by the audience. A call for the scenepainter to come on stage and take a bow usually followed. Such drops, and the scenic backdrops painted for the various plays, were the nearest things to easel paintings most members of an audience saw in their lifetime. Few of them survive today, none at all in Australia, but there are many designs for act drops to be seen in overseas theatre and other museums, in galleries, and in contemporary magazines such as the *Magazine of Art*. In 1875 Sydney's Royal Victoria installed the first advertising act drop, in which illustrations of all kinds of domestic wares, with accompanying text, took the place of art. Sustained criticism from press and public forced its withdrawal. But the advertising act drop returned towards the end of the century in variety or vaudeville theatres. In Australia, where such theatres as the Melbourne Royal and the Royal Victoria in Sydney changed their act drop every 3 years or so, it was not long before calls were made for the artist to 'move out of the classical grove' and use Australian scenes. The first of these calls was made in 1875, and there were renewed calls in 1880. But in fact, an act drop with an Australian subject had been painted for the Royal Victoria in 1870, a view of Circular Quay painted by A.Habbe and W.J.Wilson. In 1886 Sydney's Royal Standard opened with an act drop depicting yet another Italian lake scene (a favourite subject for drops), while in the same year Melbourne's new Princess's had one representing a 'voluminous curtain, as delicate in colour as material, with a medallion landscape in the centre. One of those glorious marble temples in which the Greeks experience their "cheerful sense of a noble worship" rears its Doric colonnade in the midst of a lovely landscape freshened by the waters of a perennial stream.' But all was not lost. In Sydney in the same year the new Criterion opened with an act drop showing the landing of Captain Cook. When Alfred Dampier took over the Alexandra in Melbourne for his season of Australian plays in 1890-91 he installed a new act drop which dealt 'in an emblematic manner with Australia's past and present.' The peak could be said to have been reached when, for the Melbourne production of Bedford's *White Australia* in 1909, William Anderson installed an act drop in the King's showing the Australian continent in white against a bright blue background, in its centre the Eureka flag proudly waving in the breeze. At the beginning of the century, when most Australian theatres were without 'flying' space above stage, act drops were worked up and down on wooden rollers on the same principle as the veranda blind. With the adoption of 'flown' scenery, the act drop was hauled up into the flies when not in use. (See: Flies).

Acting a la Mode. 1-act play by William Moore, Oddfellows' Hall, Melbourne 30.3.1909, initially 1 performance.

Acting manager. 18th century equivalent of the later stage manager, though for a long time 19th century theatres had both an acting and a stage manager. It was the acting manager's duty to present to the public in the best manner possible the plays decided on by the theatre proprietor or lessee; to act as go-between in the employment of actors, casting them, and arranging their salaries; and to advise, guide, and teach the less experienced members of the stock company. As time progressed and theatres grew in size and number, the acting manager's work seems to have been halved, with him becoming in effect the business manager, and the stage manager restricting himself to all matters concerned with the production and rehearsal of a play.

Actors. Never at any time during the 19th century was it difficult for the aspiring amateur to obtain a trial in the theatre, providing he could exhibit at least the glimmerings of talent. Almost every member of Barnett Levey's initial company was an amateur. Those who worked, and learned as they worked, 'stayed the distance.' Many dropped out, then as in later years, for although payment was good while they were in work, there was none at all if they had to 'rest.' But opportunities were always present for those who had talent and application. Some, of course, acted as they did everything else — in spurts of enthusiasm followed by periods of indifference. Typical of these was R.P.Whitworth, who could turn his hand to almost anything; while George Darrell could be said to have been typical of a later breed. Those amateurs who persisted were able to hold their own with visiting artists from England and America, and were often praised for the support they provided. Only towards the end of the century was a greater degree of expertise demanded than that provided by the untrained amateur. To meet the new demand for training many of the older actors opened schools, or trained groups of amateurs in the presentation of play nights. It was in this period that a kind of national pride first asserted itself with the introduction and immediate popularity of the Australian or Australian-based play, such as *The Sunny South* and its many successors. And after Federation first the *Bulletin*, and then other newspapers, began to object to such English matinee idols as Culyer Hastings and Roy Redgrave being cast as leads in Australian plays. The actor's social standing was another matter. In the early part of the century Governor Darling was prepared to label actors and their audiences 'rogues and vagabonds' if they took part in an unlicensed performance, and he obstinately refused to license dramatic performances. His successors, of course, took the opposite view, and as the century progressed the social standing of the actor improved — though not much. An outsider's view of his position in society as late as 1892 was given in the London magazine, *The Theatre:* 'Though the fashionable world of the two Australian capitals are devoted patrons of the theatre, actors as a class take a far less prominent position in social life than in London. This may be due to the fact that Australia is behind the age, and that society holds the obsolete view that the stage is not a gentlemanly calling, or to the fact that Australian actors are not socially and artistically the equals of their fellows at home.' In this year the Australian actress, Nellie Stewart, was playing lead in the comic opera *Blue Eyed Susan* at London's Prince of Wales; H.H.Vincent, an actor who had achieved great popularity during his nearly 20 years in Australia, was playing in the premiere of

Lady Windermere's Fan at the St James's; W.J. Holloway, who had started as an amateur in Australia and was largely self-taught, was standing in for Henry Irving as King Lear at the Lyceum, while Irving was away sick; Kyrle Bellew, who had also started as an amateur actor in Australia, in the northern New South Wales goldfields, was playing in his own musical and dramatic poem, *Hero and Leander,* and Herbert Fleming, who had for some 15 years featured in George Darrell's plays in Australia, was playing Nils Krogstad in Ibsen's *A Doll's House* at the Avenue. (See: Sir Ralph Darling).

Actors' wages. Information on the wages paid to actors and actresses, particularly in the first half of the century, is scant. At no time during at least the first 75 years of the century are accurate figures available for a complete theatrical company. For some of the lower grade actors there were 'accepted' rates of pay which rarely varied; for others it was often a matter of bargaining, while stars, those fortunate actors who could draw a full house to any theatre, had all the power in their hands, particularly if they could play off 1 management against another. It is known that George Buckingham, a 'utility' at Sydney Royal, in 1833 asked Barnett Levey for an increase in pay from 30 to 40s a week. This was more or less on a par with the wage of the average mechanic or tradesman of the time. Buckingham was not a star in the sense that Conrad Knowles was, yet Knowles in 1834 told the *Australian* that his weekly wage had stood at 63s a week for the past 15 months. But players such as Buckingham, Knowles, and a few others in Levey's company could also rely on an end-of-season benefit performance, which 2 or 3 times a year would, if successful, return them from £50 to £90 a benefit. In 1838 Joseph Wyatt engaged George Arabin and his wife for the Royal Victoria, at a combined wage of £3.10.0 — £2.10.0 for him and £1.0.0 for his wife. They had to pay their own fare from Hobart to Sydney, yet it was Arabin who opened the theatre as the lead in a performance of *Othello.* In 1845 George Coppin brought a company from Launceston to Melbourne, paying fares each way for all, asking only that each player should sign an agreement not to desert him until 1 season had been completed. He paid his most important actors from 30s to £2.0.0 a week. In 1859 Frank Fowler claimed that the average performer in the Melbourne theatre was receiving £15.0.0 a week. He was writing of the gold-rush days, when prices for everything rose to abnormal heights and talented actors were scarce. In 1867 a fading English star such as James Anderson was able to return to England with £3440 in his pocket for 8 weeks' work. 20 years later *Table Talk* reported that there was no recognised wage grading for actors, and so everybody got what he could. For a juvenile male lead this was said to be from £10 to £15 a week; for an 'emotional' actress £15 to £20 a week; soubrette £6 to £7 a week, and comedienne £10 to £12. At the bottom of the list came the 'walking lady and gentleman' at £4 a week each, while ballet girls and supernumeraries got 2s 6d a night. (See: Anderson, J.R. Benefit. Comic opera).

Adams, Arthur Henry (1872-1936). Born in New Zealand, Adams graduated in arts at the University of Otago, and then took up journalism. At about this time he collaborated with Alfred Hill on that composer's cantata on a Maori theme, *Hinemoa,* published in New Zealand in 1896. In 1898 Adams came to Sydney, where he first called on J.C.Williamson with the libretto of a comic opera, *Tapu,* to which Hill had written the music. As Adams later told the story in the *Lone Hand* in 1908, Williamson said he liked the work, and he engaged Adams as his 'literary secretary' at a salary of slightly less than £4 a week, 'with the stipulation that all original work done by me during my two years' engagement should become the property of my employer.' Williamson then told Adams how he thought the libretto should be recast, and he ultimately produced the opera. Leaving Williamson, Adams became in turn editor of the Red Page of the Sydney *Bulletin,* editor of the *Lone Hand,* worked for the *Sun* newspaper, and returned to the *Bulletin.* In his lifetime he published several novels, books of short stories, poems, a pantomime, and plays. Among stage works of his to achieve production were *Tapu, The Tame Cat, The Waster, The Minstrel, Doctor Death,* a 1-act play, *Pierrot in Australia* produced in Australia and at London's Little Theatre 26.1.1912, and *Mrs Pretty and the Premier.* The last was also produced in Birmingham on 4.12.1915, under the title *The Division Bell.* (See: Hill, Alfred).

Adelaide, Theatres in.

1 Royal (1838). The first theatre in Adelaide; a fit-up or room converted to theatrical use in much the same way as Barnett Levey's Royal Hotel saloon was converted to the Royal in 1832. The Adelaide, also called the Royal, was built in the ballroom above the Adelaide Tavern in Franklin Street. It had 9 boxes, apparently 3 to a wall around the 3 walls of the auditorium, and a pit. The theatre was opened on 28.1.1838 with the usual programme: an opening address, a melodrama, *The Mountaineers* (1793), two songs, and in the farce, *The Lancers* (1827). It cost 5s for a seat in the boxes, 2 for the pit. At one time 400 people were accommodated in this theatre, in a room 50ft long (less the depth of the stage) and 18ft wide. Its life was rowdy and brief.

2 Royal Victoria (1839). The actor Samson Cameron, who had earlier opened a similar theatre in Hobart, converted a shop or store in North Terrace into a theatre of the same kind as the Royal — boxes, pit, and stage. He called it the Royal Victoria. This time the row of boxes around 3 sides of the room was given the title 'dress circle.' Circle seats cost 6s, pit 3. The opening programme on 30.11.1839 was *The Stranger* (1798), a song, the third act of *Othello,* and the farce *Is He Jealous?* (1816).

Above: Queen's Theatre Adelaide 1846
Below: Exterior Adelaide Royal 1868

The *Register* thought the theatre was neatly fitted up, but that better ventilation was needed; the boxes needed to be divided with partitions, 'and more care taken as to the persons admitted to them.' Neither the dimensions nor the capacity of this theatre are known. Its life was also short.

3 Argyle Rooms (1840). Another mushroom enterprise. George Buckingham, a foundation member of Barnett Levey's Royal company in Sydney, was not engaged by Wyatt when he opened his Royal Victoria in Sydney in 1838. Buckingham lived a hand-to-mouth existence until, by the end of 1839, it was announced in the *Sydney Gazette* that he was one of the 'runaway actors' (Mrs Samson Cameron, and Lee, the comedian, were two others) who had 'bolted' to Adelaide, leaving large debts behind them. Mrs Cameron and Buckingham joined Samson Cameron at Adelaide's Royal Victoria at the end of January 1840, but not long after this the theatre closed. In May it was announced that 'Mr Solomon of Currie Street' was building the Queen's. Meantime Buckingham formed a group and opened the Argyle Rooms, in the Gilles Arcade. This makeshift theatre was advertised to open on 4.5.1840, with a company of 14 named members, including the scenepainter Edward Opie. Its size and seating capacity are not known, and mystery surrounds its fate. If it opened as planned, its career was very short, for Buckingham and the Camerons were members of the Queen's company when that theatre opened on 11.1.1841.

4 Queen's (1841). The fourth in less than 4 years, and the first 'real' theatre to be built in Adelaide. Also in Gilles Arcade, the Queen's could accommodate 1200 in its dress circle, upper circle, and pit — 700 of them in the pit. The opening programme had the usual address or prologue, the tragedy of *Othello*, a dance, and the farce *Our Mary Anne* (1838). The Queen's was also the first Adelaide theatre to provide private boxes in the dress circle, a saloon promenade in the same area, and a ladies' room. There was a company of 17 actors. Edward Opie, who designed and carried out the decorations of the auditorium, was also the scenepainter. Mr and Mrs G.Buckingham were responsible for costumes and stage properties. Dress circle seats cost 6s upper circle 5, and pit 3. Half-price was 3s, 2, and 1s 6d. By 1843 it had become obvious that Adelaide was not able to sustain a permanent theatrical company. From that year to 1850 the building was used as the Adelaide Court House.

5 Pavilion (1845). Again the need for theatricals was met by a return to the fit-up. 'The premises so well known as the Southern Cross Hotel' (*Register* 6.9.1845) were converted to the usual boxes and pit. Box seats cost 2s 6d, pit 1s 6d. The theatre, opened on 6.9.1845 with *The Married Bachelor* (1821), 'a variety of singing and dancing,' and an unknown farce called *A Tinker and a Tailor, a Soldier and a Sailor*, had a very short life.

Adelaide, Theatres in

6 Royal Adelaide (1846). Yet another pit and boxes fit-up, but this time conducted in an orderly manner. Built in premises known as the Bush Clubhouse Hotel, it was said by the *Observer* to be 'a decided improvement, as compared with many other similar places of amusement which have preceded it.' Henry Deering, an actor from Melbourne, was proprietor and manager, and for 4 months he achieved some success. Opened on 22.6.1846 with the untraceable nautical drama, *The Fatal Light Ship; or, The Wild Woman of the Waves*, a song or 2 and the farce *Perfection* (1830), it had a company of only 6 named players. Box seats cost 2s, pit 1, the nights of performance being Monday, Thursday, and Saturday. This little theatre was finally swallowed by yet another, larger theatre.

7 Queen's (1846). In October 1846 the Sydney *Atlas* reported that 'Mr Solomon, that indefatigable builder, has resolved to erect a theatre for Mr Coppin, at the Temple Tavern . . .' The billiard room of the Temple Inn was extended and converted into a 'truly snug theatre,' which in its dress boxes, lower boxes, and pit held 700 people. Named the Queen's, it was opened on 2.11.1846 with the usual melodrama, a variety of singing and dancing, and a farce. Dress box seats cost 4s, lower box seats 3, and pit 2. Half-price, at half past 9, cost 2s 6d, 1s 6d, and 1s. Although smaller than the first Queen's, this theatre also had a brief life.

8 The Dramatic Hall (1850). A small theatre opened in Leigh Street in the upstairs portion of an office building, by disaffected members of the Queen's company. They took advantage of a campaign against that theatre by the *Register* to secede and open a new theatre. The Dramatic Hall was opened on 2.2.1850 with a historical drama, a cornet solo, a comic song, a farce. Despite most favourable reviews in the *Register*, this theatre had to close for lack of support on 15.3.1850. A member of the theatre orchestra was reported to have said that 'the hall was closed because decency and propriety are at a discount among the wealthier colonists, and the stage that will truckle to the vices is the only one deemed worthy of support.'

9 Royal Victoria (1850). Adelaide had acquired a proper Court House by the end of 1850, so the old first Queen's was rebuilt and opened on 23.11.1850 as the Royal Victoria. After reconstruction this theatre emerged as a building 140ft long, and 34ft wide. The stage and dressing rooms occupied one half the length, the auditorium and front of house the other. On either side of the proscenium arch were 3 private boxes, each with its own entrance. There was also a dress circle which ran 'completely round the house' — that is, its 2 arms joined with the proscenium boxes. A pit and gallery completed the audience accommodation. There is no record of how many people this theatre could hold, though possibly it could crowd in up to 1000. The comfort and privacy of dress circle patrons was catered for with refreshment or

Adelaide, Theatres in

lounge rooms opening off the dress circle, 1 each for men and women. Auditorium lighting, in addition to 'the usual "staff" of candles,' included 'Five very handsome chandeliers.' For its opening at least, this theatre had what its predecessors had lacked, an adequate orchestra containing 'all the principal instrumental performers in the colony,' and the first night audience heard the overture to Mozart's *Don Giovanni* as a start to the night's programme. Box seats, private as well as dress circle, cost 4s, pit 2, and gallery 1. Half-price, at a quarter-to-10, cost 2s 6d and 1s. There was no half-price to the gallery. This theatre served Adelaide for 6 years.

10 Port Adelaide (1851). Opened by George Coppin in his hotel building, the White Horse Cellar, on 25.6.1851, it had pit, dress circle, and gallery. The dress circle seated 250, but the theatre's full capacity is not known. Box seats in the dress circle on the opening night cost 4s, pit 2. Half-price at 9 o'clock was 2s 6d, and 1s. The gallery was not opened until later. The theatre closed in November.

11 White's Rooms (1856). The largest entertainment area in Adelaide to this date, White's Rooms were designed to cater for public amusements of a kind not served or provided by the theatre — balls, variety and musical entertainments, public banquets, lectures, meetings, concerts. From the main entrance in King William Street patrons passed through a hallway lined with offices, to a flight of stairs. At the top of the stairs was a large landing, with a main door leading directly into the assembly room or hall, and smaller doors on either side leading to men's and women's dressing rooms, and to an anteroom 26ft long and 16ft wide. The main room or hall was 86ft long, 41ft wide, and 30ft high. To aid the acoustics, all wall and ceiling surfaces were kept plain, and mouldings avoided wherever possible. The result was a smooth-surfaced room or hall with semicircular-topped windows about 20ft up the walls, its chief decoration being the 3 ornamental chandeliers suspended from decorative centrepieces. At the far end of the room was an 'orchestra' or platform large enough to accommodate 60 performers. This, 4ft above the floor at the front, 18ft deep, and rising to a further 3 levels towards the back, each 12ins higher than the preceding one, could be reduced in size for smaller groups or solo performances. There were also retiring rooms for the performers. White's Rooms were opened with a Masonic Ball on 26.6.1856, and publicly opened with a 'grand vocal and instrumental concert' on 30.6.1856. For the next 12 years or so these rooms and the Royal Victoria met Adelaide's needs.

12 Town Hall as theatre (1868). In 1867 George Coppin brought the English Shakespearian actor, James Anderson, to Australia for a tour of the colonies. Anderson was successful in Melbourne and Sydney, but had in Adelaide what he later described as 'twelve nights . . . to very poor houses — the worst in Australia.' This was largely because Coppin could not obtain use of the Royal Victoria, and had to fit-up a theatre in

Above: Interior Adelaide Royal 1878
Below: Hudson's Bijou Adelaide 1890s

the Town Hall. His solution was a series of wooden 'steps' at one end of the hall for the audience, and a platform stage at the other, both adrift in a vast open space lined with heavy stone columns. A stage 40ft deep had the required proscenium arch, front curtain, wings, shutters (or flats), grooves, and borders. For the audience a wooden framework of ascending platforms was provided, each wide enough for chairs, about 20 rows in all, the highest being 12ft from the floor. Above this was the hall's own gallery or balcony. As Anderson later described this theatre, 'the acoustic principles were so bad, and the echoes so loud, that the actors could not be heard.'

13 Royal (1868). By 1867 the Royal Victoria had outlived its usefulness. Three partners, Sagar, Wendt, and Lazar, then built a new theatre in Hindley Street, incorporating the facade of a shop already on the site. The foundation stone of what was to be the Royal was laid in January 1868, and the building was opened on 13.4.1868. With this, civilised theatre could be said to have arrived in Adelaide. The horseshoe-shaped auditorium, 51ft long and 46ft wide, was divided into stalls to seat 144 persons, pit 470, dress circle and boxes 200, gallery 480 — seating for a total of about 1300, with room for a further 200 in the event of a crush. The stage was the width of the building, 54ft deep, and 36ft high, which meant it had no 'flies.' The proscenium opening or arch was 25ft square, with 3 boxes on either side. But although the stage had no flying space, it was equippd with traps of all kinds, and a floor built in removable sections to allow scenery, furniture, properties, and so on to be pushed up from or lowered into the cellar. The scenes, made up of the usual wings, flats or shutters, and borders — plus painted backdrops — could be moved mechanically by means of ropes, pulleys, and drums. Under the stage were 11 dressing rooms for the actors, 3 to a room, without natural light or air. The whole theatre was lighted by gas. For audience comfort there was a bar in the ground floor vestibule to serve pit and stall patrons. Dress circle patrons had their own entrance in Hindley Street, leading to a flight of stairs at the top of which were retiring rooms for both sexes, a saloon on the street front 40ft by 30ft, and a second bar. A door in the saloon's western wall gave access to a billiard room 43ft by 21ft. Gallery occupants entered from outside the building, through a restaurant and up a flight of stairs. At the foot of the stairs was bar number 3.

14 Royal (1878). In this year the *Register* welcomed news of the reconstruction of the Hindley Street Royal with the statement that while the first had taken the place of the still smaller and primitive Royal Victoria, now a larger theatre than ever was required. The 1868 theatre, all but the facade, was demolished. The new theatre could seat in its stalls, pit, dress circle, and gallery more than twice the number of the previous theatre — a total 3000, with 1000 in the gallery alone. The proscenium arch, 30ft wide and about 32ft high, framed in rich gold an

ornate act drop depicting a view of Lake Maggiore, looking over the town of Pallanza, by the Melbourne scenepainter, John Hennings. On each side of the arch were 3 stage boxes, hung with blue satin curtains. The dress circle was 'a blaze of crystal and delicately blended colour.' White and gold chairs had seats, arms, and backs of crimson plush. The walls and ceiling were panelled in pearl grey and gold paper, with gold beading and borders. 3 crystal chandeliers, and wall brackets between mirrors, provided the lighting. The approach to the dress circle was through a vestibule, up a wide staircase lighted by lamps held by half-lifesize bronze figures. At the top of the stairs was an assembly or crush room, with carpets, mirrors, and statues. Opening off this were cloak, retiring, and refreshment rooms. Behind the dress circle seats was a promenade lounge with seats. A further 200 people could be accommodated here if necessary. The stalls had American chairs with cane seats and backs, and plush-covered arms, while the pit had seats formerly used in the stalls. The general colouring of the auditorium was in blue and gold, including a blue ceiling fretted with gold stars. The stage, 73ft wide and about 70ft deep, had dressing rooms built in at the sides.

15 Academy of Music — Music Hall (1879). Side by side with a growing interest in the theatre in Adelaide was a growing interest in music hall entertainment — a programme of individual entertainments later to become known as Variety or Vaudeville. White's Rooms had proved to be inadequate for these, not least because of the flat auditorium floor and the primitive stage. A building for this purpose, given the American title of Academy of Music, was therefore built in Rundle Street in 1879, with a street frontage of 48ft, height of 55ft and depth of 106ft. Two shops, one on either side of the main entrance, occupied the ground floor street front, behind them being a billiard room. The main entrance led to a wide stairway giving access to the first floor. Two doors on the landing led to the front and back seats respectively. In the front of this first floor were women's cloak and retiring rooms, and a manager's office under a stairway leading to the gallery. The auditorium, 74ft by 49ft, included a stage as wide as the building, but only 36ft deep from the footlights to the back wall. The depth of the stage proper, excluding the forestage and proscenium, was only 25ft. The act drop framed by the proscenium arch was a copy of Turner's *A View of Rome*. Backstage there was a staircase leading to a gallery containing dressing rooms and a scenepainting area. There was said to be ample space abovestage for flying scenery. The Academy, or, as the *Register* called it, the Music Hall was opened on 2.6.1879. Disappointment was expressed with the glaring colours used in the decoration of the theatre, and with the act drop, but some of the stage scenery was said to be excellent. There is no record of the number this theatre could hold in its back and front seats and gallery.

16 Garner's (1880). With a Town Hall and a Music Hall as well as

the Royal, Adelaide now had better substitutes for the once necessary White's Rooms. But their usefulness was still far from over. In 1880 the English actor-manager, Arthur Garner, had them converted to a theatre, the decorative work being carried out by the English scene-painter and artist, George Gordon, from London's Haymarket. Facing the stage, on either side of the proscenium arch, were 2 boxes. A dress circle balcony was built in a wide sweep from one side of the proscenium to the other, the boxes being built into this, 1 on the balcony level and 1 underneath. A gallery was built at the back of the dress circle. The stalls and pit, still on the original flat floor, seated 250 and 500 respectively, the dress circle 176, and the gallery or amphitheatre (in this sense, a stepped area without seats) 400 — 1326 in all. The stage was the full width of the hall and 28ft deep. Stalls, pit, dress circle, and gallery each had their own entrance. French grey, yellow, and dark tonings were used to decorate the auditorium. The original chandeliers were left in position, but the ceiling was painted and the centrepieces coloured to agree with the general colour scheme. Garner's, as the building was now called, was opened on 17.5.1880 with the drama *George Geith* (1877), and the farce *Toddlekins* (1855). For the opening night private boxes cost £2 and £1.10s each, dress circle seats 5s, stalls 3, pit 2, and amphitheatre 1. In 1893 this building, after the abolition of the circle and boxes and a few minor alterations, was renamed Hudson's Bijou. In 1900 it was swallowed up by the Tivoli.

17 Tivoli (1900). A colourful variety theatre — stalls, dress circle, and gallery — seating 1200. Opened on 20.6.1900, this was a conversion of the former Bijou. The proscenium was 20ft 6ins wide and 22ft high, while the height from stage floor to the gridiron was 39ft. The auditorium had a dome in the ceiling, in front of the proscenium, fitted with a sliding roof for summer ventilation. The interior decorative scheme was in the French Renaissance style, in a colour range of turquoise blue, pale amber, light greys, cream, and gold. The combination of a heavy gold proscenium frame with the mirror fronts of the boxes gave this little theatre what the *Register* described as a 'handsome though tasteful and unique appearance.'

18 Empire (1909). Another small variety or vaudeville theatre, opened in Grote Street on 10.4.1909. It had front and back stalls, pit, and dress circle. The 10 rows of front stalls had a flat floor, but, beginning with the front row of the back stalls, the floor rose 5ft 6ins in 60ft to the back of the pit. The dress circle, above the pit, seated 300, stalls 500. Lighting was by means of 240 16-candlepower electric lamps.

19 King's (1911). Variety house, built in King William Street to accommodate 1600 people in the usual front and back stalls, dress circle, and gallery. Like the Empire, it had a ceiling and proscenium front of pressed metal instead of the usual wood and plaster. The general colour scheme of shades of blue and gold was emphasised by the blue plush

seats of the dress circle and front stalls, and the blue and gold stage curtain. The *Register's* claim on 25 February that 'a good view of the stage may be obtained from any part of the house' was changed after the opening night, 28.2.1911, when it was found that only those in the stalls had a good view of the stage. Complaints were also made about poor ventilation.

20 Tivoli (1913). Variety-drama theatre opened 6.9.1913 in Grote Street, seating more than 2000. The stalls area, 80ft by 63ft with a sloping floor, seated 622, dress circle 238, and gallery 1300. A stage 81ft by 63ft had a height of 53ft to the gridiron, with 12ft fly galleries on either side, and a proscenium arch 30ft by 24ft. A modern ventilating system pumped 26 000 cubic feet of air a minute into the building. The electric lighting system was served by a switchboard with more than 250 switches. The general interior colour scheme of the theatre was white and gold.

21 Royal (1914). In this year the lessees of the Royal, J.C.Williamson Ltd, decided to build a new theatre in North Terrace to counter the appeal of the new Tivoli. But costs forced a change of plan, the 1878 building being remodelled instead. The new interior had the usual stalls, dress circle, and gallery, but the previous 6 stage boxes (3 on either side of the proscenium) were increased to 4 on each side, placed along the side walls. Summer ventilation was provided by two sliding roofs, one over the centre of the auditorium, one over the back of the gallery. The interior decorative scheme, a combination of white and painted moulded plaster, plaster cherubs, and other figures, was described as 'a study in delicacy and refinement.' It included the pastel colour effects of the Louis XV period in tints of blue, cream, and gold, with red plush stage curtain and carpets. The stage boxes had moulded panels of briar roses on their sides, on a pale blue ground, with a border of deep gold. The proscenium arch, surmounted by a painted plaster cartouche with a figure representing music on either side, was 33ft wide and 35ft high. The dress circle side walls were filled with painted panels of figures in blue monochrome. The theatre was opened on 11.4.1914 with a performance of Lehar's operetta, *The Count of Luxembourg*. Seating in this remodelled theatre was half that in the 1878 theatre — 1700 (*Register* 10.4.1914). One of the reasons for this may have been that 1914 theatregoers would not endure the cramped seating conditions of 1878. Individual seats were also wider, and each row was placed to provide more leg room than before.

Admirable Crichton, The. 4-act drama by J.M.Barrie, Duke of York's, London 4.11.1902; Her Majesty's, Sydney 2.4.1904, initial 18 performances.

Admission prices. Throughout the 19th century the cost of theatre tickets in the 3 major cities — Sydney, Melbourne, and Adelaide —

varied slightly according to economic changes and supply and demand. At first, with few theatres and irregular performances, prices were high. As more and more theatres were opened and nightly performances were given, prices began to stabilise, and for many years remained at much the same level. Managers learned that increases in the ordinary charges would only be accepted to cover the increased cost of an imported star such as Sarah Bernhardt, or an overseas opera company. When Barnett Levey gave performances in his Royal Assembly Rooms in 1829 he charged 7s 6d for seats in the boxes, 5 for the pit. When he opened his saloon theatre in 1832 the charges were 5s for box seats, 3 for the pit, with half-price at 9 o'clock. The following year, when his real Royal opened, the charges were dress circle 5s, second tier of boxes 4, pit 3, gallery 2. By 1835 these prices had been changed to 5s 6d, 4, 3s 6d, and 1s 6d. The Royal Victoria, opened in 1838, for some time kept to the 5, 4, 2, and 1 pattern, but by 1853 this had become 4, 3, 2, and 1. When the Queen's opened in Melbourne it charged 5s for dress circle, 4 for upper circle, 2s 6d for pit, and 1s 6d for the gallery. In the mid-50s in Melbourne, during the gold rushes, the Queen's was charging 8s for box seats, 5 for the pit, 2 for the gallery — prices which did not survive the first reflux of diggers. 10 years later Barry Sullivan at Melbourne Royal was charging 5s for dress circle, 3 for stalls, 2 for upper or family circle, pit 1, gallery 6d. By the 1880s the 5, 3, 2, and 1 pattern was almost general in the major theatres, and remained unchanged in the 1890s. A correspondent of the London monthly *The Theatre* reported in 1892: 'There is a delightful uniformity of prices in Australian theatres. The stalls are always 3 shillings, the dress circle 5 shillings, and the gallery 1 shilling. The first few rows of the stalls are often reserved, and the price raised to five shillings.' But perhaps this uniformity is not so surprising as it may seem. The theatres presented much the same plays and light musical works, the same stars, and sometimes the same companies. Travelling expenses could be placed against the savings in not having to paint new scenery for each theatre, in having a central production and distribution point for playbills, posters, and programmes carried with each 'show,' and in contract salaries for stars and others which allowed for a nominal payment with a guaranteed tenure of employment. These tenures, more often than not, included tours of both islands of New Zealand, as well as each Australian colony. Prices in the major New Zealand theatres were — 5, 3, and 2s.

Africaine, L' (The African Girl). 5-act opera, text A.E.Scribe, music G.Meyerbeer, Opera House, Paris 28.4.1865; Covent Garden, London 22.7.1865; Prince of Wales, Sydney 21.5.1866, initial 7 performances.

After Dark. A Tale of London Life. 4-act drama by Dion Boucicault, Princess's, London 12.8.1868; Royal, Melbourne 20.2.1869, initial 29 performances.

Agamemnon. One of the Oresteian trilogy of plays by Aeschylus, first performed in Athens 458 BC. First produced in Australia in the Great Hall, University of Sydney 14.6.1886. (See: Greek play).

Aida. 4-act opera, text A.Ghislanzoni, after a story by A.Mariette, music G.Verdi, Opera House, Cairo 24.12.1871; Covent Garden, London 22.6.1876; Royal, Melbourne 6.9.1877, initial 4 performances.

Aiglon, L' (The Young Eagle). 5-act drama by Edmond Rostand, translated by Louis N.Parker, New York 1900; Her Majesty's Sydney 8.10.1904, initial 30 performances.

Akhurst, William Mower (1822-1878). Journalist and playwright. Born in London, where he had two plays produced at Cremorne Gardens before he emigrated to Australia. Arrived in Adelaide in 1849, where he worked as a journalist until 1853. From his arrival in Melbourne that year until his return to England in 1870 he wrote extensively for the Melbourne stage — farces, burlesques, pantomimes, dramas, opening and closing addresses, adaptations and localisations of overseas works — while at the same time fulfilling his duties as drama and music critic for Melbourne newspapers. Among his stage productions were *Rolla of Ours, The Mirror of Beauty, The Fall of Sebastopol, Paris the Prince and Helen the Fair* (later changed to *The Siege of Troy*), *King Arthur*, and *The Battle of Hastings*. In addition he wrote at least 14 Christmas pantomimes for the Melbourne stage, and others for Sydney, as well as a number of sketches for minstrel shows and individual performers. The texts of some of his pantomimes were published in Melbourne in the 1860s. Music he composed for a ballad and a polka was published in the *Illustrated Melbourne Post* in July-August 1863, and for a waltz in 1864. In 1870 he returned to England, where he had 9 pantomimes, 4 dramas, 2 extravaganzas, and a burlesque produced between 1871 and 1877. By this time his health was beginning to fail, and he made a sudden decision to return to Australia. He and his family embarked on the *Patriarch* in May 1878. He died when only 3 weeks at sea. (See: Nelson, Sydney; Burlesque).

Alfred the Great. 3-act dramatic and musical grand fairy spectacle in 10 tableaux, text Marcus Clarke, music Henry Keiley, Academy of Music, Melbourne 24.12.1878, initial 35 performances.

All for Gold; or, Fifty Millions of Money. 3-act drama with prologue by F.R.C.Hopkins, adapted from Eugene Sue's novel *Le Juif errant* (1844-45), Royal Victoria, Sydney 10.3.1877, initial 7 performances.

Allison, James W. (1831-1890). Nothing is known of the birthplace or early life of this man, who gave Sydney its most ornate and best-sited 19th century theatre, Her Majesty's. He was for many years a theatrical agent in Adelaide. In 1873 he went to Melbourne to gather a company of actors for Samuel Lazar's Adelaide Royal. 5 years later he was lessee of that theatre, and at roughly the same time he was managing the successful Australian tour of the American actress, Louise Pomeroy. In 1882, a year before his lease of the Adelaide Royal expired, he bought a 21-year lease of a block of land on the corner of Pitt and Market Streets, Sydney on which he proposed to build a theatre. In 1883 he was joined in this venture by the actor George Rignold, and work on the building was begun in 1884. Rignold also joined him as co-lessee of the Adelaide Royal. In the same year Allison obtained Australian rights to a number of successful English stage works, including the comic opera, *Falka*. He also bought and had transported to Melbourne the settings and curtains designed for and used by Henry Irving in his Lyceum production of *Romeo and Juliet*. These settings, as they had been in London, were the sensation of the day in Sydney and Melbourne, but the production was not. Sydney's Her Majesty's was opened in 1887, and Rignold used it for a series of large, superbly mounted melodramas, and an occasional play by Shakespeare, which set new Australian attendance records. Their partnership was dissolved by mutual consent on 13.3.1889. The following year Allison was in San Francisco, booking actors and plays for Australian theatres, when he contracted pneumonia. He died in the German Hospital in that city.

Amateur Burglar, The. 1-act play by W.J.Curtis, Criterion, Sydney 1.8.1906. (See: *Coquette, The*).

Amico Fritz, L' (Friend Fritz). 3-act opera, text 'P.Suardon' (N.Daspuro), music P.Mascagni, Constanze, Rome 31.10.1891; Covent Garden, London 23.5.1892; Princess's, Melbourne 19.10.1893, initial 2 performances.

Amilie; or, The Love Test. 3-act opera, text J.T.Haines, music W.M.Rooke (Rourke), Covent Garden, London 2.12.1837; Royal, Melbourne 20.1.1863, initial 3 performances.

Anchored. 1-act play by A.C.Stephen, Concordia Hall, Sydney 26.7.1913, initially 1 performance.

Anderson, James R. (1811-1895). Born in Glasgow, son of an actor. Took his place on the stage in early childhood. At age of 11 was sacked from the Edinburgh theatre in which he and his father were employed because he refused to play the part of a monkey in the pantomime *Perouse; or, The Desolate Island* (1801). The following year he branched out on his own, playing 'leads' with a travelling co-operative company which endured a hand-to-mouth existence in the smaller Scottish towns. He survived this, and an early manhood spent in English provincial theatres, to make his first London appearance in 1837 with W.Macready at Covent Garden. Subsequently he appeared in many of Macready's London productions. His other experiences included a spell

*Left: James R. Anderson
Below: William Anderson 1910*

in the Fleet Prison for debt; a short and disastrous term as lessee of
Drury Lane (for which he engaged the Australian-trained actress, Eliza
Winstanley); 6 successful visits to America, and an equally successful
visit to Australia in 1867-68. For this, George Coppin offered him two-
thirds of the total receipts, free passage to Australia and return, and a
guarantee that his (Anderson's) takings for an 8-week season would not
be less than £3000. He opened in Melbourne in *Hamlet* on 13.7.1867,
and gave his last Australian performance on 24.8.1868. At the end of his
tour, in Anderson's words, 'Coppin sent for me . . . that we might settle
accounts and wind up the engagement. It appeared we had taken £4663
during eight months. Coppin's third out of this came to £1551, leaving
my share £3112, to which was added £328 for expenses, making my total
£3440.' During his Australian tour Anderson appeared in *Macbeth,
Coriolanus, Ingomar the Barbarian, The Stranger, Othello, Richard III, King
Lear,* and in a play of his own, *The Scottish Chief and the Maid of Ellerslie*
(1863). He died in London after an attack by hooligans who assaulted
and robbed him. (See: Adelaide, Town Hall).

Anderson, William (1868-1940). Born in Bendigo, Anderson was the
family wage-earner by the time he was 9, supporting his invalid mother
and his brother. He was attracted to the entertainment world from his
earliest days, but with no desire to become an actor. His skills were en-
trepreneurial. He earned his first money bill-posting for theatrical and
other shows, and in selling songbooks and comic opera librettos. He
later claimed that he had made £2 and £3 a week selling these books during the Emilie Melville comic opera season in Bendigo. A year later,
aged 10, he had 3 jobs — folding newspapers at the Bendigo *Advertiser*
office at 5 o'clock each morning, making up tickets and being generally
useful at the theatre after breakfast, and selling tickets from the box
office at night. This brought him from £4 to £6 a week at a time when
the average shop-boy was earning no more than 5 to 10s a week. Later
he became a theatrical agent, booking actors and companies into the
Bendigo and other theatres. Next he leased a skating rink, made some
money, and built his own rink at a cost of £1400 — just in time to suffer
the effects of a decline in public interest in roller skating. Reverting to
the work of agent and manager for visiting theatrical companies, and
then forming his own travelling company, he next entered into a 5-year
partnership with the actor Charles Holloway, giving seasons in Sydney
and Melbourne. Then he launched out on his own, and by 1899 the
William Anderson Dramatic Company was becoming known throughout Australia as one which maintained an impeccable standard of excellence in the production of melodrama. When the new century arrived he
reached the peak of his success with the establishment of a huge entertainment centre, Wonderland City, at Tamarama Bay, next to Bondi
Beach. By 1908 he could boast that he owned Wonderland City, which

cost £30 000; had successful stage productions running in Sydney and Melbourne; had several touring companies 'on the road'; had extended leases of the Perth and Fremantle theatres, and was building his own theatre, the King's, in Melbourne. At about this time he was also funding and producing Australian plays written by members of his company, Edmund Duggan and Bert Bailey, such as *The Squatter's Daughter,* and *On Our Selection.* What he lost on the production of 'quality' plays he regained with popular plays, as when a loss on a week's run of *Cyrano de Bergerac* was recouped with 3 weeks of the melodrama, *The Worst Woman in London.* Nor did he neglect the newest craze, the moving picture, though he was not astute enough to see that ultimately this new invention would edge him and the kind of play he was expert in judging and producing, out of the theatre — thus aiding in the destruction of the 'empire' he had built up. By the 1920s he was producing overseas and Australian melodramas again, this time in Adelaide. Even as late as this his productions were so successful that he wanted to extend his activities to Sydney and Melbourne; but J. C. Williamson and others had a stranglehold in those cities, and he could not rent a theatre.

Andrews, William (1836-1878). The first Australian-born, Australian-trained actor to spend all his acting life on the Australian stage. Born in George Street, Sydney he started his acting career at the age of 19 at the Royal Victoria, playing a minor role in J.M.Morton's *Whitebait at Greenwich* (1853). At this time the tragedian G.V.Brooke made his first visit to Sydney, and Andrews transferred to his company, acting with him in Sydney, and later accompanying him to Melbourne. In 1863 he joined Barry Sullivan's company in Melbourne, where he appeared in a season of plays by Shakespeare, Sheridan, and Otway. A comedian, during his 23 years on the stage he appeared in the major Shakespeare plays, and also in such current favourites as *The Stranger, Under the Gaslight, London Assurance, The School for Scandal, Oliver Twist,* and in such 'drag' parts as Judy O'Brien, the washerwoman in Garnet Walch's 1871 extravaganza, *Trookulentos.* His notably successful comedy roles were those of Joseph Grudge in W.H.Cooper's *Colonial Experience,* and Sponge Loafer in that writer's melodrama, *Hazard; or, Pearce Dyceton's Crime.*

Anne Bolena. 2-act opera, text F.Romani, music G.Donizetti, Carcano, Milan 26.12.1830; His Majesty's, London 8.7.1831; Royal Victoria, Sydney 31.5.1875, initial 2 performances.

Anniversary Day; or, Helen's Betrothal. 3-act drama by 'a gentleman of Sydney' (J.G.Marwick), Royal Victoria, Sydney 11.6.1868, initial 2 performances. Published with the writer's *The Two Lovers,* in 'Spare Moments in Australia,' J.Sands, Sydney 1877. Copy in Mitchell Library.

Antony and Cleopatra. Tragedy by W.Shakespeare, believed to have been first performed in London in 1606 or 1607; Royal, Melbourne 8.10.1867, initial 10 performances.

Above: Apron: typical small English provincial theatre c. 1820
Below: Performance on board ship Galatea *Sydney Harbour 1869*

Apron. Up to the end of the 18th century theatre stages were lined on either side by two or more proscenium doors. Sometimes these had boxes above them for the public, sometimes there were stage-level boxes with another above, and then 1 or 2 proscenium doors. Early theatres thus had a deep forestage, the scenery inside the proscenium arch being little more than a background to the acting on the fore or apron stage. As the stage proper gained in importance and the actors moved back into the scene, behind the proscenium arch, the forestage or apron became shallower, until by the beginning of the 19th century it was little more than a space no deeper than the width of the single proscenium door on either side. Soon proscenium doors, too, were abolished, leaving only a token forestage or apron. In time this was also abolished, and the proscenium arch became a picture frame flush with the front curtain.

Arcadian Eve, An. 1-act operetta, text and music A.Plumpton, Royal, Adelaide 1.7.1895, initial 6 performances.

Arcadians, The. 3-act musical comedy, text M.Ambient, A.Thompson and R. Courtneidge, music L.Monckton and H.Talbot, Shaftesbury, London 28.4.1909; Royal, Melbourne 26.3.1910, initial 66 performances.

Archer, William (1856-1924). Author, critic, dramatist, and translator of Henrik Ibsen's plays, Archer was born in Scotland. His tenuous links with Australia include his parents' property in the north of Queensland, 'Gracemere', and the visit he made to them there in 1876-77. From this visit came his melodrama, *Australia; or, The Bushrangers,* written in collaboration with an A.G.Stanley, whose identity remains a mystery, and produced at London's Grecian on 16.4.1881. Based on the exploits of the Kelly gang in Australia, and with two repulsive bushranger characters, Black Bourke and Red Bourke, the play was a success in terms of the transpontine theatre of its day. Archer's name was never mentioned in any of the publicity for this play, which always read 'by W.A. and A.G.Stanley.' The ms held in the British Library carries the title *Australia* but no author's name. It is ironic that towards the end of a life devoted largely to trying to break the hold of melodrama on the English stage, Archer should have written another which made him for the first time in his life a wealthy man. This, *The Green Goddess,* was first produced in the USA in 1921, where it had a run of 416 performances.

Arme Jonathan, Der (Poor Jonathon). 3-act operetta, text H.Wittmann and J.Bauer, music K.Millöcker, Theater an der Wien, Vienna 4.1.1890; Prince of Wales, London 15.6.1893; Opera House, Melbourne 4.6.1891, initial 20 performances.

Arms and the Man. 3-act comedy by G.B.Shaw, Avenue, London 21.4.1894; Royal, Sydney 26.2.1910, initial 5 performances (See: *Tapfere Soldat, Der*).

Army and Navy. From the earliest days sailors whose ships were moored in Sydney Harbour, and soldiers on garrison duty in barracks at Sydney, Windsor, and Parramatta, gave public and private performances of plays in makeshift theatres. The first on record is that given on 8.1.1830 by officers of HMS *Crocodile* and HMS *Zebra* in a marquee at Fort Macquarie, on the site of the present Sydney Opera House. The plays were *Raymond and Agnes* (1809), which they called *Agnes; or, The Bleeding Nun,* and *The Miller and His Men* (1813). Three years later the Sydney *Gazette* reported a performance of *Fatal Curiosity* (1736) and *Fortune's Frolic* (1799) by sailors on board HMS *Imogene* on 25.7.1833. The next performances considered worthy of mention in the newspapers were those given at Parramatta Barracks by men of the 4th or King's Own Regiment, on 29.6.1835. They performed *Lover's Vows* (1798) and *What Next?* (1816). Some years later performances by groups of soldiers were being given in specially equipped Army theatres. By this time a high enough standard had been reached for the soldiers at Parramatta Barracks to be able to present a condensed but satisfactory performance of *The Beggar's Opera* (1728) on 13.3.1846. The production was under the direction of the composer and pianist Isaac Nathan, and his Mrs Peachum, Polly Peachum, Sukey Tawdry, and Betty Doxy were played by the eldest son of Colonel Anderson, by Captain Maine, by the eldest son of Colonel Wynyard, and by A.Macarthur Esq., respectively. After the opera the company presented a short pantomime with harlequinade, during which Lucy Lockett, played by a private of the 58th, and Polly Peachum, 'metamorphosed into elegantly dressed opera dancers,' danced a *pas de deux* described by one newspaper as 'decidedly one of the best burlesques on the Italian opera dancing we ever witnessed.'

Artist of Florence, The; or, A Family Picture. 2-act comedy by Charles Dillon and Charles Webb, adapted from a vaudeville by A.E.Scribe, Royal Victoria, Sydney 24.4.1863, initially 1 performance.

Asche, Oscar (1871-1936). Born in Australia (real name John Stanger Heiss), Asche made a name for himself on the English stage, appearing in 1893 with the Frank Benson company in Shakespearian productions. Next he joined Beerbohm Tree at His Majesty's, and then branched out on his own as actor-manager. In 1909 he and his company made their first Australian tour with a repertoire of 5 of Shakespeare's plays and 2 melodramas. In 1911 he rewrote Edward Knoblock's play, *Hajj's Hour,* renaming it *Kismet,* which he produced at London's Garrick for a successful run. The day after it closed, early in 1912, he and his company left for a second tour of Australia, when *Kismet* and *A Midsummer Night's Dream* were his major productions. He later achieved world fame with his World War I musical play, *Chu Chin Chow,* music by Frederick Norton, which had a record run of 2238 consecutive performances. As an actor he was hearty, loud-voiced, knockabout, athletic. It is said that in his production of *Othello* he 'shook Iago as a terrier shakes a rat; hauled him up and down the stage, dashed him to the ground, half-throttled him . . .' As a producer and playwright he demonstrated a remarkable grasp of popular stagecraft, and seemed to know instinctively what was and was not theatrically possible.

Aside, The. Words spoken during the course of a play and supposedly heard only by the person on the stage to whom they were addressed, or only by the audience. This was a convention adopted to let the audience know of the existence of 2 levels in the dialogue — the words spoken by the characters for all to hear, and the thoughts of those characters. In some plays the actor momentarily stepped out of character to say directly to the audience such things as 'Little does he know that I have discovered where he has taken her,' the convention being that the other actors could not hear him. Towards the end of the century a great deal of dissatisfaction with this convention was expressed by critics, audiences, and actors. But the aside also had its supporters, one of whom was the dramatist Henry Arthur Jones, who said it was as legitimate a convention as the removal of the 4th wall. When the dust of argument finally settled agreement was reached to the extent that it was admitted the aside should be used with care. Jones did not use it at all in his most popular play, *Mrs Dane's Defence* (1900), and William Archer buried it for good in 1912 when he said: 'An aside is intolerable because it is *not* heard by the other persons on the stage . . .' Its use dates at least from the days of the early Roman playwright, Plautus.

As You Like It. Comedy by William Shakespeare, believed to have been first produced in London in 1599 or 1600; Royal Victoria, Sydney 23.6.1845.

Attila. 3-act opera with prologue, text T. Solera, with additions by F.M. Piave, after Z. Werner's *Attila König der Hunnen,* music G. Verdi, La Fenice, Venice 17.3.1846; Her Majesty's, London 14.3.1848; Royal, Melbourne 17.8.1860, initial 3 performances. This opera was to have been performed at the Prince of Wales, Sydney on 12.7.1860, but a dispute caused its cancellation. 1 act only was performed the following night.

Audiences. A great many of the accepted attitudes and reactions by 19th century audiences, up to at least the 1870s, evolved in the second half of the 18th century. So it was that the early 19th century theatre in Australia had tags, lengths, benefits, half-price, hissing, bespeaks, long programmes, early starting, and a host of other carryovers from the 18th century English theatre, including, early in the century, disturbances and domination of the actors by audiences. Actors were looked on as servants of their audiences, and were abused and sometimes physically assaulted by those audiences. In Sydney in the 1830s audiences were often every bit as violent as those in England. Bottles, stones, fruit, orange peel, nutshells, and other missiles were thrown at the actors; members of the orchestra were often so heavily peppered with objects from all parts of the house that they left the orchestra pit and sought safety backstage. This was the signal for the hardier members of the audience to clamber on stage and indulge in hand-to-hand fighting with the actors. On some nights the incessant roars of displeasure from the audience made it impossible to hear the actors. On others, displeasure with an individual actor, or with the theatre manager was shown by a concerted hiss whenever either of them appeared. The pit was most often the scene of unruly behaviour, and especially of fights between those for and against a particular actor or play. In 1838, when the Royal Victoria was opened, these disturbances continued, but not to the same extent as at the earlier Royal. Yet one night in 1842, when the pit was crowded to suffocation and the audience were in an ugly mood, they took hold of a little boy and passed him over their heads from one to the other round and round the pit, buffeting and cuffing him at the same time. He finally managed to escape, 'but scarcely had their noise subsided, when a row was commenced between two ladies and their gentlemen in the upper boxes, which ended in a regular fight.' No sooner had this disturbance been settled than a drunk in the dress circle threw himself into 'theatrical attitude' and declaimed Richard's speech to Catesby. He was taken to the watchhouse. As time passed better manners prevailed. Theatres were better organised, more comfortable, and there were more of them. Only occasionally did something raise the ire of an audience, and then, as they did at one Sydney theatre in the 1850s, they tore the gas fittings off the walls and wrecked the proscenium. But by the 1890s an English visitor, writing in the London monthly *The Theatre,* reported with pride that Australian audiences so much resembled those in the better London theatres that the visitor felt sure he *was* in London. At the time, this was considered a compliment.

Auditorium, Darkening of the. A lighted auditorium during the progress of a play was normal in the 18th and early 19th century theatre. This not only helped members of the audience to see and be seen, and to read 'the bill of the play,' but also provided extra illumination for the stage. When gas came into general use for lighting it was realised that here was a medium which could be manipulated much more easily than lamps or candles. The turn of a cock could raise or lower the intensity of the light. Further, a much more dramatic and convincing stage picture could be provided if the auditorium lights were turned off, and only the stage lights were left burning. It was also discovered that while gas was expensive to use, the cost could be cut by turning out, or at least lowering the auditorium lights once the audience were seated. The first record of a darkened auditorium in the Australian theatre is that of 14.9.1835, when Edward Fitzball's *The Flying Dutchman* (1827) was first produced. The producer followed the playwright's direction for the conclusion of Act 2: '. . . the Phantom ship appears (a la Phantasmagoria) in a peal of thunder. The stage and audience part of the Theatre in total darkness.' In other words, the shape of a ship was thrown on a backcloth by means of a magic lantern, an early form of slide projector. It is not known when the practice of darkening the auditorium came into general use, but it is known that it was a recognised if only occasional practice in the 1850s. In 1859, when G.V.Brooke was lessee of Melbourne Royal, he told his stage manager to economise by getting rid of superfluous backstage staff, and by exercising the greatest care in the use of gas. The manager was told to see that the gas was turned off *'behind* when the curtain is down, and before when it is up.' Theatres also sometimes darkened their auditoriums for artistic reasons. In 1879, during a Sydney performance of *HMS Pinafore,* it was said that in the second act, representing night scenes, 'the room [auditorium] was darkened and the stage effectively illuminated by means of the lime light.' The scenepainter, the man whose work for the stage was most affected by light, should have been able to advance the most logical reasons for or against the lighting of the auditorium during a performance. Henry L.Benwell wrote in 1884: 'The scenepainter has to contend with many difficulties peculiar to his confined walk of art. The necessity of giving a brilliant light to the auditorium is often destruction to the truth and delicacy of those tints which the artist applies to his scene . . .' 4 years later he amended this statement. 'The auditorium should be lit soberly enough to see faces and features, and to read the bill or book of the play; but that utter darkness which is in vogue at some theatres is unnatural, and in a measure destroys the illusion and intensifies the glare upon the stage.' And the actors? Which did they prefer? The Sydney *Bulletin* reported in 1892: 'Actors complain of the darkening of theatres, because they like to see the happy faces before them. They might as well be playing to Dante's *Inferno,* under this cheap system.'

Australia; or, The Bushrangers. 5-act drama by W.Archer and A.G.Stanley, Grecian, London 16.4.1881, initial 24 performances, after which it did the rounds of the provincial theatres. Ms in British Library, Shelfmark ADD. 53251 (c) SCH 5358.

Australia Calls. 4-act drama by J.Lee and S.Mackay, Royal Standard, Sydney 19.5.1909. A reading for copyright purposes. The play was to have had public performances later, but was displaced by R.Bedford's *White Australia,* which dealt with the same theme — the invasion of Australia by an Asian nation. In the same year F.R.C.Hopkins published his play (anonymously) on this theme, *Reaping the Whirlwind. An Australian Patriotic Drama,* Websdale, Shoosmith, Sydney 1909.

Australia, Plays about. The late 18th and early 19th century dramatists eagerly grasped at the possibilities presented by the newly-established or discovered Australia. At first their interest was taken by navigators and explorers such as Cook, La Perouse, and Bligh; then came personalities such as Margaret Catchpole, and George Barrington, followed by convicts, bushrangers, the gold rushes, Arthur Orton the Tichborne claimant, and Ned Kelly. In between, as it were, Australia was seen dramatically as the ideal place in which to 'lose' a character, as a convict, a runaway embezzler or husband, a younger son, a gold fossicker, a murderer. Many plays had their early acts set in England and the final in Australia. Naturally, Captain Cook featured in the first English dramatic work to deal with Australia. This was the pantomime (play in dumbshow, with music, dancing, and singing), *Omai; or, A Trip Around the World,* given at Covent Garden on 20.12.1785. Next came a 4-act pantomime given in Paris at the Ambigu-Comique in October 1788, *La Mort du Captain Cook, a son troisième voyage au nouveau monde.* This reached Covent Garden the following year as *The Death of Captain Cook.* Then it was Bligh's turn, with *The Pirates; or, The Calamities of Captain Bligh,* given in 1790 at the Royal near Goodmans Fields. 2 years later an uninhabited Australia was chosen by a French dramatist for his semi-Utopian drama, *Les Emigrés aux Terres Australes.* Towards the end of the 18th century several dramatists concentrated on the French navigator, the Comte de La Perouse, the first two English plays, one by Benjamin Thompson, the other by Ann Plumptre (1799), being based on the German dramatist August von Kotzebue's *La Peyrouse.*

Australian Bunyips, The. 3-act drama by Mons. Ricard, pen-name of an unknown author, Our Lyceum, Sydney 26.1.1857, initial 2 performances. The first Australian play to have a squatter as well as a bushranger villain, and to employ a band of Aborigines to perform a Corroboree. The cast also included the Aboriginal character, King Bobby, played by a white man. The sensation scene in this melodrama is one in which the bushranger destroys the bridge and the hero falls into the rapids running through the Bunyip's Glen. He is rescued by King Bobby, who thus takes his place in Australian drama as the first of many 'sympathetic' Aborigines who rescue and protect the white man. This bridge-and-fall scene was used more than 30 years later by Alfred Dampier in the play, *The Scout,* though it dates from the bridge-over-the-chasm scene in Kotzebue's *Pizarro,* first performed at Drury Lane 24.5.1799. No copy of *The Australian Bunyips* survives.

Australian play, The. All kinds of plays were written and produced in Australia in the 19th century, more than 650 of them, but up to the year 1900 only 176 of the total output were plays with an Australian subject, setting, and characters. The majority were poor imitations of English originals. Walter Hampson Cooper was the first of only 2 representatives of the 1860s whose plays were Australian in setting and character. George Darrell was the only one in the 1870s, with his *The Forlorn Hope*, though this could be said to have a foot in both camps. In the 1880s there were no fewer than 7 plays which qualify as Australian, and 6 in the 1890s. But between 1905 and 1913 a genuine interest in the Australian play came alive. Perhaps Federation and a growth in population were partly responsible. Australians were not yet thinking as a nation, but they were beginning to think as Australians. In this period 15 Australian plays were produced to good runs. These included the record-breaking *The Squatter's Daughter* and *On Our Selection,* and *My Mate, The Man from Outback, The Girl of the Never-Never,* and *The Native Born.* The war, the end of an era, and the phenomenal growth in the efficiency of the comparatively new cinematograph brought this interest and activity to a halt. By the end of the 1914-18 war only Bert Bailey was left, still digging at the rich vein of ore in the stories by Steele Rudd (A.H.Davis), in which he appeared in films as well as on the stage. (See: Cinema. Parliamentarians).

Australians abroad. Australian actors — those born in Australia and those who made Australia their home — were nothing if not travellers. Singers, dancers, and actors travelled all over the globe under what today seem to have been the most appalling conditions, seeking audiences wherever they might be found. In their own land they travelled as far as the Gulf of Carpentaria, and as far west as Perth and Kalgoorlie. From the 1830s onward they visited China, Japan, and India, playing to the English communities in those centres. In the late 1830s the fascinating Mrs Maria Taylor, who had so scandalised the moral section of the Sydney community, made her way to India, only to die there. Blanche Lewis (nee Rose Edouin) with her husband, George, is said to have established the first theatre in Calcutta in 1867 (*Theatre,* August 1881). In 1854 they had converted Astley's Amphitheatre in Melbourne into the first Princess's. The truth is that the more talented and enterprising Australian actors could hold their own with any of their peers overseas, as they proved again and again. Though there were disdainful reactions by some English actors to the Australian theatre as a whole, most of the visiting 'stars' from England and the USA testified to the value of the support given them by local players. Only Lewis Wingfield was bitter, if not biased about his Australian experiences. He held the strange if not unique belief that the Australian population consisted of squatters and larrikins. After his visit he wrote in an article in the *New Review* (1892): 'As there is no Australian fine art, and but a meagre show of literature, so also there are no actors, any more than there are dramatists.' His peevish reaction ignored the facts. Eliza Winstanley, Mrs Charles Young (later Mrs Hermann Vezin), Herbert Flemming, Kyrle Bellew, G.Fawcett Rowe, Luscombe Searelle,

W.J.Holloway, W.H.Cooper, Alfred Dampier, F.R.C.Hopkins, Garnet Walch, and Nellie Stewart had already proved him wrong, and others were to continue to do so.

Autumn Manoeuvres. (See: *Ein Herbstmanöver*).

B

Babiole. 3-act comic opera, text L.F.Clairville and O.Gastineau, adapted R.Reece, music L. de Rille, Prince's, Manchester 10.3.1879; Bijou, Melbourne 19.7.1887, initial 8 performances.

Baby's Luck. 1-act comedietta by Marcus Clarke, Academy of Music, Melbourne 3.3.1879, initially 1 performance. Under title *The Man in Possession,* Opera House, Sydney 5.12.1885.

Back drop. Sometimes called 'drop,' sometimes 'drop scene.' Stage scene painted on canvas and hung on rollers, worked, like the act drop, on the same principle as the veranda blind. Originated in 1690. Backdrops were at first used to replace the 2 back flats or shutters which met in the middle of the stage to form the back scene, or back wall of a dwelling. The drop, being in on piece, was a way of avoiding the central join or seam exhibited when the flats met. (See: Stage setting).

Back From the Grave. 4-act drama by George Darrell, Royal, Sydney 2.3.1878, initial 13 performances.

Bailey, Albert Edward (1872-1953). Better known as Bert Bailey. Chiefly notable as Dad in the stage and film versions of Steele Rudd's *On Our Selection.* Born in New Zealand, he came to Australia in his early boyhood. At first employed in the Ashfield (Sydney) Telegraph Office, he was next floor manager of a Sydney skating rink, music hall singer, and finally actor. He joined Duggan and Smith's touring company in 1889, which covered every major town in New South Wales, Victoria, and Queensland — even as far as Normanton and Croydon at the top of the Gulf of Carpentaria. Next he joined Kate Howarde's touring company, and then the Irve Hyman company, each of which also did the 'circuit' up as far as the Gulf of Carpentaria. In this way he and

Duggan, who had formed a partnership as complementary actors and playwrights, not only learned the art of acting and character presentation in the popular theatre, but also the kind of play with the most audience appeal. On joining William Anderson's company, whose productions were restricted to the capital cities, he and Duggan collaborated on a number of plays, writing under the pen-name Albert Edmunds. These set Duggan and Bailey, but particularly Bailey, on the road to financial as well as dramatic success. From then on Bailey prospered, largely because he had decided on the kind of comic characters he wanted to represent, and the kind of play required for his purpose. For Bailey was as calculating, financially, as he as an actor. When he decided to attempt a dramatic version of *On Our Selection,* Bailey rewrote and moulded the part of Dad, which remained his for the rest of his acting life. Rightly or wrongly, he always regarded this as *his* play, and it made his fortune. Bailey retired from the stage in 1929, having played the part of Dad, and a number of other characters, for 17 years. But it was not to be the end of his acting career. He had played the character in the early silent films, and in the 1930s he played Dad again in the first talking film version of *On Our Selection,* and, for the next 10 years, in a series of 'Dad' films.

Balkan Princess, The. 3-act musical comedy, text F.Lonsdale and F.Curzon, music P.Rubens, Prince of Wales, London 19.2.1910; Royal, Sydney 10.6.1911, initial 48 performances.

Ballad opera. Typically English form of stage entertainment, with songs set to well known popular melodies. *The Beggar's Opera* is the outstanding example of the genre.

Ballet. The first ballet performances were given at Barnett Levey's Royal in Sydney, though details of their form and substance are lost to us. The first was *The Rival Lovers,* 17.1.1835, said by E.Pask to have been *The Fair Maid of Perth; or, The Rival Lovers.* Next came *The Indian Maid,* 9.2.1835, which was probably a version of *The Maid of Cashmere,* later given in Sydney as *The Rose of Cashmere,* 3.11.1845. Then followed *Don Juan; or, The Libertine Destroyed,* 21.8.1837, a version of the original Don Juan ballet by G.Angiolini to the music of Gluck (1761), and finally *Cinderella: or, The Little Glass Slipper,* 12.10.1837, which may have been a version of F.Sor's *Cendrillon.* In Melbourne, interest in ballet began to grow in the 1850s, the gold-rush years. That city's first ballet performances were produced in a shower of gold, which is to say that the delighted audiences of gold diggers at the Queen's used to throw sovereigns and nuggets on to the stage to show their appreciation. Juvenile members of the *corps de ballet* had their payment in silver, thrown to and sometimes at them. Melbourne audiences were always more interested in ballet than those in Sydney, and it is to Melbourne that the major firsts in the art belong — *La Sylphide,* 1845; *Giselle,* 1855;

La Fille mal gardée, 1855; *Ondine,* 1861. But as the century progressed performances of individual ballets lapsed, and dancers eventually found their principal source of employment in the supporting ballets given with opera performances, pantomimes, musical burlesques, comic operas, and musical comedies. Not until the visit of Adeline Genee and members of the Imperial Russian Ballet in 1913 did a real interest in ballet start to flower in Australia. In the words of E.Pask, this was 'the opening of the greatest era of ballet in this country.'

Ballo in Maschera, Un (A Masked Ball). 3-act opera, text A.Somma, based on A.E.Scribe's *Gustave III,* music G.Verdi, Apollo, Rome 17.2.1859; Lyceum, London 15.6.1861; Haymarket, Melbourne 29.1.1868, initial 9 performances. (See: *Gustave III*).

Bandit of the Rhine, The. 3-act drama by E.H.Thomas, The Theatre, Launceston 14.10.1835, initially 2 performances. Later performed at Royal, Hobart 22.10.1836. Published *The Chronicle* Office, Launceston 3.10.1835, the first play to be published in book or pamphlet form in Australia. No copy has survived.

Barbe-Bleu (Bluebeard). 3-act comic opera, text H.Meilhac and L. Halévy, music J.Offenbach, Variétés, Paris 5.2.1866; Olympic, London 2.6.1866; Princess's, Melbourne 23.4.1872, initial 16 performances.

Barbiere di Siviglia, Il (The Barber of Seville). 2-act comic opera, text C.Sterbini, music G.A.Rossini, Argentina, Rome 20.2.1816; His Majesty's, London 10.3.1818; Royal Victoria, Sydney 19.6.1843, initially 1 performance.

Barlow, Billy. The term 'a Billy Barlow' is defined in Brewer's *Dictionary of Phrase and Fable* (1974) as 'a street droll, a Merry Andrew.' The original Barlow was a half-idiot, notorious for his odd behaviour, who died early in the 19th century in a Whitechapel workhouse. His oddities have since been set out in a number of songs, the first of which, words only, seems to have been the one published in an early, undated London chapbook. The opening stanza is:

> O when I was born says old Mother Goose
> He is a fine boy, but he'll be of no use;
> My father he said that to church I should go,
> And there he had me christened Billy Barlow
>   O dear, lackaday O,
> And there he had me christened Billy Barlow.

The first recorded theatrical performance of a song of this name is of that sung by Benjain Conquest at the Pavilion, Whitechapel 11.6.1828. Frances Fleetwood says he 'sang it three or four times a night for twenty-eight weeks, first at the Pavilion and then at the Olympic, until it seemed that he would be nicknamed "Billy Barlow" for the rest of his life.' It is now possible to put the horse before the cart and discover why, at Maitland, New South Wales in 1843, the song called 'Billy Barlow in Australia' was such a success. The original was so well known to the singer's largely English audience in Australia that they could laugh at this 'new' Billy Barlow, not only because he was now very much in Australia, but also because, unlike most of his listeners, he was a 'new chum,' and was being fleeced as only new chums should be — by the old hands. George Coppin at once took up the song (the English version — there is no evidence that he ever sang *Billy Barlow in Australia*), and sang it so often throughout the colonies that his listeners tired of it. He adapted its wording to the local scene by adding topical and local comments, much as Sam Cowell (1820-1864) did in New York and London. During the Civil War the song was immensely popular. Cowell added such lines as:

And the young women there gave vent to such woe
You'd ha' thought they were parting from Billy Barlow.
  Oh, dear, oh raggedy oh!
You'd ha' thought they were parting from Billy Barlow.

The song's popularity in so many areas in the 1820s, 1840s, and 1860s is only partially explained on the grounds of its humour, its 'there but for the grace of God go I' implications. It was made the basis of a 3-act comedy, *Jemmy Green in Australia,* believed to have been written by the convict author, James Tucker, in 1845 (it was never produced), and of a farce which was several times produced.

Barlow Family, The. 1-act eccentric farce by C.A.Dibdin, Royal Victoria, Sydney 12.10.1843. Ms held in Archives Office of N.S.W.

Barrett, Alfred Wilson (1846-1904). Trained in English provincial theatres, and associated with them all his life, Wilson Barrett (as he preferred to be called) eventually starred in a number of leading London theatres. Over the years he was actor, dramatist, theatre proprietor, and theatre manager. His 27 works for the stage include comedies, dramas, an opera, and a drama set in Australia, *The Never-Never Land* (1902). As an actor he was associated with many famous 19th century melodramas, including *The Lights o' London, The Silver King, Claudian, The Sign of the Cross,* and *Quo Vadis? The Silver King,* which made him world famous, is one of 3 or 4 popular melodramas remembered for 1 particular line. One is *East Lynne,* with its 'Dead, and never called me "Mother!" ' Another is 'the long arm of coincidence,' from *Captain Swift,* while a third is the famous and much-quoted line from *The Silver King,* 'Oh God, put back Thy Universe and give me yesterday.' Barrett twice visited Australia, in 1896 and in 1902-03. The world premiere of his play *The Christian King; or, Alfred of Engeland* was given in Melbourne in 1901.

Barry, Shiel (1842-1897). Irish-born actor who began his career with W.J.Holloway in an amateur theatre they conducted in Sydney. In 1865 he went to Melbourne, where he managed to get himself 'starred' as the Irish comedian who would put all other Irish comedians into obscurity. He did not, and as he could not find work, or any sort of hard work, he eventually...

Barton, George Burnett (1836-1901). Born in New South Wales, a brother of Sir Edmund Barton, first Australian Prime Minister. Reader in English Language and Literature, University of Sydney. Author *Poetry and Prose Writers of New South Wales* (1866), *Literature in New South Wales* (1866), edited *The History of New South Wales From the Records,* vol. 1, Sydney 1889. Also wrote *Oberon; or, The Knight and the Caliphs* (1865), a fairy extravaganza.

Battle of Hastings, The; or, The Duke, the Earl, the Witch, The Why, and the Wherefore. 7-scene burlesque by W.M.Akhurst, Royal, Melbourne 29.3.1869, initial 11 performances. Text published R.Bell, Melbourne, 1869.

Bedford, Randolph (1868-1941). Journalist, miner, poet, novelist, politician, short-story writer, and dramatist. Born in Sydney, Bedford spent most of his early adult life 'knocking about' Australia. From his early years he retained a love of the theatre, and in his autobiography, *From Naught to Thirty-Three* (1944) he recalls melodramas he saw when a boy. He does not mention dates, but from his descriptions each play can be traced and shown to have been produced as he remembered it. For example on page 48 he says: 'I saw a marvellous drama at the old Gaiety Theatre in Castlereagh Street. One Reynolds had given the name of *Vanity Fair* to a melodrama . . .' Walter Reynolds did produce his drama, *Vanity Fair,* at the Gaiety, on 24.7.1882, when Bedford was 14. He later produced it in England and America. Bedford himself later took up playwriting but did not have as much success as some of his contemporaries. His interests and enthusiasms were too widespread, too diverse to be contained in any one activity. Of his 3 plays produced, the most successful in terms of the number of performances it enjoyed was *The Unseen Eye,* simply because it had about it an air of mystery and excitement the other two plays, *White Australia,* and *The Lady of the Pluckup,* lacked. Yet in *The Unseen Eye* he repeated a 'sensation' as old as Boucicault's *The Octoroon* (1859), in which a camera, unknown to the thief, photographs him in the act. Bedford thought his most important play was *White Australia,* which embodied beliefs he had many times outlined in speeches, and in a published pamphlet — the invasion of Australia by an Asian force. The invasion takes place, in Darwin first, and ultimately this highly sensational play shows 'an airship travelling through cloudland at an indefinite height above the earth and subsequently hovering over Sydney' — to drop bombs on the enemy fleet at anchor in Sydney Harbour. Randolph Bedford died in the year of Pearl Harbour (1941), when Japan took the first steps along a trail which in a few months was to bring her dangerously close to occupying first New Guinea and then Australia. (See: Reynolds, Walter).

Beggar Student, The. (See: *Bettelstudent, Der*).

Beggar's Opera, The. Ballad opera by John Gay, Lincoln's Inn Fields, January 1727; Albert, Hobart 30.3.1842.

Belisario. 3-act opera, text S.Cammarano, music G.Donizetti, Venice 4.2.1836; London 1.4.1837; Royal, Sydney 1.4.1887, initial 4 performances.

Belle Hélène, La (The Fair Helen). 3-act operetta, text H.Meilhac and L.Halévy, music J.Offenbach, Variétés, Paris 17.12.1864; Adelphi, London 30.6.1886; Royal Victoria, Sydney 31.5.1876, initial 4 performances.

Belle of Brittany, The. Two-act musical comedy, text L.Bantock and P.Barrow, music H.Talbot and M.Horne, Queen's, London 24.10.1906; Criterion, Sydney 25.2.1911, initial 25 performances.

Belle of Mayfair, The. 2-act musical comedy, text C.Brookfield and C.Hamilton, music L.Stuart, Vaudeville, London 11.4.1906; Royal, Melbourne 20.6.1908, initial 24 performances.

Belle of New York, The. 2-act comic opera, text H.Morton, music G.Kerker, Casino, New York 28.9.1897; Shaftesbury, London 12.4.1898; Princess's, Melbourne 1.4.1899, initial 28 performances. This comic opera had an initial run of 56 performances in New York, but, produced in London by the Australian, George Musgrove, it achieved an initial 693 performances, the first American musical to run in London for more than a year.

Belle-Poule, La. 3-act comic opera, text H.Crémieux, and St Alban, music Hervé (Florimond Ronger), Folies Dramatiques, Paris 3.12.1875; Royal, Sydney (as *Poulet and Poulette*) 6.10.1877, initial 3 performances.

Belle Thérèse, La. 3-act musical comedy, text M.Ordonneau and Kerroul, music G.Serpette, Folies Dramatiques, Paris 23.12.1893; Princess's, Melbourne 7.12.1895, initial 13 performances.

Bellew, Harold Kyrle (1855-1911). English-born actor who started stage career on the Solferino goldfields in New South Wales. Appeared in *Hamlet, Richard III,* and a number of comedies until his acting career ended with the exhaustion of the goldfields. He then worked for a time as a journalist in Melbourne. In 1875 he returned to England and by 1878 was with the Henry Irving company at London's Lyceum. He played Osric in *Hamlet* in 1878, and Glavis in *The Lady of Lyons* in 1879; after this he set out on his first visit to the USA. For almost 20 years he was this country's leading matinee idol. In 1888 he formed a company with the American socialite-actress, Mrs Cora Urquhart Potter. The pair toured the world's theatres for more than 10 years, reaching Australia with *Camille* and other plays popular at the time. Bellew, a handsome, graceful actor, and therefore very popular. His Mrs Potter, doubtedly beautiful, seems to have been chiefly notable for the fact that she was dressed exclusively by Worth of Paris. Bellew also wrote several plays. His *Charlotte Corday,* in which he played Marat, was one of the most popular. From 1902 until his death in 1911 he was associated exclusively with the American theatre.

Benefit. The 18th century English benefit system was still in use in the early 19th century Australian theatre. A benefit usually came at the end of a season, and was an arrangement by which each leading actor in turn was given the use of the theatre for a night, all profits, apart from the normal nightly expenses, to be his, the other actors giving their services free. The actor would draw up a long and attractive novelty programme for the night, and would have to canvass the public for their patronage, deliver playbills to the shops, and sell box and other tickets from his place of residence. If the theatre was filled on the night he made a tidy profit. But benefits were chancy things. Often by the end of a season the public had had enough of the theatre for a while, and benefit attendances were poor. The introduction of the travelling company, of the long-running play, and the abolition of seasons — theatres remaining open all the year instead of closing briefly two or three times a year — all contributed to the abolition of the benefit system. Benefits in the second half of the century were usually matinee performances for a special, mainly charitable occasion.

Ben Hur. 6-act drama by W. Young adapted from L. Wallace's novel (1880), Broadway, New York 29.11.1899; Her Majesty's, Sydney 8.2.1902, predating by nearly 2 months the London production at Drury Lane. The Sydney production ended prematurely when the theatre was destroyed by fire on 23.3.1902. Many subsequent performances were given after the theatre reopened in 1903.

Sarah Bernhardt in her Paris studio 1890

Benjamin Bowbell. (See: *Illustrious Stranger, The*).

Bernhardt, Sarah (1845-1923). French actress whose high-spirited unconventionality and sometimes absurd behaviour could not hide the excellence of her acting, or the spell cast by her voice. She made her name at the Comédie-Francaise and other Paris theatres, in plays such as Beaumarchais's *Le Mariage de Figaro* (1784), Racine's *Andromaque* (1667), and *Phèdre* (1677), Voltaire's *Zaïre* (1732), Hugo's *Hernani* (1830), and *Ruy Blas* (1838), and the younger Dumas's *La Dame aux camélias* (1852). First appeared in London in 1879, and in New York in 1880. Her visit to Australia in 1891 was a triumphal progress, from her arrival in Sydney with its official and vice-regal welcome, to her farewell in the same city some three months later. She spent a few days in Sydney after her arrival, and then left by special train for Melbourne, where she opened her Australian season on 4.6.1891 in *La Dame aux camélias*. During her tour she also appeared in *La Tosca* (1887), *Théodora* (1884), *Adrienne Lecouvreur* (1849), *Frou Frou* (1869), *Fédora* (1882), *Pauline Blanchard, Jeanne d'Arc* (1873), and *Cléopâtre* (1890). The production of Darmont's *Pauline Blanchard* in Sydney on 27.7.1891 was a world premiere. Bernhardt left Australia at the beginning of August 1891.

Bespeak. A theatrical performance requested by a town or city notability, in imitation of the royal command performance. A bespeak added importance to a normal performance, in that it drew a larger audience than usual, and in particular a larger box and dress circle audience. In Australia, when used at all, a bespeak was usually 'got up' by a group of city businessmen, as when such a group announced a bespeak for George Darrell in Sydney in 1872.

Bettelstudent, Der (The Beggar Student). 4-act operetta, text F.Zell and R.Genée, music K.Millöcker, Theater an der Wien, Vienna 6.12.1882; English version W.Beatty-Kingston, Alhambra, London 12.4.1884; Opera House, Sydney 3.6.1889, initial 24 performances.

Bill Adams, the Hero of Waterloo. 2-act musical comedy, text H.Shelley and R.Bacchus, music S.Philpot, Royal, Eastbourne 26.2.1903; Criterion, Sydney 27.5.1905, initial 10 performances.

Billee Taylor; or, The Rewards of Virtue. 2-act comic opera, text H.P.Stephens, music E.Solomon, Imperial, London 30.10.1880; Princess's, Melbourne 26.8.1882, initial 18 performances.

Birraio di Preston, Il (The Brewer of Preston). 3-act opera, text F.Guido after A.De Leuven and L.Brunswick's *Le Brasseur de Preston* (1838), music L.Ricci, Teatro della Pergola, Florence 4.2.1847; St James's, London 24.11.1857; Prince of Wales, Melbourne 4.9.1874, initially 1 performance.

Birthday, The. 3-act comedy by A. von Kotzebue, translation by

T.J.Dibdin of *Der Brüderzwist,* Covent Garden, London 8.4.1799; Royal Victoria, Sydney 11.2.1841.

Bishop, Anna (1810-1884). Famous early 19th century soprano, wife of the composer-cohductor Henry (later Sir Henry) Bishop (1786-1855). Married in 1831, she left her husband 8 years later to live and travel the world with her teacher and accompanist, the harpist Robert (Nicholas) Bochsa (1789-1856), who died during their Australian tour. The old cliche, 'has sung before the crowned heads of Europe' was in Anna Bishop's case perfectly true. From the 1830s to the early 1860s this indefatigable woman did more travelling than the majority of men and possibly of any other woman of her time. From the age of 18 onwards she regularly gave concerts and sang in opera performances in England, Denmark, Sweden, Russia, Tartary, Moldavia, Italy, Switzerland, Belgium, South America, Mexico, USA, Australia, and the East. She made her Australian debut in Sydney in 1855, and when, in 1856, George Coppin acquired the Melbourne Royal, she opened it for him with Melbourne's first season of Italian opera. Like so many others before and after it, the season resulted in a financial loss to Coppin. Resuming her travels, Anna Bishop toured South America, England, USA, Canada, the West Indies, and Honolulu. Leaving Honolulu for Hong Kong, her ship was wrecked on the voyage, and she and others managed to survive for three weeks on a coral island. They finally put off again in the two small boats which had brought them there. The smaller boat was never heard of again, but Anna, in the larger, after 13 days at sea finally reached Guam. She had lost her extensive wardrobe, her jewellery, and her library of music in the wreck. Undaunted, she set out again — Manila, Amoy, Foochow, Shanghai, Hong Kong, Canton, Singapore, India, and then back to Australia. Egypt was next, on her way back to Europe, and then to the USA. By this time her days as a singer were almost over, and she settled down to teaching.

Black Eyed Susan; or, All in the Downs. 2-act melodrama by D.Jerrold, Surrey, London 8.6.1829; Royal, Sydney 26.12.1832.

Black Rover, The. (See: *Isidora*).

Blanche of Jersey. 2-act opera, text R.B.Peake, music J.Barnett, Lyceum, London 9.8.1837; Royal Victoria, Sydney 9.6.1845.

Blind Love. 1-act drama by Bernard Espinasse, Her Majesty's, Sydney 7.6.1899.

Blue Bird, The (L'Oiseau Bleu). 5-act fairy play by M.Maeterlinck, first produced by Stanislavsky, Moscow 1908; Haymarket, London 8.12.1909, translated A.T.de Mattos; Criterion, Sydney 6.4.1912, initial 36 performances.

Blue Moon, The. 2-act musical comedy, text H.Ellis and P.Greenbank, music H.Talbot and P.Rubens, Lyric, London 28.8.1905; Princess's, Melbourne 22.6.1907, initial 36 performances.

Bobadil. 3-act comic opera, text W.Parke, music Luscombe Searelle, Opera House, Sydney 22.11.1884, initial 42 performances.

Boccaccio. 3-act operetta, text F.Zell and R.Genée, music F.von Suppé, Carl, Vienna 1.2.1879; Comedy, London 22.4.1882; Opera House, Melbourne 2.9.1882, initial 66 performances.

Bohème, La (The Bohemians). 4-act opera, text G.Giocosa and L.Illica, after H.Murger's novel, *Scènes de la Vie de Bohème,* music G.Puccini, Regio, Turin 1.2.1896; Covent Garden, London 2.10.1897; Her Majesty's, Melbourne 13.7.1901, initial 4 performances.

Bohemian Girl, The. 4-act opera, text A.Bunn based on ballet-pantomime, *La Gypsy,* by J.H.Saint-Georges, music M.Balfe, Drury Lane, London 27.11.1843; Royal Victoria, Sydney 13.7.1846.

Boldrewood, Rolf. (See: Brown, Thomas Alexander).

Bombastes Furioso. 1-act burlesque by W.B.Rhodes, Haymarket, London 7.8.1810; Emu Plains, 16.5.1825.

Bonsoir, Voison. 1-act opera, text L.Brunswick and A.de Beauplan, music F.Poise, Liége 13.12.1857; Royalty, London 29.1.1873; Prince of Wales, Melbourne 16.6.1873, initial 6 performances.

Bon Ton; or, High Life Above Stairs. 2-act farce by David Garrick, Drury Lane, London 18.3.1775; The Theatre, Sydney 1.6.1799.

Booth, Edwin (1833-1893). One of the many English and American actors to whom the gold discoveries in Australia were seen to open up theatrical opportunities, and who later made a name for themselves in their home country. Born near Baltimore, in the USA, Booth in later life was chiefly notable for his production of *Hamlet* in New York in 1864, which ran for 100 consecutive performances. Booth came to Australia in 1854 with the English-born actress, Laura Keene, and his friend and fellow-actor, D.C.Anderson. He was then not quite 21, and while the acting of the pair received high praise in Sydney and Melbourne, he was still far from the artist he finally became. The pair were praised in Australia for their portrayal of Beatrice and Benedict in *Much Ado About Nothing.* For the 11 nights they were in Sydney they acted in 9 different plays — from *The Lady of Lyons* to *Hamlet,* from *The Stranger* to *Richard III.* Unfortunately for them, they arrived in Australia at the tail end of an influx of overseas actors, and did not do well. By one of those coincidences in which theatrical as well as ordinary life abounds, Laura Keene was playing in a production of *Our American Cousin* at Ford's Theatre in Washington on the night that Edwin's brother, John Wilkes Booth, assassinated President Lincoln in that theatre — 14.4.1865.

Top left: Kyrle Bellew
Below left: Edwin Booth 1860s
Below right: Gustavus Vaughan Brooke

Boothby, Guy Newell (1867-1905). Born in Adelaide, at the age of 13 Boothby went to Christ's Hospital, London to complete his education. On his return to Adelaide he became private secretary to the mayor, and later travelled extensively in Australia and the East. At some time after 1892 he returned to London, where, between 1894 and 1907, he published 50 works of fiction, the last 2 being published 2 years after his death. Before leaving for London he had published *On the Wallaby; or, Through the East and Across Australia*, a book made up of a series of articles previously published in the South Australian *Register*. His produced plays include *The Nabob* (1889); *Memories* (1889); *Dimple's Lovers* (1890); *Sylvia; or, The Marquis and the Maid* (1890), and *The Jonquille* (1891). Though he tried to have his plays produced in London, it was not until a year before his death that a short farce of his, *In Sunny Ceylon*, was accepted for production in Manchester.

Borders. Painted canvas strips hung across the top of the stage at regular intervals to provide the necessary 'top' to a scene, and to screen the above stage space from the eyes of the audience. Usually they were painted to represent interior, sky, or foliage borders, to match the settings with which they were used. Cut cloths, q.v., sometimes did away with the need for borders in landscape and forest scenes.

Boucicault, Dionysius Lardner (1822-1890). Talented Irish-born actor, dramatist, and theatre manager. His first play was produced in 1838, when he was 16, and his last in 1884. His sensation dramas ousted the old melodramas from favour. They called for massive settings, varied tricks and effects, and demanded character acting of a kind which most actors grasped at thankfully. He made his name and his greatest successes first in the United States of America and England, and then in English-speaking countries all over the world. The popularity of his plays with audiences may be gauged from the fact that although in the 1860s in Australia 1 and 2 night runs were the normal thing, while a run of 6 nights was phenomenal, yet when Boucicault's most popular plays were produced in Australia they broke all records. They were (year of Australian performance in brackets): *Jessie Brown; or, The Relief of Lucknow* (1860), 14 performances; *The Colleen Bawn; or, The Bride of Garryowen* (1861), 12; *The Flying Scud; or, A Four-legged Fortune* (1867), 27; *After Dark. A Tale of London Life* (1869), 29; *The Shaughraun* (1875), 37. Boucicault toured Australia and New Zealand in 1885, and in characteristic forthright manner wrote an account of the economics of the tour which he published in both countries. During his lifetime he went through a fortune, and at the time of his death was teaching acting.

Bourke, Sir Richard (1777-1855). Governor of New South Wales from 1831 to 1837. Four months after his arrival in Sydney he lifted the ban on theatricals imposed by his predecessor, Governor Darling. The Sydney *Gazette* published the news in its issue of 21.4.1832 — 'We understand that his Excellency the Governor has been pleased to signify his assent to a licence being granted to Mr Barnett Levey, authorising him to give dramatic entertainments in Sydney . . .'

Box setting. An 'enclosed' room setting whose invention dates back certainly to 17th century and possibly to 16th century practice in the Italian theatre. From the 18th to the late 19th centuries stage settings in the English-speaking theatre relied to a great extent on the wings and back shutter or backcloth setting. As late as 1892, as an illustration in the *Sydney Mail* shows, this kind of setting was still in use. It was not only simple to install and work, but did not call for the construction of expensive 'flies,' or flying space for scenery above the stage. Actors made their entrances and exits through spaces between the wings, though sometimes wings were constructed with real or 'practical' doors which were used as entrances. With the box setting the wings or flats were joined edge to edge to make a continuous wall, 3 such walls making the enclosed space, or room, the fourth being the proscenium arch through which the audience watched the play. In these walls, where necessary, were practical doors, windows, and archways. A ceiling was often placed on top of this enclosed space, though its use was restricted until the arrival of electric lighting, because of fire risk in 'lighting' a room. The first mention of the use of a box setting in the Australian theatre, though not necessarily the first time one was used, was made in the *Australasian* in 1865, which noted that a scene in *The Gladiator of Ravenna* included 'what is so seldom seen on the stage, but which ought always to be seen in interiors, a real top to the apartment, shutting out the "flies," and other impertinencies that so constantly obtrude themselves to destroy the illusion.' But although use of the box setting slowly increased in Australia, all was apparently not well with its verisimilitude, at least in Melbourne, for the *Australasian* reported in 1872: 'It is hardly ever the case that a room is made to resemble what it presumably represents. Now and then there is what is called a "boxed in" apartment, but even the traditional big door in the centre, or the half-dozen doors at the sides, are practically insisted upon as imperative.' Producers still wanted the best of both worlds, a box setting but with the same number of entrances and exits as the wing and shutter setting. It was not until the social and society dramas of later in the century called for a more realistic representation of ordinary and wealthy home interiors that the box setting came into general use. (See: Multiple setting. Stage setting).

Boxes. These date from the 16th century Elizabethan theatre, when it cost a penny to stand in the pit, 2d to sit in one of the boxes in the galleries which lined 3 walls of the theatre, and 3d for cushioned front box seats. These were not, at first, 'reserved' areas. Seats, usually on benches, could be taken wherever they were available. The opera houses introduced the individual, sealed-off rooms which, in the drama theatre, were usually stage or near-stage boxes. In the ordinary boxes, those in the dress and upper circles, the original backless benches were in time replaced with chairs or backed benches seating 2 or 3 people, and later still with individual upholstered chairs. As the century progressed box seats came to be regarded as symbols of social standing, though by the second half of the century the box seat was often the worst seat in the house for seeing, particularly in the boxes set at the side of the proscenium arch. Modern building methods and design, which made it easier to replace boxes with the open gallery, and thus seat more people, banished boxes from the dress and upper circles, and finally banished them altogether.

Breaking the Spell. 1-act operetta, text H.B.Farnie, music J.Offenbach, English version of *Le Violoneux,* text E.Mestépès and E.Chevalet, Bouffes-Parisiens, Paris 31.8.1855; Lyric, London 2.5.1870; Bijou, Melbourne 1.5.1897, initial 6 performances.

Brewer, Francis Campbell (1826-1911). Author of the first history of the Australian theatre, though it deals solely with theatre in Sydney. His *The Drama and Music in New South Wales,* published by the Government Printer in 1892, was written for the World's Columbian Exposition held in Chicago in 1893, to show Americans 'how large a part the actors and musicians of that country took in the development of the kindred arts in Australia . . .' It remained unchallenged until the publication of Paul McGuire's *The Australian Theatre* in 1948, but is still a valuable work. Brewer, born in Stourbridge, Staffordshire, came to Australia with his parents towards the end of 1834. In 1836 he was articled to Edward Smith Hall of the *Sydney Monitor* to learn what was then called 'the professional art of printing.' In 1839 the *Monitor* was sold, and Brewer transferred to the *Herald,* where he completed his articles. In 1846 he went to Melbourne, and worked for a while on the *Port Phillip Patriot.* Returning to the *Herald* in 1849, he was made principal overseer of the printing department. He now began to take part in the literary work of the paper, and in time became its music and drama critic, and then its night editor. In 1877 he went to work in the *Herald*'s London office, and on returning to Sydney 2 years later was made editor of the *Herald*'s afternoon paper, the *Echo,* a position he held for 7 years. He retired in 1891, wrote his account of music and drama in New South Wales in 1892, and a year later had to give up reading and writing because of failing eyesight. He ultimately became totally blind.

Brigands, Les. 3-act comic opera, text H.Meilhac and L.Halévy, music J.Offenbach, Variétés, Paris 10.12.1869; English version H.S.Leigh (*Falscappa; or, The Brigands*), Globe, London 22.4.1871; Prince of Wales, Melbourne 7.7.1877, initial 16 performances.

Brisbane, Theatre in
   1 School of Arts (1851). The first Brisbane School of Arts Hall, used

for theatrical performances, social functions, and public meetings, was opened in Queen Street in 1851. Some years later it was dismantled and re-erected in Adelaide Street, where it was known variously as the Bijou, the Albert Hall, and the Gaiety. The building finished a varied and colourful career as Parcel Post Headquarters.

2 Mason's (1865). G.B.Mason, who in the early 1860s had a hall in Elizabeth Street known as Mason's Concert Hall, is credited with having introduced regular theatrical performances to Brisbane. In 1865 he altered and renovated his hall and opened it as Mason's Theatre, in the face of strong objections on moral grounds from an influential section of the Brisbane community. His opening programme had the plays *Perfection* (1830), *Betsey Baker* (1850), and *The Bonny Fish Wife* (1858).

3 Royal Alexandra (1866). A small theatre 'with a very good stage and scenery,' opened by J.Dinsdale in Edward Street on 27.11.1866, with a performance of *The Stranger* (1798). It remained in use for 10 or 14 years, when its name was changed to Academy of Music, or Bijou, after which it seems to have fallen into disuse.

4 Royal Victoria (1867). Opened in what had been the Victoria Concert Hall by a breakaway group of actors from the Royal Alexandra on 9.3.1867.

5 Queensland (1874). In 1871 the Melbourne theatre owner, actor, and entrepreneur George Coppin brought out a young West Indian tragedian, Morton Tavares, for an Australian tour. He was not a success in Melbourne, and he and Coppin quarrelled. Tavares won the ensuing court case, and went to Sydney, where he was an instant success in Shakespearian and other roles. By 1874 he was established in Australia and New Zealand as a popular actor, and in that year he visited Brisbane. On 21.4.1874 he opened the refurbished Royal Victoria, renaming it the Queensland, with W.S.Gilbert's *The Palace of Truth* (1870). The seating was improved, the old proscenium was replaced by one which provided a wider stage, and a cloak and retiring room was provided for ladies. As an indication of what had, perhaps, prevailed before his arrival as lessee, Tavares advised in an advertisement that the public were requested 'to acquaint the manager of any incivilities by the doorkeepers.' The Brisbane *Courier* reported that the whole of the interior of this 'dingy and cellar-like place of entertainment' had been painted in light colours, 'thus imparting a cheerful look in pleasing contrast to the old gloom that pervaded the place.' This theatre apparently had a single, flat floor divided into 3, 2, and 1s seats.

6 Royal (1881). In 1880 J.Thynne, then proprietor of the Queensland, had it pulled down and rebuilt under the name Royal. The Sydney *Bulletin* of 11.12.1880 announced that the new theatre, to be opened on the second Monday in February 1881, would seat 350 in the dress circle, 250 in the stalls, and 750 in the pit — a total 1350. It was opened,

contrary to the announced date, on 18.4.1881, and, constituting as it did the first real theatre Brisbane had ever possessed, was immediately popular. The theatre had a deep, capacious stage, its proscenium being flanked by the usual gilt-capped Corinthian columns. It was thought by the *Courier* that a mistake had been made in the shape of the dress circle, which was too much of the horseshoe, 'the heels of the shoe as it were projecting in a manner that somewhat obscures the stage for those sitting at the side.' This newspaper also commented on the extraordinary patience of the people of Brisbane in putting up for so long with the 'dingy barn' the new theatre replaced, and wondered why, in a city of close on 30 000 inhabitants, earlier moves had not been made to build a theatre. It noted with satisfaction that the Royal had a refreshment room in the dress circle, a ladies' retiring room, and a smoking room for men. Admission to the new theatre cost 4s for the dress circle, 3 for stalls, 1 for pit.

7 Her Majesty's Opera House (1888). Built in Queen Street, this theatre provided fixed seating for 2200 people, and was the first in Brisbane to present an attractive facade as well as interior. Divided into 3 floors, the building had a frontage of 66ft and depth of 248ft. The main, central entrance led to the pit and stalls, and was a passage or hallway leading to a large circular vestibule carried up the full height of three floors, each with an exterior gallery, and terminating in a 'handsome dome 80ft above the ground floor.' In the centre of the vestibule was a fountain with two basins, 1 supported by satyrs, the other by female figures. The auditorium colour scheme of green, salmon, and blue with touches of gold, had a general background of dark crimson. The pit seated 700, stalls 500, dress circle 400, and family circle 600. There were separate entrances in Queen Street to the dress and family circles. The stage, 60ft by 63ft, had the usual Corinthian column proscenium, with maroon velvet tableau curtains to match the upholstery of the dress circle and stall seats. The stage was equipped with a gridiron, and the usual grooves. There was no act drop. Occupants of the dress and family circles were able to promenade around the vestibule galleries. Interest in this new theatre was so great that dress circle seats were booked out long before the opening, and when it opened on 2.4.1888 the demand for admittance made it necessary for extra chairs to be placed along the aisles where possible. Standing room was also sold, so that when the curtain opened on the 5-act drama by W.Gillette, *Held by the Enemy* (1886) there were 2700 people in the theatre.

Briton and Boer. (See: *Jess*).

Broil at the Cafe, A. Farce by James Smith, Prince of Wales, Melbourne 22.9.1860, initially 1 performance.

Bronze Horse, The. (See: *Cheval de Bronze, Le*).

Brooke, Gustavus Vaughan (1818-1866). The most popular tragedian ever to act in Australia, and yet, by overseas standards, not a leading or star actor. Nevertheless, he was regarded in Australia as a star, and in his stay of almost 6 years he is said to have made, and lost, £50 000. Perhaps the truth is that, like the two tragedians who followed him in popularity in Australia, Barry Sullivan and Walter Montgomery, he is better described as a leading provincial actor. In 1845 the famous actor W.Macready (1793-1875) wrote of the young Brooke, with a great deal of foresight, 'one of those whom nature has gifted to a certain extent, but who will abuse her bounty . . .' which was his way of saying that Brooke would develop into a bawler, a ranter — one who would tear a passion to tatters. In 1848 E.Yates, who saw Brooke as Othello at London's Olympic, said he was 'manly, soldierly, with a voice capable of the softest modulation in love or pity, now trumpet-toned in command.' At the same time Macready, reading a highly congratulatory notice of Brooke's Othello in the London *Times,* wrote in his diary: 'I have seen this actor, and can most *purely* and truly say his acting warrants no such praise; he has no pretensions to genius, judgment, taste, or any artistic quality. He has physical advantages, but a most common mind, and no real passion . . .' Henry Morley, reviewing Brooke's Othello at Drury Lane in 1853, said he should have chosen a 'good, ranting, roaring melodrama, which he would play admirably. This would be infinitely better than making a melodrama of Othello.' The general consensus in London seems to have been, in Helen Faucit's words, that Brooke was 'a very fair actor; some thought a very good one; but never could be distinguished in his art because of his want of true dramatic instinct and imagination . . .' In Australia it was a different story, for audiences of the gold rush period took to him from the start, regarding him as the best actor they had ever seen. He introduced them to several of Shakespeare's plays never before produced in Australia, as well as appearing in the old favourites such as *Hamlet, Othello,* and *Richard III.* At his best he swayed large audiences with the force and vigour of his Othello, Macbeth, and Hamlet, and set them roaring with laughter in the farces of *The Irish Lion* (1838), *Teddy the Tiler* (1830), and *His Last Legs* (1839). Like actors before and after him, he found melodrama and Irish comedy were more popular than Shakespeare. Losing his money in unwise theatrical speculations, he left Australia in 1861, more than ever in the grip of the drink in which he had for some time been seeking refuge from his worries. Then followed hard times. The London theatre was in the doldrums, and his style of acting was outmoded. A disastrous Drury Lane season was followed by disastrous provincial appearances. In 1863, billed to star as Othello at the Royal, Marefair, Southampton, he appeared on stage so drunk he could hardly stand, and was unable to remember his lines. In Belfast the following year the curtain rose on *Richelieu* to reveal Brooke drunk and oblivious in his chair. Trying to fight his weakness, towards the end of 1865 he determined on a return visit to Australia. The ship on which he was travelling was wrecked in the Bay of Biscay, and he, refusing an offer of a place in a boat, was last seen on 11.1.1866 leaning over the ship's side stoically awaiting the end. Morley's valedictory is memorable:'Though he could not act Shakespeare, he must have been a noble fellow.' (See: Melbourne, Olympic).

Browne, Thomas Alexander (1826-1915). Known as the writer Rolfe Boldrewood, Browne was born in London and came to Australia in 1830. Educated at the Sydney Academy and Sydney College, at the age of 18 he settled on the land. A series of droughts and bad seasons resulted in heavy losses, and in 1870 he accepted an appointment as Police Magistrate and Gold Commissioner, which he held until his retirement in 1895. First began writing and publishing sketches and short stories, under the pen-name Rolf Boldrewood, in 1865. In 1881 his most popular novel, *Robbery Under Arms,* was published serially in the *Sydney Mail,* and 7 years later it was published as a book. This novel is said to have earned him £10 000. Another of his novels, *The Miner's Right,* and *Robbery Under Arms* were adapted for the stage by Alfred Dampier and Garnet Walch. *Robbery Under Arms* was an immediate success, though it bore little real resemblance to the novel, and had a happy ending. Over the next 18 years or so it had many performances throughout Australia and overseas. The stage version of *A Miner's Right,* on the other hand, had a successful first season, and after that dropped from favour.

Buchanan, McKean (1823-1872). One of the many American actors who came to Australia in a 2-way traffic between gold diggers and actors during the gold rush years, Buchanan was born in Philadelphia, the son of Paymaster Buchanan of the US Navy. Educated for the Navy, he served 3 years as a midshipman, and then made his stage debut at the St Charles, New Orleans, in *Hamlet.* In 1849 he was in England, where he had a special engagement at the Bristol Royal. In 1850 he made his first appearance in New York and Philadelphia, afterwards sailing again for England. A tall, heavily built man, he was called by some critics a 6ft 4 roarer, by others an actor of the first rank. Versatile and hard-working, on his 1853-54 English provincial tour he was said to have played '606 performances in 21 towns.' He came to Australia in 1856, appearing first in Sydney in Shakespearian and other roles. The Sydney critics regarded him as a 'great actor,' and 'a master of his art.' On his first visit to Melbourne he was described by one critic as violent, boisterous, unnatural, silly, and puerile, but on the whole his visit was a success. A few years later he returned for a second tour. From 1864 until his death he remained in America.

Burford, Charles (1820-1899). English actor who, after initial experience in London, came to Australia in 1853 and remained for the rest of his life. First came to prominence in Melbourne, playing Baradas to

James Stark's Richelieu in Bulwer-Lytton's play of that name. From then on played everything from Hamlet to the villain in melodrama. Notable for his physical resemblance to the Duke of Wellington, and his deep, sepulchral voice, his acting style was of the old melodramatic school. At one time he was a member of Barry Sullivan's Melbourne company, and also took part in such plays by Australians as *Raymond Lord of Milan, Canowindra, Anniversary Day,* and *Colonial Experience.* Burford was also a dramatist, having *The Drunkard; or Scenes in Colonial Life* (1865), and *The Mysteries of Sydney; or, Startling Revelations* (1882) to his credit. He finished his long life as a stage-door keeper; but, as the *Bulletin* wrote in reporting his death, 'as a rule the Hamlet who reaches the age of 79 is fortunate if he finds a stage-door to take charge of.'

Burglar, The. 1-act play by Katherine Prichard, Turn Verein Hall, Melbourne 5.10.1910, initially 1 performance.

Burlesque. Originally, in theatrical terms, a good-natured laugh at things theatrical which, through over-use, have stretched the gamut from utmost popularity to sheer boredom. Among these V.C.Clinton-Baddely lists rhymed couplets, bad verse, the Italian opera, Augustan tragedy, the sentimental drama, the tale of terror, the jolly Jack Tar, and so on. The conventions of melodrama are a particular target for burlesque, such as the one in which the identity of a character in a play is established by a birthmark, or a mole, or a bracelet or locket worn when the character was abandoned as a child. The essence of burlesque of this kind is not satire, but laughter. J.M.Morton's one-act *Box and Cox* (1847) is a good example. 'Satire is brimstone, but burlesque is wine.' On the musical side, the burlesque seems to have developed from, as well as with, the Christmas pantomime. In a sense the musical burlesque of the 1860s and early 1870s could be called pantomime for elders — a leg, costume, and scenic show designed to amuse and relax. Its chief features were girls in tights, ornate costumes and settings, comedy, specialty acts, dancing, and a grand finale. The story or 'book' often came from the classics, the most notable of all being *Ixion, ex-King of Thessaly,* which was given the interchangeable labels of 'burlesque' and 'extravaganza,' and introduced to American audiences by the English singer, dancer, and actress, Lydia Thompson, and her 'British blondes' in 1868. These musical extensions of the verbal burlesque were at first more refined than they later became, when they were turned into leg and nudity shows. A good example of the more sedate kind was W.M.Akhurst's *Paris the Prince and Helen the Fair,* written in 1868 for the Melbourne Royal. The book played havoc with the original story of this legendary pair, and the usual puns were glaringly present, but costumes, settings, and music made up for any disappointments a confirmed classicist may have felt. The *Argus* reported: 'The burlesque opens with a view of the exterior of the Spartan King's palace, and discloses Cupid and Hymen arranging the fate of the heroine, who presently appears with Paris and is borne off by her lover in a Phrygian gallery moored in the Eurotas. The voyage to Troy introduces some exquisitely painted panoramic views, than which nothing better has been seen in Melbourne, showing the Rock of Gibraltar, the Peak of Teneriffe, Rio De Janeiro, Tristan da Achuna, and the Cape of Good Hope, which give place to a scenic representation of Troy, with Priam and the Trojans receiving the loving pair. In the sixth scene is disclosed the wooden horse, from whose side the Grecian host emerge to open the gates of the city. Then the scene changes to the triumphal entrance of the army, and capture of Ilium, followed by the finale, a grand tableau amidst the ruins of the burning city . . .' Comic opera and musical comedy edged the burlesque off the stage.

Burn, David (1799?-1875). Came to Tasmania in 1824, where he was a landholder. Made frequent visits to Great Britain. Wrote plays, poetry, and fiction. Most of his plays are believed to have been written during his voyages. A possible exception is his *The Bushrangers,* produced at the Caledonian, Edinburgh in 1829, the ms of which is held by the Mitchell Library, Sydney. It is the only play he wrote with an Australian subject. In 1842 Burn published in Hobart his book of *Plays, and Fugitive Pieces, in Verse,* containing poems, short stories, and 5 plays. Of the plays, *Our First Lieutenant* was first produced at the Caledonian, Edinburgh in 1829 under the title *Manias and Maniacs;* his *The Queen's Love* in Sydney in 1845, and his *Loreda* in Melbourne in 1877.

Bush King, The. In 1893 a young Melbourne playwright had a 4-act drama, *The Bush King,* produced at the Surrey, London. The following year the author, W.J. Lincoln, came back to Australia and the play was produced in Melbourne for 6 performances. Nothing more was heard of it for 3 years, when it was given 5 performances at London's Novelty in 1897. 4 years later again Alfred Dampier took *The Bush King* in hand, turned it into a 5-act drama very like, or heavily influenced by his version of *Robbery Under Arms,* changed the bushranger hero's name from Captain Dart to Captain Midnight, and produced the result at Sydney Criterion on 26.1.1901. 4 years later still Dampier again altered the play, after which it was advertised as '*The Bush King,* by W.J.Lincoln and Adam Pierre,' the last being one of Dampier's pen-names. Later still the play was made into a silent film, screened at Sydney's Lyceum under the title *Captain Midnight, the Bush King* on 9.2.1911.

Bushranger, The; or, The Last Crime. 3-act drama by unknown author, Malcom's Royal Australian Amphitheatre, Sydney 24.4.1854, initial 2 performances.

Bushrangers, The. 3-act drama by David Burn, Caledonian, Edinburgh 8.9.1829. Bushrangers, Aborigines, convicts, and free settlers feature in a story set in Tasmania in 1826, dealing with the notorious bushranger, Matthew Brady, and his gang. Ms in Mitchell Library, Sydney. Published Heinemann Educational Australia Pty Ltd, Melbourne, 1971.

Bushrangers, The; or, Norwood Vale. 3-act drama by Henry Melville, Argyle Rooms, Hobart 29.5.1834. Published in April issue of *Hobart Town Magazine* 1834.

Bushwoman, The. 4-act drama by Jo Smith, King's, Melbourne 28.8.1909, initial 18 performances.

Busie Body, The. 3-act comedy by Mrs Susannah Centlivre, Drury Lane, London May 1709; The Theatre, Sydney 23.7.1796.

Business. A term used to describe movements, gestures, and stereotyped actions used by actors to add point and verisimilitude to a character. Sometimes it applied to movements and actions outside character building, but in agreement with the general setting of a play. Business was sometimes called for by a stage direction, and was sometimes implied in the text of the play, such as miming the action of making a bed, opening a parcel, and so on. Comic business, for instance, might include mimicry of other characters in the play, or of their speech habits; knockabout farce and clowning, the use of a catchphrase or a ribald or comic gesture. Knowing how and when to use business successfully was as often a matter of chance as of art or design. Bad actors, particularly bad comedians, interpreted it as a licence to hog a scene or 'improve' the playwright's lines.

Buttons; or, Wives Exchanged. 2-act comedy by H.W.H.Stephen, Royal Victoria, Sydney 24.11.1871, initial 5 performances. Given at Queen's, Sydney 30.10.1875 as *Exchange Wives;* given at Opera House, Melbourne 16.8.1884 as *Exchange of Wives*. (See: Parliamentarians).

Byron, George Gordon, Lord (1788-1824). Poet and dramatist. Was for a time on the committee of Drury Lane. 3 of his 8 plays, *Werner; or, The Inheritance, Manfred,* and *Sardanapalus* were produced in Australia. (See: Nathan, Isaac).

MUSICAL BOUQUET.

BILLY BARLOW,

SAM COWELL as BILLY BARLOW.

The Popular Comic Song,

SUNG AT ALL

PUBLIC CONCERTS.

LONDON:
MUSICAL BOUQUET OFFICE, 192, HIGH HOLBORN;
& J. ALLEN, 20 WARWICK LANE, PATERNOSTER ROW.

Nellie Stewart as Camille 1905

C

Camille. Title given in America to the play by Alexander Dumas *fils*, *La Dame aux camélias*, Vaudeville, Paris 2.2.1852. First performed in a version by W.Olwine as *Camille; or, The Fate of a Coquette*, Broadway, New York December 1853; in Australia in a revised (1854) version of Olwine's original, Olympic, Melbourne 23.6.1856. An English version of this drama was to have been performed at Drury Lane, London in 1853, but a licence was refused by the censor. English audiences had to wait 22 years for a bowdlerised version, J.Mortimer's *Heartsease*, Princess's, London 5.6.1875. An 1879 critic of his title said, 'It is difficult to discover why a heartsease should be a more righteous flower than a camellia . . .' Mortimer revised his version in 1879 for a very successful performance at the Court, London by the Polish-American actress, Helen Modjeska. Together with *The Stranger* and *East Lynne*, *Camille* was the most popular 'woman's play' of the nineteenth century. The world's leading actresses took to it as their male counterparts took to *Hamlet*. Written by Dumas first as a novel and then as a play, this story of the ill-fated Marguerite Gautier and her lover Armand Duval inspired so many different and differing stage versions, including the opera *La Traviata*, that it is difficult to trace their growth with any certainty. Famous Marguerites in Australia included Sarah Stark, Marie Duret, Marie Prevost, Mrs Brown Potter, Sarah Bernhardt, and Nellie Stewart.

Candida. 3-act drama by George Bernard Shaw, Royal, South Shields, 30.3.1895; Melbourne Repertory, Turn Verein Hall, 25.9.1911, initially 1 performance.

Captain Swift. 4-act comedy-drama by Charles Haddon Chambers,

Haymarket, London 20.6.1888; Royal, Sydney 16.2.1889, initial 12 performances.

Capuleti ed i Montecchi, I (The Capulets and Montagues). 2-act opera, text F.G.Romani after M.Bandello, music V.Bellini, La Fenice, Venice 11.3.1830; King's, London 20.7.1833; Royal, Melbourne 25.10.1887, initial 2 performances.

Carmen. 4-act opera, text H.Meilhac and L.Halévy, after story by P.Mérimée, music G.Bizet, Opéra Comique, Paris 3.3.1875; Her Majesty's, London 22.6.1878; Opera House, Melbourne 14.5.1879, initial 12 performances.

Carpenter's scene. Usually a painted cloth or drop lowered close to the proscenium arch to permit the stagehands to dismantle, or strike, the old set-scene and set the new. The opening scene in a melodrama such as *In the Ranks* (1883) is an almost full-depth interior scene. A similarly large scene could not directly follow it, for the wait while the scene change took place would have tried the patience of the audience. In the production of this play at Her Majesty's, Sydney in 1887 the ending of the first scene and the lowering of the carpenter's scene was described thus: 'Presently the side walls of the interior set hinge back at the angles, to allow of the descent in front (at which would formerly have been called the "first grooves") of a "Cloth" painted with the road to Dingley Wood — a moonlight effect of beautifully studied foliage . . .' The actors played a short comic or dramatic scene in front of this cloth, timed so that the stagehands could 'fly' the walls of the interior set, shift props and furniture, and lower and adjust the components of the new scene. The cloth was then raised in darkness and the new 'in depth' scene, gradually lighted, was revealed as Dingley Wood.

Carpet, stage. In the late 18th and early 19th centuries it was the custom to cover the stage for certain plays, usually tragedies, with a green baize carpet. This was secured by stage 'flunkeys' in full view of the audience to hooks set in a carpet-cut in the stage floor next to the footlights. For this reason, 'carpet layers' was a derisory term used to describe supernumeraries, whose task it was to lay the carpet. While they were doing this, ribald members of the audience sometimes called out 'soup, soup' to them.

Carpio. 5-act tragedy by John Finnamore, Victoria, Emerald Hill, Melbourne 5.2.1880, initial 2 performances. Also performed at the Prince's, Bradford, England 24.5.1886. Published G.Robertson, Melbourne 1875.

Case of Rebellious Susan, The. 3-act comedy by H.A.Jones, Criterion, London 3.10.1894; Lyceum, Sydney 23.3.1895, initial 17 performances.

Casino Girl, The. 2-act musical comedy, text H.B.Smith, music L.Englander, Shaftesbury, London 11.7.1900; Her Majesty's, Sydney 6.7.1901, initial 23 performances.

Caste. 3-act comedy by T.W.Robertson, Prince of Wales, London 6.4.1867; Duke of Edinburgh, Melbourne 11.4.1868, initial 12 performances.

Castle Grim. 2-act opera, text R.Reece, music G.B.Allen, Royalty, London 2.9.1865; Prince of Wales, Melbourne 11.6.1875, initially 1 performance.

Castle of Andalusia, The. 3-act comic opera, text J.O'Keefe, music S.Arnold, Covent Garden, London 2.11.1782; Royal, Sydney 19.10.1837.

Catch of the Season, The. 2-act musical comedy, text S.Hicks and C.Hamilton, music H.Haines and E.Baker, Vaudeville, London 9.9.1904; Her Majesty's, Sydney 18.12.1909, initial 24 performances.

Catching the Kellys. 1-act farce by Joseph Pickersgill, Royal, Melbourne 29.3.1879, initial 11 performances.

Catherine and Petruchio. Farce by David Garrick, adapted from Shakespeare's *The Taming of the Shrew,* Drury Lane, London 18.3.1756. This was frequently played in Australia, from 1834 to at least the end of the 1860s, and was usually billed as *Katherine and Petruchio,* but sometimes as *The Taming of the Shrew.* Its popularity lasted in England until 1886, when *The Taming of the Shrew,* with the Induction, was revived. Research has yet to be undertaken in Australia to determine which of the many 19th century productions were *Catherine and Petruchio* and which Shakespeare's *The Taming of the Shrew.*

Cathcart, Mary Francis (1833-1880). Known professionally as Fanny Cathcart throughout Australia and New Zealand, this versatile actress was the daughter of James Cathcart, an Irish-born actor well known in the theatres in the north of England. She gained her acting experience in English provincial theatres, where she first acted with G.V.Brooke. In 1854 he placed her under contract to accompany him to Australia as his leading lady. She made her Australian debut at the Queen's, Melbourne on 26.2.1855, playing Desdemona to Brooke's Othello, and quickly gained a popular following, which remained faithful to her until her death. In April 1855 her fiancé husband, the actor Robert Heir, who had been delayed in England, arrived in Australia and they were married. Heir soon became discontented with the parts he was given in Brooke's company, and he persuaded Fanny to break her contract and leave Brooke so that they could play starring roles together. Brooke took out an injunction which prevented Fanny from acting, and the pair had to live on the husband's earnings. The quarrel was patched up, and

Fanny and Robert returned to Brooke, remaining with him until he left Australia in 1861. They chose to remain in Australia, and act together. Heir died in the early 1860s on their way to New Zealand to fulfil an engagement. Fanny continued to act alone for a while, and to give readings, but in 1870 she married the actor-playwright, George Darrell, whom she had put on the road to theatrical success. He was 8 years her junior, but theirs was a happy partnership. For the next 10 years they acted together in all kinds of productions, including most of Darrell's plays, throughout Australia and New Zealand. She died in Melbourne in 1880. So well known and liked had she become by this time, as a woman and as an actress, that there was hardly an Australian or a New Zealand newspaper that did not carry news of her death.

Cavalleria Rusticana (Rustic Chivalry). 1-act opera, text G.Menasci and G.T.Tozzetti, music P.Mascagni, Costanzi, Rome 17.5.1890; Shaftesbury, London 19.10.1891; Princess's, Melbourne 25.9.1893, initial 17 performances.

Cazille. Operetta, text R.H.Horne, music C.Schmitt. Selections from this work, which was never performed in full, were given at the Masonic Hall, Sydney 8.4.1872.

Cenerentola, La; ossia, La Bonta in Trionfo (Cinderella; or, The Triumph of Goodness). 2-act comic opera, text J.Ferretti, after C.G.Etienne, based on Perrault, music G.Rossini, Valle, Rome 25.1.1817; His Majesty's, London 8.1.1820; Royal Victoria, Sydney 12.2.1844, initially 1 performance.

Cent Vierges, Les (The Hundred Virgins). 3-act comic opera, text H.C.Chivot, A.Duru, and L.Clairville, music A.Lecocq, Fantaisies-Parisiennes, 16.3.1872; English text J.Grantham, Royal, Brighton 17.10.1874; Opera House, Melbourne 27.2.1875, initial 11 performances. Another English version of this opera, by R.Reece, was given (for the British) the more moral title of *The Island of Bachelors*.

Chambers, Charles Haddon (1860-1921). The first Australian playwright to make a success on the London stage. Born at Stanmore, Sydney, and educated at Fort Street School, he became first a public servant. Finding the work unimaginative and restricting, he became in turn an insurance salesman, outback station-hand, and writer. In 1881 he went to England, returning on the ship which carried the Montague-Turner Opera Company to Sydney. His next visit to London was as manager of this company. Chambers had some success in London with his short stories, and he next turned to playwriting. His first play, a farcical comedy called *One of Them,* was produced at Margate in 1886. 2 others were produced in London the following year, but he had his first real success with *Captain Swift*. According to H.Chance Newton, Chambers tried many times to meet the actor Beerbohm Tree and read his play to him. But Tree was elusive, forcing Chambers finally to corner him in a Turkish bath. More or less a captive, Tree submitted while Chambers read *Captain Swift* to him. Luckily, Tree saw himself in the name part, and produced the play at London's Haymarket. It was a success for both of them. Miller repeats this story, saying that he had it from the English author, A.E.W.Mason, in 1933. He then continues with what is today still the best exposition of Chambers' work. The development of Chambers as a playwright is also noted by G.Rowell in his *The Victorian Theatre* (p.126) who sees a distinct continuity and growth between the four plays, *Captain Swift* (1888), *The Idler* (1890), *The Tyranny of Tears* (1899), and *Passers By* (1911). It should be added that Chambers was also fortunate in the actors who interpreted his plays — Beerbohm Tree, Charles Wyndham, George Alexander, H.B.Irving, Marie Tempest, Marion Terry, Gerald du Maurier, and Irene Vanbrugh. Between 1886 and 1922 no fewer than 22 of Chambers' plays were produced, of which the most successful were *Captain Swift*, *The Idler*, *The Fatal Card* (1894), *The Tyranny of Tears*, and *Passers By*. Most of these were published in London.

Chambers, Joseph (1837-1874). The first *premier danseur* in Australia, trained by his father. Like Samuel Lazar before him and Nellie Stewart after him, he began his stage life at a very early age. He came to Australia with his parents and sister Amy in 1842, and made his stage debut in a Naval Hornpipe at the Royal Victoria, Sydney in 1843. His father, an actor as well as dancer, had made his debut at the Olympic on 21.2.1842 in a highland fling, and his dramatic debut in Kotzebue's *The Stranger*. The young Joseph, on the other hand, rarely acted, but danced so well that the world-famous ballerina, Aurelia Dimier, chose him to partner her during her Australian tour in *Le Diable la quatre, Diana and Endymion*, and *La Fille mal gardée* when he was only 17. From then on, usually partnered by his sister Amy, he devoted himself to choreography as well as dancing, visiting each colony in turn. He finally settled in Sydney as *maître de danse* at the Prince of Wales. Here he arranged dances and ballets, and in his spare time conducted a ballet school. In 1872 the Prince of Wales was destroyed by fire, and the following year he went to the Royal Victoria to arrange ballet sequences for the comic opera, *Genevieve de Brabant*. This opened on 24.12.1873 and closed on 8.2.1874. It was his last stage work. A victim to tuberculosis, he died on 21.7.1874 after a protracted and painful illness.

Charity Begins at Home. 1-act operetta, text B.C.Stephenson, music A.Cellier, Gallery of Illustration, London 7.2.1872; Princess's, Melbourne 5.2.1887, initial 4 performances.

Charley's Aunt. 3-act farce by B.Thomas, Bury St Edmonds, England, 29.2.1892; Criterion, Sydney 26.12.1893, initial 52 performances.

Chatte Métamorphosée en femme, Le. (See: *Enchanted Cat, The*).

Cheval de Bronze, Le (The Bronze Horse). 3-act opera, text A.E.Scribe, music D.Auber, Opera Comique, Paris 23.3.1835; English version A.Bunn, Covent Garden, London 14.12.1835; Royal Victoria, Sydney 23.10.1843.

Child actors. The first 'eyrie' of children, the first of those 'little eyases, that cry out on the top of question and are most tyrannically clapped for't,' appeared at B. Levey's Sydney Royal in 1834, and most tyrannically were they clapped. In May, a group of child actors, all of them children of actor-parents or of people connected with the theatre, gave a performance of *Bombastes Furioso* (1810), a burlesque of the tragic-heroic play, by W.B.Rhodes. Unconsciously echoing the words of Rosencrantz, the *Herald* concluded its report of the performance, 'The curtain fell amidst thunderous applause.' For a few nights these child actors, 1 or 2 of whom were no more than 5 years old, put the regulars out of countenance. Almost 10 years later a second group, again the children of people connected with the theatre, gave a performance of Kane O'Hara's adaptation of Fielding's burlesque tragedy, *Tom Thumb* (1780) at the Royal Victoria. The 'star' of this production was Master Samuel Lazar, scarcely 5 years old, who grew up to become first manager and then lessee of the historic Sydney Royal, opened in Castlereagh Street in 1875. During the century there were also individual child performers, among whom A.M.Quinn stood out as the Sarah Siddons of the nursery. She was brought to Australia from San Francisco by her parents in 1854, at the age of 6, and in the following two years must have made a fortune for her parents and her mentor, the actor J.H.Vinson. She specialised in scenes from *Hamlet, The Merchant of Venice,* and *Black Eyed Susan,* and in such shorter pieces as *The Actress of All Work* (1819), in which she played 6 different characters, to the astonishment and delight of audiences throughout Australia. The same may also be said of Lily and Rose Dampier, Alfred Dampier's daughters. In 1877 they appeared, at the age of 11 and 7 respectively, in *All For Gold; or, Fifty Millions of Money,* in which they portrayed 2 orphaned children whom the villains of the piece seek to murder. The play ran for 4 weeks in Melbourne, and at its conclusion Lily and Rose each received a gold locket from the Royal management, and a gold cross from the author-adapter of the play, F.R.C.Hopkins. Later the same year Lily and Rose looked soulfully out from the cover of a piece of sheet music, *The Lily and Rose Waltzes,* composed for and dedicated to them by Master R.H.Patton, aged 13. Throughout the century there were other 'little eyases' who sought public favour, including juvenile comic opera troupes, and Master D.Pole, who at 14 unsuccessfully essayed *Macbeth,* but not so many as to warrant an Australian critic preempting or echoing Anthony Hope's despairing cry of 1904: 'Oh, for an hour of Herod!'

Children's Bread, The. 1-act play by Blamire Young, St Patrick's Hall, Melbourne 13.12.1911, initially 1 performance.

Chilperic. 3-act comic opera, text and music Hervé (Florimond Ronger), Folies-Dramatiques, Paris 24.10.1868; English version R.Reece, Lyceum, London 22.1.1870; Prince of Wales, Melbourne 25.7.1874, initial 11 performances.

Chimes of Normandy, The. (See: *Cloches de Corneville, Les*).

Chinese Honeymoon, A. 2-act musical comedy, text G.Dance, music H.Talbot, Royal, Hanley 16.10.1899; Princess's, Melbourne 30.6.1902, initial 28 performances.

Ching Chow Hi; or, A Cracked Piece of China. 1-act operetta, text W.Brough and G.Reed, music J.Offenbach, Gallery of Illustration, London 14.8.1865; Opera House, Sydney 10.1.1880, initial 12 performances.

Chocolate Soldier, The. (See: *Tapfere Soldat, Der*).

Christian, The. 5-act drama by Australian dramatist, Bernard Espinasse, adapted from Hall Caine's novel (1897), Her Majesty's, Sydney 23.9.1899, initial 37 performances. This production antedated Hall Caine's own stage version, first performed Shakespeare, Liverpool 9.10.1899. The Espinasse version was a revision of an adaptation by Wilson Barrett.

Christian King, The; or, Alfred of Engeland. 5-act drama by Wilson Barrett, world premiere Her Majesty's, Melbourne 14.9.1901, initial 12 performances. First English production Princess's, Bristol 6.11.1902.

Cigale et la Fourmi, La (La Cigale — The Grasshopper and the Ant). 3-act comic opera, text H.Chivot and A.Duru, music E.Audran, Gaîté, Paris 30.10.1886; English version F.C.Burnand, Lyric, London 9.10.1890; Princess's, Melbourne 12.2.1892, initial 27 performances.

Cinderella. 3-act extravaganza with Harlequinade, text J.H.Wood, music J.Crook, Shakespeare, Liverpool 1899; Royal, Sydney 18.3.1901, initial 41 performances.

Cingalee, The; or, Sunny Ceylon. 2-act musical comedy, text J.T.Tanner, music L.Monckton, Daly's, London 5.3.1904; Her Majesty's, Sydney 6.5.1905, initial 35 performances.

Circus Girl, The. 2-act musical comedy, text J.T.Tanner, and W.Palings, music I.Caryll and L.Monckton, Gaiety, London 5.12.1896; Her Majesty's, Melbourne 19.7.1902, initial 18 performances.

Claptrap. Sententious, patriotic, or jingoistic statement or action during the course of a play, deliberately designed to provoke applause. Typical are the lines from *Khartoum* (1885) in which the Mahdi says to the hero, 'I can see you are English by your faces,' to which the hero replies, 'Naturally, for no enemy ever yet saw it by our backs.' In *British*

Born (1872) the hero is about to be executed by the enemy when the heroine and comic man rush in and drape him in the Union Jack, crying, 'Then upon this, the British flag, fire if you dare.' The firing squad drops its muskets, and the curtain falls to the strains of *Rule Britannia*. Booth says this scene was first used in *The White Slave* (1845). It was also used in *North and South,* a play by the Australian dramatist George Fawcett, first produced at Princess's, Melbourne 3.8.1863.

Clari; or, The Maid of Milan. 2-act melodrama by J.H.Payne, Covent Garden, London 8.5.1823; Royal, Sydney 31.10.1834. John Cumberland, in his *The English Theatre* (1829), prints the text of this with the lyrics for some of the songs. In effect, *Clari* was a dramatic work for the stage to which the composer, Henry Bishop, added 22 musical numbers — solos, duets, trios, etc. It could be, and in its first Australian production was, presented as a drama without music. (See: *Guy Mannering; Paul and Virginia*).

Clarke, Marcus Andrew Hislop (1846-1881). One of the best known early Australian writers, with a wide range of work to his credit. Most famous of all is his reconstruction of the early convict days in Australia, *His Natural Life,* later re-titled *For the Term of His Natural Life.* Clarke, born in England, came to Australia in 1863, and was soon involved in journalism, writing for the Melbourne *Argus* and *Australasian*. Along with other members of a Bohemian group, including James Smith, James Neild, Robert P.Whitworth, and Garnet Walch, he turned his attention to the theatre. Between 1868 and 1872 he had 4 stage works produced: *Foul Play, Peacock Feathers, Fernande,* and *Plot*. There was then a break of 6 years before his next works for the stage were produced: *Alfred the Great: Baby's Luck; The Moonstone; The Happy Land; A Daughter of Eve,* and *Forbidden Fruit*. He also wrote 2 sketches for Harry Rickards, *Strolling on the Sands,* and *Perfection*, and 2 or 3 pantomimes. Finally he wrote, or partly wrote, the text of an opera he called *Queen Venus*. The composer, the French pianist Henri Kowalski, is believed to have changed the title to *Moustique*. Clarke's novel, *His Natural Life,* was produced in dramatised versions in Australia, New Zealand, England, and USA from 1885 to 1913. Film versions were launched in 1908 and 1911, while in 1914 Clarke's daughter, Marian, wrote and performed in a 'potted' version, *The Impostor,* in the USA. (See: Kowalski, Henri; *Moustique; Convict 1240; For a Life; His Natural Life; For the Term of His Natural Life,* and *The Term of His Natural Life*).

Class. 3-act comedy by Grosvenor Bunster, Royal, Melbourne 17.6.1878, initial 5 performances.

Claudian. 3-act drama by H.Hermann and W.G.Wills, Princess's, London 6.12.1883; Princess's, Melbourne 18.12.1897, initial 12 performances.

Clay and Porcelain. (See: *Good for Evil*).

Clerk of Clerkenwell and the Three Black Bottles, The. Melodrama by G.Almar, Sadler's Wells, London 27.1.1834; Royal Victoria, Sydney 1.7.1839. (See: Multiple setting).

Climax, The. 1-act play by Edward Dyson, Athenaeum Hall, Melbourne 15.4.1913, initially 1 performance.

Clint, Alfred (1843-1923). Son of the English marine painter, Alfred Clint (1807-1883), grandson of the portrait artist, George Clint (1770-1839), Alfred Clint came to Australia in the mid 1860s. He was at first engaged as assistant scenepainter to J.Hennings at Melbourne Royal. In his earliest work at this theatre, some of the settings for Walter Montgomery's production of *Antony and Cleopatra,* he showed himself to be a talented and original artist. After a brief stay at the Royal he branched out on his own, being appointed scenic artist at Sydney's Prince of Wales in 1869. His first work here was for W.H.Hoskins's production of *The Tempest,* for which he designed and painted 9 scenes. These included 2 'working' sea scenes (the waves falling and rising on a rocky shore), and the masque scene, in which Iris descended on a rainbow, Juno and the Graces descended in a car drawn by peacocks, and there were appearing and disappearing vision scenes. Clint remained in Sydney for the rest of his life, working in turn at the Royal Victoria, Criterion, and Her Majesty's, and at the Opera House. At all times his settings earned him the highest praise. He did the original settings for W.H.Cooper's *Sun and Shadow, Kodadad and His Brothers,* and *Hazard;* for the first Australian performance of G.Darrell's *Transported for Life,* and *The Trump Card;* for Searelle's comic operas, *Bodadil,* and *Isidora,* and for the 1887 production of *Romeo and Juliet,* in which the young Essie Jenyns received wide acclaim. Late in his life Clint and his sons established one of Australia's first scenepainting studios, at Camperdown. Up to this time scenery had always been painted in the theatre in which it was to be used. Clint was also a talented black and white artist, and did a lot of work for Sydney *Punch.* He was one of the founders of the Royal Art Society, and of the Sketch Club.

Cloches de Corneville, Les (The Chimes of Normandy). 3-act comic opera, text L.Clairville and C.Gabet, music R.Planquette, Folies-Dramatiques, Paris 19.4.1877; English version H.B.Farnie, Folly, London 23.2.1878; Academy of Music, Melbourne 23.11.1878, initial 12 performances.

Clouds, The. Comedy by Aristophanes, first performed Athens 423BC. First Australian performance by pupils of Sydney Grammar School, 20.6.1884.

Club Life. 2-act comic opera, text A.B. ('Banjo') Paterson, music E.E.P.Truman, Criterion, Sydney 12.12.1895, initial 2 performances.

Clutsam, George H. (1866-1951). A writer in the *Australasian* of 11.10.1879 reported that 'Master G.Clutsam, a native of Victoria, but now of Dunedin, New Zealand, and who is only nine years old, has composed and published a piece for the pianoforte entitled La pluie de printemps.' He was wrong on 2 counts. Clutsam was born in Sydney on 26.11.1866, so that when he published his piano piece he was approaching his thirteenth birthday. With that promising start, the young Clutsam went on to write works for the stage which were highly thought of in his day. In 1910 Thomas Beecham produced Clutsam's short opera, *A Summer Night,* at His Majesty's, London, and at Covent Garden. The London *Times* critic said there was more good music in the hour and a quarter occupied by *A Summer Night* than in many works at Covent Garden which held the stage from eight to eleven. Towards the end of 1911 Clutsam's opera, *King Harlequin,* was accepted for production in Berlin, and performed there the following year. Today there are to his credit *A Love Tangle* (1901), *Young England* (1916), *Gabrielle* (1921), *The Little Duchess* (1922), and *The Damask Rose* (1929). The most successful of all the productions with which he was concerned was the musical, *Lilac Time* (1922). Based on the life and music of F.Schubert, with music arranged by Clutsam and H.Berte, this ran at the Lyric, London for 628 performances.

Colleen Bawn, The; or, The Brides of Garryowen. 3-act domestic drama by D.Boucicault, Laura Keene's, New York 29.3.1860; Adelphi, London 10.9.1860; Royal Victoria, Sydney 20.5.1861, initial 12 performances. (See: *Lily of Killarney, The*).

Colonial Experience. 3-act comedy by W.H.Cooper, Royal Victoria, Sydney 4.7.1868, initial 4 performances. Ms in Mitchell Library, Sydney. Published Currency Press, Sydney, 1979.

Coloured fires. These were extensively used on the 19th century stage, not only to add to the realism of fire scenes in such plays as Boucicault's *The Streets of New York* (1857), or G.Darrell's *Back From the Grave* (1878), but also to add mystery and colour to pantomime transformation scenes, and to the final scenes or tableaux in burlesques, extravaganzas, comic operas, and other musical works. Four 'receipts' for these fires have been left to posterity by W.Davidge. *Red fire:* Strontia 8 oz. Potash 4 oz. Shellac 2 oz. Licopodium quarter of an ounce. *White fire:* Nitre 8 oz. Sulphur 3 oz. Charcoal quarter of an ounce. Alum eighth of an ounce. Camphor half an ounce. *Blue fire:* Nitre 8 oz. Sulphur 3 oz. Charcoal 1 oz. Antimony 1 oz. *Green fire:* Nitrate of Barytes 62½ parts. Sulphur 10½ parts. Potash 23½ parts. Orpiment 1½ parts. Charcoal 1½ parts. (See: Transformation scene).

Comedy of Errors, The. Farce by William Shakespeare, believed to have been first performed in London in 1593 or 1594; Royal Victoria, Sydney 18.1.1841.

Comic opera

Comic opera. Like burlesque, extravaganza, light opera, and operetta, comic opera is an elastic term or label with no discoverable hard and fast definition. According to one expert, Leslie Orrey, comic opera is 'a nebultus term applied to an opera that is light and amusing' — a somewhat circular definition. Another, Eric Blom, gets closer to pinning down this mercurial form of musical work for the stage with his definition, 'an exclusively French type of opera, not always comic and often by no means light, but originally always with spoken dialogue.' James Harding seems to lump comic opera and operetta together, as being one and the same, while Blom and Orrey describe operetta as partaking of light opera and musical comedy. Henry Hersee, who wrote the English texts for several operas and comic operas, wrote in the *Theatre* (1.11.1878): 'Those only are genuine operas-bouffes in which the characters are taken from mythology, history, and poetry, and are presented under ridiculous aspects.' He then quoted as typical examples *Orphée aux Enfers*, *La Belle Hélène*, *Chilperic*, and *Le Petit Faust*. Works such as *La Périchole*, *L'Oeil Crevé*, and *Le Fille de Maame Angot*, where the plot and characters are entirely imaginary, he classified as comic operas, adding that a classification which comprised 1st Comic Opera, 2nd Farcical Opera, 3rd Opéra-Bouffe, if adopted, would include in Class 1 *Les Près S. Gervais*, *La Pericholé*, *Les Cloches de Corneville*, and *Fatinitza*, while Class 2 would contain such differing works as *The Sorcerer*, *HMS Pinafore*, *La Fille de Madame Angot*, and *L'Oeil Crevé*. It seems that the only way to tread successfully through this maze is to accept the title given to his work by the composer. The alternative is the one adopted in the 19th century — to put them all together under the heading 'comic opera.' In this sense, comic opera was first produced in Australia in 1843, when Rossini's *The Barber of Seville* was given, followed by *Don Pasquale* in 1854; while the first of the French works was Offenbach's *La Grande Duchess de Gérolstein*, produced in Melbourne in 1871. Called in France an operetta, this suffered a sea change when it was produced in England, being called an extravaganza; and in Australia, where it was called a comic opera. By the 1880s comic opera had taken such a hold on Australian audiences that runs of more than 50 performances were common. By the 1890s Gilbert and Sullivan's works were being lumped together with *The Beggar Student*, *The Sultan of Mocha*, *Paul Jones*, and *Dorothy* as comic operas. And in the 1900s the comic opera was finally ousted in favour of its sister form, the musical comedy. Theatre managers, entrepreneurs, and impressarios made a great deal of money with these various musical productions, helped by the pay given the principals and lesser members of the comic opera companies, who were on stage 6 nights in every week, travelling time apart. According to *Table Talk*, in 1887 in Melbourne sopranos got from £20 to £40 a week. Nellie Stewart got only £25 a week from J.C.Williamson at a time when her voice and acting ability were filling his theatre nightly. Contraltos and mezzo sopranos got £12 to

£15; comedians £25 to £30; tenors from £25; baritones and basses £25 to £30, male choristers £3 to £4, and female £2 to £3. Conductors were paid between £20 and £30. (See: Musical comedy).

Contes d'Hoffmann, Les (The Tales of Hoffman). 3-act opera, text J.Barbier after *Les Contes Fantastiques d'Hoffmann* by J.Barbier and M.Carré, music J.Offenbach, Opéra Comique, Paris 10.2.1881; Adelphi, London 17.4.1907; His Majesty's, Melbourne 8.6.1912, initially 1 performance.

Contradiction; or, A Wife Upon Sufferance. 2-act farce by John Lazar, Royal Victoria, Sydney 6.9.1843, initially 1 performance. Copy held by Archives Office of NSW.

Convict. Like the bushranger, the convict was at first an unsympathetic figure in Australian drama. He was shown in all his real or supposed vileness in the early plays, but as the century progressed he developed into the man wrongly convicted in England of a crime committed by somebody else. Transported to Australia, through the agency of a friend or relative (frequently that of the woman he loves) his innocence is finally established and the guilty are punished. W. Cooper wrote the last of the plays about 'vile' convicts in his *Foiled; or, Australia Twenty Years Ago* (1871). G.Darrell wrote the first of the 'framed' convict plays in his *Transported for Life* (1876), in which the hero is accused of poisoning an old man for his money, is transported, and goes through a series of hardships as a ticket-of-leave holder in Australia until, in the end, virtue triumphs. In 1879 the *Sydney Morning Herald* spoke for the moralistic among its readers when it objected to the revival of Cooper's *Foiled,* on the ground that it was difficult to imagine what good object could be gained by depicting at that time 'an element which is the most repulsive in the history of these colonies, and which disappeared from the colony long ago.' The newspaper was concerned lest visitors to that year's Sydney Exhibition might 'carry away with them the wrong impressions respecting colonial history.' In Julian Thomas's *No Mercy* (1882) and Charles Haddon Chambers's *Captain Swift* (1888), the convict 'hero' commits suicide towards the end of the play, seeing this as the only solution to the social difficulties confronting him.

Convict 1240; or, Realistic Scenes from Prison Life in Australia. Drama by John A.Stevens adapted from Marcus Clarke's novel, *His Natural Life* (1874), Grand Opera House, San Francisco 18.7.1885. Retitled *A Great Wrong Righted,* New York 1.2.1886, and *A Great Wrong,* New York 26.3.1888. Stevens registered *A Great Wrong Righted,* 'a picturesque play, a prologue and five acts,' with the Library of Congress Copyright Office on 5.3.1886. The same play, reduced to 4 acts, was again copyrighted on 20.5.1913.

Coo-ee; or, Wild Days in the Bush. 4-act drama by Edward W.

O'Sullivan, Haymarket Hippodrome, Sydney 14.4.1906, initial 12 performances. (See: Parliamentarians).

Cooper, Walter Hampson (1842-1880). The first Australian exponent of the sensation drama. Born at Liverpool, New South Wales, he started his working life as a journalist on a Queensland newspaper. From this he progressed to the *Sydney Morning Herald,* and it was while he was working in Sydney that most of his plays were written and produced. Their success made him think of overseas production, and he left Australia in 1872 with 3 of the actors who had taken part in his plays, bound for San Francisco. At least 2 of his plays were produced in that city, but what could have been a successful tour, with New York as the ultimate goal, was marred by dissension among the 4, in which he was as much to blame as the others. He returned to Australia alone in 1873, and moved into politics. A rural seat, East Macquarie, was vacant and he stood for and was elected to represent it in the NSW Legislative Assembly. But he lost the seat a year later because of his politically indiscreet public statements about land selectors. He then turned to the law, and was admitted to the Bar in 1876. But real success still evaded him. Plagued, in addition, by bad health, he tried in 1880 to recapture his earlier stage success with a final play, a comedy, produced at the Royal Victoria. It was an utter failure. He died three months later. Cooper's plays include: *The History of Kodadad and His Brothers, Colonial Experience, The New Crime, Sun and Shadow, Foiled, Hazard,* and *Fuss.* (See: Hussey, Frank).

Coppin, George Selth (1819-1906). Comic actor, born and trained in England, who was also manager, producer, theatre proprietor, entrepreneur, and politician. One of the busiest and most versatile figures in the history of the Australian theatre, Coppin came to this country in 1843, when there was only one real theatre in Sydney, the Royal Victoria. He lived to see the country of his adoption dotted throughout its 6 States with attractive and comfortable theatres. Coppin played an important and influential part in the growth and development of the Australian theatre. He built and opened several theatres; he knew the tastes of his audience and, like a good chef, knew how to tempt their palate; he was an agent for overseas playwrights, an importer of actors and singers whose presence in Australia helped to lift and sustain acting standards, and was also one of the most travelled of our early actors. He started his Australian career with a successful season at the Royal Victoria, after which he moved into the hotel business, and lost his money. Next he went to Hobart, where a successful engagement enabled him to branch out as manager of his own company in Launceston. From there he brought a company back to Melbourne in 1845, where he had a season at the Queen's. In 1846 he moved on to Adelaide, where for some time he was actively associated with theatre buildings and performances. Again he lost all his money. There was only the Victorian goldfields left;

but, until he went into theatre management in Geelong, he did not find any gold. There he made enough money to pay all his creditors and finance a trip to England, where he engaged the first of his visiting stars, G.V.Brooke, and brought back to Australia a prefabricated galvanised iron building which was transformed into his Olympic in Melbourne in 1855. Next he became part lessee of the Melbourne Royal, and gave Melbourne its first Italian opera season, at a loss of £3000. Several dramatic seasons of varying degrees of success followed until 1862, when he opened his Haymarket in Melbourne. Bankruptcy followed this venture, a financial condition relieved when he brought out the famous pair, Charles and Ellen Kean. In 1864 he sailed with them to the USA as their agent, returning to Australia in 1866. From then on he brought out a succession of actors and actresses from England and America, including, ironically, the man who was to take over his theatres, J.C.Williamson. In addition, he was at different times a member of the Victorian Legislative Council and of the Legislative Assembly. Coppin always had a wide following in Melbourne, where he made his home, and when he made a round of farewell stage appearances in the early 1880s these were emotional events. But he did not retire for long. The bank crashes of the 1890s hit him very hard, and once again it was the theatre that put him back on his feet, with the production of lavishly-mounted, long-running pantomimes. He relinquished his seat in the Legislative Council in 1895. (See: Anderson, James R.; Low comedian).

Coquette, The; or, A Suicide Policy. 2-act comic opera, text W.J.Curtis and J.I.Hunt, music W.Arundel Orchard, Palace, Sydney 28.8.1905, initial 6 performances.

Coriolanus. Tragedy by William Shakespeare, believed to have been first performed in London 1607 or 1608; Royal Victoria, Sydney 11.11.1844.

Corsair, The. 2-act extravaganza, text J.Braham, music E.Rice, Bijou, New York 18.10.1886; Opera House, Melbourne 3.10.1891, initial 33 performances.

Corsican Brothers, The. 3-act drama by Dion Boucicault, adapted from the French of E.Grange and X.de Monte, who based their play on Alexandre Dumas' *Les Frères Corses,* Princess's, London 24.2.1852; Royal Victoria, Sydney 24.4.1854. Many other English versions of *The Corsican Brothers* followed Boucicault's, among them being G.V.Brooke's *La Vendetta* in 5 acts, Astor Place Opera House, New York 19.5.1852; Olympic, Melbourne 20.8.1855.

Costume. In 1705 Sir Richard Steele stated a basic theatrical truth when he wrote in his prologue to Sir John Vanbrugh's *The Mistake:*
> With audiences composed of belles and beaux,
> The first dramatic rule is, have good clothes . . .

> In lace and feather, tragedy's expressed,
> And heroe's die unpitied if ill-dressed . . .

Nowhere more than on the stage do clothes make the man, but this was a truth ignored for many years on the melodrama stage. Actors had to provide their own costumes, and more often than not the poorer actor's stage clothes and street clothes were one and the same. With burlesques, extravaganzas, pantomimes, operas, and other musical productions it was a different matter. It was soon realised that if such productions were to be successful, costumes would have to be made the responsibility of one man, usually the manager, not of individual actors. In its first few months the Sydney Royal company was frequently criticised for the incongruity of some of the costumes worn by the actors. Early in 1835, for instance, it was censured for the mixture of French, English, and Italian costumes worn in *The Honeymoon* (1805). To the impecunious actors of the time a 'fancy' costume was a fancy costume, and had to fit in with Spanish, Italian, German, or French backgrounds. A few months after this criticism was published Barnett Levey retired from the management of his theatre in favour of a group of 6 lessees, and the first thing they did was to spend a large sum on a theatrical wardrobe. The following year the actor Thomas Simes, the first resident costume designer in the Australian theatre, was in full swing, and newspapers commented on the splendour of the Oriental costumes he designed for *Blue Beard* (1798). In December that year an advertisement for 'The Grand Romantic Fairy Drama,' *Oberon and the Charmed Horn* (1832) reported that the 'whole of the dresses, banners, armour, accoutrements, and properties' were by Mr Simes. Not even the comment by one reviewer that 'Mr Collins as Badekin reminded us of a huge crayfish dressed up in a white furbelowed dimity petticoat' could detract from the importance of this, the first 1-man costume and property production in Australia. From then on the Australian theatre, apart from a few backslidings, never wanted for costume designers, property men, and wardrobe mistresses. But 'stars' continued to travel with their wardrobe trunks. In the 1870s the actor-comedian, W.H.Lingard, toured Australia and New Zealand with a personal wardrobe consisting of 12 character coats, 11 hats, 9 wigs, 14 pairs of trousers, 12 character dresses (for transvestite roles), and 3 pairs of boots and shoes.

Count Hannibal. 4-act drama adapted by Oscar Asche and F.N.Connell ('Conal O'Riordan') from S.Weyman's novel (1901), Prince's, Bristol 18.3.1909; Royal, Melbourne 15.1.1910, initial 34 performances.

Count of Luxembourg, The. (See: *Graf von Luxemburg, Der*).

Count of Monte Cristo, The. 4-act drama by Charles Dillon and George R.Morton, adapted from the A.Dumas novel (1845), Royal

Victoria, Sydney 29.1.1864, initial 6 performances. (See: *Monte Cristo; or, The Prisoner of the Chateau d'If*).

——. 3-act drama and prologue by Alfred Dampier and Garnet Walch, adapted from the A.Dumas novel (1845), Alexandra, Melbourne 18.1.1890, initial 24 performances.

Country Girl, A; or, Town and Country. 2-act musical comedy, text J.T.Tanner, music L.Monckton, Daly's, London 18.1.1902; Her Majesty's, Sydney 7.11.1903, initial 36 performances.

Creswick, William (1813-1888). Noted English Shakesperian actor who at the age of 21 was manager of the Dover Royal. He came to Australia after his best work as an actor had been done, but his tour was a complete success. Milestones in his career as an interpreter of Shakespearian roles occurred in 1839, when he started at Bristol Royal; in 1846, when he played Cassius in *Julius Caesar* in his first appearance at Sadler's Wells; in 1848, when he acted in a command performance at Windsor Castle as a member of the Haymarket company, and in 1863, when he made his first appearance at Drury Lane. He made his Australian debut at the Royal Victoria, Sydney in J.S.Knowles's *Virginius* (1820) in 1877, and played to packed houses. His Shakespearian productions included *Hamlet, King Lear, The Merchant of Venice*, and *Henry VIII*. Back in England in 1882, Henry Irving gave him a special benefit performance of *Much Ado About Nothing* at the Lyceum to mark his jubilee as an actor. Three years later Creswick made his farewell stage appearance at Drury Lane.

Crimson Thread, The. 4-act drama by George Darrell, Royal, Melbourne 11.8.1894, initial 12 performances. Later played as *The Crimes of Chicago* (1896), and *From Scotland Yard* (1897).

Crispino e la Comare; ossia, Il Medico e la Morte (The Cobbler and the Fairy Godmother; or, Death and the Doctor). 3-act opera, text F.M.Piave, music F. and L.Ricci, San Benedetto, Venice 28.2.1850; St James's London 17.11.1857; Princess's, Melbourne 11.8.1871, initially 1 performance.

Crown Diamonds, The. (See: *Diamante de la Couronne*).

Cuckoo. 3-act comedy drama by James A.Meade and John F.Sheridan, St George's Hall, Melbourne 10.11.1884, initial 11 performances.

Currency Lass, The; or, My Native Girl. 2-act musical play by Edward Geoghegan, Royal Victoria, Sydney 27.5.1844, 14 songs set to popular airs of the day, initial 2 performances. Ms held by Archives Office of NSW. Published Currency-Methuen, Sydney, 1976.

Curtain, Festoon. Type of front curtain popular during the 18th and early 19th centuries. Usually of green baize, this required neither rolling nor flying, but worked on a series of vertical draw-lines which gathered the curtain up to the top of the proscenium arch in a series of 'bunches' or festoons.

Curtain, Front. Traditionally of green baize, a usage dating from the 17th century, though sometimes red baize was used. Sydney's 1875 Royal is the first on record as having had a red baize front curtain, while the same city's 1886 Criterion had innovative red plush tableau curtains. Changes in the interior construction and decoration of theatres, and in the ways in which the stage was used were eventually responsible for the abolition of the green baize curtain.

Curtain, Tableau. Front curtain made in 2 halves, with a diagonal draw-line across each half. When drawn up these curtains bunched at either top corner of the prosenium arch. First used in England in the early 1850s, the tableau curtain was first used in Australia in the early 1880s.

Curtain, Traverse. Back curtain, usually run on rings. The oldest form of stage curtain in existence, it was sometimes in 1 piece, sometimes in 2 so that it could be parted. In the late 19th century the traverse curtain was widely used, in plain or boldly patterned materials, for quick scene changes in Shakespearian and other multi-scened productions.

Cut cloth. Painted canvas on a frame, or, if a backdrop or drop scene, canvas cut out and glued to netting or gauze, hung on top and bottom rollers, and used mainly with landscape and forest scenes. The spaces left between branches, and between leaves and clusters of leaves, for instance, were cut away to give a three-dimensional effect. Archways, colonnades, and ruins were sometimes treated in the same way. Sometimes 2 or 3 cut-cloths the width of the acting area were used with a backdrop, thus doing away with the need for wings and top borders, and avoiding the look of stiffness these sometimes presented.

Cymbeline. Tragi-comedy by William Shakespeare, believed to have been first performed in London 1609 or 1610; Royal Victoria, Sydney 13.8.1838.

Cyrano de Bergerac. 5-act verse drama by Edmond Rostand, Porte St Martin, Paris 28.12.1897; Bijou, Melbourne 2.8.1902, initial 8 performances.

Czar and Zimmermann. (See: *Zar und Zimmermann*).

Left: Marcus Andrew Hislop Clarke
Below: Anna Maria Quinn in The Middy Ashore 1855

D

Dairymaids, The. 2-act musical comedy, Text A.Thompson and R.Courtneidge, music P.Rubens and A.Tours, Apollo, London 14.4.1906; Her Majesty's, Melbourne 7.9.1907, initial 36 performances.

Dampier, Alfred (1847-1908). Born in Horsham, Sussex, son of a builder. Trained as actor in English provincial theatres. Leading actor at Manchester in 1873 when he signed a 3-year contract making him stage manager and leading actor at Melbourne Royal. By this time he was a married man with a family, having married Katherine Russell, pianist and actress, in 1868. Dampier proved to be the right choice for Melbourne, for in his first 3 years in Australia he completely won the theatre-going public, playing everything from Shakespeare to Boucicault. Also a playwright, after a few failures written by him alone he made it his practice to collaborate with a writer who had the necessary literary knowledge, while he provided the knowledge of what was and was not dramatically and theatrically effective. He opened his first Australian season with his play, *Faust and Marguerite,* in which he played Mephistopheles. Thereafter, for 30 years, he continued to entertain the public with a variety of plays written by or for him, ranging from the most popular of all, *Robbery Under Arms,* to *East Lynne.* For most of the time he had to forego production of Shakespeare's plays, in which his real interest lay, in favour of the melodramas demanded by audiences; but for a while he got over this problem by running a melodrama for 5 nights in the week and a play by Shakespeare on the sixth. Dampier's production of home-grown melodramas culminated in a Wild West drama he wrote with Garnet Walch, which owed more to the American novelist, J.Fenimore Cooper, than to anyone else — *The Scout.* Produced

Right: General Sir Ralph Darling
Below: Alfred Dampier

at Melbourne's Alexandra, which seated 2500, this drew a total audience of 31 075 over 12 nights. Dampier also became notable for the large distances of Australia and New Zealand he covered each year with his productions. No centre was considered by him too small to visit. His most popular plays, in a list of more than 30, were: *For the Term of His Natural Life; Shamus O'Brien; Jess,* and *Marvellous Melbourne.*

Dancing Mistress, The. 3-act musical comedy, text J.T.Tanner, music L.Monckton, Adelphi, London 19.10.1912; Criterion, Sydney 2.8.1913, initial 28 performances.

Dandy Doctor, The. 3-act musical comedy, text E.Marris, music D.Powell, Avenue, Sunderland 26.3.1900; Princess's, Melbourne 13.8.1904, initial 12 performances.

Dark Lady of the Sonnets, The. 1-act play by George Bernard Shaw, Haymarket, London 24.11.1910; Melbourne Repertory, Athenaeum Hall 10.12.1912, initially 1 performance.

Darling, Sir Ralph (1775-1858). A competent if somewhat strict and overbearing governor of New South Wales from 1825 to 1831, renowned in history as the official whose recall to England was celebrated with public rejoicings, and as the bureaucrat who ruthlessly and implacably countered all attempts to establish a theatre in Sydney. He introduced an Act which, in effect, banned the drama. As printed in the Sydney *Gazette* of 3.9.1828, this Act decreed that no form of public indoor entertainment for which the public paid in cash or kind could take place without authority and licence from the Colonial Secretary. From that time on all applications for a theatrical licence were rejected, only concerts being permitted, until the arrival of Darling's successor, Governor Richard Bourke.

Darrell, George Frederick (1841-1921). Real name George Frederick Price. Born in Bath, England, he came to Australia in the early 1860s and joined the rush to the Otago goldfields in New Zealand. Had his first stage experience as an amateur in New Zealand. In 1868 he returned to Australia, where he gained his first professional experience as a member of the Melbourne Royal company. The following year he was engaged by W.Montgomery for that actor's Adelaide season, and from then on he spent the rest of his working life as actor, playwright, and manager. In 1870 he married Mrs Robert Heir, the former Fanny Cathcart. Together they toured Australia, New Zealand, and the USA in Darrell's plays and in the melodramas of the day, with occasional Shakespearian performances. His wife died in Melbourne during the run of his longest-running play, *The Forlorn Hope.* Later Darrell continued his touring, sometimes alone, sometimes with his own company, and continued to produce his own plays. In 1884 his *The Sunny South* was produced at the Grand, London, and again at the Surrey, in 1898. In

1886, on a tour of New Zealand with his own company, he married the young Australian actress, Christine Peachey. Over the ensuing years he continued to tour, breaking the monotony only once when he accepted the post of general manager for Williamson and Garner in Melbourne in 1890. Two years later he and Christine embarked for London, where neither was able to obtain an engagement. Darrell finally accepted an offer of a starring tour in South Africa, during which only his plays were to be performed. His wife died in Johannesburg during the tour. Returning to Australia, Darrell achieved considerable success with his newest play, a dramatisation of Nat Gould's novel, *The Double Event.* He resumed touring, travelling again throughout Australia and New Zealand, paying one more visit to the USA and England. He produced his final play, *The Battle and the Breeze,* in Sydney in 1905. He is believed to have ended his life by suicide, his body being washed up at Dee Why on 29.1.1921. During his theatrical career he wrote and produced 35 plays, but some of these were produced under as many as three different titles. Counted by title, he wrote 55 plays. The most popular were: *Transported for Life; Back From the Grave: The Forlorn Hope; The Sunny South; The Soggarth; The New Rush,* and *The Crimson Thread.*

Daughter of Eve, A. 2-act comedy by Marcus Clarke, Bijou, Melbourne 19.7.1880, initial 5 performances.

Daughter of St Mark, The. 3-act opera, text A.Bunn, after J.de Saint-Georges, music M.Balfe, Drury Lane, London 27.11.1844; Royal Victoria, Sydney 31.5.1852.

Davis, Arthur Hoey (1868-1935). Born at Drayton, Queensland, Davis was educated at Emu Creek State School. Moving to Brisbane in 1886, he gained employment in the Sheriff's Office, and in 1902 was promoted Under-Sheriff. The following year he left the public service and started to write for a living, adopting the pen-name Steele Rudd. His earliest work was published in Brisbane newspapers, and then he began to write for the Sydney *Bulletin,* which encouraged him in his work. His first collections of stories about the Rudd family, *On Our Selection* (1899) and *Our New Selection* (1903) were published in the *Bulletin* library series. His first book made him famous. People all over Australia recognised in its 'selection' characters the kind of people they had seen or met in real life. In due course Steele Rudd published a total 23 books. E.Morris Miller writes of his work: 'He broke new ground in presenting the daily life of small settlers, both within the home and on the land, without the foil of the large station . . . It brought home to young Australians the fact that the stalwart pioneers of the bush were not solely the grandees of the large stations.' Several attempts were made to turn Rudd's successful 'On Our Selection' stories into a stageplay, and after about 5 years of false starts a version advertised as having been written by Beaumont Smith and Albert Edmunds opened at the Palace, Sydney on 4.5.1912. The play was an instant and long-standing success. William Anderson, who put in £300 towards the cost of staging the play, drew a return of £6000 in three years. Winifred Hamilton, writing in the early 1930s of Rudd and the play, said nobody knew how much Bailey and Grant, the theatre manager, made out of it, but at the time she was writing 'the creator of the play has nothing but a pension of £1 per week from the Federal Government.' She said Rudd had written her a memorandum setting out that he had signed an agreement with Bailey for royalties of £6 a week (£1 a night) and 5 per cent of the gross weekly takings after the first £600. In a capital city, if the play made £1000 a week, Rudd received £26 for the week. He said the highest weekly royalty he ever received was £30. In 1915 the *Bulletin* published a paragraph in which it was said that the play, *On Our Selection,* had been a 'little gold mine' to Steele Rudd. He quickly replied that 'unfortunately, I am not one of those to whom *On Our Selection* is a little gold mine.'

Dead Timber. 1-act play by Louis Esson, St Patrick's Hall, Melbourne 13.12.1911. Published, with *The Woman Tamer* and *The Sacred Place,* Fraser and Jenkinson, Melbourne 1912.

Deakin, Alfred. (See: Parliamentarians).

Death of Marlowe, The. 1-act verse tragedy by R.H.Horne, Royal, Melbourne 12.7.1860, initially 2 performances. This was a world premiere, as the play had not previously been produced. The first London performance was given by the Irving Amateur Dramatic Club in 1887. Horne first published the play in 1837. A revised version was published in 1870.

Deering, Olly (1836?-1906). Son of actor parents, during his adult life as an Australian actor he earned a name as one of the most reliable, hard working members of the profession. A handy 'general' actor, but with more push and intelligence than the average, he could turn his talents to comedy or villainy with equal ease. One of his earliest roles was that of the new chum in W.H.Cooper's *Hazard; or, Pearce Dyceton's Crime,* and from then on he seems to have concentrated on Australian productions. He acted in most of G.Darrell's plays in Australia and New Zealand, and acted and sang for two years in Luscombe Searelle's comic operas, *Bobadil,* and *Isidora.*

Deirdre. 1-act play by W.B.Yeats, Abbey, Dublin 24.11.1906; Bryceson Treharne's Elder Conservatorium students, Lyric Club, Adelaide 17.8.1909, initially 1 performance.

Democrat, The; or, Under the Southern Cross. 4-act drama by Edmund Duggan, Royal Standard, Sydney 18.9.1891, initially 1 performance. The author rewrote the play into five acts, changed its title to *The Eureka Stockade; or, The Fight for the Standard,* and produced it at the Royal, Adelaide 27.11.1897, where it had 7 performances. Rewritten again, this time with the title *The Southern Cross,* and still in 5 acts, the play was performed at the Victoria, Newcastle 28.9.1907. Transferred to the Criterion, Sydney 5.10.1907 it ran for 18 performances. The play enjoys the distinction of being the first of only 2 plays in 19th century Australia to deal with the Eureka rebellion.

Devil To Pay, The; or, The Wives Metamorphos'd. 3-act ballad opera by C.Coffey and J.Motley, music anon., Drury Lane, London 6.8.1731. Cut to one-act version in 1732, and in this form produced at Emu Plains 11.6.1827.

Devil's Disciple, The. 3-act drama by George Bernard Shaw, Prince of Wales, London 26.9.1899; Repertory, Sydney 2.10.1913, initial 6 performances.

Devil's Opera, The. 2-act opera, text G.Macfarren senior, music G.A.Macfarren, Lyceum, London 13.8.1838; Royal Victoria, Sydney 3.12.1846.

Diamants de la Couronne, Les (The Crown of Diamonds). 3-act comic opera, text A.E.Scribe and J.de Saint-Georges, music D.Auber, Opera Comique, Paris 6.3.1841; English version T.H.Reynoldson, Princess's, London 2.5.1844; Royal, Melbourne 12.4.1861, initially 1 performance.

Dick. 2-act comic opera, text A.Murray, music E.Jakobowski, Globe, London 17.4.1884; Opera House, Melbourne 6.8.1887, initial 29 performances.

Dillon, Charles (1819-1881). Child of a deserted actress mother, Dillon took the name of his stepfather, the actor Arthur Dillon, and began his acting life at a very early age. Despite several physical imperfections he was able to transcend all his shortcomings in his acting, which gripped his audiences the moment he came on stage. In 1833, as a boy of 14, he was stage manager of the City of London Theatre. 10 years later he was a recognised star. From 1850 to 1856 he was lessee of various provincial theatres, and then he leased the London Lyceum, from 1856 to 1858. His first season in this theatre featured such plays as *Belphegor the Mountebank* (1851), *The Three Musketeers* (1850), *Virginius* (1820), *King Lear, Othello,* and *Macbeth.* But his improvidence, and his habit of borrowing money at from 100 to 200 per cent brought disaster. In 1860 he went to the USA to see if he could mend his fortunes, but had bad luck from the start when, in a storm at sea, one of his legs was broken. By 1863 he was in Australia, where he stayed for 4 years. He left towards the end of 1867, having played in Sydney and Melbourne to appreciative audiences, who regarded his Belphegor and Lear as revelatory interpretations. Back at Sadler's Wells, London in 1868 he found he had been away for so long that younger men had taken his place. He was seldom seen again in London, but ended his acting life doing the rounds of the provincial theatres. He wrote 3 plays, produced at London's Marylebone in 1844 — *The Mysteries of Paris, Life's Highway,* and *The Female Bluebeard.* While he was in Australia he co-authored with Charles Webb *The Artist of Florence,* and with George R.Morton *Night and Morning,* and *The Count of Monte Cristo.* Dillon gave Australia its first performance of Lord Byron's *Manfred,* and Sydney its first performance of *Werner,* and *Sardanapalus.*

Dimple's Lovers. 1-act operetta, text Guy Boothby, music Cecil J.Sharp, Government House, Adelaide 2.9.1890.

Dind, William (1813-1895). Born in London, Dind began his adult life with the Army in West Africa. Later he came to Tasmania, and then to Sydney, where he at first became acting manager of the Royal Victoria in 1840. Eventually he became lessee of that theatre, and then took over as manager of the first Prince of Wales, opened in 1855. When this was destroyed by fire in 1860 he again leased the Royal Victoria. A new Prince of Wales was opened on the site of the old in 1863, and Dind not long afterwards became lessee of both theatres. He exercised in his control of Sydney's 2 major theatres what could be called a benevolent despotism. The *Bulletin* obituary notice recorded that 'he was a genial, hearty old gentleman, of stainless honour; and the "profession" has never had a better friend.' When the second Prince of Wales was also destroyed by fire, in 1872, Dind gave up and retired from theatrical activities. He bought a hotel on the North Shore, where he spent the rest of his life. He became first an alderman and then mayor of East St Leonards Municipal Council, founded in 1868.

Dinorah. (See: *Pardon de Ploermel, Le*).

Diplomacy. 4-act drama by B.C.Stephenson and C.Scott, based on V.Sardou's *Dora* (1877), Prince of Wales, London 12.1.1878; Bijou, Melbourne 12.4.1890, initial 12 performances.

Doctor Death. 1-act play by Arthur H.Adams, Criterion, Sydney 6.7.1912, initially 1 performance. Published in the *Lone Hand* 5:27 (1909), 257-268.

Doctor's Dilemma, The. 4-act tragedy with epilogue by George Bernard Shaw, Court, London 20.11.1906; Royal, Melbourne 24.3.1914, initially 2 performances.

Doctor of Alcantara, The. 2-act comic opera, text B.E.Woolf, music J.Eichberg, Museum, Boston 7.4.1862; French, New York 25.9.1866; Connaught, London (as *The Village Doctor*) 1.11.1879; Opera House, Sydney 26.12.1879, initial 13 performances.

Dog drama. A form of melodrama popular in the first half of the century, in which dogs rescued drowning people (and, in some plays, drowned them), discovered criminals, released prisoners, and fed the

Charles Dillon as Othello

hungry by stealing food. Typical dog dramas produced in Australia were: *The Dog of Montargis; or, The Forest of Bondy* (1814); *Jack Robinson and his Monkey* (1828); *The Dog of the Convent* (1831), and *The Cherokee Chief; or, The Shipwrecked Sailor and His Dog* (1833).

Dollar Princess, The. 3-act musical comedy, text B.Hood, adapted from A.Willner and F.Grunbaum, music L.Fall, Knickerbocker, New York 6.9.1909; Daly's, London 25.9.1909; Her Majesty's, Melbourne 9.4.1910, initial 30 performances.

Doll's House, A. (Et Dukkehjim). 3-act drama by Henrik Ibsen, translated W.Archer, Novelty, London 7.6.1889; Princess's, Melbourne 14.9.1889, initial 11 performances.

Don, Sir William (1825-1862). Baronet amateur actor who, in the words of the American actor, J.Jefferson, 'would walk ten miles to help an old woman or to escape from a tailor.' As Jefferson describes him, he could have been the model for Captain Versatile Fluent in W.H.Cooper's *Colonial Experience*. Though handsome, and 6ft 6 tall, he owed his stage success more to his title than to his acting ability. Jefferson, at one time manager of the Savannah theatre in the USA, engaged Sir William, believing he was just the kind of draw needed to make a success of his opening season. He knew his public. The theatre was crowded night after night by the fashionable, all of them eager to see the tall, acting 'Sir.' Speaking of Sir William's acting, Jefferson said he was an unmistakeable amateur. Typically, before Sir William could make his appearance Jefferson had to send £50 to Charleston to redeem Sir William's wardrobe. He had lost all his money at the national game of poker. Sir William was the only son of the sixth baronet of Newtondon, Berwickshire. During his 3 years as an officer in the Fifth Dragoon Guards he incurred such large gambling and other debts that the estate had to be sold. The sale realised £85 000, but was not enough to meet his debts. He took up acting because it seemed to him the most obvious way of earning a living, acting at first in the smaller theatres in the north of England, then, in the early 1850s, in the United States. By 1857 he was back in England, at the Bristol Royal, having in the meantime married the English actress, Emily Saunders. Here his creditors caught up with him again, and he had to spend a fortnight in the Bristol Debtors' Prison. Released on bail, he acted for a week at Birmingham, and returned to Bristol for a benefit performance, after which he made a characteristic curtain speech to the packed audience. It contained advice to the 'fast young gentlemen present' to keep out of debt. 'Dear young gentlemen,' he concluded, 'take this long monumental warning before you.' Sir William and Lady Don visited Australia in 1861, where they first appeared in Sydney in the dramas *The Daughter of the Regiment* (1848) and *The Rough Diamond* (1847). Later, in a burlesque, he took the part of Queen Elizabeth, his wife playing Leicester. It is said that she was taller than average, but looked like a fairy beside her husband. There followed a season in Melbourne, and then in Hobart, where Sir William died in 1862. His wife continued her acting career as Lady Don, in America and England, finishing up as a music hall entertainer.

Don Checco. 2-act comic opera, text A.Spadetta, music N.de Giosa, Nuove, Naples 11.7.1850; Masonic Hall, Sydney 25.12.1884, initial 2 performances.

Don Giovanni; ossia, Il Dissoluto Punito (Don Juan; or, The Rake Punished). 2-act comic opera, text L.da Ponte after G.Borati's *Il Convitato de Pietra,* music W.A.Mozart, Prague 29.10.1787; His Majesty's, London 12.4.1817; Royal, Melbourne 21.10.1861, initial 8 performances.

Don John of Austria. 3-act opera, text J.L.Montefiore, music Isaac Nathan, Royal Victoria, Sydney 3.5.1847, initial 2 performances.

Don Pasquale. 3-act comic opera, text G.Rieffini after A.Anelli's *Ser Marc' Antonio,* music G.Donizetti, Italien, Paris 3.1.1843; Her Majesty's, London 29.6.1843; Royal Victoria, Sydney 12.10.1854, initial 1 performance.

Dorcas. 3-act comic opera, text H. and E.Paulton, music W.Hydes and C.Lockname, Royal, Kilburn 21.2.1898; Criterion, Sydney 30.11.1901, initial 6 performances.

Dorothy. 3-act comic opera, text B.C.Stephenson, music A.Cellier, Gaiety, London 25.9.1886; Princess's, Melbourne 20.8.1887, initial 29 performances.

Double Event, The: or, A Tale of the Melbourne Cup. 4-act drama by George Darrell, after Nat Gould's novel of the same title, Royal, Melbourne 1.4.1893, initial 18 performances.

Douglas. 5-act tragedy by J.Home, Edinburgh, December 1756; Drury Lane, London 28.2.1815; Emu Plains 20.11.1830.

Drag. 19th century slang term for the clothes worn by actors playing female roles. Said to have been derived from the drag of a skirt or petticoat on the ground as opposed to the free movement of trousers. (See: Men as women. Women as men).

Dragons de Villars, Les. 3-act opera, text J.P.Lockroy and E.Cormon, music A.Maillart, Lyrique, Paris 19.9.1856; performed in Germany as *Das Glöcklein des Eremitens,* in Australia, St George's Hall, Melbourne 9.6.1877, as *The Hermit's Bell,* initial 10 performances.

Drama, The. With remarkably few exceptions, the plays presented to the audiences which filled the theatres of the English-speaking world in the 19th century had practically no literary merit. Their merit lay in their stageworthiness. They could involve an audience in the basic emotions, and keep them on the edge of their seats. A great many of these plays were published, not because of their literary value, but as acting editions and copies which lovers of the theatre could read when they wanted to revive memories of performances by their favourite actors. Towards the end of the century, when copyright laws began to provide some form of protection to authors, the publication of plays by successful playwrights provided a handy supplementary income. Before this, literary plays *were* written and published, the only remarkable thing about most of them being their lack of stageworthiness. The 19th century theatre was popular theatre, a theatre for the masses; and its plays, like their sensation scenes, aimed for instant impact with straightforward to obvious character parts, and obvious morality. The good were very good, the bad very bad, yet providence always ensured that virtue triumphed over vice. Such plays have been branded as rubbish in the present century, usually because of out-of-context comparisons made with plays of the 18th and earlier centuries. It is as if we were to blame Noel Coward for not being Friedrich Dürrenmatt. George Colman the Younger (1762-1836) had an apt reply for everyone who complained to him about the decline of the drama in the 19th century. Countering first with the statement that such a decline has always been attributed to the drama, he would add, '. . . few regular shoemakers are inclined to take the trouble of making shoes, when they find so much encouragement given to them for cobbling.' The plays of the 19th century need to be seen in their social as well as theatrical context. What was it about the everyday life of the 19th century playgoer that forced him to seek again and again the solace of what we today would call 'pie in the sky' plays? Why did these plays, with few exceptions, always embody the proposition that 'to be rich and well-born is, almost inevitably, to be wicked; to be poor and humble is all but a guarantee of virtue?' Why were their characters rarely human beings, but rather a quality or proposition to which human beings could attach themselves, or to which they could aspire? Though we may feel superior to such theatrical fare, modern entertainment as represented by much of our stage, film, and television fare is not so very different from it. As Daniel Mayer says: 'Only when we accept the possibility that for every literary, philosophic, and consciously artistic theatrical piece there are some dozens of inartistic, energetic, mindless, unliterary dramatic genres which enjoy a vast popularity and which appeal, not necessarily to persons of refinement and educated taste, but to the greater part of the population, perhaps to the entire population, do we begin to see the theatrical expressions of an age in a more accurate perspective.' (*Western Popular Theatre*).

Dress circle. Term first used in England to denote an area of the theatre set apart exclusively for those wearing formal dress. The first use of the term, or its equivalent, in the Australian theatre occurred when the *Sydney Monitor,* reporting the reconstruction of B.Levey's original Royal, said in its issue of 9.3.1833 that 'the dress row of boxes will be a great acquisition.' Advertising the reopening of this theatre, Levey used the term 'dress circle' for the first time. In the Australian theatre it was always the most expensive and smallest area in the house, and its clientele, until the arrival in the late 1880s of society drama, opera, and operetta performances, were more noticeable for their absence than for their attendance. It is possible to read play review after review in which the phrase 'house full' or 'house crammed, except for the dress circle' regularly occurs. This could be construed, at least partly, as a value judgment made by 'society' on the quality of the fare offered, though snobbery and moral attitudes were contributing factors. Command performances brought a full dress circle 'to honour the vice regal party,' as did performances by well known and popular visiting English and Continental stars — particularly to those who had played before Queen Victoria.

Dreyfus; or, Vive la France. 4-act drama by Walter Bentley and George Rignold, Criterion, Sydney 21.10.1899, initial 13 performances.

Drill: A Parade of Girls of the World. 3-act comedy by H.W.H.Stephen, Royal Victoria, Sydney 6.10.1877, initial 5 performances.

Drink. 5-act drama adapted by C.Reade from W.Busnach and O.Gastineau's stage version of Emile Zola's *L'Assommoir,* Princess's, London 26.6.1879; Royal, Melbourne 22.5.1880, initial 12 performances.

Drop scene. (See: Backdrop).

Duchesse de Chevreuse, The; or, A Duel in the Olden Times. 3-act drama by Jacob L.Montefiore, translated from J.P.Lockroy and E.Badon's *Un Duel sous le cardinal de Richelieu* (1832), Royal Victoria, Sydney 22.8.1843, initially 1 performance.

Duchess of Coolgardie, The. 5-act drama by E.Leigh and C.Dare, Drury Lane, London 19.9.1896; Criterion, Sydney 5.11.1898, initial 12 performances.

Duchess of Dantzic, The. 3-act comic opera, text H.Hamilton, music I.Caryll, Lyric, London 17.10.1903; Her Majesty's, Sydney 2.1.1909, initial 48 performances.

Duchess of Malfi, The. 5-act tragedy by J.Webster, believed to have been first performed in London at some time between 1612 and 1614. Produced Sadler's Wells, London in rewritten version by R.H.Horne 20.11.1850; Royal Victoria, Sydney 26.9.1855, initially 1 performance.

Due Foscari, I (The Two Foscari). 3-act opera, text F.M.Piave after Lord Byron's drama (1821), music G.Verdi, Argentina, Rome

3.11.1844; Her Majesty's, London 10.4.1847; Haymarket, Melbourne, 13.2.1868, initially 1 performance.

Due Studenti, I (The Two Students). 3-act opera, text U.Catani, music Alfred Plumpton, Alexandra, Melbourne 24.12.1887, initially 3 performances.

Duggan, Edmund (1866-1938). Actor and dramatist. Brother of the actress Eugenie Duggan, brother-in-law of William Anderson, and partner with Bert Bailey — Duggan never reached the heights achieved by any one of them. Born in Ireland, he was brought to Australia at an early age, and spent the first 10 years or so of his acting life in the 'backblocks' with companies or groups of itinerant actors who were in some ways like the earlier English barnstormers. Randolph Bedford has told how he first met Duggan in Wagga Wagga in 1886, when Duggan was about 24 and Bedford 18. Duggan was then a member of a travelling company of 6 men and 2 women which lived a hand-to-mouth existence presenting shortened versions of well known melodramas adapted to their abilities. They could, and did, tailor any play to last from half an hour to 2 and a half hours. Theirs was a vagabond but happy existence, as Bedford saw it, and he joined them for a while. In an interview published in 1911 Duggan told of some of his early adventures in the bush, in which he made it clear that he and other actors wandered the length and breadth of inland Australia, sometimes uncomfortably close to starvation. In a further interview in 1912 he told of similar travels with Alfred Dampier and his company, and of taking his own company as far as the Gulf of Carpentaria, and of a disastrous tour of Victoria in the depths of winter. But Duggan proved that he had ambition and talent when he managed to produce his first play in Sydney in 1891, *The Democrat; or, Under the Southern Cross,* even though he lost his money in the venture. In 1907 the first of several collaborations between Duggan and his fellow actor, Bert Bailey, under the pen-name Albert Edmunds, produced the record-breaking *The Squatter's Daughter.* It made a lot of money for the 3 men principally involved, Duggan, Bailey, and W.Anderson. Other plays by the 2 followed, providing Duggan with comparative comfort and success. This happy situation continued until at least 1928 when, his fortunes still tied in with those of his brother-in-law, he played the lead in Steele Rudd's *The Rudd Family,* presented in Adelaide, Sydney, and Melbourne — but he died a poor man. Other plays by Duggan, written either alone or with a collaborator, are: *The Man From Outback; On Our Selection; The Term of his Natural Life; Lady Audley's Secret; My Mate,* and *The Native Born.*

Duke's Motto, The. 5-act drama translated from F.Soulier's *Le Bossu* by James Smith, Haymarket, Melbourne 6.7.1863, initial 5 performances.

Dyson, Edward (1865-1931). Australian-born writer who was in turn miner, sub-editor of *Life* magazine when he was 21, poet, novelist, short-story writer, and dramatist. He published 12 books of short stories between 1898 and 1929. His most popular short story, written when he was 18 and reprinted many times after it first appeared in the *Bulletin*, 'A Golden Shanty,' he dramatised in 1913. He dramatised another of his short stories, 'Factory 'Ands,' in 1916. His 1-act play, *The Climax,* was performed in Melbourne in 1913.

Poster for The Double Event

E

Earl and the Girl, The. 2-act musical comedy, text S.Hicks, music I.Caryll, Adelphi, London 10.9.1903; Criterion, Sydney 27.7.1905, initial 24 performances.

East Lynne. Many adaptations of Mrs Henry Wood's novel of this name (1861) were made for the stage in England, America, and Australia. As a play it rivalled *Uncle Tom's Cabin* in popularity, and could truthfully be described as the manager's saviour, for after a failure he had only to run a week or two of *East Lynne* to recoup his losses. The first adaptation was done in America by Clifton W.Tayleure and performed at a matinee in 1862. The first English stage version was by W.J.Archer, Britannia, London 12.11.1864, under the title *Marriage Bells; or, The Cottage on the Cliff.* Many other versions followed (Nicoll lists 15 under the title *East Lynne*), while in Australia Alfred Dampier turned his hand to yet another version as late as 1900. The first performance of *East Lynne* in Australia, probably in the Oxenford version, was given at the Haymarket, Melbourne 2.9.1867.

Ebreo, L'. 3-act opera with prologue, text A.Boni, founded on Bulwer-Lytton's *Leila,* music G.Apolloni, Fenice, Venice 23.1.1855; Prince of Wales, Melbourne 13.3.1873, initial 2 performances.

Edmunds, Albert. Pen-name adopted by Edmund Duggan and Bert Bailey in writing their successful early 20th century melodramas. Actor members of the William Anderson Company, who had served their apprenticeship with all kinds of touring companies, the 2 were astute and experienced enough to sense the growing interest in Australian scenes and characters on the stage, and to exploit it. Duggan was the writer of the partnership, Bailey the actor-comedian with an uncanny stage sense. Together they wrote, produced, and acted in such successful works as

The Squatter's Daughter; or, The Land of the Wattle (1907); *The Man From Outback; or Stockwhip and Stirrup* (1909); *On Our Selection* (1912), and *The Native Born* (1913). After this last and least successful play the partnership seems to have been dissolved by mutual consent.

Eldorado. Comic opera in 5 tableaux, text H.B.Farnie, music by several hands, Strand, London 19.2.1874; Opera House, Melbourne 24.10.1874, initial 7 performances.

Electric lighting. In 1857, while Melbourne's Amphitheatre (Astley's) was being converted to the first Princess's, it was said that its entrance was to be lighted by the electric light. This, if it happened (and there is some doubt that it did), constituted the first use in Australia of the carbon-arc electric light, or electricity without a dynamo or generator. Perhaps in this instance, as with the early gas experiments in Sydney, promises were made or results expected which could not then be fulfilled. As Bergman explains it, the arc lamps of this period consisted of two horizontal or vertical, point-to-point carbons connected to an electric current source (a battery or accumulator) and which produced between them an intense arc of bluish-white light. The Place de Concord in Paris was lighted with an arc lamp in 1844, and by 1854 the light was being used in Paris with night construction work. The arc light was first seen in Sydney on 3.2.1879, when it was exhibited in Sydney Harbour by the French warship, *Victoreuse*. On 25.2.1879 the working of this light was exhibited at Sydney Post Office. Its first public use was made in 1882, when the Sydney Arcade was lighted with electricity. 2 years later the Sydney Post Office was illuminated with Edison's incandescent light. The first use of electric lighting in the theatre appears to have been in Melbourne in 1882, when it was announced that the Australian Electrical Company was to light the vestibule and auditorium of the Opera House. The following year the Sydney Royal was similarly lighted. But for some years to come electricity was used in conjunction with gas lighting, for electricity was not only unreliable, artists, actors, and managers had not yet learned how to cope with its harsher, and sometimes yellower light. (See: Gas lighting. Stage lighting).

Elisir d'Amore, L. (The Love Potion). 2-act opera, text F.Romani, based on A.E.Scribe's *Le Philtre*, music G.Donizetti, Canobliana, Milan 12.5.1832; Lyceum, London 10.12.1836; Royal, Melbourne 26.7.1856, initial 3 performances.

Emerald Isle, The; or, The Caves of Carric-Cleena. 2-act comic opera, text B.Hood, music Sir Arthur Sullivan and E.German, Savoy, London 27.4.1901; Her Majesty's, Melbourne 17.3.1903, initial 18 performances.

Emperor, The. 2-act comic opera, text W.J.Curtis, music W.Arundel Orchard, Palace, Sydney 7.11.1906, initial 6 performances.

Emu Plains. Government farm for convict labour established about 36 miles (56 kilometres) from Sydney, where convicts, with the approval of an indulgent superintendent, in 1825 established their own theatre. Its use was restricted to officials of the farm and their families, and to the 'gentry' living nearby. *Howe's Weekly Commercial Express* of 25.7.1825 reported that 'the audience were select, composed of the neighbouring gentry and their families, who declared themselves highly gratified with the evening's amusement, and retired expressing their approbation by a magnificent donation which we hope will prove a stimulus to this *corps dramatique* . . .' The Emu Plains convict theatre seems to have been most active during 3 different years, 1825, 1827, and 1830. But here again records are scanty, and may also be faulty. As with Sidaway's theatre, it seems reasonable to assume that other plays were given besides those of which a record exists. From a first-hand description of this theatre and of a performance, left by 1 of the convicts thought to have been involved in its conduct (see the novel, *Ralph Rashleigh* by James Tucker), it is apparent that it was in some ways a duplicate of the 1789 Sydney convict theatre. The building was constructed of slab and bark, the gaps in the walls being filled with mud, and the interior whitewashed with local pipeclay. The rough wooden seats or benches in the pit and boxes, and the framework or the stage scenery, were made from local timber. Canvas for the scenes was had from 'fragments of bags, prisoners' duck clothing, bed ticks, etc., and painted in distemper with pipeclay, charcoal, and various coloured earths.' Tin was used to make lamps and candlesticks, oil and candles being provided by farm officials. But the governor of the day, Lieutenant General Ralph Darling, was eventually forced to close the theatre. The people of Sydney were envious and annoyed because Emu Plains, a convict centre, had a theatre, but not Sydney. On 2.11.1830 Superintendent John Maxwell of Emu Plains received a curtly worded letter from the Colonial Secretary ordering that theatrical performances be discontinued, and that the performers be assigned to private service. (See: Jamison, Sir John; Sydney, Theatres in).

Enchanted Cat, The. (la Chatte Métamorphosée en femme). 1-act opera bouffe, text A.E.Scribe and A.Duveyrier, music J.Offenbach, Bouffes-Parisiens, Paris 19.4.1858; Drury Lane, London 23.6.1863; Opera House, Sydney 6.9.1879, initial 6 performances.

Enchantress, The. 3-act opera, text A.Bunn after J.H.de Saint-Georges, music M.Balfe, Drury Lane, London 14.5.1845; Royal Victoria, Sydney 23.6.1851, initially 1 performance.

Enemy of the People, An. 5-act drama by Henrik Ibsen, trans. W.Archer, Haymarket, London 14.6.1893; Melbourne Repertory, Royal, 27.6.1914, initially 1 performance.

England versus Australia. 1-act play by William Moore, Oddfellows' Hall, Melbourne 30.3.1909, initially 1 performance.

England's Hope. 4-act drama by Bernard Espinasse, King's Melbourne, 23.12.1911, initial 24 performances.

Erminie. 3-act comic opera, text C.Bellamy and H.Paulton, music E.Jakobowski, Royal Comedy, London 9.11.1885; Princess's, Melbourne 26.12.1887, initial 6 performances.

Ernani. 4-act opera, text F.M.Piave, based on Victor Hugo's *Hernani* (1830), music G. Verdi, Fenice, Venice 9.3.1844; Her Majesty's, London 8.3.1845; Princess's, Melbourne 23.5.1857, initially 1 performance.

Espinasse, Bernard. Author of the plays: *In the Dark; Mr Harris; The Magic Cloak; Her Good Name; The Three Musketeers* (with George Rignold); *Blind Love; The Christian; The Ivy Leaf; England's Hope, The Master of Angestroom,* and *Ned Kelly; or, The Bushranger.*

Esson, Thomas Louis Buvelot (1879-1943). One of the earliest exponents of the modern movement in the drama in Australia. Esson, with one foot in the 19th and another in the 20th century, was nevertheless uninfluenced by the purely commercial world of the melodramatic theatre. Like the pioneers among whom he is numbered he found only a limited audience for his work. Chief among his plays, up to 1914, was his comedy *The Time is Not Yet Ripe* (1912), which had 1 performance in July and 1 in December 1912, and was then allowed to drop out of sight until the third quarter of the present century.

Estrella. 3-act comic opera, text Walter Parke, music Luscombe Searelle, tryout Prince's, Manchester 15.5.1883; second tryout Gaiety, London 24.5.1883; Folies Dramatiques, London 6.6.1883, initial 24 performances; Royal, Sydney 27.9.1884, initial 18 performances.

Euchred. 3-act drama by H.W.H.Stephen, Royal Victoria, Sydney 23.3.1872, initial 5 performances.

Eugene Aram; or, St Robert's Cave. 3-act melodrama by W.T.Moncrieff, adapted from Bulwer-Lytton's novel (1832), Surrey, London 8.2.1832; Royal, Sydney 5.12.1836.

——. 4-act drama by Alfred Dampier, adapted from Lytton, Royal, Melbourne 29.7.1874, initial 2 performances.

Eureka Stockade, The. (See: *The Democrat; or, Under the Southern Cross*).

——. 4-act drama by Edward W.O'Sullivan, Standard, Sydney 9.4.1898, initial 6 performances. Later rewritten, retitled *The Eureka Rebellion; or, The Fight at the Eureka Stockade,* Haymarket Hippodrome, (a tent theatre) Sydney 8.6.1907, initial 6 performances. (See: Parliamentarians).

Eva; or, Leaves From Uncle Tom's Cabin. 4-act drama by Frank Fowler, Lyceum, Sydney 25.8.1856, initial 4 performances. (See: Quinn, Anna Maria).

Evangeline. 3-act extravaganza, text J.C.Goodwin, music E.E.Rice, Niblo's, New York 27.7.1874; Court, Liverpool 11.6.1883; Opera House, Melbourne 27.4.1891, initial 32 performances.

Everyman. 16th century English morality play, revived London 1901; Town Hall, Melbourne 26.10.1905, initially 1 performance.

Extravaganza. (See: Burlesque).

Convicts' theatre advertisement Emu Plains 1830

```
Proprietor of Bank Stock.
                JOHN BLACK, Cashier.

            CONVICTS' THEATRE,
                EMU PLAINS.
                BY PERMISSION.

   ON the Evening of Saturday, the 30th
      November, this private Theatre will
   be opened with the celebrated national
   Tragedy of
                    DOUGLAS.
        CHARACTERS.        PERFORMERS.
   Young Norval,        William Toogood.
   Lord Randolph,       William Toogood.
   Glenalvon,           William W.
   Officer,             Joseph Hill.
   Old Norval,          William W.
   Servant,             Samuel Fenton.
                    WOMEN.
   Lady Randolph,       C. Holden.
   Anna,                J. Matthews.
   Between the Pieces, sundry Amusements.
       To conclude with the Farce of the
                    PADLOCK.
   Don Diego            John Northall.
   Leander,             James Dennison.
   First Scholar,       Samuel Fenton.
   Second Scholar,      Henry Aldis.
   Mungo,               William Toogood.
                    WOMEN.
   Leonora,             J. Matthews.
   Ursula,              J. O'Connor.
   Doors open at 7, to commence at half-past 7
```

Mitchell Library

Above: Scene from Faust *Prince of Wales Sydney 1864*
Below: Scene from La Fille de Madame Angot *Sydney Royal 1877*

F

Fair Penitent, The. 5-act tragedy by N.Rowe, Lincoln's Inn Fields, London May 1703; The Theatre, Sydney 4.2.1796.

Fairy Lake, The; or, The Magic Veil. 3-act opera, text C.Selby adapted from *Le lac des fees* by A.E.Scribe and A.H.Melesville, music D.Auber, Strand, London 13.5.1839; Royal Victoria, Hobart 17.7.1843, initially 1 performance. This version had music by Auber, Hérold, Boildieu, Marschner, and Rossini arranged by F.Howson.

Falka. 3-act comic opera, text H.B.Farnie after E.Leterrier and A.Vanloo, music F.Chassaigne, Comedy, London 29.10.1883; Opera House, Melbourne 24.4.1886, initial 42 performances.

Fall of Sebastopol, The; or, The Campaigners. 3-act drama by W.M.Akhurst, Royal, Melbourne 17.8.1857, initial 6 performances.

Fanciulla del West (The Girl of the Golden West). 3-act opera, text G.Civinini and C.Zangarini, after D.Belasco, music G.Puccini, Metropolitan, New York 10.12.1910; Covent Garden, London 29.5.1911; Her Majesty's, Melbourne 11.6.1912, initially 1 performance.

Fanny's First Play. 3-act comedy by George Bernard Shaw, Little, London 19.4.1911; Little, Sydney 5.5.1913, initial 36 performances.

Fatal Curiosity. 3-act tragedy by G.Lillo, Haymarket, London May 1736; HMS *Imogen*, Sydney Harbour 25.7.1833.

Fatinitza. 3-act operetta, text F.Zella nd R.Genée, founded on A.E.Scribe's *La Circassienne*, music F. von Suppé, Carl, Vienna 5.1.1876; Alhambra, London 20.6.1876; Opera House, Sydney 26.12.1882, initial 19 performances.

101

Faust. 5-act opera, text J.Barbier and M.Carré, based on Goethe's drama, music C.Gounod, Lyrique, Paris 19.3.1859; Her Majesty's, London 11.6.1863; Prince of Wales, Sydney 3.3.1864, initial 4 performances.

——. 5-act drama by Gilbert Parker, based on Dion Boucicault's *Faust and Marguerite,* Her Majesty's, Sydney 31.3.1888, initial 42 performances.

Faust and Gretchen. 4-act operetta, text R.Jaentsch, music M.Heuzenroeder, Albert Hall, Adelaide 19.3.1883, initially 1 performance.

Faust and Marguerite. 3-act drama by Alfred Dampier, adapted from Goethe's *Faust,* Royal, Melbourne 20.9.1873, initial 9 performances.

Favorite, La. 4-act opera, text A.Royer and G.Vaez after F.T.de Baculard d'Arnaud's *Le Comte de Comminges,* music G.Donizetti, Opera House, Paris 2.12.1840; Drury Lane, London 18.10.1843; Princess's, Melbourne 8.11.1858, initially 1 performance.

Fawcett, George. (See: Rowe, George Fawcett).

Fedora. 4-act drama by V.Sardou (1882), translated by H.Merivale, Haymarket, London 5.5.1883; Her Majesty's, Melbourne 28.7.1900, initial 12 performances.

——. 3-act opera, text A.Colautti, after V.Sardou, music U.Giordano, Lirico, Milan 17.11.1898; Covent Garden, London 5.11.1906; Her Majesty's, Melbourne 14.12.1901, initial 2 performances.

Fernande. 4-act drama by Marcus Clarke, adapted from V.Sardou's comedy (1870), Princess's, Melbourne 24.11.1871, initial 2 performances. Sardou's play was turned by Clarke into a drama for the tragic actress Mary Gladstane.

Fille de Madame Angot, La. 3-act comic opera, text P.Siraudin, L.F.Clairville, and V.Koning, music A.C.Lecocq, Alcazar, Brussels 4.12.1872; St James's, London 17.5.1873; Prince of Wales, Melbourne 24.9.1874, initial 26 performances.

Fille du Régiment, La. 2-act comic opera, text J.Hde Saint-Georges and J.F.Bayard, music G.Donizetti, Opéra Comique, Paris 11.2.1840; Her Majesty's, London 27.5.1847; Royal Victoria, Sydney 20.10.1851, initially 1 performance.

Fille du Tambour-Major, La (The Drum-Major's Daughter). 3-act comic opera, text A.Duru and H.Chivot, music J.Offenbach, Folies Dramatiques, Paris 13.12.1879; Alhambra, London 19.4.1880; Prince of Wales, Melbourne 27.12.1880, initial 102 performances.

Films. (See: Motion pictures).

Fires of St John, The. (Originally *Johannisfeuer,* also translated as *Midsummer Fires*). 4-act drama by H.Sudermann, translated M. and W.H.Harned, Her Majesty's, Melbourne 24.6.1905, initial 6 performances.

Fit of the Blues, A. 1-act operetta, text and music V.Robillard, Strand, London 29.10.1873; Opera House, Melbourne 28.2.1874, initial 9 performances.

Flats. Painted canvas scenes on frames, each half the width of the stage's acting area. They were used as back scenes in conjunction with wings and borders, but were also used from the second groove to the last, depending on the kind of scene required. The direction in 19th century published plays, 'the scene opens' and 'the scene closes' meant simply that the two flats were pulled off at either side of the stage to reveal a new scene behind them; or that two were pushed on somewhere in front of the back scene, to close out an old scene with a new one. These movements of the scenery — wings as well as flats — were made in full view of the audience. Very often, when an actor spoke a line such as 'Let us go and see if she is in the garden,' the scene would 'open' to reveal the garden, and the actors would walk into it. Later, flats were tall canvas-covered frames used to build box and other settings when the use of the groove system of stage setting was abandoned. (See: Box set).

Fledermaus, Die (The Bat). 3-act operetta, text C.Haffner and R.Genée, from *Le Réveillon* by H.Meilhac and L.Halévy and *Des Gefängnis* by Bendix, music J.Strauss junior, Theater an der Wien, Vienna 5.4.1874; Alhambra, London 18.12.1876; Queen's, Sydney 17.10.1877, initial 3 performances. (See: *Night Birds, The*).

Flemming, Herbert (1856-1908). Began stage work as an amateur at the Bijou, Notting Hill, with another amateur who later achieved considerable fame — Beerbohm Tree. In 1876 left England for Australia, but finished up in Christchurch, New Zealand. Here he engaged in minor business enterprises, all of which failed, and finally was offered a professional engagement as juvenile lead by W.Hoskins, then conducting the Christchurch Royal. Flemming always acknowledged that in the next 6 months he received from Hoskins essential coaching in every description of stage work, forming the foundation on which he built a total 16 years of practical experience in theatres throughout Australia. Leaving Hoskins to join Mrs Scott Siddons and her company as juvenile lead, Flemming visited every Australian colony, playing in everything from *Romeo and Juliet* to the most insignificant melodrama. In the course of his subsequent Australian experience he at one period played 21 different parts in 18 nights, played secondary roles in G.Darrell's melodramas, and joined Janet Achurch's company, where he gained further experience in Shakespeare and Ibsen. He returned to London in 1893 with this company, calling on the way and playing in Sumatra, the East Indies, Singapore, Calcutta, Benares, Delhi, Bombay, Aden, Ismailia, Cairo, and Malta. For the next 2 years in London he found no difficulty in getting work, playing, among other roles, Nils Krogstad in *A Doll's House,* Lord Chudleigh in C.H.Chambers and W.O.Tristan's *The Queen of Manoa,* James Cook in *Clever Alice* (an adaptation by B.Thomas of A.Willbrandt's *Die Maler*), Maurice de Saxe in *Adrienne Lecouvreur,* and 206 performances as Robert Overston in H.Pettitt's *A Woman's Revenge.* He also played in the single matinee performance of *A Life Policy,* a dramatisation by the Australian (Tasmanian) writer, Helen Davis, of her novel, *For So Little,* published in England. His final part for 1894 was that of Dick Marston to Alfred Dampier's Captain Starlight in *Robbery Under Arms* at the Princess's. Towards the end of 1895 he joined Miss Fortescue's company as lead in a tour of South Africa, organised by Luscombe Searelle. 'Miss Fortescue,' the stage name by which she was always known, was a noted beauty of the day whose real name was Emily May Finney. She was the first to play Lady Ella in *Patience,* and Celia in *Iolanthe.* Flemming spent some years in South Africa, and when he met the monologist Mel. B.Spurr in 1903, who was making a successful South African tour, he became his agent and booked him for a tour of the Australian colonies. The tour ended with Spurr's death in Melbourne in 1904. Flemming next formed his own touring company, a venture in which he lost all his money just before his death in 1908.

Flesh and the Devil, The. 5-act tragedy by George Rignold, translated or adapted from V.Sardou's *La Patrie,* Criterion, Sydney 17.6.1899, initial 8 performances.

Fligende Holländer, Der. (The Flying Dutchman). 3-act opera, text and music Richard Wagner, Dresden 2.1.1843; Drury Lane, London 23.7.1870; Princess's, Melbourne 29.4.1901, initially 1 performance.

Flies. Galleries or gangways half-way up the top portion of the stage, and usually all around it, where scenes, cloths, curtains, light battens etc., are 'flown.' These are pulled up from the stage floor on ropes and pulleys set in the gridiron immediately under the stage roof. The ropes are then tied to the pinrail in the flies until the scenes, etc., are required to be lowered again . (See: Gridiron).

Float. (See: Footlights).

Floradora. 2-act musical comedy, text O.Hall, music L.Stuart, Lyric, London 11.11.1899; Her Majesty's, Melbourne 15.12.1900, initial 93 performances.

Flying Dutchman, The; or, The Phantom Ship. 3-act nautical drama by E.Fitzball, Adelphi, London 1.1.1827; Royal, Sydney 14.9.1835. (See: *Fliegende Holländer, Der.;* Projected scenery).

Flying Dutchman, The; or, Vanderdecken. 5-act drama by K.Russell

(Mrs Alfred Dampier), Victoria, Newcastle 4.9.1880, initially 1 performance.

Flying Jib; or, The Derby Day. 3-act drama by Robert P.Whitworth, Prince of Wales, Auckland, New Zealand 28.7.1868, initial 5 performances.

Flying Scud, The; or, A Four-legged Fortune. 4-act drama by Dion Boucicault, Holborn, London 6.10.1866; Royal, Melbourne 16.3.1867, initial 27 performances.

Foiled; or, Australia Twenty Years Ago. 3-act drama by Walter H.Cooper, Prince of Wales, Sydney 22.4.1871, initial 22 performances.

Footlights. Commonly known as the 'float.' A row of lights at the front of the stage, at the actors' feet, but just above the heads of the orchestra. In the 18th century theatre the front of the stage was illuminated by one or more chandeliers suspended over the proscenium. This, it was found, impeded the view of those seated in the upper portion of the house, and when the actor David Garrick was lessee of Drury Lane he removed the chandeliers and substituted a frame of lamps known ever since as footlights. In the early English theatre footlights were of two kinds — a trough of oil on which floated small triangular saucers containing wicks or candles which fed on the oil; and tallow candles. This float could be lowered mechanically to the understage area, where wicks were trimmed and oil replenished. In large theatres such as Drury Lane and Covent Garden comparatively little discomfort was felt by actors or audience in their use, but in small theatres such as Barnett Levey's Sydney Royal the fumes from oil lamps and guttering candles were sometimes overpowering. When Sydney's Royal Victoria opened in 1838 it used oil lamps, but not candles, for a new kind of lamp had come into general use, the Argand lamp. This not only gave a steadier, brighter light than before, but was also smokeless if properly tended. The new lamp had a circular wick which allowed air to pass up its centre. It was also protected by a glass chimney. In 1841 the Royal Victoria was lighted by gas, and the float contained instead of oil lamps a series of open, naked gas jets on a long pipe, giving not only light but also a great deal of heat. In Melbourne the Olympic was still using oil lamps as late as 1856, as a *Punch* 'ode' of that year indicates:
>Now fade the oil-fed foot-lights on the sight . . .

But in the same city the Royal had been opened the year before with gas lighting. And gas continued in general use until the advent of the electric light and the safer enclosed light bulb.

For a Life. 4-act drama by J.J.McCloskey, from Marcus Clarke's novel, *His Natural Life* (1874), Queen's, Manchester 19.7.1886; Surrey, London 6.5.1889. Nicoll says this was produced under the title *His Natural Life* at Leicester on 7.8.1896, but there is no record of this performance having taken place. Although McCloskey, an American actor-playwright, registered 48 of his plays with the Library of Congress Copyright Office, *For a Life* was not among them, indicating that it was written for a specific actor or manager for production in England only.

For Life; or, The Foster Brothers. 4-act drama by Wybert Reeve, Royal, Melbourne 1.5.1880, initial 6 performances.

For the Term of His Natural Life. Drama in 6 tableaux and prologue by Thomas Somers (Thomas Walker) and Alfred Dampier, from Marcus Clarke's novel, *His Natural Life* (1874), Royal Standard, Sydney 5.6.1886, initial 42 performances. Revised version, using names of Walker and Dampier, Her Majesty's, Sydney 30.11.1895, initial 19 performances. This version was last staged at the King's, Melbourne by William Anderson in 1909.

——. Drama in prologue and 7 tableaux by William T.K.South, Royal, Wellington, New Zealand 6.10.1886, initial 2 performances.

——. Drama in prologue and 4 acts by Edmund Duggan, Royal, Adelaide 6.12.1897, initial 6 performances.

——. 4-act drama by unknown author, Adelphi, Sydney 1.11.1913, initial 18 performances. (See: *Convict 1240; His Natural Life; Strong as Death;* Parliamentarians).

Forbidden Fruit. 2-act comedietta by Marcus Clarke, adapted from A.-H.-J.Duveyrier (pseudonym of M.Melesville) and P.-F.-A.Carmouche's *Le Fruit défendu* (1848), Bijou, Melbourne 31.7.1880, initial 5 performances.

Forlorn Hope, The. 4-act drama by George Darrell, People's, Melbourne 26.12.1879, initial 37 performances.

Formosa; or, The Railroad to Ruin. 4-act drama by Dion Boucicault, Drury Lane, London 5.8.1869; Prince of Wales, Sydney 13.11.1870, initial 17 performances.

Forster, William. (See: Parliamentarians).

Fortune Teller, The. 3-act comic opera, text H.B.Smith, music V.Herbert, Shaftesbury, London 9.4.1901; Royal, Sydney 17.1.1903, initial 35 performances.

Fortune's Fool. Comedy by F.Reynolds, Covent Garden, London 29.10.1796; The Theatre, Sydney 1.6.1799.

Fortune's Frolic. Farce by J.T.Allingham, Covent Garden, London 25.5.1799; Royal, Sydney 29.12.1832.

Forza del Destino, La (The Force of Destiny). 4-act opera, text F.M.Piave after *Don Alvaro* by A.P.de Saavedra, music G.Verdi, St Petersburg 10.11.1862; Her Majesty's, London 22.6.1867; Prince of Wales, Melbourne 10.6.1878, initial 2 performances.

Foul Play. 4-act drama by Marcus Clarke, adapted from the novel by

Charles Reade and Dion Boucicault (1868), Duke of Edinburgh, Melbourne 7.12.1868, initial 6 performances.

Fountain, The. 3-act comedy by G.Calderon, Aldwych, London 28.3.1909; Melbourne Repertory, Turn Verein Hall, 2.10.1911, initially 1 performance.

Fourth wall. A term used to describe the non-existent wall (the proscenium arch) through which an audience views a domestic drama. It is as old as c.1580, when the Italian author of *Dialogues on Stage Affairs,* Leone di Somi, wrote in his fourth dialogue that while there was a 'certain beauty' in seeing a room on the stage, yet such a room was contrary to reality 'in that the room is lacking (as it must) a fourth wall.' Some 300 years later the 'naturalists' in the 19th century theatre had become so obsessed by the 'presence' of this supposed fourth wall that they placed actors and furniture on the stage so that the 'picture' looked as though someone had indeed lifted the fourth wall to find out what was going on in the room. But the theatre is a world of conventions, and the public has always accepted this — from the earliest times when it accepted without demur the pushing on-stage by visible stagehands of the 2 halves of a back scene and the placing of furniture by servants, to the present, when hundreds of spotlights and floods suspended over the stage and around the auditorium are accepted as 'normal' lighting.

Fra Diavolo; ou, L'Hôtellerie de Terracine (Brother Devil; or, The Inn at Terracina). 3-act comic opera, text A.E.Scribe, music D.Auber, Opera Comique, Paris 28.1.1830; Drury Lane, London 1.2.1831; Royal Victoria, Hobart 3.10.1842, initially 1 performance.

Francesca Vasari. 3-act tragedy by John Finnamore, Royal, Melbourne 17.4.1867, initial 2 performances. Published by W.H.Williams, Melbourne 1865. Copy in Mitchell Library, Sydney.

Freischutz, Der. (The Freeshooter). 3-act opera, text F.Kind, based on a tale in the *Gespensterbuch* of J.A.Apel and F.Laun (1811), music C.M.von Weber, Schauspielhaus, Berlin 18.6.1821; Lyceum, London (as *The Seventh Bullet*) 22.7.1824; Royal Victoria, Sydney 15.9.1838.

French Maid, The. 2-act musical comedy, text B.Hood, music W.Slaughter. Bath 4.4.1896; Her Majesty's, Sydney 4.9.1897, initial 36 performances.

Fun On the Bristol; or, A Night at Sea. 3-act musical comedy, text John F.Sheridan, music by various hands, Royal, Manchester 15.5.1882; Gaiety, Sydney 16.3.1884, initial 40 performances.

Fuss. A Tale of the Exhibition. 3-act comedy by Walter H.Cooper, Royal Victoria 5.4.1880, initial 5 performances.

ROYAL VICTORIA THEATRE

First Night of the 'Royal Masquer.

On MONDAY EVENING, MAY 12, 1845

Will be presented, an entirely new and original Drama, entitled

THE ROYAL MASQUER

OR, THE FLOWER OF CLYDE.

Written by the Author of the "Hibernian Father," "Currency Lass," &

Jamie Jamieson (a universal genius, a dabbler in all professions, but now practising as a tinke
Mr. GRIFFITHS
Cranstoun (Laird of Govan) Mr. SAVILLE   Andrew Fleming (a farmer) Mr. FENTO
Sir Mark Livingstone (the King's confidant) .... Mr. GROVE
Malcolm (a young student of Glasgow) .... Mr. JAMES
Davie Launder (landlord of the "Fox and Goose") .... Mr. COLLI
Hans Schnapsen (a smuggler) .... Mr. DEERING
Nicol Muckleman and Sam Maxwell (smugglers, accomplices of Hans Schnapsen) Mess
RILEY and DOUGLASS
Simon Snipe (a philanthropic tailor, a practical illustration of purely benevolent emigratio
Mr. SIMES
Dame Fleming (wife of Andrew, and mother of Effie) .... Mrs. GIB
Meenie Launder (a warm-hearted Scotch lassie) .... Madame LOUISE
Effie (the Flower of Clyde, daughter of Andrew Fleming) Mrs. O'FLAHERTY

A SONG BY MADAME CARANDIN.

Playbill for The Royal Masquer *(Geoghegan)* 1845

G

Gaiety Girl, A. 2-act musical comedy, text O.Hall, and H.Greenbank, music S.Jones, Prince of Wales, London 14.10.1893; Princess's, Melbourne 13.4.1895, initial 18 performances.

Galatea. (See: *Schöne Galathee, Die*).

Gagging. A word with 2 or more meanings. The first is 'the substitution of any sort of nonsense by an actor who has forgotten an author's lines.' The second is 'the addition of words or topical phrases or puns to an author's lines.' In the first half of the 19th century gagging in the first sense was rife in most theatres because of the length of the nightly programmes. In some theatres the prompter was often the hardest worked member of the company. Gagging in the second sense was most often used by actors when they wanted a quick or cheap audience reaction, or when they wanted to score off a public figure or another member of their profession. In well conducted theatres, gagging of any kind by an actor was subject to a fine, taken from his weekly wage, but it was a practice so much resorted to in the early Sydney theatre that even fines could not eradicate it. Again and again, until at least the late 1840s, newspapers continually complained of 'too much gagging.'

Garibaldi, the Hero of Palermo. 3-act drama by James Smith, Prince of Wales, Melbourne 8.9.1860, initial 7 performances.

Gas lighting. That far-seeing theatre enthusiast, Barnett Levey, as early as 1826 was indulging in dreams of his theatre being lighted with gas. Perhaps he was inspired by the experiments with gas conducted by a Sydney chemist that year, and the successful lighting of a Sydney shop in 1828. No doubt, had Levey lived he would have been the first in Australia to light a theatre with gas. As it was, the honour became Wyatt's, at his Royal Victoria in Sydney. The first theatre in England to use gas, on the stage, was the Lyceum on 6.8.1817. Sydney's Royal Victoria, opened in 1838, was lighted by Argand oil lamps. Even the central chandelier in the ceiling was made up of 24 Argand lamps. In July 1841 the lighting was changed to gas, not only in the auditorium but also on the stage. The only exception was the central chandelier, which held the original oil lamps until a gasalier was obtained. Gas lighting on the stage remained in use for some time after the introduction of electricity, because actors and scenepainters favoured its soft light as opposed to the harsh and sometimes yellow early electric light. As late as 1888 gas lighting was still being used on most Australian stages, while in 1900 the Sydney theatre architect C.Backhouse gave a talk to the Insurance Institute of NSW in which he took it as the accepted thing that every new theatre built would have its stage lighted by gas. He said every theatre should have an independent gas service despite the installation of electric light. In describing the gridiron above the stage he said that 'from it hang all the sky borders, cloths, gas borders, etc . . .'

Gay Gordons, The. 2-act musical comedy, text S.Hicks, music G.Jones, Aldwych, London 11.9.1907; Royal, Melbourne 21.12.1910; initial 39 performances.

Gay Grisette, The. 2-act musical comedy, text G.Dance, music C.Kiefert, Royal, Bradford 1.8.1898; Royal, Melbourne 4.2.1911, initial 30 performances.

Gay Lord Quex, The. 4-act comedy by A.W.Pinero, Globe, London 8.4.1899; Royal, Sydney 26.8.1899, initial 13 performances.

Gay Parisienne, The. 2-act musical comedy, text G.Dance, music I.Caryll, Opera House, Northampton 1.10.1894; Her Majesty's, Sydney 31.7.1897, initial 30 performances.

Geisha, The. 2-act musical comedy, text O.Hall, music S.Jones, Daly's, London 25.4.1896; Princess's, Melbourne 17.12.1898, initial 42 performances.

Genevieve de Brabant. 5-act comic opera, text A.Jaime and E.Tréfeu, music J.Offenbach, Bouffes-Parisiens, Paris 19.11.1859. Revised version by H.Crémieux, Menus-Plaisirs, Paris 26.12.1867; Philharmonic, London 11.11.1871; Prince of Wales, Melbourne 11.9.1873, initial 15 performances.

Gentleman in Black, The. 3-act opera, text E.Searle, music H.Marsh, Royal, Melbourne 24.7.1861, initial 3 performances.

Gentleman Joe. 2-act musical farce, text B.Hood, music W.Slaughter, Prince of Wales, London 2.3.1895; Lyceum, Sydney 24.8.1895, initial 12 performances.

Geoghegan, Edward (1813-?). Convict playwright of the 1840s whose

7 plays, performed at the Royal Victoria, Sydney earned him a total of £6. One of his plays, *The Hibernian Father,* had 7 performances. The return to the theatre owner, J.Wyatt, must have been considerable. Geoghegan arrived in Australia on the convict ship *Middlesex* from Ireland in 1840. A medical student in Dublin, he was accused and found guilty on a charge of 'obtaining goods under false pretences,' and was sentenced to be transported for 7 years. On arrival in Sydney, because of his background, he was given the post of dispenser in the medical department at Cockatoo Island. This was a more or less privileged position, and he was able to persuade the doctor in charge to give him a weekly pass to Sydney. Thus he was able to make contact with an actor he had known in Dublin, F.Nesbitt, and, through him, with the Royal Victoria. Writing to the Colonial Secretary in 1846 to ask for a licence for a play of his called *The Jew of Dresden* (it was never performed), Geoghegan listed 7 plays written by him in 4 years and performed at the Royal Victoria. He claimed that 3 of these were his original work, and 4 were adaptations. The plays were: *The Hibernian Father* (1844), *The Currency Lass* (1844), *The Last Days of Pompeii* (1844), *A Christmas Carol* (1845), *Captain Kyd; or, The Rover of the Seas* (1845), *The Royal Masquer; or, The Flower of the Clyde* (1845), and *La Fitte the Pirate; or, The Outlaws of Barritaria* (1845). When he regained his freedom, Geoghegan moved to Melbourne. *A trip to Geelong* by Edward Geoghegan, Princess's, Melbourne 15.7.1861, was possibly his last work for the stage.

German drama. The most popular and most frequently performed German play in Australia was August Friedrich von Kotzebue's *Menschenhass und Rhue,* translated by B.Thompson as *The Stranger* (1798). This was closely followed by Mrs N.A.Lovell's translation of Baron Eligius von Münch-Bellinghausen's *Der Sohn der Wildnis,* which she called *Ingomar, the Barbarian* (1851). The Baron, who wrote under the pen-name Friedrich Halm, also wrote *Der Fechter von Ravenna,* translated by a Melbourne journalist under the title *The Gladiator of Ravenna.* Other German plays frequently seen on Australian stages were Kotzebue's *Das Kind der Liebe,* translated by Mrs Inchbald as *Lovers' Vows* (1798); his *Die Spanier in Peru,* translated by R.B.Sheridan as *Pizarro* (1799), and his *Der Brüderzwist,* translated by T.J.Dibdin as *The Birthday* (1799).

Geschiedene Frau, Die. (The Girl on the Train). 3-act operetta, text V.Leon, music L.Fall, Carl, Vienna 23.12.1908; Vaudeville, London 4.6.1910; Criterion, Sydney 4.11.1911, initial 72 performances.

Gilbert and Sullivan. W.S.Gilbert (1836-1911), dramatist, and Arthur Sullivan (1842-1900), composer, first collaborated on what Gilbert called a 'dramatic cantata' — *Trial by Jury* (1875). Next came their first comic opera, *The Sorcerer* (1877), but it was not until the production of their operetta, *HMS Pinafore* (1878), that they really struck gold. The initial London run of this work achieved 571 performances, as against

131 for *Trial by Jury* and 178 for *The Sorcerer*. Such was the tremendous popularity of *HMS Pinafore* that it was pirated throughout the English-speaking world, including Australia. In 1879 it was said that more than 300 companies in the USA were performing *HMS Pinafore* with success. This work was first performed in Australia by the Kelly and Leon Minstrel Troupe at the Sydney School of Arts on 3.5.1879. The success of their production persuaded several Melbourne people to embark on *Pinafore*. This time two companies, one headed by W.H.Lingard and his wife, Alice Dunning, and the other by Richard Stewart and his three daughters, Docy, Maggie, and Nellie, opened on the same night, 7.6.1879. Quite by coincidence, on the same night Kelly and Leon presented the first performance of *Pinafore* in Brisbane. If all this was not enough, on 23.9.1879 the sailors of HMS *Wolverene*, then in Sydney Harbour, gave a performance of the operetta on their ship. This was apparently not a pirated performance, for early in August J.C.Williamson had returned to Sydney from an overseas trip with the sole Australian rights to *Pinafore,* and the 'pirates' were made to disgorge.

Gioconda, La. 4-act opera, text A.Boito after Victor Hugo's *Angelo,* music A.Ponchielli, Scala, Milan 8.4.1876; Covent Garden, London 31.5.1883; Royal, Melbourne 5.1,1.1887, initial 9 performances.

Giovanni. 3-act opera, text Alfred Hill and Harriet Callan, music Alfred Hill, Repertory, Sydney 3.8.1914, initial 6 performances.

Gipsy Love. (See: *Zigeunerliebe*).

Girl Behind the Counter, The. 2-act musical comedy, text L.Bantock and A.Anderson, music H.Talbot, Wyndham's, London 21.4.1906; Royal, Melbourne 17.4.1909, initial 24 performances.

Girl From Kay's, The. 3-act musical comedy, text O.Hall, music C.Cook, Apollo, London 15.11.1902; Princess's, Melbourne 4.6.1904, initial 18 performances.

Girl From Wayback, The. 4-act drama by P.Lytton and W.E.Vincent, Palace, Sydney 31.8.1912, initial 18 performances.

Girl in the Taxi, The. 3-act musical comedy, text F.Fenn and A.Wimperis, adapted from the German of G.Okonkowski, music J.Gilbert, Lyric, London 5.9.1912; Her Majesty's, Sydney 8.8.1914, initial 60 performances.

Girl of the Golden West, The. 4-act drama by D.Belasco, Belasco, New York 14.11.1905; Elephant and Castle, London 29.9.1905; Royal, Sydney 7.11.1908, initial 11 performances (See: *Fanciulla del West*).

Girl of the Never Never, The. 4-act drama by Jo Smith, King's, Melbourne 26.12.1912, initial 20 performances.

Girl on the Film, The. 3-act musical comedy, text J.Tanner, music

W. Kollo, Gaiety, London 5.4.1913; Her Majesty's, Sydney 19.12.1914, initial 42 performances.

Girl on the Train, The. (See: *Geschiedene Frau, Die*).

Girl Who Loved a Soldier, The. 4-act drama by Wilton Welch, Adelphi, Sydney 27.7.1912, initial 18 performances.

Girls of Gottenberg, The. 2-act musical comedy, text G. Grossmith, Jr., and L. Berman, music I. Caryll and L. Monckton, Gaiety, London 15.5.1907; Her Majesty's, Melbourne 26.10.1907, initial 43 performances.

Girofle-Girofla. 3-act operetta, text A. van Loo and E. Letterrier, music C. Lecocq, Alcazar, Brussels 21.3.1874; Opera Comique, London 6.6.1874; Prince of Wales, Melbourne 22.5.1875, initial 13 performances.

Giving out the play. At Barnett Levey's Sydney Royal in the 1830s, and in other Australian theatres for some time afterwards, the English custom of giving out the play was followed at the end of each performance. This consisted of an announcement from the stage of the programme for the next performance at that theatre. (See: Playbill).

Gladiator of Ravenna, The. 5-act tragedy by William Jaffray, translated from F. Halm's (Baron E. von Meunch-Bellinghausen) *Der Fechter von Ravenna* (1859), Royal, Melbourne 1.7.1865, initial 12 performances.

Goatcher, Phillip W. (1852-1931). Born in London, Goatcher began his working life in a law office. Having natural ability as an artist, and a strong inclination to the theatre, he gave up the law and gained employment at London's Sadler's Wells. Here he indulged his enthusiasm for scenepainting, though in what capacity is not known. Tiring of this, and urged by a spirit of adventure, he somehow made his way to St Petersburg, possibly working his passage on a ship. Returning to London, he next signed on board a ship bound for Australia. He made a second visit in 1867, but this time he left ship at Melbourne and walked all the way to Ballarat. Here he soon found the local theatre, where he spent some time with John Hennings, then the resident scenepainter. But although Hennings recognised his assistant's talent, and helped him all he could, he was unable to persuade him to stay. The urge to travel had again gripped Goatcher, and this time he went to the New Zealand goldfields, finishing up, not with a cradle and a dish, but with charcoal and a paint brush at Captain Butt's theatre in Shortland. His next move was to San Francisco, where he first met J.C. Williamson, and then on to New York, where he was engaged as assistant to the talented Matt. Morgan at Niblo's Gardens. This proved to be his real training ground. As a result of the work he did and the training and experience he gained at Niblo's he was able to move on to important engagements at theatres

Above: Phillip W. Goatcher,
Scenic Artist at the Theatre Royal, Melbourne
Right: John G. Griffiths as Iago 1854

in Boston, St Louis, Philadelphia, and other major US centres. He moved on again after a few years, this time back to London, where he painted at the Princess's, Drury Lane, and Covent Garden until, in 1875, he returned to the USA. Working at first in Philadelphia and other centres, he returned to New York as resident scenepainter at the famous Wallack's. Here he remained for 10 years, when he again returned to London and worked on most of the popular stage productions of the time at the St James's, Adelphi, and other theatres. In 1890 J.C.Williamson, on a visit to London, invited Goatcher to Australia as scenepainter for the Firm. From then on he was associated with most of the J.C.Williamson opera, comic opera, and drama successes, and made Australia his permanent home. In 1896 he was commissioned to design and carry out work on the decoration of the interior of the new Sydney theatre, the Palace, which he did in Indian style. This completed, he worked in several theatres until, in 1906 or thereabouts, he moved to Perth, where he became a landowner and established a successful painting and decorating business in the city with one of his sons. But that he could still be prevailed upon to return to the theatre was demonstrated in 1911, his jubilee year as a scenic artist, when he returned to Melbourne to paint for several important productions, including the J.C.Williamson premiere in that city of *The Chocolate Soldier*. Noted for his painting of act drops, it was said that the satin curtains he painted for the Sydney Lyceum act drop in that year puzzled many viewers, who thought they were made of real satin. (See: Act drop; *Chocolate Soldier, The*).

Gold and Alloy. 5-act drama by Walter Reynolds, Academy of Music, Melbourne 6.4.1878, initial 6 performances. Title changed to *Tried and True*, People's, Melbourne 27.9.1879, initial 6 performances.

Golden Belt, The. 4-act drama by H.W.H.Stephen, Queen's, Sydney 20.11.1875, initial 6 performances.

Golden Shanty, The. 4-act drama by Edward Dyson, Palace, Sydney 30.8.1913, initial 12 performances.

Goldfields, Theatre on the. There are few descriptions in existence of the temporary theatres sometimes erected on the goldfields with the dual purpose of entertaining the diggers and making a fortune for the players. The following, reprinted in the *Age* from the *Ararat Advertiser* in 1857, is therefore the more valuable. 'About 3 months back the first theatre on Ararat was commenced to be built. Poles were driven in the ground, on which calico was stretched for the walls, whilst the roof was composed of the same material, without even a necessary fly to resist the weather. The stage itself was but a poor affair, the floor having too steep an incline, with only about 18 ins beyond the wings. A very small calico tent formed the dressing room for the ladies, from which they emerged, crossed a small space, and ascended a ladder to the stage. The calico walls certainly helped to increase the number of the audience if it did not swell the manager's exchequer; for numbers of boys and men nightly stood outside and witnessed the performance through convenient holes. In wet weather the "theatre" had a most dismal and wretched appearance; the rain came through the roof, trickled down the rafters, and formed pools of water in different parts of the pit and "stalls." We need not say the audience on such occasions was very, very small . . .'

Gondoliers, The; or, The King of Baritaria. 2-act comic opera, text W.S.Gilbert, music Sir Arthur Sullivan, Savoy, London 7.12.1889; Princess's, Melbourne 25.10.1890, initial 48 performances.

Good for Evil. 3-act drama by F.R.C.Hopkins, Princess's, Dunedin, New Zealand 16.10.1876. Last act only, Royal, Melbourne 27.7.1877. Originally published as *Clay and Porcelain; a Drama of the Present Day,* Charlwood, Melbourne 1875. Copy in Mitchell Library, Sydney.

Gordon, George (1839-1899). William, George, and John Gordon are honoured names in the history of scenepainting. William, who had been a pupil of the great Clarkson Stanfield, achieved his greatest fame with the settings he did for Madame Vestris at London's Olympic, and for Charles Kean's Shakespearian productions at London's Princess's — *King John, Henry VIII,* and *A Midsummer Night's Dream.* His son, George, was his assistant in 1858 when William painted the settings for the Bristol Royal production of *A Midsummer Night's Dream.* George came to the fore as a scenepainter in his own right during the Bancrofts' seasons in London, for which he painted some outstanding settings for Shakespearian and modern dramas. He painted some of the first 'carpenters' scenes' for the Bancrofts' production of *The Merchant of Venice,* and designed solidly built-up settings for the modern plays, *Peril* (1876), and *Diplomacy* (1878). The hall setting for *Peril,* with a huge staircase and gallery, was so solidly built that it could not be 'changed,' and a small boudoir scene required for the same play had to be built inside it. Trained as an architect as well as an artist, George Gordon excelled in interior settings, as he demonstrated when he came to Australia in 1879 as scenepainter to Arthur Garner's London Comedy company. At the end of this company's 200-night Sydney season the *Mail*'s critic wrote that most of the plays presented were little more than 'table and chair pieces,' but that 'if there be a star in the company, Mr George Gordon, the scenic artist, is that star, and him the management have to thank for much of their success; while Australian theatregoers and scenepainters have to thank him for an education in stage setting.' When 'the firm' — Williamson, Garner, and Musgrove — was formed in 1882 he was appointed chief scenepainter. Early in 1880 Gordon, who had decorated the interior of London's Gaiety and Prince of Wales, did the interior decoration of Garner's in Adelaide, for which he also painted a striking act drop. In 1886 he designed and decorated the interior of Melbourne's new Princess's, making it one of the city's outstanding showplaces. The new theatre's first manager, Harry Musgrove, in 1926 wrote of Gordon: 'He made, I remember, a special trip to England and there bought the carpets, the chairs, and many fittings made to his own design.' Gordon died on his 60th birthday, as the result of injuries received in a fall from a tram.

Gordon, John Cameron (1872-1911). Came to Australia with his father, George Gordon, in 1879. At the age of about 18 took up scenepainting for a living, and soon proved himself to be every bit as talented as his father and his grandfather. His work over the years for all kinds of productions — operas, comic operas, dramas, burlesques and pantomimes — earned him high praise. His article, 'Scene painting in Australia' (*Lone Hand*, 2.11.1908), illustrated with 4 examples of his work, could be called the final credo of the 19th century scenepainter. At the time of his death he was working on the settings for a revival of the drama, *Ben Hur*, at Her Majesty's, Sydney.

Götterdämmerung. (See: *Ring des Nibelungen, Der*).

Gould, Nat (1857-1919). Born in England, this famous racing novelist — '. . . we may go to him for what may be termed the moral system of the racecourse' says E.Morris Miller — spent 12 years in Australia as a young man. Arriving in 1884, he worked as a journalist on a number of Brisbane and Sydney newspapers. Like Hornung before him, the impressions he thus gained of Australia remained with him for the rest of his life. A large percentage of his published work deals with Australia. His most famous or best known novel, *The Double Event* (1891), achieved new popularity when it was made into a play by G.Darrell in 1893. Although he published more than 120 novels, 3 or 4 non-fiction works, and 14 annuals, Gould had only one play produced — *The Chance of a Lifetime,* Elephant and Castle, London 27.10.1909.

Graf von Luxemburg, Der. (The Count of Luxembourg). 3-act operetta, text A.M.Willner and R.Bodansky, music F.Lehár, Theater an der Wien, Vienna 12.11.1909; Daly's, London 20.5.1911; His Majesty's, Melbourne 5.4.1913, initial 31 performances.

Grand opera. A rather pretentious title for serious opera, which has no spoken dialogue. Its secondary definition, as the words imply, is opera on a large scale, lavishly mounted. As a term it does little more than distinguish between comic and serious opera, though both can be 'grand' in one sense, and overlooks the many different kinds of opera which are neither comic nor grand. Even the word 'opera' is hardly the right kind of bed in which, like Procrustes, to fit *Clari, Orpheus aux Enfers, Faust,* and *Der Ring des Nibelungen.*

Grande-Duchesse de Gerolstein, La. 3-act comic opera, text H.Meilhac, and L.Halévy, music J.Offenbach, Variétés, Paris

12.4.1867; Covent Garden, London 18.11.1867; Princess's, Melbourne 27.2.1871, initial 15 performances.

Great Wrong Righted, A. (See: *Convict 1240*).

Greek drama. The first public performance of a Greek play, at the University of Sydney, was of the *Agamemnon* of Aeschylus. Given by students in the Great Hall on 14.6.1886, it was nevertheless not the first Greek play performed in Sydney. Sydney Grammar School pupils gave a performance of the comedy by Aristophanes, *The Clouds,* at their school on 20.6.1884. The University production had music especially composed for it by Hector McLean, and Professor Walter Scott of the University provided a printed English translation of the play for sale to members of the audience who had no Greek. B.N.Jones, a well known actor of the time, stage-managed the production.

Greenroom. A room in the theatre set aside for the use of the actors, in which they rested between scenes, entertained visitors, made social contact with their fellow actors, occasionally rehearsed, and listened to play-readings by the manager. Originally a place where the reigning stage favourites could hold court, with quite marked class distinctions, it began to fall into disuse as dressing rooms changed from the 'table, chair, and mirror for all-comers' concept to the comfortably furnished and private individual room. The greenroom was never much used in Australia, though it was provided in some theatres. More often than not it became the room in which the dusty overflow from the property room, wardrobe, or scene dock was stacked.

Greville, John R. (1834-1894). Born in Dublin, Greville made his first stage appearance at the Royal Phoenix in that city as an amateur in 1851. In 1852 he emigrated to Melbourne. Here he sang once at a Saturday night concert at the Queen's, and then left Melbourne to try his fortune on the goldfields. He stuck it for 6 months before exchanging the uncertainty of gold-digging for the certainty of employment in Bendigo as a shop assistant. 6 months later again, in 1853, he was acting for a living at Bendigo's Cairncross. In a further 2 years he was stage manager at the Charles Napier, Ballarat. For some years afterwards he alternated between Melbourne and Adelaide, having a wide following in both centres. In 1858 he became manager of the Melbourne Princess's, and later went into partnership with George Coppin and John Hennings. From 1870, when he appeared in Walter H.Cooper's *Sun and Shadow,* he seems to have concentrated on or to have been chosen for roles in plays written in Australia, including the Hopkins-Dampier *All for Gold;* Darrell's *Transported for Life* and *Man and Wife;* Bunster's *Class;* Pickersgill's *Catching the Kellys;* Reeve's *For Life,* and Thomas's *Michael Strogoff.* Late in his acting life he transferred to George Rignold's company at Her Majesty's, Sydney where he appeared in that actor's production of *Henry V* and other plays.

Gridiron. Placed, ideally, twice the height of the proscenium above the stage, the gridiron is made of a series of beams and walking surfaces carrying the blocks, sheaves, or pulleys with ropes which are used in raising and lowering curtains, act drops, back drops, and light battens. Anything thus pulled up into the flies is said to be 'flown.'

Griffiths, John Gordon (1810-1857). Born in Shropshire, Griffiths had his initial stage training in Scottish theatres. Transferring to the English provincial theatres, he later became manager of the Shrewsbury circuit. Acting for a while in London, he was seen there by Joseph Wyatt, who was looking for new talent for his Royal Victoria in Sydney. The last of Wyatt's imports, he made his debut in *Hamlet* in January 1843. He never acted anywhere else but in the Royal Victoria, appearing in plays by local writers and in Shakespearian and other productions. At first given a hostile reception by Sydney audiences, who did not like his Hamlet, he won their favour in other roles, and, apart from Conrad Knowles, was soon considered to be *the* Sydney actor. He was made manager of the Royal Victoria in 1854, and of the Prince of Wales in 1855. On his retirement from the stage towards the end of 1855 he bought and conducted the Pier Hotel at Manly, NSW.

Ground piece, ground rows. Low cut-outs or profile pieces placed on the floor of the stage, usually in front of a backdrop or backscene, and painted to represent grass, stones, flowers, a low fence, and so on. Besides giving a third-dimensional effect to the scene, these also provided a handy place in which to mask extra lighting.

Guarany, Il. 4-act opera, text and music A.Gomes, Scala, Milan 19.3.1870; Covent Garden, London 13.7.1872; Opera House, Melbourne 17.11.1888, initial 6 performances.

Guerin, Mrs James. (See: Yates, Theodosia).

Guillaume Tell. (William Tell). 4-act opera, text V.J.de Jouy and H.L.Bis, based on Johann Schiller's drama (1804), music G.Rossini, Opera House, Paris 3.8.1829; Drury Lane, London 1.5.1830; Royal, Melbourne 9.12.1867, initial 11 performances.

Gustave III; ou, Le Bal Masqué, (Gustavus III; or, The Masked Ball). 5-act opera, text A.E.Scribe, music D.Auber, Opéra, Paris 27.2.1833; Covent Garden, London 13.11.1833; Royal, Sydney 29.1.1838. (See: *Ballo in Maschera, Un*).

Guy Mannering. 3-act melodrama, text D.Terry and Sir Walter Scott, from that author's novel (1815), music and vocal numbers H.Bishop and J.Attwood, Covent Garden 12.3.1816; Royal, Melbourne 17.12.1855, initially 1 performance. (See: *Clari; or, The Maid of Milan*).

H.M.S. Pinafore *Sydney 1879*

H

Habbe, Alexander Christian (1829-1896). One of several outstanding scenic artists who made their home in Australia. Born in Copenhagen, Denmark, he came to Australia during the gold rush years of the early 1850s. Having no success at gold-digging, he went to the Montezuma at Ballarat as scenic artist. From there he moved on to the Melbourne Royal in 1858, and about a year later was scenepainter at the Royal Victoria, Sydney. In the early 1860s he and W.J.Wilson formed a partnership and painted the decorations, scenery, and act drop for Sydney's new Prince of Wales. In 1867 they converted the Lyceum, York Street into an Alhambra-style ballroom. Two years later they turned the ballroom back into a theatre, this time renaming it the Adelphi. Here they painted the scenery for a number of sumptuous productions, including melodramas, pantomimes, and a production of the play, *Faust,* which ran for 6 weeks. At the end of 1870 Habbe and Wilson took over the Royal Victoria, and engaged in a number of successful productions. Habbe's settings for *London Assurance* earned him high praise and the usual curtain calls by the audience. The same applied to the settings he later did at this theatre for Marcus Clarke's *Foul Play.* Towards the end of 1871 he did the settings for Garnet Walch's extravaganza, *Trookulentos,* scenery which the *Sydney Mail* described as 'remarkably brilliant'. One of his last big undertakings for the Sydney stage was the scenery for the first Australian production of *The Duchess of Gerolstein.* Soon after this Habbe returned to Melbourne, where he worked in various theatres until the cancer which ended his life made work no longer possible.

Half-price. A practice begun in the 18th century, by which theatre patrons were admitted after the third act at half the normal admission price. Very often, because of the exigencies of the programme, half-price was fixed at 'after nine o'clock,' or 'after nine-thirty.' At first patrons were allowed free entry after the third act of a play; then a small charge was made, and later again programmes were made longer to justify the imposition of a half-price charge. The custom lasted in the English theatre to as late as the 1870s, though it seems to have been dropped in Australia in the late 1850s.

Hall, George William Louis Marshall (1862-1915). Musician, composer, poet, dramatist, and literatteur. The son of a London surgeon, his musical ability manifested itself at an early age, and by the time he was 16 he had already published a book of songs. A student of the Royal College of Music, extracts from his early operatic and orchestral works were performed in London in 1893 and in 1898. Appointed first incumbent of the Ormond Chair of Music at the University of Melbourne in 1890, he took up the post the following year, and from then on devoted himself to raising the standard of musical training and performance in Melbourne. Between 1893 and 1912 he conducted 111 orchestral concerts; established and conducted the Conservatorium of Music; published several books of poems; fell out on many occasions with the music critics; was dismissed from the University in 1900 because of what was called 'the libidinous character of his poems and other writings,' and his disbelief in Christianity; established his own Marshall Hall Conservatorium, and produced his 3-act opera, *Stella*. In 1913 he was in London trying to secure performance of his operas. He was not successful, and finally had to accept the performance of a truncated version of *Stella* at the Palladium in 1914, sandwiched between vaudeville acts. In 1914 he was again offered the Ormond Chair of Music, which he accepted. A year later he died after an operation for appendicitis. Among his musical compositions are symphonies, instrumental works, songs, and 3 operas — *Harold*, *Stella*, and *Romeo and Juliet*. His published writings include 4 books of poems, and two tragedies, *Aristodemus,* and *Bianca Capello.*

Hamlet. Tragedy by William Shakespeare, believed to have been first performed in London in 1600 or 1601; Royal, Sydney 18.8.1834.

Handsome Ransom, The; or, The Brigand's Bride. 2-act operetta, text Francis R.Hart, music Sir William Robinson, Government House, Perth 11.1.1894. Later altered, the title changed to *Predatoros; or, The Brigand's Bride,* and produced as 2-act comic opera, Princess's, Melbourne 12.11.1894, initial 3 performances. Text, under the title *Predatoros; or, The Brigand's Bride,* published J.Arbuckle, Melbourne 1894. Sir William Robinson was governor of Western Australia.

Hänsel and Gretel. 3-act opera, text A.Wette from a fairytale by the brothers Grimm, music E.Humperdinck, Hof, Weimar 23.12.1893; Daly's, London 26.12.1894; Princess's, Melbourne 6.4.1907, initially 1 performance.

Above: Joseph Bland Holt 1878
Right: John Hennings 1881

Harpur, Charles (1813-1868). Notable chiefly as one of the early Australian poets, but in his youth he toyed with the stage, as actor as well as playwright. Born at Windsor, NSW, he was the son of a schoolmaster and was trained to follow his father's calling. But he rebelled, and at the age of 20 was engaged as an actor by Barnett Levey, appearing at the Sydney Royal in minor roles in such plays as *The Miller and His Men, The Mutiny at the Nore,* and the burlesque, *Chrononhotonthologos.* He was not a success as an actor, and after suing Barnett Levey for back pay he said was owing to him (he lost the case), he and the Royal parted company. But while he was at the Royal he must have been working on his first and only play, *The Tragedy of Donohoe.* He was next a post office clerk, and then he settled down and became a schoolmaster in the Hunter River district. He finished his life as a gold commissioner at Nerrigunda. (See: *Tragedy of Donohoe, The*).

Havana. 3-act musical comedy, text G.Grossmith, Jr., and G.Hill, music L.Stuart, Gaiety, London 25.4.1908; Her Majesty's, Sydney 13.3.1909, initial 18 performances.

Hazard; or, Pearce Dyceton's Crime. 3-act drama by Walter H.Cooper, Royal Victoria, Sydney 15.7.1872, initial 24 performances.

Hedda Gabler. 4-act drama by H.Ibsen, translated by W.Archer, Vaudeville, London 20.4.1891; Her Majesty's, Melbourne 20.7.1900, initially 1 performance.

Helen's Babies. Comedietta by Garnet Walch, after J.Habberton's novel (1876), Royal, Melbourne 20.7.1877, initial 7 performances. This play, which featured Dampier's 2 little daughters, was produced by him in the USA in 1877, and in England in 1878.

Hennings, John (1833-1898). Born in Bremen, Germany. At the age of 14 Hennings was apprenticed to an interior decorator in Dusseldorf, much of whose work was done in the various chateaux or castles along the Rhine. He later did a course in architecture and perspective at the Dusseldorf Academy. Soon after this he was 'thrown on his own resources,' and earned a living travelling through Europe painting flower and fruit decorations. He had his introduction to the theatre in Vienna, where he painted some garlands for use in the opera *L'Enfant prodigue,* by Auber. He then emigrated to Australia, arriving in Melbourne on his 20th birthday. Here he obtained his first engagement at the Queen's, painting the settings for that year's pantomime. Subsequently he was associated in his work with such figures of the period as G.V.Brooke, Barry Sullivan, and W.S.Lyster. He was also notable for the artistry of his pantomime transformation scenes, which every year earned him new superlatives. He was at various times part lessee of Melbourne Royal, and was painting up to a few days before his death. Among the many notable productions for which he painted settings were *Faust and Marguerite* in 1858 and 1873, *Sardanapalus, All For Gold, No*

Mercy, Estrella, and *For the Term of His Natural Life.* He also painted a number of act drops for Melbourne and other theatres. In 1880 he was co-lessee of the Royal Victoria, Sydney with G.Coppin and J.R.Greville when it was destroyed by fire. From the earliest work he did for Coppin and Brooke at Melbourne Olympic up to the time of his death he was regarded as the first scenepainter in Australia.

Henry IV, Part I. Historical drama by William Shakespeare, believed to have been first performed in London in 1589 or 1590; The Theatre, Sydney 8.4.1800.

Henry V. Historical drama by William Shakespeare, believed to have been first performed in London in 1598 or 1599; Royal Victoria, Sydney 14.2.1857.

Henry VIII. Historical drama by William Shakespeare, believed to have been first performed in London in 1613; produced by amateurs in Sydney 7.1.1836; first professional production Royal Victoria 20.5.1844.

Her Good Name. 1-act drama by Bernard Espinasse, Her Majesty's, Sydney 6.8.1898, initial 6 performances. Produced at the Imperial, London 17.4.1902.

Herbstmanöver, Ein (Autumn Manoeuvres). 3-act operetta, text K.von Bakyonyi, music E.Kalman, Vigszinhaz, Budapest 22.2.1908; English version by H.Hamilton, Adelphi, London 25.5.1912; Her Majesty's, Sydney 28.6.1913, initial 28 performances.

HMS Pinafore; or, The Lass That Loved a Sailor. 2-act operetta, text W.S.Gilbert, music A.Sullivan, Opera Comique, London 25.5.1878; School of Arts, Sydney 3.5.1879, initial 12 performances. (See: Gilbert and Sullivan).

Hermit's Bell, The (See: *Dragons de Villars, Les*).

Heuzenroeder, Moritz (1849-1897). German-born composer who made his home in Adelaide in 1872, after study at the Royal Academy, Stüttgart. Taught piano and singing, gave concerts and recitals, and wrote the music for the following operas, all of which were produced in Adelaide: *Singvogelchen, Onkel Beckers Geschichte, Faust* and *Gretchen, The Windmill, Immomeena.*

Hibernian Father, The. 5-act tragedy by E.Geoghegan, Royal Victoria, Sydney 6.5.1844, initially 1 performance.

Hill, Alfred (1870-1960). Born in Richmond, Victoria, Alfred Hill was taken at an early age to New Zealand with his family, where he had most of his early training and experience as a musician. He studied music in Leipzig from 1887 to 1891, receiving a diploma with honours, and came to Australia to take up the post of conductor of the Sydney Liedertafel.

This band of amateur singers assisted in 1900 with the production of his opera, *Lady Dolly*. Hill's next venture was his Maori opera, *Tapu; or, The Tale of a Maori Pah*. Accepted for production by J.C.Williamson, work began on it in 1899, but at this time Williamson had the popular English comic opera success, *The Geisha* on his hands, and he temporarily shelved *Tapu*. The opera consequently had its first production in Wellington, New Zealand in 1903. The following year it was produced in Auckland and Hobart. It was produced in Sydney the following year, but this production was far removed from the opera conceived and written by Hill and Adams. Among other things, it had by this time additional lyrics by Bert Royle, Williamson's New Zealand representative. Hill tried again in 1905 with a comic opera called *A Moorish Maid*. Auckland and Wellington performances were artistically and financially successful, £1000 being taken in Auckland in one week. But for its Australian performance in 1906 *A Moorish Maid*, like *Tapu* before it, was 'improved,' this time by the George Stephenson Musical Comedy Company. At some time between 1906 and 1910 Hill left the Liedertafel and became conductor, sometimes deputy-conductor, of musical comedy and opera companies for Williamson and others. Towards the end of 1910 he gave this up, and decided to revive *A Moorish Maid*. Remembering its success in Auckland and Wellington, he, or some person unknown, rewrote the text, and the revival opened at the Standard, Sydney on 26.12.1910. In 1914 Hill told the *Theatre* magazine that, apart from the little money he got from his comic opera, *A Moorish Maid*, and the £100 Williamson paid him for *Tapu*, 'composition has brought me nothing.' In this year his 1-act play, *Wattle Tree Farm* was also produced. *Giovanni* was his last opera in this period, though he later wrote and produced *The Rajah of Shivapore, Auster,* and *The Ship of Heaven*. The ABC Music Library holds the score of his unperformed comic opera of 1893, *The Whipping Boy*.

His House in Order. 4-act comedy by A.W.Pinero, St James's, London 1.2.1906; Little, Sydney 24.1.1914, initial 37 performances.

Her Majesty's Guest. 3-act musical comedy, text and music J.H.Darnley, Princess of Wales, Kennington 26.3.1900; Princess's, Melbourne 25.11.1911, initial 12 performances.

His Natural Life. There were a number of stage versions of Marcus Clarke's novel, *His Natural Life* (later retitled *For the Term of His Natural Life*) performed under various titles on the world's stages. The first, *Convict 1240*, was written by an American and performed in the USA in 1885. It was later retitled *A Great Wrong Righted*. The second, *His Natural Life*, was written by an Englishman and performed in Australia in 1886. The third, called *For the Term of His Natural Life*, was written by an Australian and performed in Australia in 1886. The fourth version was also by an Australian performed in Australia. The fifth, *For a Life*, was written by an American and performed in England in 1886. The sixth, *For the Term of His Natural Life,* written by an Australian, was performed in New Zealand in 1886. The seventh, *His Natural Life,* by two Australians, was performed in Australia in 1891; and eighth, *His Natural Life,* by an Australian, was performed in Australia in 1896; the ninth, also by an Australian, *For the Term of His Natural Life,* was performed in Australia in 1897; the tenth, by an Australian, *His Natural Life,* in Australia in 1906, and the eleventh, in 1913, by an unknown author. Performed under the last title were:

——. Drama in prologue and 5 acts by George Leitch, Royal, Brisbane 26.4.1886, initial 11 performances. Ms in Mitchell Library, Sydney.

——. Drama in prologue and 4 acts by Inigo Tyrrell, Mechanics' Institute, Williamstown, Victoria 14.6.1886, initially 1 performance.

——. Drama in prologue and 5 acts by W.South, revised version of his earlier *For the Term of His Natural Life,* Gaiety, Sydney 26.2.1887, initial 5 performances.

——. 4-act drama by Frank Gerald and Stilling Duff, Royal, Broken Hill 11.4.1891, initial 2 performances.

——. Drama in prologue and 5 acts by Dan Barry, Her Majety's Opera House, Brisbane 22.6.1891, initial 8 performances.

——. 4-act drama by E.I.Cole, Haymarket Hippodrome, Sydney 24.11.1906, initial 6 performances. (See: *Convict 1240; For a Life; For the Term of His Natural Life; Strong as Death*).

Hissing. A practice indulged in by audiences in the 18th century theatre and carried over into at least the first half of the nineteenth century. A concerted hiss from a packed audience was sufficient to stop or condemn a play or actor. Never very much used by Australian audiences, it was nevertheless used particularly to greet the entry on stage of the villain, as his 'applause' after a particularly nasty piece of villainy, and to show the audience's dislike of him during the course of a play.

History of Kodadad and His Brothers, The; or, The Disguised Prince. 1-act extravaganza by Walter H.Cooper, Prince of Wales, Auckland 1.5.1867. Published by W.Fairfax, Brisbane 1866. Copy in Yale University Library.

Hobart, Theatres in.
 1 Freemason's Tavern. In its issue for December 1833 the *Hobart Town Magazine* announced that a group of actors had just arrived in Hobart, and they were to give their first performances on December 28. The group was led by Samson Cameron and his wife, who rented the 'new large room of the Freemason's Tavern' and had it fitted up as a theatre. On December 24 Cameron advertised that the theatre would open that night with *The Stranger* (1798) and *The Married Bachelor* (1821).

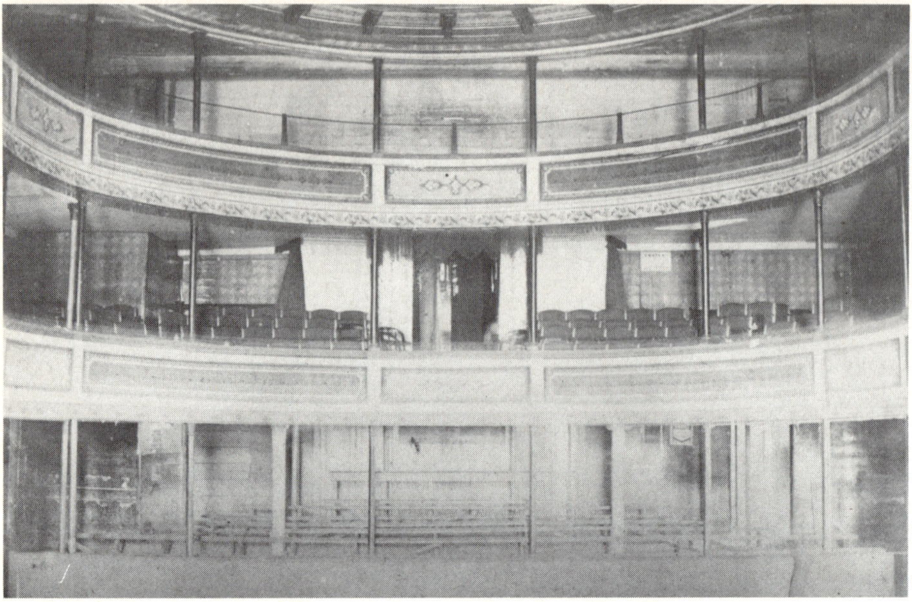

Allport Library

Above: Auditorium Hobart Royal 1862
Below: Proscenium Hobart Royal 1862

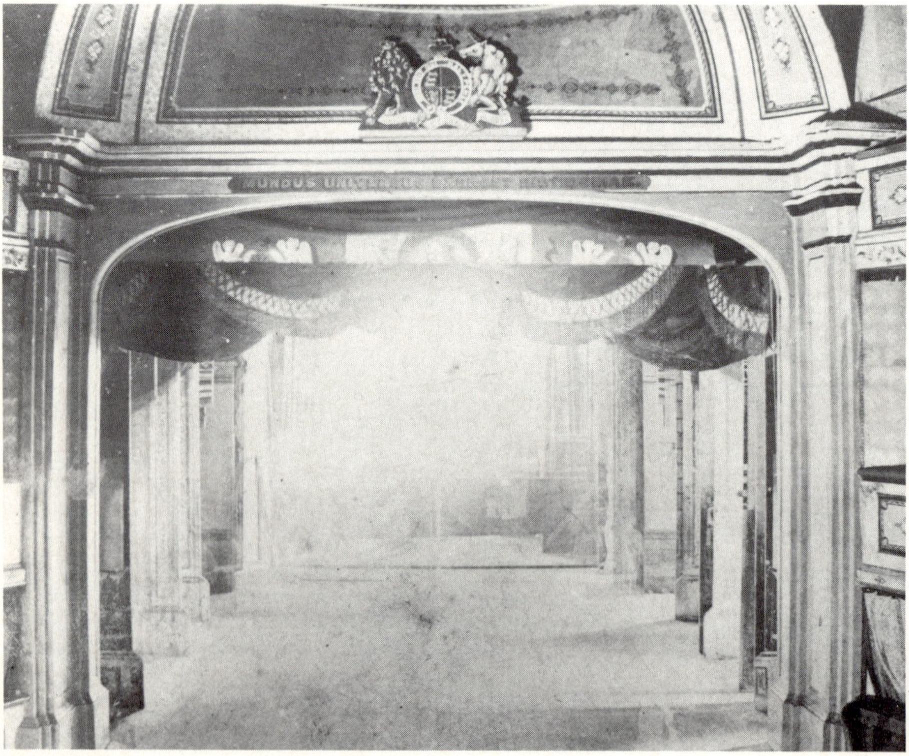

Allport Library

Admission cost 6 shillings for adults and 4 for children. As usual, the room had been fitted up with a gallery, the floor or pit seats 'being elevated in progression.' The stage was 18 to 24 ins from the floor, with a 'chaste' proscenium and an act drop depicting classical ruins. This theatre remained in intermittent use until May 1834.

2 Royal, Argyle Street. Having announced the advent of the first theatre in Hobart, the *Hobart Town Magazine* in January 1834 announced plans for a rival establishment, the Royal, in the Argyle Rooms. This was to accommodate 500 people in boxes, pit, and gallery. The following month the result of a survey of the building was published in the *Tasmanian and Austral Asiatic Review,* when it was said the building was to be used for concerts and other amusements, and that it was 'capable of being constructed into a public theatre . . .' This suggests that it was not first opened as a theatre. It was opened on 14.2.1834 with a concert followed by 2 acts of a pantomime, when its interior was described as 'a noble room of accurate dimensions, admirably calculated for theatrical purposes, as it admits of abundant stage room . . .' In April, although the Freemason's Tavern and the Royal were in use, it was announced in the *Hobart Town Magazine* that a site for yet another theatre had been decided on in Campbell Street. In May the Camerons and their company left Hobart for Launceston. Meantime the drama continued in Argyle Street with the production of *The Bushrangers; or, Norwood Vale* in May 1834. Then, as if to show there were audiences in Hobart still untapped, a young actor named Mackay, who had been with the Sydney theatre, and the Hobart Royal, announced that he was to open his own theatre in Roxborough House. Nevertheless, although there were now 2 rivals in the offing, the Royal carried on. In 1836 it was taken over by John Meredith, who had been bound over to keep the peace after a fracas in the Sydney Royal. A little more than a year later this Hobart Royal closed for lack of support.

3 Roxborough House. Towards the end of October 1834 the *Colonial Times* advised its readers that Mackay had rented a room in Roxborough House, where he proposed to give dramatic performances. 'The room we believe to be well adapted for the purpose, and it is being fitted up with a good deal of taste.' The theatre was opened on 4.11.1834 with 2 short comedies, *The Gallery Slaves,* and *The Wags of Windsor.* Reporting a bumper house, the *Times* added that 'the room is by far too small for the purpose.' After a few more performances the theatre was closed at the end of the month.

4 Royal (1837). The Campbell Street theatre announced in 1834 was not ready for opening until 1837, all kinds of building and other disputes hindering its completion. It was finally opened on 6.3.1837, when admission prices were boxes 5s, pit 3s, gallery 2s. The plays produced were *Speed the Plough* (1801), and *The Spoiled Child* (1790). Little is known of the interior design of this theatre, except that when opened it was still

unfinished., 'It is of that convenient size (like Vestris's little Olympic) which does not distress the senses either of hearing or seeing, whilst on the other hand, it is large enough to produce scenic and dramatic effect,' said the *Hobart Town Courier*. From a report in the *True Colonist* of 10.3.1837 it appears that the theatre had a gallery, upper boxes, lower boxes, and pit. In May the public was advised that the shareholders were losing money on their investment. This lack of support was attributed to the poor quality of the acting. For the next 20 years or so the theatre had a history of intermittent use. At some time in this period it was named the Victoria.

5 Albert (1842). Mrs Anna Clarke, an actress and manageress, in 1842 returned to Hobart from a visit to England, where she had recruited some new members for her company, established in 1840. Early in March she had the Argyle Rooms converted to a theatre, which she named the Albert. It opened on 29.3.1842 with Mrs Clarke, Signor Carandini, Frank and John Howson, Mrs F.Howson, and Miss Young as its principals. The opening performance consisted of the opera, *The Quaker* (1777), dances, musical items, and scenes from the play, *Jack Sheppard* (1839). Admission cost 10s to any part of the small house. The theatre and its company were so successful that Mrs Clarke transferred in July to the Victoria, which she first had redecorated, at the same time having extra boxes installed.

6 Royal (1856). The Campbell Street theatre was rebuilt or reconstructed in 1856 to such an extent that when finished it was almost a new building. To allow for a larger gallery, the front of the building was brought out to the line of the area, or sunken portion of the frontage which lighted the basement front rooms. The auditorium was provided with a pit, private boxes, dress circle, and a gallery to seat 300. A dome in the ceiling was 33ft above the floor of the pit. The interior colour scheme was in white relieved by blue, with mouldings of burnished gold. The draperies of the dress circle, private boxes, and slips (box-like areas on the sides of the gallery) were of blue and gold damask, the seats being covered in blue damask. Above the proscenium arch was a group representing the seasons, supported on either side by arabesque scrolls in blue and gold. The interior of the central dome, ribbed with gold moulding, was divided into 8 compartments, one containing a portrait of Shakespeare, the remaining 7 depicting his Seven Ages of Man. The fronts of the private boxes, dress circle, and gallery were divided into panels ornamented with classic figures, and bordered in blue and gold. The theatre's original name, Royal, was restored, and when the 'new' theatre opened private boxes cost £2.2.0, or 5s for a single seat, dress boxes 4s, pit 2, gallery 1.

7 Royal (1862). The interior of the 1837 theatre was again remodelled in 1862, along what was felt to be more democratic lines. The pit was enlarged by removing the private boxes at the back. Originally it was

planned to convert the 3 front rows of the pit into stalls, but the idea was abandoned because it was felt the division would make an invidious distinction. The dress circle was left as before, with its central box for the governor, but the gallery was abolished and replaced with boxes for families which did not want to go to the trouble of dressing for the dress circle. All the old pictorial decorations in the dome and on the fronts of the tiers were replaced with what was called Louis Quatorze decorations in white and gold relieved by pale greens and pink. Nights of performance were announced as Monday to Friday only, as it was felt that Saturday night performances would interfere with what was a late shopping night. Five years later the decoration of the interior was again changed, this time mostly with the use of wallpaper. An innovation was the Latin motto painted across the top of the proscenium arch. All the boxes were abolished, apart from the governor's. The gallery again became a gallery, and the pit was divided into stalls and pit. In 1882 other minor changes were made, and an outside stairway covered with a galvanised iron roof was constructed for access to the gallery. The auditorium was repainted, the tier fronts being decorated with landscape medallions on a ground of white with grey stiles. The dome was painted to represent a cloudy sky, in which floated 5 female figures in rich draperies. A representation of Shakespeare's Seven Ages was painted above the proscenium. The governor's box was given a Brussels carpet, the dress circle linoleum, and the rest of the house retained the familiar boards.

8 Royal (1890). Structural alterations were made to the theatre again in 1890, keeping pace with the growth in the size of the population and in the number of travelling companies and individual artists visiting the city. In this year the height of the walls, and therefore of the room, was raised and the rear of the building extended, the whole designed to provide a more spacious auditorium and backstage area. The interior of the theatre was demolished, including the proscenium and stage. When work on the alterations was complete it was said that whereas the old theatre had seated 700 to 800 people, the new would seat 1200. This accommodation was provided in stalls (320), pit (directly behind the stalls), dress circle (200), and gallery. The governor's box was abolished, the orchestra was placed in a sunken well close to the proscenium. The new stage measured 47ft wide and 52ft deep. The proscenium arch was in bronze and gold, to provide a picture-frame effect, and above it was a coved surface divided into three panels, on which were painted representations of Music (right), Painting (left), with William Shakespeare in the centre. The dress circle ceiling was in grey and straw colour as a foil to the walls, which were papered in a silver and gold floral design. The stage had fly-floors or galleries 21ft above the stage floor, while the gridiron was 40ft above the stage floor. The floor itself had sunken footlights, 2 quarter traps, a grave trap, and a 16ft by 4ft

trap for use in raising or lowering scenery, props, etc., to or from the stage floor. A separate platform was built below the fly-floors to take the winches which raised and lowered the front curtain and act drop. Gas lighting was used throughout. In the auditorium the 'dingy mythological personages of doubtful divinity and most queer anatomy' painted in the dome were removed, and the whole was painted a graduated cerulean blue spangled with gold stars. The general auditorium colour scheme was in white, gold, turquoise blue, and touches of Pompeian red. The backed bench seats of the old stalls were replaced with folding chairs, a comfort not extended to the pit and gallery. The dress circle also had folding chairs, but these were upholstered in maroon rep. The 'new' theatre was opened on 4.10.1890.

9 Royal (1912). The final change to this theatre made in the period under survey took place in 1912, when theatrical performances of all kinds were in a state of flux throughout the country. Once again the interior was demolished. The entrance was widened, and a storey added to the front of the building. The auditorium was enlarged to seat 1250 people. The height of the dress circle from the floor of the building was increased, the gallery was raised 7ft, and the dome 10ft. The dress circle had seats for 250, the gallery for 500, while the pit was abolished and the floor of the building given over entirely to front and back stalls. New tip-up seats were used everywhere except in the gallery, where there were tiers or wide wooden steps on which the public sat, as in Sydney and Melbourne theatres. The proscenium was made 6ft higher and 6ft wider, and the whole theatre was lighted with electricity. Modelled plaster was used extensively in the decoration of the auditorium. The proscenium coves, and dress circle and gallery fronts were finished in the Louis XV style, in soft tints with gold and silver enrichments. The central proscenium entablature had a plaster cherub, seated in a shell, playing a flageolet. The dome in the ceiling was divided into 20 panels, shaded from pale grey to pale blue. Ten of the panels had portraits of composers painted on them. Colours used in decorating the auditorium were predominantly gold and bronze, with shades of red, rose, grey, cream, and ivory.

Holloway, William John (1843-1913). Born in London, he was taken from school at the age of 9 and apprenticed to a watchmaker. At 11 he had a new job, holding stencils for a wallpaper stainer who hand-printed floral wallpapers. In 1856 he emigrated with his family to Australia, where his father took up land outside Sydney. William soon tired of farming, and at 14 got himself a job in Sydney driving a horse and cart. Soon after this he gained an apprenticeship with a firm of shipbuilders, as a boilermaker. In the meantime he and a fellow apprentice, Shiel Barry, were attending the theatre whenever they could, and building their own, a galvanised iron shed, on a vacant piece of land near their workplace at Pyrmont. Here, under the most primitive conditions, he and others gave performances of melodramas that were in every way successful. It was not long before Holloway obtained an engagement with a professional company for a season in Brisbane. From then on he devoted himself entirely to the stage. In 1869 he was a member of the company formed in Sydney by the visiting Shakespearian actor Walter Montgomery. When Montgomery left, Holloway joined the company formed by the former Salder's Wells actor, W.H.Hoskins. After a visit to India, he returned to Australia in 1871, and ultimately formed his own company. Leading members of this were his wife, the actress Kate Arden, and his stepdaughter Essie Jenyns. In 1888, for family reasons, he gave it all away and went to London. There, in 1892, he became a member of Henry Irving's company at the Lyceum, playing Kent in *King Lear*. Irving fell sick during the run of this production. His understudy, Hermann Vezin, declined to accept such a difficult part as King Lear at short notice, and Holloway was asked if he would read the part for a night or two. Instead, he learned it in 5 hours, and was repaid for his work by wild applause and curtain calls. With his customary generosity, once he had recovered Henry Irving shared the rest of the run with Holloway, playing on alternate nights. (See: Jenyns, Essie).

Holt, Joseph Bland (1853-1942). Born at Norwich in England, Holt came to Australia with his mother and father in 1854. His father was the English provincial actor Clarance Holt (1826-1903). While in Australia the young Holt was educated at the Church of England Grammar School at Brighton, Victoria. When, in 1862, his actor parents moved on to Dunedin in New Zealand, his education was continued at Otago Boys' High School. In 1864 the family returned to England. Three years later Joseph became a professional actor, taking the stage name Bland Holt. He travelled extensively in England and the USA with various companies. In 1876 he returned to Australia, where from then on he made his home. His forte was comedy, and his most notable roles at Sydney's Royal Victoria in 1876-77 were Dogberry; the Gravedigger in *Hamlet;* Launcelot Gobbo, and the comedy roles in G.Darrell's *Transported for Life, The Trump Card,* and *Man and Wife.* In December 1877 he moved to Melbourne, where he played clown in the annual pantomime. He thus alternated between Sydney and Melbourne, acting wherever there was an opening, until 1880, when he first branched out as a producer with the Australian premier of *The New Babylon* (1878) at the Royal Victoria, Sydney. From then on, except for a break in 1886, when he joined his father in a tour of English provincial theatres, he produced throughout Australia and New Zealand a succession of melodramas of the Drury Lane class, including many 'localised' as Australian melodramas. In 1909, sensing great changes in the world of the theatre as he had known it, and a growth of interest in the cinema, Bland Hope retired from acting; unlike his father, who, in his 70th year, was acting in the successful Drury Lane melodrama, *The Duchess of Coolgardie*

(1896). Bland Holt was chiefly notable for the careful and expert way in which he staged 'large' overseas melodramas — plays which relied on built-up scenery, large casts, and the realism of live animals and actual objects such as a motor car. The emphasis in all his productions seems to have been on action rather than acting or dialogue, and the hardest worked members of the company were the sceneshifters.

Honest Man's Fortune, The. Tragi-comedy by Francis Beaumont (1584-1616) and John Fletcher (1579-1625), believed to have been first acted in London in 1613. It was first published in 1647. In 1849 Samuel Phelps, then conducting a season of legitimate drama at Sadler's Wells, London, commissioned R.H.Horne to 'adapt the play to present-day requirements.' The version Horne prepared ran for 38 performances, one of the actors in it being William H.Hoskins. In 1862, when Horne and Hoskins were living in Australia, Hoskins produced the Horne version of the play at the Royal, Ballarat on 12.9.1862 for 2 performances. On the first night the flamboyant, bohemian Horne, dressed in Elizabethan costume, delivered a 67-line prologue he had written especially for the occasion.

Hopkins, Francis Rawdon Chesney (1849-1916). Born at Colaba, near Bombay. Educated at Southampton College, England. Was a writer for the English press before he emigrated to Victoria in 1865. In Australia he went on the land, and for some years had a pastoral holding on the Murray River. He seems to have devoted his spare time to writing of all kinds — poems, short stories, essays, and plays. His first play to be produced was an adaptation of Eugene Sue's novel, *The Wandering Jew*, which Hopkins called *All For Gold; or, Fifty Millions of Money* (1877). Reviewing this, the critic for the *Australian* said that Hopkins in the past 2 years had offered several plays to the management of Melbourne Royal, but all of them had been rejected on the ground that as he was an Australian author he was not likely to have written a play worthy of acceptance. Alfred Dampier produced *All For Gold*, and also other plays by Hopkins — *Good for Evil*, last act only (1877), *Only a Fool* (1880), *Michael Strogoff, the Courier of the Czar* (1882), and *L.S.D.* (1882). In the meantime Hopkins also edited *The Australian Ladies' Annual* (1878); published a book of essays, *Confessions of a Cynic, Social, Moral, and Philosophical* (1882), a book of verse *Gum Leaves Old and Gum Leaves New* (1902), and 2 books of short stories, *Birds of Passage* (1908), and *The Opium Runner* (1909). When A.Dampier went to the USA and England in 1877-78 he produced *All for Gold* in Birmingham on 15.7.1878, and Garnet Walch's *Helen's Babies* on 5.8.1878. *Helen's Babies* was also produced in London at the Gaiety on 15.9.1878, and *All For Gold* at the Surrey on 21.2.1881.

Horne, Richard Henry (1803-1884). Born in London and educated at Sandhurst. Later became midshipman in the Mexican Navy. Served in the war against Spain, then went to the USA. In 1828, after his return to England, he had his first poem published, and from then on he was bent on a literary career. In 1837 his first plays were published, *Cosmo de Medici,* and *The Death of Marlowe.* Several other works followed, and in 1843 he published his epic poem, *Orion,* which achieved notoriety principally because the first 3 editions were sold for a farthing a copy. In 1847 he married, and, continuing with his literary work, published stories, poems, a novel, and, in 1848, his third play, *Judas Iscariot.* In 1852 he came to Australia, where he was first a commander of the gold escort in Victoria, then Commissioner of Crown Lands for the goldfields. He continued his writing in Australia, including a dramatic poem, *Prometheus, the Fire Bringer* and a lyric masque called *The South Sea Sisters* written for the opening of the Intercolonial Exhibition in Melbourne in 1866. In 1867 he decided to substitute Hengist for the Henry in his name, and as Richard Hengist Horne wrote a cantata for the welcome to Australia of the Duke of Edinburgh. Two years later he returned to England, where he continued writing and publishing. He was granted a civil pension in 1874. Plays by Horne produced in Australia are: *The Duchess of Malfi* (1855), *The Death of Marlowe* (1860), *A Spec in China* (1866), *The Honest Man's Fortune* (1862), and the opera *Cazille* (1872).

Hornung, Ernest William (1866-1921). Chiefly notable for his novels dealing with Raffles, the 'gentleman burglar.' Born in England, he came to Australia in 1884 and took up a situation as tutor in an inland NSW station. It was here that he began work on his first novel, *A Bride From the Bush,* published in 1890. During his brief stay in Australia Hornung gathered impressions that were to stay with him all his life. As E. Morris Miller has noted, nearly two-thirds of his novels, of which at least 30 were published, refer in varying degrees to Australian incidents and experiences. Hornung wrote 2 plays, the first, written with E. Presbury, *Raffles, the Amateur Cracksman,* Comedy, London 12.5.1906, 353 performances; the second, *Stingaree, the Bushranger,* Queen's, London 1.2.1908, 24 performances.

Hoskins, William Henry (1816-1886). Born at Newton-Solney, near Burton-on-Trent, he was at first intended for the church, but adopted the law. At the age of 19 he gave up his studies and ran away to Southampton, where he made his stage debut. From then on he got his training and experience in provincial theatres. In 1837 he undertook the management of the Royal at Worthing, for what turned out to be a disastrous year. Programmes were excellent, but attendances were not. Then followed appearances at Covent Garden; a return to the provinces, and then, in 1846, he was engaged by Samuel Phelps as a member of his Sadler's Wells company. Here he quickly made a name for himself in all kinds of supporting roles, principally in Shakespeare's plays. Later he transferred to the Olympic. In 1850 he married Julia Harland, a well known opera singer, and in 1856 they came to Australia. Then began long years of travelling throughout the colonies and New Zealand, for Hoskins decided to make Australia his home. Over the years, as theatre lessee, manager, or actor he put on beautifully staged productions of Shakespeare's plays in Sydney, Melbourne, Ballarat, Adelaide, and throughout the major New Zealand cities. His most notable production was *The Tempest,* with lavish settings and costumes, and with which he regularly lost money. In Sydney in 1868 he produced, and played the part of Versatile Fluent in, W.H.Cooper's *Colonial Experience.* After the death of his first wife he married, in 1874, the actress Florence Colville. In March the following year they went to New Zealand, and stayed until 1881. He could be said to have brought the theatre, in the full sense of that statement, to Christchurch, and to have enlivened the existing theatrical scene in Wellington and Dunedin. In the process he made, and lost, a fortune. Bad seasons followed good, and devoured his reserves. Even nightly changes of programme made little difference. In a letter to the *Australasian* in Melbourne in 1875, Hoskins said that in a season of 72 nights at Wellington he had produced 67 different plays. He continued to act in Australia until his retirement from the stage in 1884, by which time he had earned the title so often awarded to thespians past their 50s — 'an actor of the old school.'

Hotel, The; or, the Double Valet. Farce by T.Vaughan, Drury Lane, London 21.11.1776; The Theatre, Sydney 16.1.1796.

Howson, Frank (1817-1869). The cleverer of two brothers (the other was John) who came to Australia from England in 1842. From an early age Frank Howson displayed a talent for vocal and instrumental music, but as a young man he joined a Lancer Regiment, part of the British Legion which fought in the Carlist wars in Spain (1834-1840). On his return to England he and his brother determined to emigrate to Australia. Here their talents were given every opportunity for development. Frank was a good actor as well as a singer and musician, appearing in Australia in such plays as *Macbeth, The Merry Wives of Windsor, Hamlet, The Hunchback, The Lady of Lyons,* and *Money.* He also composed and sang at the Royal Victoria, Sydney the patriotic song, *Our Happy Land of Gold.* While manager of Sydney's Prince of Wales in 1855 he adapted the music of Spohr's opera, *Faust* (1816) to the drama of *Faust and Margaret* (1854). His knowledge of opera, particularly of English opera, was very wide. Among operas he produced in Australia, in collaboration with his brother John and the leader of the Royal Victoria orchestra, John Gibbes, in alphabetical order, are: *The Barber of Seville, Blanche of Jersey, The Bohemian Girl, The Bronze Horse, The Daughter of St Mark, The Daughter of the Regiment, Don Pasquale, The Devil's Opera, L'Elisir d'Amore, The Enchantress, The Fairy Lake, Fra Diavolo, Der*

Above: Frank Howson in Jenny Lind at Last 1847
Below: Punch cartoon of Coppin, Brooke, etc. 1855

Freischutz, Lucia di Lammermoor, Maritana, The Marriage of Figaro, Masaniello, The Mountain Sylph, The Night Dancers, Norma, The Siege of Rochelle, and *La Sonnambula.* As the *Sydney Morning Herald* wrote of him in 1855, the list of operas he had produced in Sydney in the 10 years 1845-1855 'exhibits quite sufficient to prove how sedulously and how well this gentleman has laboured in the cause of musical science since he first joined the banners of Mr Wyatt . . .' With the word 'banners' the *Herald* was acknowledging that Howson had worked in both of Wyatt's theatres, the Royal Victoria and Prince of Wales. But it should not be assumed that all these were productions of opera in the modern sense. The Howsons and other early enthusiasts had to cope with every imaginable difficulty — a shortage of sheet music; difficulty in getting and training a chorus; tenors having to sing baritone roles, sopranos singing tenor roles, and inadequate orchestras. More often than not operas also had to be given in shortened versions, so as to fit in with the long programmes demanded at the time. But there were also times when Howson was able to produce an opera as written, with all the necessary soloists, a chorus, an adequate orchestra, and appropriate costumes and settings. In 1866 Howson and his family (his daughter Emma, and his two sons, Frank A. and J.Jerome Howson) went to the USA, making their first stop at San Francisco. Here Howson formed Howson's English and Italian Opera Troupe, which gave its first performances in Maguire's Opera House in that city. Three years later, while in Omaha on his way to New York, he was taken ill. He died there of cancer on 16.9.1869.

Huguenots, Les. 5-act opera, text A.E.Scribe and E.Deschamps, music G.Myerbeer, Opera House, Paris 29.2.1836; Covent Garden, London 20.6.1842; Royal, Melbourne 15.11.1862, initial 19 performances.

Hume, Fergus (1860-1932). Born in New Zealand and intended for the Bar, Hume came to Australia in the early 1880s and settled in Melbourne. There he wrote his first novel, *The Mystery of a Hansom Cab,* published in Melbourne in 1886. It was the first of about 140 murder-mystery novels written by Hume, and the most successful. When it also proved a success in London, Hume decided to move to that city. A dramatic version of *The Mystery of a Hansom Cab,* was first produced in Australia in Melbourne on 25.8.1888. (See: *Mystery of a Hansom Cab, The*).

Hunchback, The. 5-act drama by J.S.Knowles, Covent Garden, London 5.4.1832; Royal Victoria, Sydney 20.4.1843.

Hussey, Frank (1831-1889). Actor, singer, comedian, and Negro impersonator whose chief interest to the theatre historian lies in his involvement with the Australian dramatist, W.H.Cooper. Born on the island of Nantucket, New York, Hussey is said to have been a grandson of the American President, Benjamin Franklin. Working at first in an office, he soon tired of it and took to the stage for a living, at a time when the minstrel show in America was enjoying the first flush of a popular vogue. He travelled to California as manager of a minstrel show, and later headed a troupe of performers sent to France to take part in the Paris Exhibition of 1857. Afterwards he toured Great Britain, Europe, India, China, Japan and South Africa. He paid his first visit to Australia in 1870 with a troupe known as the Weston-Hussey Minstrels. While he was performing in Sydney at the Prince of Wales, the Australian dramatist, W.H.Cooper, was supervising the production of his play, *Sun and Shadow*, at the Royal Victoria. The men met as fellow professionals, and no doubt Hussey spoke enthusiastically if a little optimistically of the opportunities there would be for Cooper with his plays in the USA. From their friendship came the play *Hazard; or, Pearce Dyceton's Crime*, into which Cooper wrote a dual role for Hussey — that of Tatwell the gambler who, when necessary, assumes a disguise as Jake the Negro. Advertisements for the play carried the lines '. . . the unrivalled Ethiopian comedian, Mr Frank Hussey, will make his first appearance in drama, in a sensational play, written expressly for him by Walter H.Cooper, and entitled *Hazard* . . .' Two weeks later it was announced that Cooper, Hussey and his wife, and J.Bartlett, who played a part in *Hazard* and was also stage manager, were to leave for a tour through the USA with Cooper's plays. The tour was a disaster. Disagreement between Hussey and Cooper started in Auckland and continued all the way to San Francisco. Both men were egotists; both were short-tempered. But despite this, *Hazard*, and *Foiled* were performed in San Francisco, beyond which Cooper refused to go. He returned to Sydney, and Hussey toured with *Hazard* to Salt Lake City, Sacramento, Stockton, and San Jose. Bartlett went east with *Foiled*, which he had retitled *Magdalen*. Hussey, who had married the Australian actress, Blanche Clifton, continued in his managerial and acting roles in the USA with varying degrees of success until, having developed heart and lung trouble, he returned to Australia in the early 1880s. While performing in Launceston in 1887 he decided the climate there was better for him than that on the mainland, and he retired there from the stage. (See: Cooper, W.H.).

Hygiene. Michael Baker says that in 1892 at Covent Garden in London 'there was insufficient lighting and ventilation behind the scenes, and that nine dressing rooms as well as the whole *corps de ballet* (some one hundred persons in all) had the use of a single lavatory.' In Sydney a writer in *Society* in 1887 said that actors had the scantiest accommodation for their comfort in most of the theatres, 'and in some cases no provision for the decencies of nature.' It is likely that latrines in most of the early theatres were located only in the hotels or pubs attached or built into each theatre. In 1877 the Royal Victoria in Sydney was said to be 'very old, very dirty, and very full of fleas.' In 1885 it was said that when the Melbourne Royal was built in 1872 it was suggested that there should be lavatories and baths installed for the actors. 'The suggestion was regarded as preposterous,' the writer said, implying that in 1885 it was still so regarded. The truth is that at least until the end of the 1880s the comfort of actors was the last thing Australian theatre proprietors thought about. In 9 theatres out of 10 dressing rooms were placed in the basement, where the only light was oil or gaslight and the air breathed by the actors came to them through the fanlights in each room, heavily laden with gas fumes. This is true of Sydney's Criterion, opened in 1886, whose basement also had 5 WCs and 3 urinals for the use of audience and actors alike, and a room or area containing gas meters and the oxygen gas tanks for the lime and arc lights. All this in an unventilated area. On the other hand, some theatres had their dressing rooms above the stage, where the actors had to use several flights of crude ladder-like stairways every time they went up and down, and where, no matter what the season, the rooms were always stifling because of the rising heat and fumes from the open gas lights on stage. Her Majesty's in Sydney, opened in 1887, had 18 dressing rooms, well ventilated but situated on the first, second, and third floors, from all of which access to and from the stage was gained by winding wooden stairs, an obvious fire hazard. But as time progressed government pressure, on the grounds of health and fire precaution, resulted in better and safer conditions for actors and audiences. Special directives to proprietors made it clear that if the required changes or alterations were not made, the theatre's licence would not be renewed. Faced with the cost of the suggested alterations, proprietors of some of the older, more run-down and less popular theatres, simply closed them.

Hypocrite, The. 3-act comedy, chiefly an alteration of Colley Cibber's *The Non-Juror* (1717) by Isaac Bickerstaffe, Drury Lane, London 17.11.1768; Royal, Sydney 26.10.1835.

I

Ideal Husband, An. 3-act drama by Oscar Wilde, Haymarket, London 3.1.1895; Lyceum, Sydney 13.4.1895, initial 6 performances.

Idler, The. 4-act drama by Charles Haddon Chambers, Lyceum, New York 11.11.1890; Garrick, Sydney 31.1.1891, initial 12 performances.

Illustrious Stranger, The; or, Married and Buried. 2-act musical farce, text J.Kenney and J.Millingen, music Isaac Nathan, Drury Lane, London 1.10.1827; Royal, Sydney 28.5.1835. Sometimes also performed as *Benjamin Bowbell,* sometimes as *Married and Buried.*

Image Breaker, The. 3-act comedy by Alfred Buchanan, St Peter's Hall, Eastern Hill, Melbourne 25.4.1914, initially 1 performance.

Immomeena. 2-act comic opera, text H.Congreve Evans, music Moritz Heuzenroeder, Royal, Adelaide 7.10.1893, initial 3 performances.

Importance of Being Earnest, The. 3-act comedy by Oscar Wilde, St James's, London 14.2.1895; Princess's, Melbourne 10.8.1895, initial 6 performances.

In the Dark. 1-act drama by Bernard Espinasse, Richmond Town Hall, Victoria 28.8.1893, initially 1 performance.

In the Shadow of the Glen. 1-act play by J.M.Synge, Molesworth Hall, Dublin 8.10.1903; Adelaide Repertory, Lyric Club 16.8.1909, initially 1 performance.

In Town. 2-act musical comedy, text A.Ross and J.T.Tanner, music F.O.Carr, Prince of Wales, London 15.10.1892; Princess's, Melbourne 4.5.1895, initial 18 performances.

Ingomar the Barbarian. 5-act drama by Mrs G.W.Lovell, a translation of Baron E.von Münch-Bellinghausen's *Der Sohn der Wildnis,* Drury Lane, London 9.6.1851; Royal Victoria, Sydney 1.7.1853.

In the Ranks. 5-act drama by G.R.Sims and H.Pettitt, Adelphi, London 6.10.1883; Her Majesty's, Sydney 24.12.1887, initial 83 performances.

Iolanthe; or, The Peer and the Peri. 2-act fairy opera, text W.S.Gilbert, music A.Sullivan, Savoy, London 25.11.1882; Royal, Melbourne 9.5.1885, initial 42 performances.

Ione. 4-act opera, text G.Peruzzini, based on Bulwer-Lytton's *The Last Days of Pompeii* (1834), music E.Petrella, Scala, Milan 26.1.1858; Royal, Melbourne 1.8.1870, initial 3 performances.

Irish Widow, The. 2-act comedy by David Garrick, Drury Lane, London 23.10.1772; The Theatre, Sydney 8.4.1800.

Isidora. 3-act comic opera, text and music Luscombe Searelle, Bijou, Melbourne 7.7.1885, initial 18 performances. Later re-titled *The Black Rover,* Globe, London 23.9.1890, initial 40 performances.

Ivy Leaf, The. 1-act drama by Bernard Espinasse, Palace, Sydney 27.4.1901, initially 1 performance.

J

James, John Stanley (1843-1896). Born in Staffordshire, England, he began his working life as a journalist in London. Tiring of this, he became a clerk on the London and North Wales railway. Having achieved the rank of stationmaster, he then returned to London and freelance journalism. When the Franco-Prussian war broke out in 1870 he went to Paris. Here he became mixed up in local politics, and was arrested as a spy. On his release he returned to London and a certain notoriety, which his stories from Paris had gained him. Tiring of London again, he left for the USA, where he first adopted the name 'Julian Thomas.' Unsuccessful in America, he next emigrated to Australia, where he arrived in 1875 almost penniless. He kept himself alive with occasional journalism in Melbourne until he obtained a permanent post on the *Argus*. He wrote for this daily, and for its sister weekly, the *Australasian* for many years under the pen-name 'the Vagabond.' His many articles on social conditions in Sydney and Melbourne in the last quarter of the century are today valuable records for the historian. Between 1876 and 1890 he published a number of books, including accounts of his travels in the South Seas and in the East. As a vagabond, a bohemian, James naturally made friends with the actors and other stage people of his day, and while he was in Sydney in 1880 he wrote his first play, for and with his friend, the actor Alfred Dampier — *The Nihilists; or, Russia As It Is*. This was reasonably successful, but his next play, written alone, was the most successful in terms of the number of performances it received — *No Mercy*. But Dampier and James, by virtue of their calling, were nomads. Each had to keep moving about Australia, New Zealand and other countries to make a living, and although they continued to meet occasionally in Adelaide, or Melbourne, or in the Victorian provincial cities, James wrote no more

Above: Essie Jenyns 1883
Right: John Stanley James 1882

for the theatre; but over the next few years he presided at various performances of his *No Mercy,* and of *The Nihilists* under its new title, *England and Russia; or, The White Hand.*

Jamison, Sir John (1776-1844). A wealthy landowner of the early days, Sir John, by reason of his support for the convict theatre at Emu Plains, may safely be called Australia's first patron of the theatre. He used to entertain lavishly at his princely mansion on the Nepean, *Regentville,* and, when it could be arranged, after dinner would take his guests to the theatre. He had inherited on the death of his father in 1811 a number of grazing properties, among which was one of 1000 acres at Penrith. Here, about 1825, he built *Regentville,* which he named after the Prince Regent, who had appointed him a knight bachelor in 1813. He became one of the founders of the Bank of New South Wales, along with Barnett Levey and others; a member of the Legislative Council; first president of the Australian Patriotic Association; founder and president of the Sydney Turf Club; one of the founders of Sydney College (now the Sydney Grammar School), and a large shareholder in the Bank of Australia. A *bon viveur,* with a town as well as a country residence, he kept open house for local and visiting celebrities, including the Governor and the Chief Justice, and his 'table' was the talk of Sydney. Some idea of the life enjoyed at this period by the 'gentry' is to be gained from the occasional social notes in the newspapers. On 10.7.1830, for instance, the *Sydney Gazette* reported that the district of Penrith had been the scene of extraordinary gaiety the previous week. On the Monday, a party of nearly 30 ladies and gentlemen had dined at 'the seat of George Cox, Esq.,' and attended the ball which followed. On the Wednesday the party was entertained at *Regentville,* on the Friday there was a picnic for which no fewer than eight carriages were needed for the 53 guests, while on the Saturday 'the amusements of the gala week were wound up by a trip to the Emu Theatre, where *Rob Roy* and *John Bull* were performed to an overflowing house . . . The audience exceeded 200 . . .' And James Tucker, in his novel of convict life at this time, *Ralph Rashleigh,* describes a performance in the Emu Plains theatre, at the conclusion of which 'the Knight of Regentsville,' as Sir John was known, and his party made substantial gifts to the theatre musicians and actors, which worked out at 15 shillings for each. (See: Emu Plains).

Jefferson, Joseph (1829-1905). American character actor, notable for his performance in *Rip Van Winkle* (1859), in which he had little real success until Boucicault took the play in hand and gave it dramatic shape (1865). On the stage he was, according to T.Allston Brown, an 'able exponent, if not the leader, of that natural school which reproduces without caricature, acts without exaggeration — is, and not merely seems to be.' Born in Philadelphia, the son of actor parents, Jefferson made his stage debut as the child in *Pizarro.* His first appearance as an adult was at the National, New York in 1849. Gradually he built up a reputation as one of the most original and reliable comic actors. In 1862 he came to Australia, opening in Sydney in February that year in *Rip Van Winkle*. Then followed *Our American Cousin* (1858), *The Cricket on the Hearth* (1859), *The Heir at Law* (1797), *The Octoroon* (1859), and *The Poor Gentleman* (1801), all of which had roles he had made peculiarly his own. He later said of the stock company which supported him at the Royal Victoria that 'I plainly saw that I had my work cut out if I expected to stand prominently forward amidst such surroundings.' His Sydney success was repeated in Melbourne, and after a tour of New Zealand and South America he made his first professional visit to London. Here Boucicault doctored *Rip Van Winkle* for him. He opened in the new version at the Haymarket on 4.9.1865, and was rewarded with a run of 107 nights. From then on he never looked back.

Jennings (Jenyns), Essie (1866-1920). A naturally talented actress, stage name Essie Jenyns, whose life story could be called the first Cinderella story of the Australian stage. She was born near Gympie, Queensland. Her father, a doctor, was an alcoholic, and very early in Essie's life her mother left him, and obtained a position as governess on a squatting station. Sometime afterwards her father was killed in a drunken brawl in South America. Her mother later moved to NSW, where she became matron of the Randwick Institute. Next she bought a partnership in a boarding house, in which the star boarder was the English actor, William Creswick, who fell in love with and married the second partner, a Mrs Bellenfanti. With the partnership about to be broken up, Creswick suggested to Essie's mother that she should go on the stage. Adopting the stage name of Kate Arden, she did quite well for herself, and when Esssie was 5 Kate married the Australian actor, William J.Holloway. She was a manager, and so was he, and between them, by dint of thrift and hard work they enjoyed a successful theatrical career. It reached its peak when the young Essie took to the stage at the age of 15. She first drew attention in some of G.Darrell's plays, and after a couple of years her parents took her to London, ostensibly for her health's sake, where she saw among other stars of the day Sarah Bernhardt, and the American actress Mary Anderson, under whose spell she fell completely. Essie's later Juliet and her Parthenia in *Ingomar the Barbarian* were obviously based on Mary Anderson's interpretations. Returning to Australia in 1885, Essie suddenly leapt into theatrical prominence and popularity, so much so that by 1887 a firm of Sydney photographers could boast that it had sold 15 000 photographs of her in some of her roles. But beneath the surface success discontent was brewing. The hard, slogging work night after night; the learning of long, difficult roles, and the feeling that she was feeding the ambitions of others rather than her own became irksome. Her stepfather, it appeared, had an ambitious plan to present her to London audiences, where she was to challenge Mary Anderson in Juliet and other roles. Essie had other plans. She had fallen in love with John R.Wood of Newcastle, member of a wealthy family with brewery and coal-mining interests. In 1888, after triumphant Melbourne and Sydney seasons in *Romeo and Juliet, Twelfth Night, Much Ado About Nothing,* and *Cymbeline,* she suddenly and unexpectedly broke it to her parents that she was going to marry John. They were furious, but could do nothing. They sailed for London a few days after her marriage, which was a social event, in St Andrew's Cathedral, Sydney. From then on Essie led what many would describe as the ideal life, the first few years of her marriage being spent on extensive tours of Europe. The young couple finally made London their home. During World War I they were living at Kingston Hill, London, and she rented a billiard room and garden near her home for use by Australian soldiers on leave from France. Early in her married life she had given her support to the establishment of the kindergarten movement in her husband's home city, Newcastle, NSW, and it was while she was on a return visit to Australia with the idea of reviving the movement that she contracted appendicitis. She died soon after an operation.

Jess. 6-act drama by Alfred Dampier and J.H.Wranghan, from Rider Haggard's novel (1887), Gaiety, Sydney 3.3.1888, initial 16 performances. Given as *A Transvaal Heroine,* 5-act drama by Alfred Dampier, Her Majesty's, Sydney 14.3.1896; and as *Briton and Boer,* 5-act drama by Alfred Dampier, Alexandra, Melbourne 17.1.1900.

Jessie Brown; or, The Relief of Lucknow. 3-act drama by Dion Boucicault, Wallack's, New York 22.2.1858; Britannia, London 11.4.1859; Prince of Wales, Sydney 30.4.60, initial 14 performances.

John Bull; or, The Englishman's Fireside. 3-act comedy by G.Colman the Younger, Covent Garden, London 5.3.1803; Emu Plains, 3.7.1830.

John Gabriel Borkman. 4-act drama by Henrik Ibsen, translated W.Archer, Strand, London 3.5.1897; Melbourne Repertory, Turn Verein Hall, 29.6.1911, initially 1 performance.

Jolie Parfumeuse, La. 3-act comic opera, text H.Crémieux and E.Blum, music J.Offenbach, Renaissance, Paris 29.11.1873; Alhambra, London 18.5.1874; Prince of Wales, Melbourne 17.11.1875, initial 9 performances.

Jonathan Bradford; or, The Murder at the Roadside Inn. 3-act melodrama by E.Fitzball, Surrey, London 12.6.1833; Royal, Sydney 26.12.1834. (See: Multiple setting).

Jonquille, The. 4-act drama by Guy Boothby, Royal, Adelaide 14.8.1891, initially 2 performances. Published by W.J.Thomas, Adelaide 1891.

Joseph of Canaan. 4-act drama by George Walters, Her Majesty's, Sydney 24.8.1895, initial 24 performances. Published by Akhurst, Sydney 1895, and by G.Robertson, Melbourne 1897. This play was also licensed for production in Glasgow, Scotland on 12.9.1913.

Joy. 3-act drama by J.Galsworthy, Savoy, London 24.9.1907; Melbourne Repertory, Athenaeum Hall 1.10.1914, initial 3 performances.

Juive, La. (The Jewess). 5-act opera, text A.E.Scribe, music J.F.Halévy, Opéra, Paris 23.2.1835; Drury Lane, London 29.7.1846; Prince of Wales, Melbourne 15.4.1874, initial 6 performances.

Julius Caesar. Historical drama by William Shakespeare, believed to have been first performed in London in 1599 or 1600; Royal Victoria, Sydney 4.9.1838.

Regentville, Sir John Jamison's country seat Penrith c. 1825

K

Kean, Charles (1811-1868). Son of the famous English actor, Edmund Kean (1787-1833), Charles was more notable as the producer of ornate, accurately staged classics and melodramas than as an actor. He made his first stage appearance at the age of 16, and by the time he was 37 he had given several command performances before Queen Victoria at Windsor Castle. For some years after this he stage managed most of the performances given at the castle. The most successful period in his life was during his lesseeship of the Princess's, 1850-59, when he staged a series of Shakespearian and other productions which drew crowded audiences night after night. Modern critics have dismissed his work as 'upholstered Shakespeare' — Shakespeare with pantomime transformation scenes, tableaux, and ballets. His were, indeed, sumptuous productions, with historically accurate settings and costumes — the work of an antiquarian. But Kean knew his audiences and his times, and his productions were right for both. He and his wife embarked on a tour of Australia and the USA in 1863. During their stay in Australia, from October 1863 to July 1864, they appeared in Melbourne, Sydney and other centres in most of their favourite plays — *The Wife's Secret* (1848), *Louis XI* (1855), *The Merchant of Venice*, *Henry VIII*, *Hamlet*, *Macbeth*, *Rchard III*, *The Jealous Wife* (1761), *King John*, *King Lear*, *Money* (1840), *The Stranger* (1798) and others. At this time Kean and his wife were in the autumn of their life and talent, but, like all good professionals, could still hold an audience spellbound, and teach the not-so-old a great deal about acting and stage production. It was not for nothing that a Sydney newspaper, reviewing Kean's production of *The Wife's Secret* at the Prince of Wales, wrote: 'We imagine the audience received a lesson on Wednesday as to the manner in which a piece should be produced. It was evident a mastermind had regulated all the accessories. The scenes

Left: Laura Keene
Below: Mrs Charles Kean as Hermione in The Winter's Tale

were shifted without the preliminary whistle; the delay between the acts was exceedingly short; there were no listeners at the wings, nothing which could possibly distract the attention of the audience . . . moreover, the actors did not hang over the footlights, but kept the centre of the stage, addressing each other and not the audience . . .'

Kean, Mrs Charles (1806-1880). Five years older than her husband, Ellen Kean (the former Ellen Tree) was, as so often happened with such 19th century stage partnerships, the better actor. She made her first London appearance in 1822, and later was praised by Hazlitt. Like Charles, she made a number of successful visits to the USA before they were married, so that by 1842, when they became man and wife, they were able to start out with a capital of £30 000 between them. After her marriage Ellen submerged herself in her husband, content to live and to act only for him. She was his stage manager, his valet, his arbiter, his nurse, and his wife. One of the many stories told of her devotion concerns an actor in their company who had dared to make a loud noise during one of Charles Kean's important scenes. Later, when he came to her to make his apologies, he told her he had already apologised to Kean, and had been forgiven. Mrs Kean is said to have surveyed him with regal calm and replied: '*He* has forgiven you, but' — pointing heaven wards — 'will you be forgiven up there?' There were few critics who did not recognise and acknowledge her ability as an actress. No matter how incongruous she may sometimes have looked on stage (she played Hermione wearing a crinoline hoop), audiences forgot her appearance in her acting. She and her husband endeared themselves to audiences in Australia and the USA as they had done in England, as actors and individuals. By the 1860s they were an eccentric though lovable couple, as this description of them by the American actress, Clara Morris, indicates: 'As they came down the street together, Mrs Kean majestically towering above her lord and master, looked like an old-time frigate with every inch of canvas spread, while at her side Charles puffed and fretted like a small tug. The street boys were a continual torment to him but Mrs Kean appeared serenely unconscious of their existence, even when her husband made short rushes at them with his gold-headed cane, crying, "Go away — you irreverent little brutes — go away!" and then puffed laboriously back to her again as she sailed calmly on.'

Keane of Kalgoorlie. 4-act drama by E.W.O'Sullivan and Arthur Wright, founded on Wright's novel (1907), Haymarket Hippodrome (tent theatre), Sydney 18.4.1908, initial 12 performances. (See: Parliamentarians).

Keene, Laura (?1826-1873). English-born actress who first came into prominence as a member of the 'bevy of beauty' engaged for the London Lyceum production of *A Chain of Events* (1852). The bevy consisted of the theatre lessee, Madame Vestris, and Miss Julie St

George, Miss Foote, and Miss Laura Keene. The play ran for more than 3 months. This was long enough for Laura to tire of it and the theatre. In September the same year she made her first appearance in New York, and from then on made America her home. Early in 1854 she played in San Francisco for the first time. Here she leased the Union, and embarked on theatre management. Things were going well with her, but again she abruptly changed her mind. The Starks had returned to San Francisco from Australia with big stories of the money to be made there. She sailed for Australia with the young Edwin Booth, and D.C.Anderson. Here they opened in Sydney on 23.10.1854, but while critics were favourable, audiences were poor. So they moved on to Melbourne, where they first had to wait before they could procure a theatre. Opening on 20.11.1854, they stayed for 5 nights only. On returning to the USA Laura again entered on management in San Francisco. Her she introduced the public to *Camille,* with Booth playing Armand. Next she moved on to New York, finally finishing there with her own theatre. Her most important production was T.Taylor's *Our American Cousin* (1858), the play which introduced the fictional Lord Dundreary (with his whiskers) to the world. In April 1864 Laura began a short season at Ford's, Washington, winding up with a benefit for herself in which *Our American Cousin* (billed as having been played more than 1000 times) was the main feature. During the course of this production President Abraham Lincoln was assassinated by the brother of Edwin Booth, John Wilkes Booth.

Kelly, Ned (1855-1880). Inevitably a subject for theatrical exploitation, this bushranger and his gang attracted the lunatic fringe among writers for the stage, rather than the serious dramatist. These ranged from the inept enthusiast to the out-and-out opportunist, only a few of whom achieved the financial success which constituted their main purpose in writing. The first of these plays was by a journalist, J.Pickersgill, who, in his *Catching the Kellys,* apparently set out to make fun of the police. This was first performed at the Royal, Melbourne on 29.3.1879, and ran for 11 performances. The next venture, a burletta called *The Kellys,* by an unknown author, was ignored by all the newspapers when it was produced at the People's, Melbourne on 12.3.1880. In the same year a writer with the unlikely name of Marmaduke Evendale wrote a drama in three acts called *The Capture of the Kelly Gang,* which was to have been produced at the Queen's, Sydney on 5.7.1880. The theatre was packed for the opening night, but before the performance could start the theatre was closed by order of the Colonial Secretary. Next came, again in Melbourne, 'the grand moral drama' *Ostracised,* by E.C.Martin, first performed at the Princess's on 6.8.1881 for a run of 29 performances. This seems to have been the first of the Kelly plays written to present him as a 'hero,' and when, under the title *Ostracised; or, The Downfall of Crime,* it was performed at the Victoria

Hall, Sydney on 8.4.1882 it shared the same fate as *The Capture of the Kelly Gang*. The Colonial Secretary was not going to permit Kelly's exploits to be presented as entertainment. It was 16 years before the next Kelly play, *The Kelly Gang,* was presented, this time at the Alexandra, Melbourne on 12.3.1898, for 12 performances. A more or less innocuous drama, it also supported the earlier 'hero' myth. Its success led to the production of A.Denham's *The Kelly Gang; or, The Career of Ned Kelly, the Ironclad Bushranger of Australia* at the Opera House, Sydney on 22.7.1899, where it ran for 6 performances and was then transferred to the larger Criterion, for a further 28 performances. Two other Kelly plays, presented in the same year, were scotched by Denham, who took out an injunction against them. They were *The Career of the Kelly Gang* by F.H.Greene, Royal, Adelaide 7.8.1899, and *Outlaw Kelly* by L.Booth, Victoria, Newcastle 12.8.1899. In the first the Kelly gang were presented as men more sinned against than sinning, and in the second nothing so ignominious as hanging was allowed to end the hero's life. He died 'perforated in a hundred places with the iron hail fired by the vindicators of the law.' These were the last attempts at the Kelly story in the theatre during the period under review. Kelly's next step was into the grey world of the motion picture film.

King Arthur; or, Lancelot the Loose, Gin-ever the Square, and the Knights of the Round Table and other Furniture. Burlesque extravaganza by W.M.Akhurst, Royal, Melbourne 31.10.1868, initial 26 performances. Published R.Bell, Melbourne 1868.

King Dodo. 2-act comic opera, text J.Francis after F.Pixley, music G.Luders, F.Weierter and others, Daly's, New York 12.5.1902; Criterion, Sydney 10.6.1905, initial 13 performances.

King John. Historical drama by William Shakespeare, believed to have been first performed in London in 1596 or 1597; Royal Victoria, Sydney 6.2.1843.

King Lear. Tragedy by William Shakespeare, believed to have been first performed in London in 1605 or 1606; Royal, Sydney 23.1.1837.

King of Cadonia, The. 2-act musical comedy, text F.Lonsdale, music S.Jones, Prince of Wales, London 3.9.1908; Her Majesty's, Melbourne 12.6.1909, initial 36 performances.

King's Dragoons, The. 3-act comic opera, text J.W.Jones, music J.Crook, Royal, Manchester 1.11.1880; Opera House, Melbourne 18.11.1882, initial 23 performances.

Kismet. 3-act drama by E.Knoblock, Majestic, Erie, Philadelphia 9.1.1911; Daly's, New York 16.1.1911. Oscar Asche, offered the play for use under his own conditions, rewrote it, with music by C.Wilson, Garrick, London 19.4.1911; Royal, Melbourne 6.4.1912, initial 48 performances.

Kitty Grey. 3-act musical comedy, text J.S.Pigott after M.M.Mars and Hennequin's *Les Fêtards*, music H.Talbot and L.Monckton, Vaudeville, London 25.4.1900; Princess's, Melbourne 25.6.1904, initial 17 performances.

Knight for a Day. 2-act musical comedy, text R.B.Smith, music R.Hubbell and F.Hart, Wallack's, New York 16.12.1907; Her Majesty's, Sydney 9.7.1910, initial 12 performances.

Knowles, Conrad (1810-1844). Originally articled as a clerk, at the age of 18 he left England for Western Australia as one of a band of ill-fated Swan River colonists. Finding no prospects of any kind in Perth, he took ship to Hobart, where he became a tutor. He is said to have fallen in love with one of his charges, the resultant 'scandal' forcing his retirement to Sydney. At this time Barnett Levey was forming his first company for the opening of his Royal. Although he was the son of a Wesleyan minister, and was staying in Sydney with Wesleyan friends, to all of whom the theatre was anathema, Knowles could not resist his particular 'call.' He appeared in the forefront of Levey's company, adopting at first the surname 'Cooper,' when the theatre opened in 1832. From then until his death 12 years later he was rarely off the stage, earning in the course of his work more praise than adverse criticism. During this period he established his place in theatrical history as Australia's first Hamlet and first Othello. He was at various times stage and acting manager of the Sydney Royal and Royal Victoria, and wrote and published at least one play, *Salathiel; or, The Jewish Chieftain*. Towards the end of his hard-working life he tried to revive the theatre in Melbourne, without success.

Kowalski, Henri (1841-1916). Highly popular concert pianist, composer, and conductor, described by F.C.Brewer as 'a Frenchman, a journalist, a jolly good fellow.' Born in Paris, he showed an early interest in music and was soon studying piano under the celebrated Antoine Francois Marmontel, and composition under Napoleon-Henri Reber and Michele Enrico Carofa. Early in his adult life he was appointed a court musician to Napoleon III. In the 1860s he toured Spain, Germany, and England, and then spent from 1870 to 1879 in the USA, with occasional trips home to Paris. In 1880 he determined on a visit to Australia, where his concerts were an immediate success, and where he took a very active interest in musical affairs. In this year he was also adviser to the Melbourne International Exhibiton. He returned to Paris in 1882, where he is said to have supervised the production of his opera, *Gilles de Bretagne*. Later he claimed that the opera he had written to Marcus Clarke's libretto, originally called *Queen Venus* but changed to *Moustique* when it was produced in Australia, had been produced in Brussels. There is no evidence to support this claim. Kowalski wrote more than 100 compositions for the piano, including a Marche

Hongroise, composed in 1864 and said to have sold more than 500 000 copies. During his stay in Sydney and Melbourne in 1881 his 3-act lyric drama or opera, *Vercingetorix; or, Love and Patriotism,* was given its first performance. Eight years later *Moustique* had its first Australian performance in Sydney, with the composer conducting. Kowalski made several visits to Australia. In 1895 he was appointed conductor of the Sydney Philharmonic Society. He established the Orpheus Club, and in 1896 he wrote the music for an oratorio written by A.B.Wood, the text of which, *Future Life,* was published by W.A.Pepperday, Sydney the same year.

Laura Keene with Edwin Booth 1854

Above: Alice Lingard 1884
Right: Samuel Lazar

L

Ladies' Prerogative, The. Vaudeville by W.M.Akhurst, music Sydney Nelson, Protestant Hall, Melbourne 11.1.1853.

Lady Barmaid, The. 2-act musical comedy, text F.Bowyer and W.Sprange, music J.Crook, Opera House, Southport 1.7.1895; originally called *The New Barmaid,* songs by F.Weierter were added and the title changed for the production at the Criterion, Sydney 31.1.1903, initial 12 performances.

Lady Dandies, The. 3-act comic opera, text after V.Sardou by B.Hood, music H.Felix, Daly's, London 27.10.1906; Her Majesty's, Sydney 21.3.1908, initial 43 performances.

Lady Dolly. 2-act comic opera, text Margery Browne, music Alfred Hill, Palace, Sydney 31.3.1900, initial 6 performances. Text published John Sands, Sydney 1900.

Lady Inger of Ostrat. 5-act drama by Henrik Ibsen, translated C.Archer. World premiere Her Majesty's, Melbourne 20.4.1901, initial 6 performances. First English performance Scala, London 29.1.1906.

Lady Madcap. 2-act musical comedy, text P.Rubens and N.Davis, music P.Rubens, Prince of Wales, London 17.12.1904; Princess's, Melbourne 3.8.1907, initial 12 performances.

Lady of Lyons, The; or, Love and Pride. 5-act drama by Bulwer-Lytton, Covent Garden, London 15.12.1838; Royal Victoria, Sydney 15.4.1839.

Lady of the Pluckup, The; or, The Days of Eighty-four. 3-act drama by Randolph Bedford, Princess's, Melbourne 23.9.1911, initial 7 performances. Adapted from his novel, serialised in the Melbourne *Argus* in 1893.

Lady Windermere's Fan. 4-act comedy by Oscar Wilde, St James's, London 20.2.1892; Lyceum, Sydney 19.5.1894, initial 8 performances.

Land of Heart's Desire, The. 1-act play by W.B.Yeats, Avenue, London 29.3.1894; Repertory, Adelaide 24.9.1908, initially 1 performance.

Land of Nod, The. 2-act musical comedy, text F.Adams and W.Hough, music J.Howard, New York, New York 1.4.1907; King's, Melbourne 20.12.1913, initial 54 performances.

Last Days of Pompeii, The. 3-act drama by E.Geoghegan, adapted from Bulwer Lytton's novel (1834), Royal Victoria, Sydney 29.7.1844.

Last Edition, The. 1-act play by William Moore, Oddfellows' Hall, Melbourne 30.3.1909, initially 1 performance.

Lazar, John (1801-1879). On his arrival in Australia in 1837 publicity issued by the Sydney Royal claimed that Lazar had acted at Drury Lane and Covent Garden, a doubtful claim. He made his first Australian appearance as Shylock in *The Merchant of Venice*, a performance which earned praise and blame in equal measure. From then on he became an important figure in the Australian theatre. Versatile and hard-working, he played in an enormous number of different roles in his stage career. While manager of the Royal Victoria he encouraged Australian playwrights, and himself wrote a farce, *Contradiction; or, A Wife Upon Sufferance,* as well as two or three pantomimes. He was in turn manager of the Sydney Royal (1837), Royal Victoria (1838), Queen's, Adelaide (1841), Royal Victoria, Sydney (1843), and partner with George Coppin in the Victoria, Adelaide (1850). While engaged in commercial pursuits in Adelaide he was Mayor of that city from 1855 to 1857. Following bad times in the next decade, he migrated to New Zealand, where he was town clerk first in Dunedin, and then in Hokitika.

Lazar, Samuel (1838-1883). Born in Sydney, made his first stage appearance at the age of 5 in a juvenile production of *Bombastes Furioso* (1810) at Sydney's Royal Victoria, where his father, John Lazar, first appeared the year Samuel was born. At the age of 13 Samuel played Richard in the Cibber version of Shakespeare's *Richard III*. Not long afterwards he decided that his future lay with the managerial rather than the acting side of the theatre. He was for several years manager of a stock and station agency in Adelaide, and in 1868 was one of the three partners who built the Royal in Adelaide. Early in 1875, after having leased and managed the Adelaide Royal with some success, he came to Sydney and leased and managed the Queen's in York Street, which he extensively remodelled for the first appearance in Sydney of

J.C.Williamson and Maggie Moore in *Struck Oil.* At the same time he acquired a lease of the ground on which the Prince of Wales had stood before its destruction by fire. Here he built the Sydney Royal, which, in name at least, occupied the site for almost 100 years. He managed this theatre for some years, until bad health forced his retirement in 1882. In 1874 he published in Adelaide the text of one of his annual pantomimes; two more in Sydney in 1875; and one each in 1877 and 1878.

Led Astray. 6-act drama by Dion Boucicault, adapted from O.Feuillet's *La Tentation,* Union Square, New York 6.12.1873; Gaiety, London 1.7.1874; Royal, Melbourne 27.4.1875, initial 4 performances.

Leete, Henry Benjamin. (See: Rickards, Harry).

Legitimate drama, The. A term originally applied to plays with spoken as opposed to sung dialogue, or a play with music, an opera. The term, like 'Theatre Royal,' arose from the interpretation or misinterpretation of the Theatre Licensing Act of 1737, which decreed that only the 2 patent theatres, Covent Garden and Drury Lane, could present plays in London. Smaller, lesser theatres were restricted to singing, dancing, dumb-show, or equestrian entertainments. Theatre proprietors gradually overcame the restrictions in this Act by ignoring them when they could, or by presenting plays with musical accompaniment and a few songs — known as the 'illegitimate drama.' Such plays were called burlettas, a name which included genuine musical works for the stage as well as what were quite plainly legitimate plays with songs and spectacular effects added. Meantime, constant lobbying went on for a change in the law, resulting first of all in modification, and finally, in 1843, in the Theatre Regulation Bill, which abolished monopolies and privileges. But the term 'legitimate drama' continued in use for many years afterwards. From about 1850 onwards it seems to have held the connotation 'the serious as opposed to the melodramatic and comic drama.' (See: Theatre Royal).

Leitch, George (1842-1907). This actor, playwright, and theatre lessee seems to have faced division in himself over what name to adopt. His real name, George Goodyear, was not used after he became an actor. At different times during the ensuing years he wrote and acted under the names George Ralph Walker, George Leitch Walker, R.Andre Leitch and George Leitch, the last being the name by which he was best known. Trained as a civil engineer, he gave this up in favour of the stage and gained his experience in a number of English provincial theatres. He made his first London appearance at the Standard in *The Two Orphans* (1874), followed by engagements at the Crystal Palace, Adelphi, and Strand. He then toured South Africa, and later moved to Australia. By this time he had had 8 works for the stage produced in England, between 1873 and 1881, all written under the name George Ralph Walker. While in Australia he appeared in all the major theatres as actor, actor-manager, and playwright. He was the first to exploit, if not to see, the possibilities in a stage version of Marcus Clarke's *His Natural Life,* which he first produced in Brisbane. It was then produced in turn in Sydney, Melbourne, Adelaide and New Zealand until it was swamped under the tide of other versions. His other plays, produced in New Zealand as well as in Australia, included *The Pearl Divers,* and *Wanda,* the last being a dramatised version of Ouida's novel of that title. (See: *His Natural Life*).

Length, or side. In an era when printed copies of plays were the exception, and usually only one copy was available, it was time-consuming and costly to write out copies of the complete play by hand for the whole cast. The problem was solved by writing out the lines for each character. These were written on separate pieces of paper called lengths, or sides (two halves of a foolscap sheet, divided down the middle), 42 lines to the length, with cues. So that, of the plays produced up to about 1850, all most of the actors knew about them were the lines each had to speak, and the cues for entrance, speech, and exit. It was a system which made the 3-plays-a-night programme possible, if actors were a 'quick study,' and did not outlast the popularity of such programmes.

Leopold, George (?-1904). Pantomimist, ballet dancer, actor, and singer; one of three brothers who came to Australia in 1857 under contract to G.Coppin. A talented family, consisting of Tom, Henry, and George, and Henry's wife, Fraulein Fanny, they had danced with some success in Europe. In Australia they made their first appearance in the harlequinade of the annual pantomime at Melbourne Royal. For the next 3 years they provided Australian audiences with some of the first classical ballets ever seen in Australia. In 1861 they visited India, returning to Australia the following year. In 1866 they joined the Lyster Opera Company, providing ballets for the various operas. Four years later the eldest brother, Tom, died. The family disintegrated, and George graduated to the dramatic stage. He and Tom had for a brief while in 1868 acted in *Hamlet, King John,* and *Antony and Cleopatra.* After Tom's death George appeared in W.H.Cooper's *Sun and Shadow,* and *Colonial Experience,* among other works. In 1879 he played in his first singing role in a performance of *HMS Pinafore,* and in 1884-85 he had acting and singing roles in L.Searelle's comic operas, *Bobadil,* and *Isidora.* From then on he continued as an actor. At the time of his death he was a member of one of the lesser touring companies. Towards the end of 1904 the Hobart *Mercury,* quoting a paragraph in the Melbourne *Sporting and Dramatic News,* said he had left an estate of £2814 to his family, his will being proved under his real name — George Wooldridge.

Levey, Barnett (1798-1837). The first free male Jewish settler to arrive in Australia, Levey also founded the regular, professional theatre. He came to Sydney in 1821 in search of his brother, the wealthy emancipist,

Solomon Levey, who financed his establishment as a business man in his (Solomon's) former shop in George Street. Barnett Levey ultimately built his foolishly grandiose Colchester Warehouse on this site, incorporating his Royal Hotel and theatre, with a huge mill on top of the 5-storey building. Besides being a business man, Levey was also a stagestruck singer and comedian. In 1825-26 he took part in a number of concerts, singing comic songs and giving recitations which were voted by many in the audience to be the best part of the evening's entertainment. By 1828 his theatre was ready for use. He had a scenepainter working on the stage scenery, and a corps of actors rehearsing the opening programme. And then his troubles began. He and Governor Darling became implacable enemies. The vital difference between them was that Darling held the power, and he used it. He refused to licence dramatic performances, and it was not until he was replaced by Governor Bourke in 1832 that Levey at last got a licence to conduct dramatic performances in his theatre. (This hand-written licence is held in the Archives Office of NSW). But by that time Levey no longer owned a theatre. His buildings had been sold at auction by the mortgagor. Undaunted, he fitted up the saloon of the Royal Hotel as a theatre, and the first professional performance in Australia was given there on 26.12.1832. Meantime he found ways and means of having his original Royal reconstructed and renovated, and this was opened as the Royal proper on 5.10.1833. Regular performances were given here until a few weeks after his death, when J.Wyatt, proprietor of the new Royal Victoria, bought Levey's theatre from his widow and closed it. It was destroyed by fire in 1840. (See: Sydney, Theatres in).

Liebe Augustin, Der (Princess Caprice). 3-act operetta, text R.Bernauer and E.Welisch, music L.Fall, Berlin 3.2.1912; Shaftesbury, London 11.5.1912; Her Majesty's, Melbourne 17.10.1914, initial 6 performances.

Lieschen and Fritzchen. 1-act operetta, text P.Boisselot, music J.Offenbach, Ems 21.7.1863; Bouffes-Parisiens, Paris 5.1.1864; Covent Garden, London 27.12.1869; Opera House, Melbourne 12.3.1875, initially 1 performance.

Life and Death of Captain Cook, The. 5-act drama by John Perry, Gaiety, Sydney 28.1.1888, initial 6 performances. Winner in competition organised by Alfred Dampier to mark Australia's first century.

Light That Failed, The. 2-act drama by George Darrell, from Rudyard Kipling's novel (1891), Royal, Perth 24.6.1899, initial 6 performances.

——. 3-act drama by George Fleming (Julia Constance Fletcher), Lyric, London 7.2.1903; Her Majesty's, Sydney 23.4.1904, initial 15 performances.

Lights o' London, The. 5-act drama by G.R.Sims, Princess's, London 10.9.1881; Royal, Sydney 2.9.1882, initial 31 performances. 5 years later George Rignold staged this at Her Majesty's, Sydney for an initial run of 60 performances.

Lily of Killarney, The. 3-act opera, text J.Oxenford and Dion Boucicault, based on Boucicault's *The Colleen Bawn* (1860), music J.Benedict, Covent Garden, London 8.2.1862; Prince of Wales, Sydney 16.7.1863, initial 4 performances.

Limelight. A form of spot or floodlight so bright it fathered the phrase used to this day to describe someone very clearly to be seen — 'in the limelight.' Its chief characteristic was its sharp, brilliant whiteness compared with the yellow oil, candle, or gas lighting. Invented in 1826, it was first used on the stage in 1837 by William Macready, and by the 1850s was widely in use in the London theatres. The light was produced in front of a reflector by 'impinging a small hot flame on a block of lime.' At first a mixture of alcohol and oxygen was used to produce the flame. Later this was replaced by an oxy-hydrogen flame. The first discoverable reference to the use of the limelight in the Australian theatre appeared early in 1863, when it was reported that the limelight was used in two of the tableau scenes in a production of *Uncle Tom's Cabin*, '. . . being entirely new to Sydney.' From then on, particularly in the 1870s, its use became fairly general, especially in pantomimes. One of its most consistent users was Alfred Dampier, whether he was playing Mephistopheles in *Faust and Marguerite*, or the Ghost in *Hamlet*. (See: Coloured fires. Electric lighting. Transformation scene).

Linda di Chamounix (Linda of Chamonix). 3-act opera, text G.Rossi, music G.Donizetti, Karntnertor, Vienna 19.5.1842; Her Majesty's, London 1.6.1843; Princess's, Melbourne 6.5.1857, initially 2 performances.

Lingard, Mrs William Horace (1847-1897). Talented English singer, dancer, and actress who received her early training at the Grecian, London when she was Alice Dunning. She received lessons in voice production from Guiseppe Operti, who later composed the music for the first American musical comedy, *The Black Crook* (1866). In this year she married W.H.Lingard (1838-1927), an English music hall singer and comedian. Two years later he went to the USA, where he appeared with a certain degree of success at the Theatre Comique, New York. He sent for his wife to join him, and they first appeared together at the Academy of Music, Brooklyn, towards the end of 1868. From then on they undertook regular tours, except for occasional stints at theatres in which Lingard assumed the management. In 1870 they were in San Francisco, where Alice distinguished herself in a performance of *Frou Frou*. The pair then starred in a series of plays in the same theatre, Maguire's Opera

House. Touring continued, with a return to San Francisco in 1875, where Alice and her sister-in-law, Dickie Lingard, made a big success in N.H.Jackson's *The Two Orphans*. This was said to have netted $11 000 in seven performances. In 1878 Alice and her husband, a lesser talent, came to Australia, where she was an immediate success. They appeared in a round of plays and musical productions in Melbourne and Sydney, including *HMS Pinafore, The Sorcerer,* and a 1-act operetta written by Lingard, with music by G.Operti, *I Ladroni*. From Australia they travelled to New Zealand, where they repeated their Australian programmes, with the addition of the first performance of Lingard's *The Wreck of the Pinafore,* music by Luscombe Searelle. By 1881 they were back in the United States, where Alice again enchanted American audiences with her beauty and talent. In the 1890s, back in London again, she appeared at Drury Lane in *A Million of Money* (1890), in the title role of *Vida* (1892) at the Prince of Wales, and, full circle, in John Oxenford's version of *The Two Orphans* (1874) at the Adelphi in 1894. (See: Searelle, Luscombe; *Wreck of the Pinafore, The*).

Little Christopher Columbus. 2-act burlesque opera, text G.Sims and C.Raleigh, music I.Caryll, Lyric, London 10.10.1893; Lyceum, Sydney 4.11.1899, initial 24 performances.

Little Duke, The. (See: *Petit Duc, Le*).

Little Jack Sheppard. 3-act musical burlesque, text H.P.Stephens and W.Yardley, music M.Lutz and others, Gaiety, London 26.12.1885; Opera House, Melbourne 27.12.1886, initial 53 performances.

Little Lord Fauntelroy. 3-act comedy by E.V.Seebohm, from Mrs F.H.Burnett's novel (1886), Prince of Wales, London 23.2.1888; Princess's, Melbourne 19.10.1889, initial 48 performances.

Little Michus, The. 3-act musical comedy, text A.Vanloo and C.Duval, music A.Messager, Daly's, London 29.4.1905; Her Majesty's, Sydney 2.6.1906, initial 30 performances.

Little Minister, The. 4-act comedy-drama by J.M.Barrie, founded on his novel (1891), Haymarket, London 6.11.1897; Princess's, Melbourne 4.6.1898, initial 24 performances.

Living Statues, or Poses Plastiques. Reproduction by actors of the poses or attitudes of works by notable sculptors. The first in the field seems to have been Giovanni Batista Belzoni, who at Oxford in 1813 performed 'several striking attitudes . . .' in imitation of classical statuary. At about the same time the talented equestrian, Andrew Ducrow, while performing in Belgium presented his *poses plastiques* on horseback, striking attitudes as Mercury or Zephyr on the back of his horse. Belzoni abandoned the world of entertainment, and it was largely Ducrow who captured, and held, the public interest with his horseback poses. In 1828 he brought these 'down to earth' with a series of living statue poses on the stage. In the course of time these 'statue' performances appeared on the legitimate stage, in the music hall, and in the vaudeville theatre. Charles Selby, in his 3-act drama, *The Marble Heart* (1854) used Canova's sculpture group, 'Graces', for his living statuary. In the published version of the play he prints at the end of the first act instructions on preparing 'statues'. He is careful to state that they should not be *too* naked. 'The statues are *doubles,* and can be produced without expense or difficulty. White calico drapery (the *best* material to represent marble), white stockings, white thread wigs, braided in the Grecian style; the heads and arms (in the absence of white cotton bodies and sleeves) whitened, like the necks and faces, with bismuth.' *(Copy in State Library of NSW)* Joseph Simmons appears to have been the first to perform living statues in Australia, at Sydney Theatre Royal in 1836.

Loder, George (1814-1868). Noted pianist and conductor who played accompaniments for Madame Anna Bishop at some of her London concerts. He also conducted at the entertainments she and the harpist, Bochsa, gave in New York, where the singing of the one and the solos of the other were complemented by full orchestra and chorus. He came to Australia in the 1850s, and was for a time conductor with the Lyster Opera Company. Early in 1857 he conducted the opera season which inaugurated the opening of Melbourne's Princess's, *Norma* being the first opera presented. Later in the same year he was conductor of the opera season at Sydney's Royal Victoria. In September a special performance of *Der Freischutz* was given at Sydney Prince of Wales for his benefit. Loder spent the rest of his active life as opera and theatre conductor, occasionally teaching. In 1864 he conducted the first performance in Australia of Gounod's *Faust* for Lyster at the Sydney Prince of Wales. 4 years later, alone and forgotten by all except a few friends, he died of consumption in Adelaide. His only surviving relative, his sister Kate (Fanny) Loder, was in London. Eleven years after his death some of his friends erected a 'neat, plain gravestone' over his and his wife's grave in the West Terrace cemetery.

Lohengrin 3-act opera, text and music Richard Wagner, Weimar 28.8.1850; Covent Garden, London 8.5.1875; Prince of Wales, Melbourne 18.8.1877, initial 8 performances.

Lombardi alla Prima Crociata, I (The Lombardi on the First Crusade). 4-act opera, text T.Solera after poem by T.Grossi, music G.Verdi, Scala, Milan 11.2.1843; Her Majesty's, London 12.5.1846; Prince of Wales, Melbourne 25.5.1874, initial 3 performances.

London Assurance. 5-act comedy by Dion Boucicault, Covent Garden, London 4.3.1841; Royal Victoria, Sydney 8.5.1854.

London Merchant, The; or, The History of George Barnwell.
Tragedy by George Lillo, Drury Lane, London June 1731; as *George Barnwell; or, The London Apprentice,* Emu Plains, 8.5.1830.

Lonely Lives (Einsame Menschen). 5-act drama by G.Hauptmann (1891) translated Mary Morrison, Strand, London 1.4.1901; Melbourne Repertory, Athenaeum Hall 19.3.1912, initially 1 performance.

Long runs. Many Australian plays (plays written in Australia by residents) achieved long runs, but such runs must be seen against the population of the centre in which they were performed, and the year of their production. A run of a week in the Brisbane of the 1870s would have been unusual, but only fair in Sydney or Melbourne. When Walter H.Cooper's three plays, *Sun and Shadow, Foiled,* and *Hazard* achieved runs of 21, 22, and 24 respectively for their opening productions in Sydney in the early 1870s they created a record. And when, in Melbourne in the same decade, Marcus Clarke's *Alfred the Great* and George Darrell's *The Forlorn Hope* achieved 35 and 37 performances respectively they, too, created records. In the 1880s Darrell's *The Sunny South* had an opening run of 36 performances; Gilbert Parker's *Faust* 42; Dampier and Kehoe's *Shamus O'Brien* 42; Dampier and Wranghan's *Marvellous Melbourne* 36, and Parker's *The Vendetta* 24. In the 1890s *Robbery Under Arms* ran for 42 performances; *The Scout* 25; *The Kelly Gang* 34, and *The Christian* 31. It was in the first decade of the new century that a play by an Australian achieved the longest initial run of all. This was *Parsifal,* with 51 performances in 1906. *The Squatter's Daughter* had 36 performances in 1907; *The Man From Outback* 30 in 1909, *My Mate* 23 in 1911. Then, in 1912, came *On Our Selection,* whose long opening run had to be broken because the theatre ceased to be available. It had an initial run of 42 performances in Melbourne.

Some long runs were achieved by light operas and musical comedies, among them *The Arcadians* 66; *Boccaccio* 66; *La Fille du Tambour Major* 102; *Floradora* 93; *The Girl on the Train* 72; *The Girl in the Taxi* 60; *The Land of Nod* 54; *Little Jack Sheppard* 53; *The Merry Widow* 66; *Miss Hook of Holland* 54; *The Orchid* 65; *Our Miss Gibbs* 85; *Paul Jones* 68; *The Quaker Girl* 90; *A Runaway Girl* 54; *The Sunshine Girl* 60; *The Chocolate Soldier* 52.

Loreda. 3-act drama by David Burn, St George's Hall, Melbourne 29.10.1877. This was an amateur production, so was a subsequent one at the Royal, Melbourne 4.5.1878.

Lough Deargh's Shrine; or, The Cave of Penance. 4-act tragedy by G.F.Pickering, Royal Victoria, Sydney 13.12.1847. (See: Parliamentarians).

Louise. 4-act opera, text and music M.Charpentier, Opéra Comique, Paris 2.2.1900; Covent Garden, London 18.6.1909; Her Majesty's, Melbourne 28.8.1913, initially 1 performance.

Love in a Village. 3-act comic opera, text I.Bickerstaffe, music various composers, Covent Garden, London 8.12.1762; Royal, Sydney 22.2.1836, initially 1 performance.

Love Laughs at Locksmiths. 2-act operatic farce, text G.Colman the Younger, original music E.Mehul, new music Michael Kelly, Haymarket, London 25.7.1802; Olympic, Melbourne 25.9.1855, initial 4 performances.

Love's Labor's Lost. Comedy by William Shakespeare, believed to have been first performed in London in 1594 or 1595; Royal, Melbourne 9.4.1860.

Lover's Vows (Das Kind der Liebe). 5-act drama by A.von Kotzebue, translated Mrs E.Inchbald, Covent Garden, London 11.10.1798; King's Own Regiment, Parramatta Barracks, 29.6.1835.

Low comedian. Member of a stock company whose primary role was that of the country bumpkin, comic servant, noodle, or Billy Barlow. A favourite role with low comedians, who could also when called on take over more serious roles, was that of Paul Pry in the play of that name by D.W.Jerrold (1826).

L.S.D. 5-act comedy-drama by F.R.C.Hopkins, Gaiety, Sydney, 20.3.1882, initial 3 performances.

Lucia de Lammermoor. 3-act opera, text S.Cammorano, after Sir Walter Scott's *The Bride of Lammermoor* (1819), music G.Donizetti, San Carlo, Naples 26.9.1835; Her Majesty's, London 5.4.1838; Queen's, Melbourne 12.12.1853.

Lucrezia Borgia. 2-act opera, text F.Romani, based on Victor Hugo's tragedy, *Lucrece Borgia* (1833), music G.Donizetti, Scala, Milan 26.12.1833; Her Majesty's, London 6.6.1839; Royal, Melbourne 7.12.1855, initially 1 performance.

Luisa Miller. 3-act opera, text S.Cammarano, based on Schiller's *Kabale und Liebe* (1784), music G.Verdi, San Carlo, Naples 8.12.1849; Sadler's Wells, London 3.6.1858; Royal, Melbourne 23.11.1859, initial 7 performances.

Lurline. 3-act opera, text E.Fitzball, music W.V.Wallace, Covent Garden, London 23.2.1860; Royal, Melbourne 1.4.1861, initial 5 performances.

Lustige Witwe, Die (The Merry Widow). 3-act operetta, text V.Leon and L.Stein, music F.Lehar, Theater an der Wien, Vienna 28.12.1905; Daly's, London 8.6.1907; Her Majesty's, Melbourne 16.5.1908, initial 66 performances.

Lustigen Weiber von Windsor, Die (The Merry Wives of Windsor). 3-act opera, text S.H.Mosenthal after William Shakespeare, music

C.Nicolai, Opera, Berlin 9.3.1849; Her Majesty's, London 3.5.1864; Queen's, Sydney 6.10.1877, initial 4 performances.

Lying Valet, The. 2-act comedy by David Garrick, Goodman's Fields, London November 1741; Emu Plains, 11.7.1825.

Lyster, William Saurin (1827-1880). Born in Dublin, the son of Captain Chaworth Lyster, there was nothing about W.S.Lyster's early life that can be seen as a preparation for its second half, in which he was head of an opera company. An invalid in his youth, he had to make long voyages for his health's sake (one was made to Australia in 1842). Later he was a member of the American merchant navy, after which he served in Nicaragua as one of General Walker's filibusters. After his army service he turned to acting, appearing at one time with Edwin Forrest, regarded by Americans as the greatest living tragedian. The production was R.M.Bird's *The Gladiator* (1831), in which Forrest played Spartacus and Lyster one of his fellow gladiators. Giving up acting, Lyster in 1856 formed the New York Opera Company, travelling with it throughout the USA with great success for the next four or five years. In 1861 he brought to Australia the first full-time opera group with a consistently high standard of performance to visit this country. Opening in Melbourne in March, the Lyster Opera Company gave 108 performances before the end of the year. After the first Melbourne season the company visited Sydney, opening in August at the Royal Victoria. From then on the company had annual seasons in Sydney and Melbourne, interspersed with visits to the other colonies and to New Zealand until 1867, after which there was a change of format and of name. These included seasons by the Lyster Smith Opera Company (1870), and the Lyster and Cagli Company (1872). In 1873 W.S.Lyster became, in effect, a company. The Opera House Company, founded in Melbourne, bought in Lyster's library, costumes and goodwill, and appointed him managing director. He died in Melbourne on 27.11.1880.

Above: Nellie Stewart as Mam'zelle Nitouche 1894
Below: Exterior Melbourne Royal 1855

M

Ma Mie Rosette. 2-act romantic opera, text J.Prével and A.Liorat, music P.Lacome and I.Caryll, Folies Dramatiques, Paris 4.2.1890; English version C.Dance, Globe, London 17.11.1892; Princess's, Melbourne 16.6.1894, initial 36 performances.

Macbeth. Tragedy by William Shakespeare, believed to have been first performed in London in 1605 or 1606; Royal, Sydney 7.9.1835.

——. 4-act opera, text F.M.Piave and A.Maffei, after Shakespeare, music G.Verdi, Pergola, Florence 14.3.1847; Prince of Wales, Sydney 5.7.1860, initial 3 performances.

McCloskey, J.J. (See: *For a Life*).

McCron, Francis Nesbitt (1809-1853). Born in Manchester, educated in Ireland, where he studied to become a surgeon. Tiring of hospital life he took to the stage, appearing in several English theatres with success, and finally in Glasgow. He returned to Ireland in 1840, and at the end of that year eloped with and married the daughter of an old and respected family. The pair came to Sydney in January 1841. Unable to obtain other employment, he again sought a theatrical engagement. At first he was unsuccessful, but in 1842 the Royal Victoria had not only to cope with competition from the new Olympic, but also lost its 2 leading actors to that theatre — C.Knowles and Eliza Winstanley. In desperation the manager of the Royal Victoria decided to give McCron, who had adopted the stage name of Francis Nesbitt, a trial. As far as Sydney was concerned, a star was born. He made his debut in the title role of Sheridan's *Pizarro* (1799) on 3.3.1842, and there was not one voice to condemn his performance. A week later the *Gazette* spoke for everybody when it said of Nesbitt that 'with the exception of a few passages [in Richard III] his acting was quite equal to that of any of the leading men of the London theatres, far superior to anything that this colony has ever witnessed.' But Nesbitt, it was soon revealed, was an alcoholic, and his lapses increased as each year passed. He toured the colonies, and then, in 1848, sailed for San Francisco. Back in Australia again in 1852, he tried to regain his former popularity, but his bouts of drunkenness militated against this. In 1853 he went to Victoria. Soon after arrival there he had to be carried from the stage during a performance of *William Tell* at Geelong. He died shortly afterwards in the Geelong Hospital.

Machinist. Backstage 'engineer' — the man who made things work. Stage machinery for creating wonders in the way of stage pictures, and for lifting and lowering individuals, and groups of fairies, demons, gods, spirits, and mortals is as old as the ancient Greek and Roman theatres, and as new as the latest Broadway spectacular. In the theatre of the eighteenth and at least the first half of the 19th century a good machinist was worth his weight in gold. He devised systems by which complete stage settings composed of wings, borders, and back shutters or cloths, could be changed by the turn of a winch or drum. Such a system may still be seen in use at the court theatres at Drottningholm in Sweden and at Litomyšl in Czechoslovakia. The machinist also exercised his ingenuity in transformation scenes used in pantomimes and in special burlesque and other productions, working in collaboration with the scenepainter, stage carpenter, and property man. In the second half of the 19th century, with the introduction of elaborate, free-standing and built-up stage settings, the machinist was no longer necessary. Manpower, which was cheap, replaced the winch, and stagehands were kept busy bringing in from either side of the stage, lowering from the flies, and pushing up from the cellar or understage area the various pieces which, when assembled, made up the scene. The process was reversed at high speed when the scene ended, and began again with the setting of the next scene. Hughes says that at various times Henry Irving had a backstage staff of 90 stagehands, 32 propertymen, 19 gasmen, and 20 limelightmen at the Lyceum for some productions. George Rignold was one of the few actor-producers in Australia who employed a large backstage staff. (See: Transformation scene).

Mackay, James Alexander Kenneth. (See: Parliamentarians).

Madame Butterfly. 1-act tragedy by D.Belasco and J.Long, from a story by Long, Herald Square, New York 5.3.1900; Duke of York's, London 28.4.1900; Her Majesty's, Sydney 27.7.1903, initial 11 performances.

Madama Butterfly. 2-act opera, text G.Illica and L.Giacosa, after Belasco and Long, music G.Puccini, Scala, Milan 17.11.1904; Covent Garden, London 10.7.1905; Royal, Sydney 26.3.1910, initial 24 performances.

Madame Favart. 3-act comic opera, text A.Duru and H.Chivot, music J.Offenbach, Folies Dramatiques, Paris 28.12.1878; Strand, London 12.4.1879; Royal, Sydney 17.9.1881, initial 18 performances.

Madame l'Archiduc. 3-act comic opera, text A.Millaud and L.Halévy, music J.Offenbach, Bouffes Parisiens, Paris 31.10.1874; Opéra Comique, London 13.1.1876. Prince of Wales, Melbourne 26.5.1877, initial 6 performances.

Madame Midas, the Gold Queen. 4-act drama by Phillip Beck and Fergus Hume, after Hume's novel (1888), Stratford, 7.7.1888; Her Majesty's, Sydney 23.3.1889, initial 23 performances.

Madame Sans-Gene. 3-act comedy by V.Sardou and E.Moreau, adapted by J.C.Carr, Lyceum, London 10.4.1897; Bijou, Melbourne 24.12.1898, initial 27 performances.

Maestro de Capella, Il. 2-act comic opera by F.Paer, Paris 1821; Royal, Melbourne as *The Music Master; or, La Prova d'un Opera* 4.2.1856; Prince of Wales, Sydney 5.5.1857. The Italian defies an exact English rendering. It can be 'chapel master,' 'musical director,' even 'conductor.'

Magda. 4-act drama by L.N.Parker, a translation of H.Sudermann's *Die Heimat* (1893). Lyric, London 3.6.1896; Royal, Sydney 10.3.1900, initial 6 performances.

Magic Cloak, The. 1-act operetta, text Bernard Espinasse, music E.P.Truman, Paddington Town Hall, Sydney 16.10.1896, initially 1 performance.

Magistrate, The. 3-act farce by A.W.Pinero, Court London 21.3.1885; Royal, Sydney 1.5.1886, initial 24 performances.

Maid Marian and Robin Hood. 3-act comic opera, text H.B.Smith, music R.de Koven, Park Hall, Camden Town, London 20.9.1890; Prince of Wales, London 5.2.1891; Princess's, Melbourne 16.6.1894, initial 19 performances.

Major Barbara. 3-act drama by George Bernard Shaw, Court, London 28.11.1905; Melbourne Repertory, Athenaeum Hall, 24.9.1913, initial 2 performances.

Makeshifts. 1-act play by Gertrude Robins, Gaiety, Manchester, 5.10.1908; Melbourne Repertory, Turn Verein Hall 25.9.1911, initially 1 performance.

Make-up. Basic substances used in facial make-up before the adoption of greasepaint were bismuth or French chalk powder; Fuller's Earth; chrome, vermilion, and bluepowders, and burnt cork, the whole being supplemented with coloured crayons or water paints. The coloured powders were sometimes used with a grease or oil base. Sticks of greasepaint were first marketed at the end of the 1870s or the beginning of the 1880s, but at first were not widely used. By 1882 a *homade au visage,* or wig paste was available to those who wished to use it. Wigs, beards, moustaches, and false skull and hairpieces, and noses of varying degrees of realism were always in use. The introduction of gas lighting called for many changes in the former use of make-up, as it was found that this form of lighting bleached some colours and darkened others. Electric lighting called for further adjustments, especially in the early days, when it had a bluish quality as opposed to the yellow of the gas flame.

Mam'zelle Nitouche. 3-act operetta, text H.Meilhac and A.Millaud, music Hervé (Florimond Ronger), Variétés, Paris 26.1.1883; Trafalgar Square, London 6.5.1893; Lyceum, Sydney 11.8.1894, initial 18 performances.

Man and His Makers. 4-act drama by W.Barrett and L.N.Parker, Lyceum, London 7.10.1899; Her Majesty's, Melbourne 3.8.1901, initial 6 performances.

Man and Superman. 3-act drama by George Bernard Shaw, Court, London 23.5.1905; Melbourne Repertory, Athenaeum Hall, 6.12.1912, initially 1 performance. This was given at Sydney Royal 20.12.1913 for a run of 15 performances.

Man and Wife. 5-act drama by George Darrell, from the Wilkie Collins novel (1870), Victoria Hall, Brisbane 5.6.1871, initial 2 performances.

Man From Outback, The; or, Stockwhip and Stirrup. 4-act drama by Albert Edmunds, King's, Melbourne 1.5.1909, initial 30 performances.

Man of Destiny, The. 1-act play by George Bernard Shaw, Grand, Croydon 1.7.1897; Sydney University Dramatic Society, Royal 19.7.1907, initially 1 performance.

Manfred. 3-act tragedy by George Gordon, Lord Byron, Covent Garden, London 29.10.1834; Royal Victoria, Sydney 10.7.1863, initial 7 performances.

Manola. 3-act comic opera, text H.B.Farnie from the French of E.Letterier and A.Vanloo, music C.Lecocq, Strand, London 11.2.1882; Opera House, Melbourne 26.12.1882, initial 29 performances.

Manon Lescaut. 4-act opera, text M.Praga, D.Oliva, G.Ricordi and others, music G.Puccini, Regio, Turin 1.2.1893; Covent Garden, London 14.5.1894; Her Majesty's, Melbourne 13.9.1913, initially 1 performance.

Manteaux Noirs, Les. 3-act comic opera, text W.Parke and H.Paulton, from the French of A.E.Scribe, music Bucalossi, Avenue,

London 3.6.1882; Opera House, Sydney 11.7.1883, initial 36 performances.

Manxman, The. 5-act drama by W.Barrett, from Hall Caine's novel (1894), Grand, Leeds 22.8.1894; Princess's, Melbourne 8.1.1898, initial 15 performances.

Mariana; or, The Thirty Thieves. 2-act musical comedy, text W.Risque, music E.Jones, Terry's, London 1.1.1901; Princess's, Melbourne 24.5.1902, initial 31 performances. Also called *Miss Mariana; The Thirty Thieves.*

Marionettes. Another manifestation of the Italian theatre, marionettes (*fantocci* or string puppets) were introduced into England by Italian showmen after the Restoration. According to F.S.Quadrico (*Theatre Notebook* 5:3 (1951) 65-67), by the middle of the 18th century the English had excelled their masters and had theatres (stages) with figures 4ft high and finely dressed. The first mention of marionettes in Australia was made in 1852, when it was announced that a show would be opened in the saloon of the Royal Hotel, George Street, Sydney 'with five scenes and almost 200 mechanical figures.' The scenes consisted of views of Waterford, Rome, the Alps, China, and the interior of the Great Exhibition in London. Accompanying figures to each scene went through a series of everyday movements and activities. A different act-drop was exhibited between each scene, and the whole had an orchestral accompaniment. Admission cost two shillings for front seats, one for back. By the following year the Royal Marionette Theatre, as it was called, had moved to the vacant Olympic Circus building in Castlereagh Street. For the opening on 11.4.1853 admission charges were increased to three shillings for box seats, two for reserved seats, and one for the pit. The first programme in the new setting consisted of the burlesque *Bombastes Furioso* (1810), a number of scenes with moving figures as before, and a recital by a group of singers. This entertainment received general newspaper support, with frequent 'puffs,' including the following:

> The stage is small, but fitted up with care,
> And has about it elegance of air,
> Where horses once played many a circus freak
> Brown's able puppets do all things but speak.
> That want, however, human beings supply,
> They act the mouth — the puppets limb and eye;
> Each to the other gives a certain grace —
> Who doubts the fact? Go, sceptic, view the place,
> If unconverted then, 'tis understood
> Your head is like the puppets' — made of wood.

Soon after its opening at the Olympic Circus the Royal Marionette Theatre was apparently destroyed, or partly destroyed by fire, and nothing more was heard publicly of its proprietor, Albany Brown.

Maritana. 3-act opera, text E.Fitzball after the melodrama, *Don Cesar de Bazan,* by A.d'Ennery and P.Dumanoir, music V.Wallace, Drury Lane, London 15.11.1845; Royal Victoria, Sydney 19.4.1849. The combined Sydney and Melbourne performance figures between 1849 and 1908 show this to have been the most popular of all the operas of the period. *Maritana* was performed 236 times in Sydney and 224 in Melbourne — a total 460 performances between 19.4.1849 and 7.11.1908.

Marjorie. 3-act comic opera, text L.Clifton and J.Dilley, music W.Slaughter, Prince of Wales, London 18.7.1889; Princess's, Melbourne 20.12.1890, initial 10 performances.

Marmondelle the Moor. 5-act tragedy by Thomas Walker, Royal, Sydney 22.7.1893, initial 6 performances. (See: Parliamentarians).

Marriage of Figaro, The. 4-act comic opera, text T.Holcroft, after L.da Ponte, Mozart's music 'adapted' by Henry Bishop, Covent Garden, London 6.3.1819; Royal, Sydney 11.5.1833. In this version Bishop omitted the original overture and eight of Mozart's best numbers, substituted 10 of his own, and 6 dances. He even altered the few Mozart pieces he retained. (See: Nozzi de Figaro, Le).

Married and Buried. (See: *Illustrious Stranger, The*).

Martha, oder Der Markt von Richmond. (Martha; or, Richmond Market). 4-act comic opera, text F.Riese (pseud. 'W.Friedrich'), after J.H.V.Saint-George's ballet-pantomime *Lady Henrietta; ou La Servante de Greenwich,* music F.von Flotow, Karntnertor, Vienna 25.11.1847; Drury Lane, London 4.7.1849; Royal, Melbourne 24.6.1856, initial 4 performances.

Martyrs, Les. (See: *Poliuto*).

Marvellous Melbourne. 5-act drama by Alfred Dampier and J.H.Wranghan, Alexandra, Melbourne 19.1.1889, initial 36 performances. Rewritten and re-titled *Slaves of Sydney,* Royal, Sydney 13.5.1893, initial 6 performances.

Masaniello. A title used indiscriminately for various stage works. The correct sequence seems to be:
17.2.1825 — Drama by the English dramatist, G.Soane, with music by H.Bishop, Drury Lane, London.
27.12.1827 — *Masaniello; ou, Le Pecheur Napolitain,* opera by M.E.Carafa, text C.Moreau and A.M.Lafortelle, Opera Comique, Paris.
29.2.1828 — *La Muette de Portici,* opera by D.Auber, text A.E.Scribe and G.Delavigne, Opera House, Paris.
The confusion with these productions is twofold. The title *Masaniello* has been used for all of them, and Henry Bishop not only wrote the music for the drama, but apparently also, at a later stage, 'arranged' or

adapted the music of Auber's opera as he did Mozart's *Le Nozze di Figaro*, to the disadvantage of both. All that can be done now is to record the fact that the first musical stage production called *Masaniello* was performed at the Royal Victoria, Sydney 8.9.1838, the work being credited to Auber and Bishop. (See: *Muette de Portici, La*).

Mascotte, La. (The Mascot). 3-act operetta, text A.Duru and H.C.Chivot, music E.Audran, Bouffes Parisiens, Paris 28.12.1880; Royal, Sydney 25.10.1882, initial 48 performances.

Masked Ball, The. (See: *Gustavus III; Un Ballo in Maschera*).

Masks and Faces; or, Before and Behind the Curtain. 2-act comedy by C.Reade and T.Taylor, Haymarket, London 20.11.1852; Royal Victoria, Sydney 25.9.1856.

Mason, Charles Kemble (1805-1875). Born in England, the son of Jane, a younger sister of John Philip Kemble, and said to have been physically very like his famous uncle. Made his first stage appearance as Young Norval in John Home's tragedy of *Douglas* (1756) at Covent Garden in 1823. From 1829 to 1831 leading man at Bristol Royal. Made American debut at Philadelphia in 1834. In Australia from 1853 to the beginning of 1857. At first, Australian critics complained of his inability to remember his lines, and the gagging or ad-libbing in which he indulged. At this time this was apparently an ingrained weakness of his. Kathleen Barker quotes his cousin, Fanny Kemble's account of her experience when acting with him at Bristol in 1831. But by 1856 the *People's Advocate* in Sydney, which had been one of his severest critics, was able to report a considerable improvement. As well as appearing in several of Shakespeare's plays, and giving public readings in Shakespeare, Mason also acted in *Werner, Guy Mannering,* and other popular plays of the period. He was given a farewell benefit in Sydney in 1857, and later that year was acting in San Francisco. In 1864-65 he was back in New York, at the Wintergarden, where he played the Ghost in Edwin Booth's production of *Hamlet*. His final stage engagement seems to have been during a season with Mrs Scott-Siddons in Philadelphia in 1869.

Mastersingers, The. (See: *Meistersinger von Nürnberg, Die*).

Matilda of Hungary. 3-act opera, text A.Bunn, music V.Wallace, Drury Lane, London 22.2.1847; Royal Victoria, Sydney 7.3.1850.

Matinee. Dating in England from about the 1850s, matinees were at first called 'morning performances,' a direct translation of the French *matinée*, even though those performances did not start until after midday. In the late 1870s or 1880s the Anglicised matinee was adopted, even though these were still afternoon performances. Strictly speaking, a matinee is an afternoon representation of an evening performance, but in the 19th century Australian theatre, from about the 1880s, matinee performances of pantomimes and comic operas were curtailed versions of evening performances. Sometimes matinees were given once a week, on Saturday; sometimes twice, on Wednesday and Saturday.

Matrimonio Segreto, Il (The Secret Marriage). 2-act opera buffa, text G.Bertati after G.Colman and D.Garrick's drama of that name, music D.Cimarosa, Burgtheater, Vienna 7.2.1792; London 11.1.1794; Prince of Wales, Sydney 21.9.1871, initially 1 performance.

Maximilian; or, The Empress and the Traitor. 3-act historical drama by R.P.Whitworth, Haymarket, Melbourne 28.10.1867, initial 5 performances.

Mayor of Garret, The. 2-act farce by S.Foote, Haymarket, London 20.6.1763; Emu Plains, 8.5.1830.

Mayor of Tokio, The. 2-act musical comedy, text R.Carle, music W.Peters, Hippodrome, New York 4.12.1905; Adelphi, Sydney 2.5.1914, initial 16 performances.

Measure for Measure. Tragi-comedy by William Shakespeare, believed to have been first performed in London in 1603 or 1604; Royal, Melbourne 22.10.1860.

Medieval theatre. Based on a principally vernacular religious drama which drew for its stories on the Bible. Mystery, miracle, and morality plays or pageants of the period were closely associated with the church all over Europe. The plays were conducted in cycles, principally by the trade guilds, the York cycle, for instance, being made up of 42 separate pageants. (See: *Everyman. Trial Before Herod, The*).

Meistersinger von Nürnberg, Die. 3-act music-drama, text and music Richard Wagner, Munich 21.6.1868; Drury Lane, London 30.5.1882; Her Majesty's, Melbourne 16.8.1913, initially 1 performance.

Melba, Nellie (1861-1931). Name adopted by the later world famous soprano, Mrs Charles Armstrong, in tribute to the city of Melbourne where she was born at Richmond on 19 May, and christened Helen Porter Mitchell. In 1881 her mother and youngest sister died, and the following year she went to Queensland with her father, David Mitchell, a master builder. Here she met and married Charles Frederick Nesbitt Armstrong. The marriage was not a success, and in 1884 she returned to Melbourne and began earnest consideration of her future career as a singer. Receiving initial lessons from Mary Ellen Christian and Pietro Cecchi in Melbourne, in 1886 she went to London, and then to Paris. Here the famous mezzo-soprano, Madame Mathilda Marchesi recognised her potential and undertook her training. She made her operatic debut as Gilda in *Rigoletto* at Brussels on 12 October 1887, and from then on began the deliberate and determined climb to world success which ultimately made her *prima donna assoluta*. She adopted the surname Melba in the same year. Her first London appearance was as Lucia in *Lucia di Lammermoor* at Covent Garden on 24.5.1888. Paris was next, the following year, where she sang Ophelia in *Hamlet*. She made her first appearance with the famous Monte Carlo Opera at the Monte Carlo Theatre as Juliet in Gounod's *Romeo and Juliet* on 15.12.1890. 3 years later she made her New York debut at the Metropolitan Opera House. In 1900, after a lapse of 10 years, she returned to Monte Carlo as *prima donna assoluta* to sing Violetta in *La Traviata*. 2 years later she sang the role of Mimi in that theatre's first performance of *La Boheme*, her Rodolfo being the famous tenor, Enrico Caruso. It is said that her fee of 6000 francs per performance at Monte Carlo in 1900 had two years later jumped to 8400 francs a performance. This meant that in 1900 she received 23 650 francs for her Monte Carlo appearances, and 42 000 in 1902. The truth is that although she was one of the most remarkable sopranos of her era, she was also a woman with tremendous drive and business acumen. She always insisted on being paid more than the other stars who sang with her, even Enrico Caruso, and when she began to make gramophone recordings her stipulation was that her records should always be sold for a shilling more than anyone else's. In 1918 Nellie Melba was created Dame Commander of the British Empire for her work for the Red Cross during World War I. She made her last appearance in America in 1920, and her last in London two years later. She died in Sydney on 23 February.

Melbourne, Theatres in.
1 Royal Pavilion (1841). Melbourne's theatrical development in many ways paralleled Sydney's. On 8.1.1841, when Melbourne was barely 6 years old, and under the control of Sydney, it was announced that a wooden theatre 65ft long and 35ft wide was to be built in Bourke Street, alongside the Eagle Inn. The building had a pit, a series of boxes built around the walls on the veranda principle, and a gallery. This Royal Pavilion Saloon, as it was at first called, was opened with a concert on 12.4.1841. Box tickets were 10s 6d, pit 7s, and gallery 4. Some days before this concert the proprietor, Thomas Hodge, was advised that Sir George Gipps in Sydney had refused a theatrical licence for the Pavilion. Despite this, Hodge held a second concert, the management being in the hands of G.Buckingham from the Sydney theatres. The Melbourne police magistrate threatened to have performers and audience brought before him and charged as 'rogues and vagabonds,' if there were any more performances. Following this, several applications were made for a licence, without success, and finally Hodge decided to force the government's hand. He held another concert on New Year's Eve, and on 26.1.1842 was fined the maximum £50, or 6 months' imprisonment. Less than a month later Buckingham was able to advertise that permission had been granted for an amateur performance on 21.2.1842 at the 'Theatre Royal Melbourne,' as the

*Left: Auditorium
Melbourne Royal 1869*

*Above: Exterior Melbourne
Olympic 1855
Right: Exterior Melbourne
Royal 1872*

Pavilion was now called, in aid of the hospital fund. The plays, the first to be given in Melbourne, were *The Widow's Victim* (1835), and *The Lottery Ticket* (1826). In August 1842 the pit and stage of the theatre were lowered to give more height to the interior, and thus allow increased accommodation. An upper tier of boxes was also installed, giving the theatre pit, boxes, upper tier of boxes, and gallery. Admission charges were: Boxes and upper boxes 5s (half-price 3), pit 4s (half-price 2s 6d), gallery 2s 6d (half-price 1s 6d). In August 1843 C.Knowles succeeded Buckingham as manager. Until his death the following year he tried without success to make the theatre pay. He was succeeded in turn by S.Cameron (9.7.1844) and F.Nesbitt (1845). Then came competition, the one thing the shaky Royal could not combat. It was used as a theatre for the last time on 24.4.1845.

2 Queen's (1845). The *Port Phillip Herald,* which first announced that John Thomas Smith was building a brick and stone theatre on the corner of Queen and Little Bourke Streets, in 1845 fed the public with regular paragraphs about its progress. One of these, dealing with the opening performance, said the theatre was 'elegantly decorated' and the stage scenery 'beautifully painted.' A later paragraph said the theatre was 'the most complete theatre in the colonies.' Its final puff said the building was strong and durable, the accommodation and decorations creditable, 'and will be made very pleasing and comfortable.' Which was another way of saying that, like many before it and others to come after it, the Queen's was opened before work on its interior was completed. 'The decorations are not intended for daylight, and as such they have not that grand effect upon the observer by day, but we opine they will have good effect by lamp or candle light,' the *Port Phillip Patriot* reported. The theatre had three 'floors' — pit, boxes, and gallery. Admission charges were 5s for the boxes, 4 for pit, and 3 for the gallery. It was estimated that between 800 and 900 people could be accommodated. 2 days after the opening the *Port Phillip Gazette* said the theatre was 'beautifully decorated, and when the arrangements are complete — which we learn will be in the course of a fortnight — the Queen's will be the most tastefully fitted up theatre in the colonies.' The theatre was opened on 21.4.1845 for a benefit performance for the actor John Davies (or Davis), who doubled as actor at the Royal and reporter on the *Port Phillip Gazette.* The first of the regular dramatic performances was given on 1.5.1845. One of the theatre's most successful seasons was that conducted by George Coppin in the late 1840s, but the theatre did not have a long life. It was popular during the gold rush years, but competition from new theatres proved too much for it. The building itself lasted into the present century as a furniture factory.

3 Royal Amphitheatre (1854). Construction of this wooden amphitheatre on the corner of Spring and Little Bourke Streets was begun in 1854. It was called Atley's Amphitheatre, after buildings of that name

Above: Smoking room Her Majesty's Melbourne 1900
Below: Crush-room (lounge) Her Majesty's Melbourne 1900

in London devoted to equestrian entertainments. The building was 110ft long, 80ft wide, and about 40ft high. At one end it had a semicircular gallery called the half-crown gallery; at the other was a stage for dramatic performances. On either side of the quadrangle between stage and gallery were rows of pit seats and dress circle boxes, and in the centre of it was a circle for equestrian and circus events. The amphitheatre was opened in September 1854 with a series of concerts, pending the arrival of an equestrian company from London, due in November. The amphitheatre was not a success, and in 1856 the building, then described by the auctioneers as built 'substantially of stone,' was offered for sale. George Coppin, convinced there was an audience for variety and other entertainments as well as for drama, leased the building in February 1856, when the *Argus* announced that it was to become a 'regular temple of the drama.' The interior was remodelled, redecorated, and lighted with gas. Under its new guise, as the Royal Amphitheatre, admission to the opening performance cost 3s for side boxes and stalls, 2 for the pit and promenade, and 1 for the gallery. The Bacchus Minstrels gave the opening programme, and later there were dramatic performances of various kinds. But by 12.4.1856 Coppin had to announce that after a season of 8 weeks the amphitheatre would have to close because of lack of support. The building was then used intermittently until work was begun in 1857 on transforming it into the first Princess's.

4 Royal (1855). The first 'grand' theatre to be built in Australia, and said to have been large enough to rival in size and accommodation London's Drury Lane and Covent Garden. In fact, like Sydney's Royal Victoria, for many years its size made it a losing proposition for lessees. When the *Argus* announced in May 1855 John Black's proposal for a theatre with a frontage in Bourke Street and extending back to Little Bourke Street, it said the cost would be about £60 000. When it was finally opened on 16.7.1855 the ensuing shortage of and consequent high cost of labour and materials because of the gold rushes was said to have forced this figure up to £95 000, though the accuracy of these figures is doubtful. The Royal, as it was called, had stalls (the first seven rows on the ground floor, seating 200), pit (1,100), and a range of 3 galleries or tiers above. The first was the dress circle (460), the second and upper circle (600), and the third the gallery (700). The gallery also had its sides partitioned off into boxes called 'slips' or 'side slips' (150) In addition, there were 15 private boxes (90), 7 in the dress circle, 2 in the upper circle, and 3 on each side of the proscenium, so that this theatre could comfortably seat 3300, or more if there was a crush. The proscenium, a 12ft deep area between the orchestra and the proscenium arch, was 45ft wide, and had two large Corinthian columns on either side, supporting an entablature ornamented with medallions picked out in gold, and surmounted by the Royal coat of arms. These columns were

transparent, and were lighted inside. The proscenium arch was 38ft wide (curtain), the stage having back flats 21ft high and 14ft wide, and wings 21ft high and 8ft wide. This gave each back scene a width of 28ft, extended on either side by the 8ft of the wings. The act drop was a copy of Turner's reconstruction of ancient Rome, surrounded by a frame in gold. The ceiling of the auditorium was a huge circle enclosing two smaller circles, with a radiating glory or halo as a centrepiece. The convex fronts of the tiers were decorated with rosettes and wreaths in relief. The back and side walls of the dress and upper circles were papered in dark crimson, while the walls of the pit were covered with a 'representation of oak panelling.' 16 brackets were distributed around the front of the upper circle and gallery, from each of which was suspended a small gas chandelier or gasalier, with five burners each. Although the theatre was 40ft high from the floor of the pit to the tie beam of the roof, this height did not continue to the stage, which, when the theatre opened, was only 30ft high. There was a bumper house for the opening on 16.7.1855, but few of them after that. The gold boom was almost over, and the big spenders of the early 1850s were dwindling away. In April 1856 the Royal was put up for sale, for the owner was bankrupt. The following month Coppin, gifted with a great deal of theatrical foresight, was announced as the buyer for £21 000. After minor alterations, including a new proscenium, he opened with a season of opera, which at once put him in the red. Over the next few years lessees and managers followed one after the other, and the theatre was many times renovated and cleansed, but failures outnumbered successes, and managers who broke even or made a profit were the lucky few. In March 1872 the theatre was destroyed by fire.

5 Olympic (1855). While he was in England in 1854 the actor and entrepreneur George Coppin bought in Manchester an iron building 'complete in every way at a cost of about £5000.' This was a prefabricated iron structure made up of iron uprights and principals, and sheets of corrugated iron, used by Coppin as the shell of his Olympic on the corner of Stephen and Lonsdale Streets. The true picture of this theatre is contained in the report published in the *Age* of 5.6.1855, and the illustration of its exterior, in which the curved roof of the original iron auditorium is plainly to be seen. The *Age* reported: 'The exterior portion of the theatre is of iron, and was, together with a large portion of the woodwork, constructed in England; it remained, however, for our colonial artists to design the actual form and figure of the interior arrangements . . .' These consisted of a pit (the first few rows were stalls), dress circle of boxes 24ft deep facing the stage, and boxes 8ft deep along each side wall. They also included the 33ft wide proscenium arch with its gilded Corinthian columns or pillars on either side, the auditorium colour scheme of green, pink, and French white, and the medallions with scenes from Shakespeare, Otway, and Lord Lytton

which decorated the fronts of the dress circle and side boxes. The height of the auditorium from the pit floor to the roof was variously given as 26ft to 30ft. According to the *Argus* this theatre seated 1150: 450 in the dress circle and boxes, and 700 in the pit and stalls. Brick and glass additions were made to the front and sides of the auditorium, including a hotel and grog shop, and a stage with neither cellar nor flies was built on to the back. Reports on this theatre's dimensions conflict, no two of them agreeing on all points. It seems to have been a rather uncomfortable auditorium, hot in the summer and cold in the winter, without a ceiling — there was simply the low-pitched corrugated iron roof painted blue-white dotted with gold stars. Seats in the boxes and stalls were backed, and covered with crimson cloth; the rest were backless benches. Lighting for the first few months was by oil lamps, gas being installed six months after the theatre was opened. By April 1856 this theatre had, at least in Coppin's eyes, fulfilled its purpose, and he tried to sell it. Writing in 1872 of the 1855 building as he had known it, a correspondent in the *Australasian* said it was 'like a dissenting chapel in the severely evangelical neighbourhood of a very unpicturesque manufacturing town in the south of England.' In 1886 another writer in the same weekly said that internally the Olympic had 'resembled a chapel with a rectangular gallery for its dress circle . . .' In 1857 the theatre became a dance hall. 2 years later it was reopened as a theatre for a brief spell. In 1860 the building was converted to a Turkish baths. By 1890 it was being used as a furniture warehouse, and in 1894 it was demolished. It could be said that the Olympic lived only while it housed the Shakespearian actor, G.V.Brooke, for whose use it was built. A set of farewell verse published in Melbourne *Punch* at the end of Brooke's season in 1856 provides a pen-picture of the theatre, and of the regard in which Brooke was held.

> Now fade the oil-fed foot-lights on the sight,
>   And darkness falls upon the chandelier;
> And, with a thrifty haste, each globe of light
>   Is dowsed, that decorates the sole box tier . . .
>
> Behind that sombre baize, that curtain green,
>   Stage-sweepers ply the dust-compelling broom;
> Each weary actor, vanish'd from the scene,
>   Disrobes himself in yonder dressing-room . . .
>
> To me, while musing 'neath this iron roof,
>   Whereon the patt'ring rain falls thick and fast,
> Comes the box-keeper, with a mild reproof,
>   And asks why I should linger to the last. . . .
>
> 'Next week we'll miss him in the 'tin stew-pot,'
>   Behind the foot-lights where he used to be,
> Another actor like him we ha'nt got,
>   To draw, there's none like this here G.V.B.'

Above: Auditorium Melbourne Princess's 1857
Below: Exterior Melbourne Princess's 1857

6 Princess's (1857). The first attempt to turn the Royal Amphitheatre into the Princess's was a half-hearted affair. Once again the theatre was opened before work was completed on it, and there were many complaints. The interior was converted into stalls and pit, and what seems to have been one gallery or tier with boxes in front and the dress circle behind. The stage was brought forward to give it greater depth, for the theatre was to be opened with a season of opera. The proscenium was flanked on either side by almost lifesize statues: Music, and Drama, while the general colour scheme of the auditorium was white and gold. Gas lighting was used, with several small gasaliers suspended from the pillars supporting the roof. An advertisement for the opening on 16.4.1857 said the theatre could provide accommodation for 2500. The opera was a success on the opening night, the theatre was not. Ventilation was bad, the house was poorly lighted, and promises of 'magnificence' had not been kept. One critic wrote that managers were foolish to speak extravagantly of 'enormous expenditure,' 'total remodelling,' and so on and then to present the public, as the manager of the Princess's had done, with what was plainly a makeshift. After a few years the first of many changes were made in the Princess's. In 1861 the pit floor was raised and the stalls area enlarged. A new proscenium and act drop were installed, and a gas chandelier hung from the centre of the ceiling. But the Princess's was not a popular theatre, and before its complete renovation was announced in 1865 had been vacant for almost 2 years. This time the interior was gutted, the ceiling was raised to a height of 32ft, and the dress circle was rebuilt with a curved front instead of the previous octagonal shape. A new stage, 58ft deep and 79ft wide was installed, with a proscenium arch 33ft wide and 32ft high. The slightly curved or domed ceiling was painted with figures reclining among clouds. The seating was changed so that the dress circle held 350, stalls 350, boxes 250, and pit 700. Again there was public interest for a while, followed by indifference, and the theatre had long periods of disuse until, in 1886, it was demolished.

7 Prince of Wales (1860). In the 1850s there was a building in Lonsdale Street known as Tattersalls. Over the years it had been used as ballroom, stables, saleroom, and vegetable market. Then, in 1858, an American circus company transformed the building into the American Hippodrome, seating about 1000, and devoted to circus performances. It was opened on 6.7.1858, and apparently consisted of pit and gallery, with a circus ring. The popularity of the circus waned, and by May 1860 the Americans were transforming the building into the Prince of Wales, with dress circle, boxes and pit designed to accommodate 1500. The stage, 68ft wide and 60ft deep, had a detachable equestrian circle or ring which could be taken up in eight minutes. The new theatre was opened on 24.5.1860 with a programme of equestrian acts, vaudeville, and ballet. By July it had changed over to drama. 2 months later the

proprietor or proprietors were in the Insolvency Court, and the theatre fell into the familiar now open, now closed pattern. At one period the pit was boarded over level with the stage and the building used for promenade concerts. After this it reverted to drama, to opera, and to the circus. Finally an attempt was made early in 1862 to revive public interest by renovating and repainting the building, and changing its name to Marsh's Royal Lyceum. At the end of 1862 its scenery, properties, and fittings were sold by the mortgagees, and the Prince of Wales ceased to exist.

8 Haymarket (1862). Opened in Bourke Street on 15.9.1862, this theatre had seating for 2500 in its stalls, pit, dress circle, and upper circle, with room for 400 more if required. In the same building, on the street front above the main entrance, was the Apollo Music Hall, said to have accommodated 1500. The theatre and hall were approached through a courtyard-vestibule having a fountain in its centre, the whole open to the sky, but surrounded by a covered walk. The stalls-pit area of the theatre measured 70ft by 62ft, the height from the floor of the stalls to the ceiling being 50ft. The pit had backed benches, while the stalls and dress circle seats were covered in crimson damask, and the upper circle seats in green morocco leather, making a bright contrast with the general colour scheme of white, gold, and blue. The front of the dress circle was only 35ft from the stage, which had a depth of 80ft 6ins. The auditorium was lighted by an ornate crystal chandelier hanging from the centre of the ceiling, and by ornamental brackets around the front of the dress circle. This, and the front of the upper circle, was ornamented with white and gold scrollwork on a blue satin ground. The painted ceiling was divided into panels by an ornamental frieze painted to imitate raised ornament. In each of the 4 panels was a painted medallion representing the seasons. There were no stage boxes (these were in the front of the dress circle) and as a result there was a depth of only 4ft between the front of the stage and the proscenium arch, which was like a picture frame of curved gold fretwork on a white ground. The surmounting entablature, decorated with the masks of Tragedy, Comedy, and Farce, was supported by four slender gold-twined columns. Opened in a blaze of glory, the theatre never really took on with the public. The acoustics were bad, and because the dress circle was carried so close to the stage, the pitites could neither see nor be seen by the other occupants of the theatre. Towards the end of its brief life it was more often closed than not.

9 Duke of Edinburgh (1868). New name given to the Haymarket in January that year in compliment to the visiting Duke. The theatre was destroyed by fire three years later.

10 Royal (1872). Plans to build a theatre to replace the burnt-out Royal of 1855 were announced in May 1872, the foundation stone was laid in June, and the theatre was opened on 6 November. The new

Above: Promenade saloon Academy of Music Melbourne 1876
Below: Exterior Melbourne Haymarket 1862

building was 12ft higher than the old. All entrances, except that to the gallery, were in Bourke Street. A central entrance through a 26ft long hallway led to the main vestibule, 66ft long and 32ft wide, giving access to the pit, stalls, dress, and upper circles. On the dress circle floor there was the usual cafe, billiard room, and saloon. The auditorium was 85ft deep, 62ft wide, and 60ft high from the floor of the pit to the dome in the ceiling. The pit seated 1000 (more when there was a crush) on plain wooden forms; the stalls 550 on cane-bottomed seats; the dress circle 550 in upholstered seats covered with rep; the upper circle 650 in seats covered with American leather (cotton-based kind of oil cloth), and the gallery 1200 on wooden forms. Melbourne still had the largest theatre in Australia. The ceiling had a central dome 42ft in diameter, from which hung a large chandelier. The dome was painted with London and Melbourne scenes, and with portrait busts of G.V.Brooke and W.Montgomery. The ceiling above the stalls was painted with a representation of G.Reno's fresco, *Aurora*. The picture-frame proscenium was 28ft wide and 31ft high, with fluted columns on either side supporting an entablature painted with representations of musical instruments. The stage was 120ft deep and 62ft wide. The theatre was opened before work on it was completed, and there were complaints about its many inconveniences. Changes were made from time to time. In 1880, while the seating was the same as in 1872, the depth of the stage was said to be only 90ft, with a height of 48ft to the gridiron. There was a property room 72ft by 24ft; a scene dock of the same size with about 120 scenes, and a painting room 40ft by 24ft. The stage floor had 9 traps. The scenes, that is the flats and/or backdrops, measured 25ft by 18ft 9ins. In 1891 the proscenium was brought forward 10ft into the auditorium, which was redecorated. Major reconstruction was also carried out in 1904.

11 Prince of Wales Opera House (1872). This theatre in Bourke Street, more often referred to as the Prince of Wales, and sometimes simply as the Opera House, was opened on 24.8.1872. It seated 2500 in stalls, pit, dress circle, family circle, and gallery — a figure increased on occasion to 3000. There were three entrances in Bourke Street, one to the dress circle through a vestibule 50ft by 15ft, lined with rows of Doric columns, with an enriched cornice, a coved ceiling decorated with gold stars on a blue ground, tiled floor, and polished bluestone staircase to the dress circle. A second entrance led to the gallery, and a third to a vestibule giving access to pit, stalls, and family circle. The stalls were entered through a corridor or passageway under the pit which opened on either side of the auditorium. This gave more room to the pit, and free passage from one side of the stalls to the other without having to walk through the audience. The *Illustrated Australian News* said the height of the auditorium from pit floor to central dome was 50ft; the proscenium was 28ft wide, and the stage 63ft wide and 65ft deep. The *Argus* said the

proscenium was 28ft wide and 30ft high; the stage 63ft wide and 70ft deep, and the distance from the front curtain to the front of the dress circle was 45ft. A large gas 'sunlight' in the central dome provided the only lighting for the auditorium, doing away with chandeliers and light brackets. The main auditorium colour scheme was in white and gold. In 1882 this theatre was lighted with electricity, but it led a chequered existence, housing everything from opera to the most amateurish entertainments. In 1893 it became a variety house for a while, and was renamed the Alhambra and Varieties. It ended its life as a livery stable, and was demolished in 1900.

12 Academy of Music (1876). Small, elegantly decorated theatre to seat about 1500, built over an arcade which ran between Bourke and Little Collins Streets. The theatre, suited for productions in which 'great stage display is not essential,' had no pit, the ground floor being given over entirely to stalls. Eight feet above this was the dress circle, and above this the family circle and gallery in the one tier. A wide approach corridor to the theatre, 120ft long, was fitted up as a promenade or saloon. This had a tesselated floor and was decorated with gilt framed mirrors, statuettes, and Japanese vases filled with artificial flowers. A corridor on the eastern side was fitted up as a billiard room and bar. The auditorium ceiling was painted with classical figure subjects by the scenepainter, Harry Grist. Opened on 6.11.1876, the building was renamed the Bijou 4 years later.

13 Bijou (1880). Name given to the former Academy of Music. In 1882 the *Imperial Review* reported that this theatre was a fire trap, as the whole of its audience was assembled upstairs. 7 years later the theatre was destroyed by fire, but without loss of life.

14 Alexandra (1886). A theatre to seat 2800, built in Exhibition Street and opened on 1.10.1886. Work on the building started in June 1885, but completion was delayed because of a shortage of money. The 77ft by 87ft auditorium (the *Age* gave the dimensions as 67ft by 77ft) had a flat floor to its stalls and pit, the height from the floor to the ceiling being 47ft. Above the pit was a tier containing the dress and family circles, while a second tier contained the upper circle. There were no stage boxes. The flat stage was 50ft deep, and 54ft to the gridiron. It was one of the first to be built without the groove system for scenery. The proscenium opening of 33ft by 29ft was 5ft wider than that at the Royal. The prevailing colour in the auditorium was pale blue, with light amber-coloured walls. Seats were upholstered in crimson, and the ornamental grille in front of each tier was in gold with a crimson backing. The dome in the centre of the ceiling was pale blue powdered with silver stars. The proscenium was framed in two large gold mouldings, with a coved space between, the main colours being in gold, cream, and bronze green. The theatre was lighted by gas and electricity, the central light in the auditorium being a 'lightning spray of electric light.' By 1891 this

theatre was said to have been in such a bad state of disrepair that it had to be redecorated throughout. Up to the first few months of 1900 it was Melbourne's principal melodrama theatre, greatly favoured by Alfred Dampier and William Anderson. For a brief period in 1897 it was known as the Queen's. J.C.Williamson Ltd took over the theatre in 1900.

15 Princess's (1886). 8 months after the first Princess's was destroyed by fire a new one, built by Williamson, Garner, and Musgrove, was ready for use. This had an imposing architectural exterior, and was replete with every comfort and convenience. The auditorium, lighted with the mixture of gas and electric lights usual at this time, consisted of stalls, dress, and family circle, the first two of which terminated in private stage boxes between the usual Corinthian columns. This theatre was said to seat the same number as the Royal. The prevailing colours of the interior were peacock blue, warm cream, and dead gold. The proscenium was framed in rich gold, above it being a group of figures on a gold ground representing the muses. The act drop was painted to represent the involved folds of a voluminous stage curtain, a medallion in the centre being painted with the usual classical temple subject. On either side of the proscenium arch were alcoves or lunettes, each covered with a painting of allegorical figures. Between acts the paintings slid aside to reveal a fern grotto with a trickling stream of water. According to the *Argus,* 'a current of cool air flowed into the building from the four openings.' Then the covering or ceiling over the dome of the auditorium 'silently disappeared,' letting the 'vitiated atmosphere' out and fresh air in. Besides its attractive interior this building also had a grand entrance foyer which was said to have the same effect on the visitor as that experienced by one 'ascending the corresponding portion of the house in the Grand Opera of Paris, the Stadt Theater in Frankfurt, and the Grand Theatre in Bordeaux . . .' The theatre was opened on 18.12.1886. Almost ten years later it was redecorated in what was called modern Renaissance style, with a colour scheme of electric blue, amber, fawn, grey, and gold. The sliding roof was painted to represent a heliotrope and white striped satin velarium, and the dome itself was encircled by a painted balustrade over which leaned children holding bands or festoons of flowers. The whole of the stage arch was recoloured, and the proscenium decorated with painted fruits, flowers, and musical instruments. The dress circle seats were upholstered in electric blue plush, and the floor laid with Wilton carpet.

16 Bijou (1890). This, the second by this name, was opened on 5.4.1890. It seated 1700 people in an auditorium 44ft high and 80ft deep, having 3 levels, the ground floor (stalls), dress, and family circles. The front of each tier was 40ft from the stage, while the stage itself, 50ft wide, had a ceiling 58ft above. Lighting throughout was by means of 670 incandescent electric lamps and 3 arc lights. The auditorium had central

lights in the dome, and bunches of light in the form of poppies at various angles in the ceiling. On either side of the proscenium arch were 3 stage boxes. The front curtain was of terracotta-coloured velvet. When lifted it revealed an act drop painted to represent a lace curtain, with the usual medallion in its centre, this time of Comedy banishing Melancholy, against a background of classical architecture. The nude figures in this were painted by Tom Roberts. An enormous saucer-shaped area in the centre of the ceiling had a ventilating grille around its perimeter. Special provision was made for the speedy clearing of this theatre in the event of fire, with passages leading from the auditorium and under the stage to Little Collins Street. Unfortunately, because of space problems, the actors had to endure cramped conditions backstage in small and meagre dressing rooms, reached from the stage by very steep 'tiny iron spiral staircases like corkscrews.' The general appearance of this theatre, according to the *Age,* was 'one of comfort and brightness rather than of splendour or magnificence . . .'

17 Her Majesty's (1900). In May 1900 J.C.Williamson leased the Alexandra, and an army of workmen under the supervision of the architect, W.Pitt, at once set about transforming it into Her Majesty's. The formerly level stalls floor was relaid with a slope of 3ft from the pit to the orchestra. The stage was lowered almost 2ft, and another private box was constructed at each end of the dress circle. For the comfort of the actors (for this was to be primarily a light opera theatre) suites of dressing rooms, cloak rooms, and offices were installed and furnished. Lavish use of gold paint, plush curtains and upholstery, and new carpeting completed the more obvious changes made to this theatre.

18 Opera House (Tivoli) 1901. The entertainer and entrepreneur, Harry Rickards, built this theatre in Bourke Street, between Swanston and Russell Streets on the site of the earlier Prince of Wales Opera House at a cost of £35 000. Opened on 18.5.1901, the theatre seated 2000 in its stalls, dress circle, and gallery or amphitheatre, the last 2 being combined in the same tier. The auditorium was designed and decorated in the Moorish style, in a colour scheme of red, blue, old gold, ivory, and cream, with gold and silver leaf. The theatre was, in fact, a blaze of colour from its electric light bulbs to the 2 wide corridors leading from Bourke Street to the dress circle and stalls entrances. These were decorated with salmon pink and turquoise blue frescos picked out with gold. The dress circle was reached by 2 marble staircases, the space between these being occupied by a fountain set in a fernery beneath an arcade of Moorish arches. The *Argus* description of this colourful theatre continues: 'The sliding shutter of the roof has a groundwork of turquoise blue, interlaced with ornaments of old gold, white, brick red, and gold; the dome has panels between ribs of silver leaf, upon which are painted scrollwork patterns of Moorish design, with lines and stiles of salmon pink, and finished with fretwork in imitation of old ivory. The portion

over the proscenium is handsomely picked out, showing ornamental plaster in relief, and etched with gold and silver leaf. Each private box is similarly ornamented, having side panels in old ivory and columns of silver and gold, with the overhanging canopies in dull silver.' The dress circle walls had 'handsome gold paper richly embossed with flowers,' and a dado of raised plaster work coloured to represent antique beaten metalwork. Designed as a variety or vaudeville house its name was soon changed to the Tivoli.

19 King's (1908). Built at a cost of £32 000 to seat 2200, this theatre in Russell Street, between Bourke and Little Collins Streets, was opened on 11.7.1908. The lessee was William Anderson, formerly of the Alexandra. A vestibule paved in black and white marble tiles, and with a Victorian marble dado in 3 colours around its walls, led to the stalls and dress circle entrances. From it led a white marble stairway to a commodious dress circle lounge, its walls papered in blue and gold and having 3 large painted panels, the 2 end ones depicting Pomona and Ceres respectively, the centre one a group of cupids with flowers. The auditorium contained the usual stalls, dress circle, and gallery, and was decorated in what was called the modern French Renaissance style, with a lavish use of fibrous plaster. Over the proscenium a large panel depicted Aurora with the children of Joy and Happiness, painted in flesh tints against a background of blue threaded with gold lines to give a tapestry effect. 'The fronts of the boxes are treated with floral devices,' the *Argus* reported, 'and over each a cupid is shown with trumpet in hand.' The seats and balcony rail in the dress circle were upholstered in blue velvet, to match the front curtain, which had a central monogram in gold silk surmounted by a crown. The stage, 4 storeys high, had dressing and wardrobe rooms on the right-hand side of each storey, while the stage or fly gallery held the switchboard and dimmers controlling the theatre's more than 3000 electric lights. It was proudly announced that all but the very topmost seats in this theatre had backs, while a fresh step in theatrical enterprise in Australia was the provision of a ladies' dressing room for gallery patrons. (See:. Seating capacity).

Melodrama. The stock-in-trade of the popular theatre, which deals in 'that drama produced by and offered for the enjoyment or edification of the largest combination of groupings possible within that society. Often it happens that for these groupings the adjective "lower" is significantly appropriate: lower per capita income, lower level of education and literacy, lower interest in or knowledge of aesthetic criteria, lower level of political influence' (David Mayer). While it is true that at least 95 per cent of 19th century drama is melodrama, it is equally true that by thus confining it to one century its continuing growth and blossoming in today's film, radio, and television studios is overlooked. Melodrama shares the world of make-believe with the fairy tale. In it virtue always vanquishes vice, and there is almost always a happy ending. As Booth says: 'Right to the end of its history both English and American melodrama identified virtue with toil, simplicity, and poverty; vice with riches, idleness, and property. These attitudes are understandable when we consider the lot of a member of the working class in the early 19th century (and later), a harsh and a poor one at best, crushed under a massive edifice of authority, power, and wealth dependent on him for its strength and giving him nothing in return but a bare and hard existence.' For this as well as for other reasons melodrama should be neither despised nor denigrated. It fulfils a real need in human nature, and has its own logic and approach. 'The best writers of melodrama were by no means wanting in literary merit, though none emerges as an artist of the first rank; it is unjust to dismiss their work because a few of the melodramas that are now remembered for their absurdities of plot and language have given the term "melodrama" a pejorative cast. If melodrama does not accord with a high ideal of literature, it suggests that the theatre can get along without obviously literary content for a surprisingly long time, but that it cannot endure without emotion and passionate appeal' (Robertson Davies). The actor, author, and drama critic, Hesketh Pearson, who could be said to have had a foot in both camps, should have the last say. Writing in 1950, he suggested: 'But perhaps the chief reason that he [the actor John Martin-Harvey, 1863-1944] never became a West End favourite was that the type of play he did, which called for his type of acting, was going out of fashion . . . Harvey would now be called a "ham" actor by all those who confuse the underacting of today with natural acting. As a matter of fact he was perfectly adapted to the class of play he produced, and if *The Only Way* or *The Breed of the Treshams* were staged at the present time they would be utterly ineffective because no modern actor could put them over. It is well to remember that both Shakespeare and Shaw wrote their plays for "ham" actors; that is to say, for men who knew how to deliver a long speech with the rhetorical flourish necessary to maintain interest and the vocal control to build up the climax.'

Melville, Henry (1800-1873). Real name Henry Saxelby Melville Wintle. Born in England, Melville came to Australia in 1827. He established himself in Tasmania as a newspaper proprietor, publisher, and landowner. He printed and published, among other works, the first novel to be published in Australia, *Quintus Servinton: A Tale Founded on Incidents of Real Occurrence* (1831), written anonymously by Henry Savery. Melville's play, *The Bushrangers; or, Norwood Vale,* was published by him in his *Hobart Town Magazine* (Vol. 3, April 1834, pp.82-96), which no doubt led to its production, in an extended version, in the Argyle Rooms, Hobart on 29.5.1834 and 2.6.1834, and at Launceston 24.11.1835. Slight though this is, it is of value as the first play by a resident Australian produced in Australia, and also as the first to deal with a typically Australian subject — the interplay between bushrangers, white settlers, and Aborigines. Melville left Tasmania in 1849 for the Australian mainland, where he remained for a while before returning to England. There he interested himself, until his death, in occultism and the lost mysteries of Masonry.

Memories. 1-act play by Guy Boothby, Albert Hall, Adelaide 25.9.1889, initially 1 performance.

Men as women. From the days of the boy actors who played the feminine roles in Shakespeare's plays, men have played women on the stage. In today's parlance, Edward Kynaston (c.1650-1706) could be ranked as the first of the famous 'drag' actors. Such actors have burlesqued, caricatured, or imitated women. Sometimes they have been so successful in their imitations as to deceive not only members of their own sex but women as well. Among the first to play a burlesque female role on the Australian stage was Joseph Simmons, in the part of the Italian prima donna, Angelica Catalani, in *The Mock Catalani in Little Puddleton*. And one of the first and most successful of the many 'serious' imitators on the Australian stage was the American Francis Leon, known as 'the only Leon.' When he first appeared in Melbourne in 1878 the *Argus* reported that ladies in the audience 'were most positive in claiming him as "one of themselves".' His slight figure and small hands and feet aided him in the deception, 'while his singing, instead of dispelling the illusion assisted it.' His mimicry of the contemporary soprano, Ilma de Murska, 'would have justified almost anyone in believing the performer a lady with a powerful soprano voice.' Francis Leon went on to play Josephine in the first Australian performance of *HMS Pinafore*. Prior to his arrival in Australia several actors had disported themselves in burlesque feminine roles, including Bland Holt, who in 1876 played the goddess Minerva in Burnand's *Ixion* (1863), and Emma, an elderly lady, in the pantomime *Alpine Apples; or, Harlequin Intelligence; or, Swiss A.B.C.* (See: Drag).

Merchant of Venice, The. Comedy by William Shakespeare, believed to have been first performed in London in 1596 or 1597; Hobart Theatre, Freemason's Hotel, February 1834.

Merry Duchess, The. 2-act comic opera, text G.Simms, music F.Clay, Royalty, London 23.4.1883; Royal, Sydney 23.8.1884, initial 18 performances.

Merry Freaks in Troublous Times. (See: Nagel, Charles).

Merry Monarch, The. 3-act comic opera, text J.Goodwin, after E.Chabrier's *L'Etoile*, music W.Morse and E.Chabrier, Broadway, New York 18.8.1890; Princess's, Melbourne 26.12.1891, initial 24 performances.

Merry Widow, The. (See: *Lustige Witwe, Die*).

Above: Noted female impersonator J. F. Sheridan
Right: American female impersonator Francis Leon 1879

Merry Wives of Windsor, The. Comedy by William Shakespeare, believed to have been first performed in London in 1598 or 1599; Royal Victoria, Sydney 14.10.1839.

——. The opera (See: *Lustigen Weiber von Windsor, Die*).

Messenger Boy, The. 2-act musical comedy, text J.T.Tanner and A.Murray, music I.Caryll and L.Monckton, Gaiety, London 3.2.1900; Palace, Sydney 8.10.1902, initial 21 performances.

Michael Strogoff, the Courier of the Czar. 4-act drama by F.R.C.Hopkins, adapted from the Jules Verne novel (1880), Gaiety, Sydney 4.2.1882, initial 18 performances. Later produced under the title *Russia As It Is,* Royal, Melbourne 6.5.1882, 6 performances.

Midas. 2-act burletta, text K.O'Hara, music anon., Crown Street, Dublin 22.1.1762; Royal Victoria, Sydney 13.5.1839, initially 1 performance.

Midsummer Night's Dream, A. Lyrical comedy by William Shakespeare, believed to have been first performed in London in 1595 or 1596; Prince of Wales, Sydney 6.5.1864.

Mignon. 3-act opera, text J.Barbier and M.Carré, from Goethe's *Wilhelm Meister,* music A.Thomas, Opéra Comique, Paris 17.11.1866; Drury Lane, London 5.7.1870; Gaiety, Sydney 25.7.1881, initial 10 performances.

Mikado, The; or, The Town of Titipu. 2-act comic opera, text W.S.Gilbert, music Sir Arthur Sullivan, Savoy, London 14.3.1885; Royal, Sydney 14.11.1885, initial 34 performances.

Milestones. 3-act drama by A.Bennett and E.Knoblock, Royalty, London 5.3.1912; Royal, Melbourne 22.3.1913, initial 36 performances.

Miller and His Men, The. 2-act melodrama by I.Pocock, Covent Garden, London 21.10.1813; officers and men of HMS *Crocodile* and HMS *Zebra,* Fort Macquarie 8.1.1830.

Miner's Right, The. 5-act drama by A.Dampier and G.Walch, adapted from R.Boldrewood's novel (1890), Alexandra, Melbourne 14.2.1891, initial 26 performances.

Miner's Trust, A. 3-act drama by Jo Smith, Palace, Sydney 31.10.1908, initial 7 performances.

Mirror of Beauty, The; or, Little Snow White and the Seven Dwarfs. Burlesque extravaganza by W.M.Akhurst, Queen's, Melbourne 5.10.1855, initial 6 performances.

Miss Decima (Miss Hellyitt). 3-act operetta, text M.Boucheron, translated and retitled by F.C.Burnand, music E.Audran, Bouffes

Parisiens, Paris 12.11.1890; Criterion, London 23.7.1891; Lyceum, Sydney 7.3.1896, initial 11 performances.

Miss Hook of Holland. 2-act musical comedy, text P.Rubens and A.Hurgon, music P.Rubens, Prince of Wales, London 31.1.1907; Royal, Melbourne 18.4.1908, initial 54 performances.

Mock Catalani, In Little Puddleton, The. 1-act musical burletta, text Charles Nagel, words and music of 3 songs by the author, remainder set to popular airs of the period, Royal Victoria, Sydney 4.5.1842, initial 3 performances. Text published by James Tegg, Sydney 1842. Copy in British Library, Shelfmark 1344 K8.

Mock Doctor, The; or, The Dumb Lady Cur'd. 2-act ballad opera, text Henry Fielding, songs set to popular airs of the day, Drury Lane, London June 1732; Emu Plains, 16.5.1825.

Money. 5-act comedy by Bulwer-Lytton, Haymarket, London 8.12.1840; Olympic, Melbourne 24.1.1856.

Monsieur Choufleuri restera chez lui là . . . (M.Choufleuri Will Stay at Home). 1-act operetta, text Duc de Morny and others, music J.Offenbach, Présidence du Corps Legislatif, Paris 31.5.1861; Bouffes Parisiens, Paris 14.9.1861; Queen's, Sydney 16.12.1878, initial 6 performances.

Monsieur de Poureaugnac. Comedy by Molière, written as a court entertainment in 1669. Performed in French before the Duke of Edinburgh by students in the Great Hall, University of Sydney 24.1.1868.

Monte Cristo; or, The Prisoner of the Chateau d'If. 4-act drama by Alfred Dampier from the novel by Alfred Dumas (1844), Royal Standard, Sydney 27.11.1886, initial 5 performances. (See: *Count of Monte Cristo, The*).

Montefiore, Jacob Levi. (See: Parliamentarians).

Montgomery, Walter (1827-1871). Real name Richard Tomlinson, born in Long Island, USA, but lived in England from an early age. Began acting career as an amateur in London, then moved to the provinces in the early 1850s, acting in Bath, Bristol, Birmingham, and other centres. His first professional appearance in London was in *Othello* at the Princess's in 1863. Switching to public readings from Shakespeare, after a time he appeared at Drury Lane in *King John, Henry IV, Manfred, Faust,* and *Comus.* Acting with him was Mrs Hermann Vezin, the former Australian actress, Mrs Charles Young. 2 years later he played Hamlet at the Haymarket. He also appeared as Iago to the Othello of 'the African Roscius,' Ira Aldridge, the son of a Senegal chief. The following year he was with Helen Faucit in *As You Like It,* and *The Hunchback.* Then followed an Australian tour from 1867 to 1869, when he created a sensation with his Hamlet a la Fechter, with blonde wig, and engendered a series of heated letters and public discussions on the question of Hamlet's sanity. He also gave Australia its first production of *Antony and Cleopatra*. Acting and reading in every colony, and helping and training amateurs such as George Darrell, and W.J.Holloway, he rallied a big following because of his somewhat eccentric behaviour as well as his acting ability. An instability in his character finally led him to take his own life in a London hotel in 1871, 2 days after his marriage to an American actress.

Moonstone, The. 5-act drama by Marcus Clarke, from the Wilkie Collins novel (1868), Royal, Melbourne 13.10.1879; initial 5 performances.

Moore, Maggie (1851-1926). Stage name adopted by the American-trained actress Margaret Virginia Sullivan, who in 1873 married the actor and entrepreneur, J.C.Williamson. Expert in comedienne and soubrette roles, Maggie had a big following, and was a genuine favourite with Australian audiences. She made her first appearance with her husband in *Struck Oil* at the Melbourne Royal on 1.8.1874, and toured with him in this play throughout the world. When she left Williamson in 1891, breaking up their marriage, she took with her the script of their successful, money-making play and continued to act in it for some years. There was dispute over ownership of the play, a matter which was never resolved, though Williamson always inclined to the view that its success was entirely due to his efforts. The majority of newspaper reviews of their performances do not support this contention. Two opinions of Maggie Moore's ability as an actress, written by contemporaries, follow: 'She was the foundation of the Williamson fortunes and the keystone of the Firm,' Harry Musgrove wrote of her in 1926, adding that J.C.Williamson owed to her the great success that came his way, little though he was disposed to admit it. Another who knew the Williamsons, the Musgroves, and all the stars of the day as well as she knew her own sisters, was Nellie Stewart, who bluntly wrote in her autobiography: 'It was Maggie Moore and *not* J.C.Williamson who made J.C.Williamson in Australia. Let us remember what we owe her . . . A very fine woman and an honour to the theatre . . .'

Moore, William George (1868-1938). 1 of the leaders in the 1-act play movement in Melbourne in the early part of the 20th century. Was also author of 6 one-act plays which achieved production. Art and drama critic for the Melbourne *Herald*, art critic for Sydney *Daily Telegraph*, author of *Australian Art* (1934), and editor with T.Inglis Moore of *Best Australian One Act Plays* (1937). His produced plays were *Acting a la Mode; The Only Game; England versus Australia; The Last Edition; The Tea-room Girl*, and *The Mysterious Moonlight*.

Moorish Maid, A. 2-act comic opera, text J.Y.Birch, music Alfred

Hill, His Majesty's, Auckland 26.6.1905; Palace, Sydney 28.4.1906, initial 7 performances.

Moral attitudes. Actors and dramatists trod an artfully mined field in the 19th century theatre. Theirs was a largely unmapped area mined by the followers of the various religious sects, the various political groups, and by those reviewers who thought it their main task to save a sinful world from the results of its own moral turpitude. Certain plays could always be relied on to bring out these baying watchdogs in full cry, among them *Don Giovanni in London, Jack Sheppard, The Stranger,* and *Camille.* The first 2 were not only regarded as evil in subject, but, what was worse, they presented the spectacle of women playing men, women in trousers instead of skirts. The last 2 dealt with 'loose' women — with women who, in the ambiguous phrase of the period, were no better than they should have been. The *Sydney Monitor* said in 1837 of *Don Giovanni in London* that 'it is a disgrace to any woman of chastity to be present at the performance of this lewd entertainment.' It seems that, well into the third quarter of the century, whatever it was women had it was certainly not legs, for these were never seen. If actresses showed their legs, and many did, they offended. In the same year the *Gazettte* unequivocally stated that 'the father, however much he may be pleased with dramatic entertainments himself, must hesitate before he takes his innocent daughter, or his yet unpolluted son, to witness the performance of females whose shameless indelicacy has been the topic of every tongue — the subject of every pen.' Twelve years later, although the doom-sayers were still in full cry, theatre-lovers had at least one champion in the aptly-named *People's Advocate,* which said in the face of the clamour about the performance of *Jack Sheppard* that it emanated from 'those thin-skinned ones who assume a virtue which they do not possess.' This writer said the drama in question clearly showed the reward of virtue and the punishment of vice — 'What drama can do more?' it asked. Moving forward 20 years or so, the Melbourne *Argus* of 27.2.1875 is to be found noting without comment the odd fact that 'while in Australia it is considered sinful for a clergyman to witness a performance of *Hamlet,* a prominent minister of the gospel at Cleveland, Ohio, has written a letter to Mr Lawrence Barrett, a well known American actor, complimenting him on his performance of the character of James Harebell in a drama entitled *The Man o' Airlie.*' At the same time in Sydney the *Town and Country Journal* was claiming that 'of late years it has very frequently been necessary for a gentleman to attend the performance of a play before determining whether it was a suitable one for his wife to witness.' A year later still, a Sydney weekly, the *Stockwhip,* reached the height of bad taste when it complained of 'those women who, dressed in scant costumes, nearly half nude, with a liberal display of leg, and the hair under the armholes contrasting with the colour of the hair of their heads, steeped in champagne and soda water, and doubtless as strong as the smell of a polecat, who draw crowded houses, and gain the thundering applause of those whose humour chimes in with such scenes.' And the abuse continued in this way until at least the end of the century, to the accompaniment of the construction of ever-larger theatres, ever brighter lights, higher kicking dancers, faster music, and the increased enjoyment of increasing audiences. (See: Theatre, Opposition to the).

Morocco Bound. 2-act musical comedy, text A.Branscombe and A.Ross, music F.O.Carr, Shaftesbury, London 13.4.1893; Lyceum, Sydney 1.9.1894, initial 24 performances.

Morton, George Ross (1837-1869). English-born writer and journalist, for some time connected with the NSW press. From 1865 he was editor of Sydney *Punch*. He was the son of the dramatist Thomas Morton, and nephew of J.M.Morton, who together wrote *All That Glitters Is Not Gold* (1851); and grandson of Thomas Morton senior, whose most famous play was *Speed the Plough,* first performed in Australia in 1834. G.R.Morton, with C.Dillon, wrote two plays, both produced at Sydney's Royal Victoria just after Morton's death — *Night and Morning,* and *The Count of Monte Cristo.*

Mosè in Egitto (Moses in Egypt). 3-act opera, text A.Tottola, music G.Rossini, San Carlo, Naples 5.3.1818; Her Majesty's, London 22.4.1822; Prince of Wales, Melbourne 6.5.1873, initial 5 performances.

Moser, Thomas (1831-1900). *Sydney Morning Herald* journalist, novelist, and *litterateur* who collaborated with the composer, Hector McLean, on the comic opera, *Populaire* (1886). In his early days as a journalist in New Zealand he published *Mahoe Leaves, being a Selection of Sketches of New Zealand and its Inhabitants,* Wellington 1863, reprinted 1888. Returning to Sydney, he worked on Sydney *Punch,* and contributed to the publications *Punch Staff Papers* (1872) and the *Vagabond Annual* (1877), which was dedicated 'to all vagabonds in Australia, contributors being the Vagabond himself, Marcus Clarke, F.R.C.Hopkins, H.W.H.Stephen, and B.Stephens. In 1884 his novel, *The Parsonage Girl* was published in Sydney, and in 1886 the text of the opera *Populaire* was published.

Motion pictures. Sydney and Melbourne audiences first saw films of people moving as they did in real life in 1895, when Thomas Edison's first continuous pictures were shown in his patent Kinetoscope. This was a viewing apparatus only. The following year both cities saw examples of the work done with the Lumière Brothers' Cinematographe — camera and projector in a single apparatus. From then on motion pictures, with their almost continuous improvements, were to take such a hold on audiences as ultimately to 'oust the legitimate.' In 1906 Harry Rickards showed at the Melbourne Opera House one of the earliest attempts to marry the motion picture and sound — the Gaumont

Chronophone. The *Sydney Mail* reported that although this had not reached perfection it was well on the way towards it. In fact, sound pictures were not perfected until the late 1920s. By 1907 silent motion pictures had become so popular that the Glaciarium ice-skating rink in Sydney's Railway Square was converted to a picture show — a theatre for showing pictures — to seat 3000. In May the following year a *Bulletin* writer complained that the 'flickergraph' had ousted the touring companys in the affections of country people. In the same year Sydney's first motion picture theatre, the first to be built solely for the showing of films, was opened at Railway Square. Called the Bijou Picture Palace, it opened on 29.8.1908 with a programme consisting of a history of the Dreyfus case; a love story set in Mexico, and several shorts dealing with buckjumping, woodchopping, and comedy subjects. In March 1909 the *Bulletin* reported that in Melbourne the Athenaeum Hall, the Bijou, Wirth's Olympia, the Glaciarium, and the Continental Garden had all gone over to what it called 'sillymatographic exhibitions.' It said the Town Hall was used for the same purpose at times, while St Kilda had 4 picture shows of its own and South Melbourne 2. In 1913 the *Sydney Morning Herald* noted that Sydney then had 4 motion picture theatres properly so called, and 'between 70 and 80 cinematograph shows,'; while the *Mail* noted of Edison's Kinetophone at the Lyceum that 'the reproduction of voices or of other sounds has been made perfectly simultaneous with the fitting actions as shown on the screen.' The first film made in Australia was of the 1896 Melbourne·Cup. When a start was made on making feature films, those of former Australian stage successes predominated, among them *The Story of the Kelly Gang, Eureka Stockade, Robbery Under Arms, For the Term of His Natural Life, The Squatter's Daughter,* and *Thunderbolt.* Two of the earliest producers were the former dramatists Beaumont Smith and W.J.Lincoln.

Mountain Sylph, The. 2-act opera, text T.J.Thackeray, music J.Barnett, Lyceum, London 25.8.1834; Royal Victoria, Sydney 11.5.1846.

Mountebanks, The. 2-act comic opera, text W.S.Gilbert, music A.Cellier, Lyric, London 4.1.1892; Princess's, Melbourne 1.4.1893, initial 30 performances.

Moustique. 3-act comic opera, text Marcus Clarke, music H.Kowalski, Opera House, Sydney 2.7.1889, initial 10 performances.

Moving panorama. (See: Panorama, moving).

Mrs Dane's Defence. 4-act drama by H.A.Jones, Wyndham's London 9.10.1900; Royal Sydney 7.8.1901, initial 10 performances.

Mrs Doolley's Joke. (See: *Mrs Goldstein*).

Mrs Goldstein. 3-act musical comedy, text J.F.Sheridan and P.Finn, music F.Weierter, Criterion, Sydney 20.9.1902, initial 30 performances. In 1905 the title was changed to *Mrs Dooley's Joke.*

Mrs Pretty and the Premier. 3-act comedy by Arthur H.Adams, Melbourne Repertory, Athenaeum Hall 26.9.1914, 2 performances.

Much Ado About Nothing. Comedy by William Shakespeare, believed to have been first performed in London in 1598 or 1599; Royal Victoria, Sydney 28.10.1854.

Muette de Portici, La (The Dumb Girl of Portici). 5-act opera, text A.E.Scribe and G.Delavigne, music D.Auber, Opera, Paris 29.11.1828; Drury Lane, London (as *Masaniello*) 4.5.1829; Royal Victoria, Sydney 8.9.1838. (See: Masaniello).

Multiple setting. Also known as a divided setting. A setting on more than one level, divided horizontally or vertically, or both — what has been called an exploration of the vertical dimensions of stage space. Its first use in Australia was for the melodrama, *Jonathan Bradford; or, The Murder at the Roadside Inn* (1833), given at Sydney Royal on 26.12.1834. Act 1, Scene 5 of this shows 4 rooms of the George Inn (2 on the ground floor, 2 on the first storey) in which separate actions take place simultaneously. The 2 ground floor rooms are seen in exterior and interior views. Another 2-level play, also produced in Australia, was *Walter Brand; or, The Duel in the Mist* (1833), in which the lower level showed a cellar under a street, the full width of the stage. Above was a view of the open street by moon and lamplight. Other plays, such as *The Clerk of Clerkenwell* (1834), had multiple settings which were simply 2 rooms of a house showing the dividing wall in the centre, one room alongside the other. There were also settings with one room above another. All these were, in a sense, a reduced form of the box setting, and must have been substantial structures to take the weight of the actors involved. When Barnett Levey produced *Jonathan Bradford* he closed the theatre to members of the press because a reporter had given away one of his publicity 'lurks.' Even before the first performance Levey had had playbills printed with the message: 'The public are respectfully informed, that owing to the crowded state of the house, and the approbation bestowed on the 5th scene of *Jonathan Bradford* on witnessing the performances in 4 different parts of the stage at the same time, it will be repeated.' (See: Box setting).

Musgrove, George (1854-1916). One of the few 19th century Australian theatre men not activated solely by the profit motive. He demanded a high standard of artistic excellence in his productions, whether of comic or serious opera, Shakespeare or melodrama, and was not above keeping a financially unprofitable production on stage because he enjoyed it as a work of art. Musgrove, a nephew of the impressario, W.S.Lyster, was born in England but came to Australia with his parents in 1866. On leaving school he at first worked in a solicitor's office. He married in 1874, a marriage which was not a success. Soon afterwards he took over as treasurer for his uncle, at the same time learning the profession which was to be his for the rest of his life. In 1880 he branched out as manager in his own right, and from then until a few years before his death he seemed to possess the golden touch with most of his theatrical ventures. He not only bought the rights to English productions he saw in London, but came back to Australia in 1880 with a complete company and launched J.Offenbach's *La Fille du Tambour Major* on a delighted public. It was during the Adelaide production of this comic opera that he first met the actress Nellie Stewart, with whom his life was bound up until his death. In 1882 he joined A. Garner and J.C.Williamson to form what was later known as 'the Triumvirate', founders of the long-lived J.C.Williamson Company. In 1888 he went to London to book plays, operas, actors, and singers for the company's theatres, in the face of competition from America. He came back with another successful comic opera, *Dorothy*. But it was not long before the cautious, not to say timid J.C.Williamson and the adventurous G.Musgrove ceased to see eye-to-eye. They parted, and Musgrove took over the Sydney Royal for a series of successful musical productions. Two years later he and Williamson were together again, this time as Williamson and Musgrove Ltd, and together staged a succession of dramatic and musical works. In 1896 Musgrove was based in London as agent for 'the Firm.' The following year he took a lease of London's Shaftesbury in the name of the firm, but without first letting Williamson know. In 1898 he launched the record-breaking musical comedy, *The Belle of New York* at the Shaftesbury, from whose success he made a great deal of money. In 1900 he and Williamson parted for good, and he returned to Australia to become one of Williamson's heaviest competitors in the fields of comic and grand opera. Between them they presented first Australian performances of most of the world's major operas and lighter musical works. Only towards the end of his life did Musgrove seem to lose the ability he had always had to forecast what would and what would not appeal to Australian and New Zealand audiences.

Music. Very few historians of the 19th century theatre have concerned themselves with the use of music as an adjunct to and support for the drama. Usually this lack of interest in, or sometimes deliberate avoidance of the subject is excused on the grounds that 'music is a specialist subject.' The answer to such a claim is that it was never a 'specialist subject' to audiences. People responded always to the way in which the music added emphasis to words, situations, and movements. When the avenging hero, with dread purpose, cried: 'Die (followed by a crashing chord in the orchestra) traitor!' (followed by another), and the heroine cried out, 'No! (tremolo violins), no! (more tremolo), don't

Above: Auditorium Melbourne Academy of Music 1876
Below: Interior Sydney Music Hall 1895

stain your hands with his blood!' (plaintive music) the audience felt, without being able to say exactly how or why, that they were being caught up and whirled to an area of life that was philosophically truer than life itself. At first theatre orchestras, or 'bands' as they were often called, were primitive. They just managed to provide the necessary background to the songs, dances, and plays which made up the normal night's performance. Their main quality in these early days seems to have been of the 'wake up,' or 'startle,' and the 'dreamy' kind. Reading through some of the melodramas produced at Levey's Royal in Sydney in the 1830s, and at the Royal Victoria from the 1840s on, one finds that in most of them music 'cues' are marked quite plainly in the text. In the first act of *A Tale of Mystery* (1824) such directions as 'hunting music,' 'music to express contention,' 'confused music,' 'music expressive of terror,' 'music of sudden joy' are given. These directions occur throughout the play, with the final curtain falling 'to slow and solemn music.' The simpler direction 'music' occurs throughout *The Vampire; or, The Bride of the Isles* (1820), while no fewer than nine songs (some of them duets) are used to set the mood for the various scenes. *The Flying Dutchman; or, The Phantom Ship* (1827) also has music cues marked throughout, and, as befits it subject, songs and an invisible chorus. Turning to later plays, such as *The Colleen Bawn* (1860) it is found that things are much the same as they were in the 1820s, the first direction for Act 1 being 'music — seven bars before curtain.' Directions continue all through the play, including such things as 'music through dialogue,' and 'music change.' Thus every orchestra or band leader had to be a 'cobbler,' had to be able to build musical bridges — often little more than a simple modulation — between the most telling scenes. From some of these play directions it is possible to see that a dramatic and foreboding use was also made of silence. When the Sydney Royal reopened for a new season in May 1835 its orchestra consisted of a leader and 4 other violins, flute, 'cello, piano, 2 clarinets, 2 bassoons, bugle, and drums. When the Royal Victoria opened in Sydney in 1838 it had an orchestra of 19 players — an ideal number for a theatre of its size. But, it soon transpired, this was a piece of opening night bravado, and the orchestra was soon reduced to half that number. It can safely be said that from then on to the end of the century economics governed the size of theatre orchestras, except during the occasional grand opera season. Only in the 1840s was an opera season hampered by an inadequate orchestra, but in this decade there were also inadequate if enthusiastic singers, and often band parts had to be written with the aid of a singer singing a particular aria or solo from memory. In 1854 the Royal Victoria had an orchestra of 17. This went down again in the post-goldrush years. In 1874 the *Town and Country Journal* complained of the inadequacy of the opera orchestra. In the 1860s, it said, there had been opera orchestras of 23 and 21 players. Now there was an orchestra made up of 2 first violins, no second, a tenor, no cello, a double-bass, and a piano played by the conductor. By the 1880s, with the construction of new, more ornate and comfortable theatres, and improvements in stage presentation, most theatres had from adequate to good orchestras, and retained them. In Melbourne in 1887, when comic operas and musical comedies were very popular, the ideal opera orchestra was put at 25 to 30 players, with the norm said to be 'the leader and two first violins, two violas, first and second flutes, first and second clarinets, two 'cellos, two double basses, one oboe, one bassoon, two cornets (sometimes three), two trombones, two horns, and the drum.' At this time Melbourne players had their own Professional Orchestra Society of Australia to look after their interests. Travelling companies were a different matter, particularly dramatic companies. In 1877, on one of his frequent New Zealand visits with his own company, G.Darrell's theatre 'orchestra' consisted of violin, clarinet, cornet, bass, and piano, while in Wellington in 1880, according to G.A.Kennedy, the average theatre orchestra consisted of piano, violin, and cornet, with the occasional addition of a double bass.

Music hall. In Australia this form of entertainment was never as popular as it was in England, nor did it take the same form. More often than not it was housed in a plain, spartan building, and provided entertainment for audiences which wanted light music, gaiety, ribald and sentimental songs, recitations, comedy and animal turns, and a chorus of girls. In the 1860s these halls were little more than pot-shops where bedraggled performers whose theatrical days were over sang and danced at intervals, while waiters urged everyone seated at the tables to 'fill 'em up again!' The introduction of this form of entertainment in Sydney from the 1860s parallels a Melbourne movement which began in the 1850s during the gold rushes. But 'musical nights' in pubs and hotels were first held in Sydney in the late 1830s. The first so-called music hall in Sydney seems to have been the Royal Alhambra, opened in King Street in the mid-1860s, which was little more than a grog shop. Next came the Scandinavian Hall in Castlereagh Street, in the same decade. This, though it was also more grog shop than music hall, outlasted the Alhambra. There was also an Alhambra Music Hall attached to the Victoria Hotel in Pitt Street in 1868. But the true music hall of the last quarter of the century supplied neither food nor drink. It was first opened at the Haymarket, Sydney in 1884 as the Academy of Music. A hall with a small stage at one end, it seated about 600. A year later, after alterations and renovations, it became the Alhambra Music Hall, able to seat 900. By 1887 this had taken on the appearance of a theatre, with a wood and canvas painted proscenium, in a hall 82ft long, 40ft wide, and 32ft high. The front seats were called the dress circle, behind which were the stalls, with a gallery above. The Alhambra, which was really a variety house, maintained its popularity well into the present century, finishing its days as a cinema or 'picture show.' The largest music hall in Sydney was Lawler's, opened in George Street in 1895 between Bathurst and Liverpool Streets. Located above a row of shops, this had a hall 92ft long, 40ft wide, and 30ft high, was ornately finished, and had a stage 42ft wide and 30ft deep. This hall, which seated 1000, was never successful, and after its first few weeks was unable to fight the double disadvantage of being at the wrong end of the city, and upstairs.

Music Master, The. (See: *Maestro di Capella, Il*).

Musical comedy. A hybrid form of stage entertainment which had its beginning in the mists of theatrical time, and its flowering in the 20th century. Nobody invented it, but many people improved on each successive manifestation, the most notable of them being George Edwards. Tradition has it that the first real musical comedy was *In Town* (1892). In America, some historians have placed the birth of musical comedy in the year 1866, with the production of *The Black Crook*. Others regard this work as a very weak link in the long chain that leads to *Oklahoma* and *West Side Story*. Brilliant stage pictures, hosts of pretty girls, light and appealing music, startling dance sequences, and comedy, comedy, comedy, were said to be the ingredients for success. The finished work, in the 19th century at least, was a compound of all that had gone before in the way of burlesques, extravaganzas, musical plays, and comic operas; and yet with a form that was different from all, a shape which was further improved upon when, after World War I, American theatre practitioners took it over. The actual title or label, 'musical comedy,' was first used on the programme of *A Gaiety Girl* in 1894.

My Lady Molly. 2-act comic opera, text G.H.Jessop, music S.Jones, Royal, Brighton 11.8.1902; Her Majesty's, Melbourne 9.5.1903, initial 12 performances.

My Mate. 4-act drama by Edmund Duggan, King's, Melbourne 4.2.1911, initial 23 performances.

Mystery of a Hansom Cab, The. 5-act drama by F.T.Vale, adapted from Fergus Hume's novel (1886), Alexandra, Melbourne 25.8.1888, initial 6 performances. Vale later reduced this to a 3-act version.
——, 4-act drama by George Darrell, Royal, Adelaide 6.10.1888, initial 7 performances. Given as *Midnight Melbourne* Opera House, Brisbane 20.7.1889.

Mysterious Moonlight, The. 1-act play by W.Moore, Turn Verein Hall, Melbourne 15.5.1912, initially 1 performance.

N

Nabob, The. 2-act comedy by Guy Boothby, Albert Hall, Adelaide 25.9.1889, initially 1 performance.

Nabucco (Nabucodonosor). 4-act opera, text T.Solera, music G.Verdi, Scala, Milan 9.3.1842; Her Majesty's, London (as *Nino*) 3.3.1846; Prince of Wales, Sydney 16.6.1860, initially 1 performance.

Nagel, Charles. So far, very little has been discovered about this early playwright. He was commissioned in England as an Ensign in the 97th Regiment, the Queen's Own Royal West Kent, on 10.6.1826, and promoted to Lieutenant on 18.12.1829. He retired from the army with that rank in 1837, which entitled him to use the courtesy rank of Captain. He then emigrated to Australia. In April 1842 he was appointed a magistrate of the Territory in New South Wales (JP). He is known to have written to the Colonial Secretary early in the 1840s seeking a public service post, because the financial depression and drought had reduced him to penury. He did not get the position. It appears from this that at some time between 1837 and 1842 he became a landholder, as retired officers were at this time entitled to buy land under a price remission scheme. In 1846 he was officially recommended for a post in the public service. His plays include *The Mock Catalani, in Little Puddleton, Merry Freaks in Troublous Times* (never performed, but published by T.Forster, Sydney 1843. Music for this was written by Isaac Nathan) and *Shakespericonglommorofunnidogammoniae*.

Naked Truth, The. 5-act drama by George Darrell, Opera House, Melbourne 12.5.1883, initial 12 performances.

Nathan, Isaac (1792-1864). English composer and singer. Born in Canterbury, he died in Sydney. Nathan studied music with Domenico Corri (1746-1825), composer of 2 or 3 operas and music for the theatre.

He also trained as a singer, and sang at Covent Garden and the major provincial theatres. In 1814 he asked Lord Byron to send him some poems so that he could set them to music. The two collaborated on a total of 26 poems, which achieved fame as Hebrew Melodies. Soon after his first marriage, to Elizabeth Worthington, he became music librarian at the court of the Prince Regent, and Princess Charlotte's singing teacher. He was involved in one or two minor court intrigues, and later played a leading part in a mysterious 'under cover' assignment for the British government, an affair which to this day is still largely a mystery. After it he claimed £2326 from the government, but instead was given £326 and dismissed. In 1840 he hurriedly left England with his second wife and 8 children for Australia. Although from then on he worked hard at a variety of occupations, he soon found he had come to a land which was not only in the depths of a financial depression, but whose people had little real regard for music. But he persisted, writing songs and piano pieces, sometimes using Aboriginal themes, lecturing, forming, training and conducting choral groups, establishing a music academy, and writing and publishing several books. In 1844 he had to be rescued from bankruptcy by his friends. Three years later he had one of his bitterest disappointments in the failure of his opera, *Don John of Austria*. He was alighting from one of Sydney's horse-drawn trams in 1864 when it started again before he was clear of the rails, and he was crushed beneath its wheels. Nathan's stage works include music for the comic operas *Sweethearts and Wives* (1823); and *The Alcaid; or, The Secrets of Office* (1824); for the operatic farce of *The Illustrious Stranger; or, Married and Buried* (1827), for the music drama *Triboulet the King's Jester* (1834), the operatic drama *Merry Freaks in Troublous Times* (1843), and the opera *Don John of Austria* (1847).

Native Born, The. 4-act drama by Albert Edmunds, Royal, Adelaide 1.3.1913, initial 6 performances.

Naughty Nancy. 2-act musical comedy, text O. Bath and G.W. Preston, music R.E. Lyon and G.W. Preston, Savoy, London 8.9.1902; Criterion, Sydney 26.6.1905, initial 17 performances.

Ned Kelly; or, The Perils of the Bush. 2-act drama by unknown author, Britannia, London 23.10.1880. The first Ned Kelly play to be produced in England. Ms in British Library, Shelfmark ADD 53240 (H) SCH 3588.

Ned Kelly; or, The Bushrangers. 4-act drama by Bernard Espinasse and Harry Leader, Vaudeville, London 25.9.1902; also produced at the Grand, Islington 30.5.1904, as *The Bushrangers*.

Neild, James Edward (1824-1906). Born in Yorkshire. When he left school he was apprenticed to his uncle, a medical practitioner in Sheffield. On completing his apprenticeship he was enrolled at London

Dr J. E. Neild 1898

University College, and was ultimately qualified to practise by the Society of Apothecaries. In London he frequented the theatres, and became a personal friend of William Hoskins at Sadler's Wells. Neild was appointed medical officer at Rochdale. In 1853 he took the position of ship's medical officer on a clipper bound for Australia. He settled in Melbourne, and began the busy life which he continued to pursue until within a few years of his death — doctor, journalist, theatre critic, publisher, forensic expert, university lecturer, and a prominent figure in Melbourne's social life. He obtained his MD degree at the University of Melbourne in 1864, and in 1879 the degree of Bachelor of Surgery. He also lectured in forensic and psychological medicine, and as a pathologist is said to have made more than 8000 post mortem examinations. In between he was Melbourne's leading and most knowledgeable theatre critic for more than 30 years, and a member of the Bohemian circle which included Marcus Clarke, Adam Lindsay Gordon, R.P.Whitworth, R.H.Horne, G.Walch, and others. His work as theatre critic brought him into close contact with actors and actresses from all over the world, many of whom regularly corresponded with him.

Nell Gwynne. 3-act comic opera, text H.B.Farnie, music R.Planquette, Avenue, London 7.2.1884; Opera House, Melbourne 17.7.1886, initial 18 performances.

Nelson, Sydney (1800-1862). Singer, executant, composer, teacher, and music publisher. Born in London, he came to Australia in 1852, by which time he had to his credit the music for *The Middle Temple* (1829), *The Grenadier* (1831), *Cousin Joseph* (1835), *Domestic Arrangements* (1835), and *The Cadi's Daughter* (1851). He had also achieved some notoriety with his songs, including the most popular of all, *The Pilot*. Opening in Melbourne, he gave a series of musical entertainments with his son and daughters, and later collaborated with William M.Akhurst on several vaudevilles, including *Ladies' Prerogative, Quite Colonial,* and *The Rights of Women.*

Nemesis; or, Not Wisely But Too Well. 2-act operatic extravaganza, text H.Farnie, songs set to airs from French comic opera, Strand, London 17.4.1873; Opera House, Melbourne 2.2.1874, initial 23 performances.

Nesbitt, Francis. (See: McCron, Francis Nesbitt).

New Crime, The; or, 'Andsome 'Enery's Mare's Nest. 1-act farce by Walter H.Cooper, Royal Victoria, Sydney 7.8.1868, initially 1 performance.

New Sin, The. 5-act drama by B.M.Hastings, Royalty, London 20.2.1912; Melbourne Repertory, Athenaeum Hall 6.12.1913, initial 2 performances.

Never-Never Land, The. 5-act drama by Wilson Barrett, Victoria,

Brighton 9.4.1904. The author drew on his Australian experiences for this play.

New Barmaid, The. (See: *Lady Barmaid, The*).

New Rush, The. 5-act drama by George Darrell, Bijou, Melbourne 27.12.1886; initial 17 performances. Later played as *Caradoc's Crime* (1891), *The Queen of Coolgardie* (1897), *The King of Coolgardie* (1897), *The Road to Ruin* (1905), and *The Land of Gold* (1907).

Night and Morning; or, The Lights and Shadows of Human Life. 4-act drama by Charles Dillon and G.R.Morton, adapted from Bulwer Lytton's novel (1841), Royal Victoria, Sydney 19.11.1863, initial 2 performances.

Night Birds, The. 3-act musical comedy, text G.Unger, music J.Strauss, an adaptation of *Die Fledermaus,* Lyric, London 30.12.1911; Criterion, Sydney 15.6.1912, initial 42 performances.

Night Dancers, The. 2-act opera, text G.Soane, music E.Loder, Princess's, London 28.10.1846; Royal Victoria, Sydney 15.11.1847, initially 1 performance. Operatic version of the ballet *Giselle*.

Nino. (See: *Nebucco*).

No Mercy. 4-act drama by Julian Thomas, adapted from P.Giacometti's *La mort civile* (1867), Gaiety, Sydney 4.3.1882, initial 11 performances. (See: James, John Stanley).

Noces de Olivette, Les (Olivette). 3-act comic opera, text H.Chivot and A.Duru, music E.Audran, Bouffes Parisiens, Paris 13.11.1879; Strand, London 18.11.1880, Royal, Sydney 13.8.1881, initial 30 performances.

Norfolk Island. Towards the end of February 1788 Captain Phillip, Australia's first governor, divided his settlement and sent a group under Lieutenant Philip Gidley King to Norfolk Island, which lies north west of New Zealand. They were to establish a colony and grow wheat. The idea was that they should make themselves self-supporting and thus relieve the drain on the main body at Sydney Cove. This little colony survived its infancy, and in May 1793 a group of free men and convicts on the island sought permission of Lieutenant-Governor King to open a playhouse. This was given, and plays were presented once a month and on public holidays. No record of these performances has survived. All that is known is that on 10.3.1794 King advised Home Secretary Dundas in London that he had had to close the theatre because of disturbances caused by the soldiers. Norfolk Island was abandoned after 1803 and became a whaling station. Then, in 1825, it became a penal station, and before long the words 'Norfolk Island' were synonymous with all that was depraved and degrading in the convict penal system. In an attempt to better conditions on the island a prison reform specialist,

Captain Alexander Maconochie, was appointed superintendent, and took up his post on 17.3.1840. One of his ideas was to grant a holiday, an organised holiday, on the Queen's birthday. That year it was celebrated with the hoisting of the colours, the issue of special rations, theatrical performances by volunteer prisoners, and punch and fireworks at night. As convicts before them had so often done, the men transformed one of the huts into a theatre and called it the Royal Victoria, Norfolk Island. The programme was made up of 2 acts of *The Castle of Andalusia* (1782), a musical interlude, and the play of *The Purse; or, Benevolent Tar* (1794). The entertainment pleased everybody but the man who held the real authority, and who was not present — Sir George Gipps, Governor of New South Wales. He was so furious when he heard of the liberties permitted the convicts that he effectively put a stop to any further performances. All that remains today of that happy birthday celebration in 1840 is the handwritten playbill of the performance, which is held in the Public Record Office in London. The composer of this stuck rigidly to the format followed in the printed handbills of the theatres at home, many examples of which he had no doubt held in his hands in happier days.

Norma. 2-act opera, text F.Romani, music V.Bellini, Scala, Milan 26.12.1831; King's, London 26.6.1833; Royal Victoria, Sydney 16.2.1852.

Nozze di Figaro, Le (The Marriage of Figaro). 4-act opera, text L.da Ponte, based on Beaumarchais's *La Folle Journée, ou Le Mariage de Figaro*, music Mozart, Burgtheater, Vienna 1.5.1786; His Majesty's, London 18.6.1812; Royal, Sydney 11.5.1833, with Mozart's music arranged and adapted by H.Bishop. Given 'with original music' Royal Victoria, Hobart 21.1.1845.

O

Oberon; or, The Elf-King's Oath. 3-act opera, text J.R.Planche, based on Wieland's poem and the medieval French romance *Huon de Bordeaux,* music C.Weber, Covent Garden, London 12.4.1826; Royal, Sydney 26.12.1836.

Oberon; or, The Knight and the Caliphs. 1-act extravaganza by G.B.Barton, Prince of Wales, Sydney 19.12.1865, initial 2 performances. Burlesque version of Weber's *Oberon* set to popular airs. Published Mason, Sydney 187? Copy in Mitchell Library, Sydney.

Oeil creve, L' (One in the Eye). 3-act comic opera, text H.B.Farnie, music Hervé (Florimond Ronger), Opéra Comique, London 21.10.1872; Opera House, Melbourne 28.2.1874, initial 12 performances.

Old Guard, The. 3-act comic opera, text H.B.Farnie from E.Goudinet and G.Duval's *Les Voltigeurs de la Eme,* music R.Planquette, Renaissance, Paris 7.1.1880; Avenue, London 26.10.1887; Princess's, Melbourne 11.4.1891, initial 42 performances.

Olio. In newspaper advertisements and playbills of the 1830s and 1840s can often be seen, after the main play of the night has been listed, the words 'olio,' or 'musical olio.' This meant that the play would be followed by a variety section, a melange, or an interlude — in the case of olio — or an interlude restricted to song, in the case of a musical olio. Then followed the afterpiece, usually a comedy or farce. The use of the olio with dramatic performances did not last beyond the 1840s, though it was still to be found in minstrel shows, in which song-and-dance-men, jugglers, contortionists, dancers, and instrumentalists took part. Usually these olios concluded with a 'stump speech' — an impromptu comic or burlesque speech on a topical or amusing subject in which malapropisms and double meanings abounded. Olio was originally a Spanish word meaning 'a mixed dish,' 'hotchpotch,'or 'stew.'

Olivette. (See: *Noces d'Olivette, Les*).

Onkel Beckers Geschichte. 1-act operetta, text and music by Moritz Heuzenroeder, Albert Hall, Adelaide 3.11.1882, initially 1 performance.

Only Dust. 3-act comedy by Wybert Reeve, Bijou, Melbourne 22.5.1886, initial 23 performances. Said to have been based on a translation of an Italian original prepared for him by the Italian actor, Signor E.Majeroni.

On Our Selection. 4-act comedy-drama by Beaumont Smith and Albert Edmunds, based on the *On Our Selection* stories of Steele Rudd, Palace, Sydney 4.5.1912, initial 12 performances. The most popular and widely performed 19th century Australian play. Its first performances could have been extended to more than 40 had a theatre been available. As it was the company had to move on because their lease of the Palace expired. Successful performances were given in Newcastle, Toowoomba, Brisbane, and Adelaide before a Melbourne season which lasted for 42 performances. Given at Lyric, London 24.8.1920, initial 31 performances. (See: Davis, Arthur Hoey).

O'Neil, Nance (1874-1965). American born and trained, Nance O'Neil earns a place in the history of the Australian theatre as the actress who introduced Australian audiences to Henrik Ibsen's *Hedda Gabler* and *Lady Inger of Ostrat,* and to Hermann Suderman's *Magda* (*Die Heimat*) and *St John's Fire* (*Johannesfeuer*).

Only a Fool. 3-act drama by F.R.C.Hopkins, adapted from the A.Dumas novel *Chicot the Jester* (1846), Royal, Melbourne 12.2.1880, initial 2 performances.

Only Game, The. 1-act play by William Moore, Oddfellows' Hall, Melbourne 30.3.1909, initially 1 performance.

Only Way, The. 4-act drama by F.Wills, adapted from the Charles Dickens novel, *A Tale of Two Cities* (1859), Lyceum, London 16.2.1899; Royal, Sydney 23.12.1899, initial 18 performances.

OP and PS. (See: Stage directions).

Open Gate, The. 1-act play by Charles Haddon Chambers, Comedy, London 25.3.1887; Repertory, Sydney 18.10.1913, initially 1 performance.

Opera. From the earliest days, attempts were made to present opera (chiefly English and Italian) to a music-hungry public. Until 1861 most of these productions consisted of little more than selected arias sung by principals. They were opera produced and sung in the face of incredible difficulties — inadequate rehearsal, poor accompaniments, inadequate settings and costumes, sopranos singing tenor roles, and, in at least one instance, the conductor singing the tenor role while conducting. There were also occasions when sheet music was unavailable, and the melodies were taken down as sung, and then orchestrated. In only a few instances did it prove possible to present full orchestra-principals-chorus productions. Not until the arrival in Australia of W.S.Lyster and his company in 1861 did Australia see complete opera productions, including, with many of them, the supporting ballets. It was Lyster and his corps who established a record for an opera production — *Les Huguenots* ran in Melbourne for 19 consecutive performances. Later notable impresarios were George Musgrove and J.C.Williamson, the first of whom introduced some of Wagner's major works to Australian audiences. A survey made to discover the most frequently performed operas in Sydney and Melbourne between 1849 and 1914 has revealed the following combined totals: *Maritana* 460; *Faust* 417; *The Bohemian Girl* 320; *Il Trovatore* 301. Among the light and comic operas and musical comedies, the most frequently performed were: *HMS Pinafore* 418; *Our Miss Gibbs* 300; *The Mikado* 299; *Floradora* 286. (See: Comic opera. Grand opera; Howson,F.; Lyster, W.S.).

Orchard, W.Arundel (1867-1961). Composer and musician. Succeeded Alfred Hill as conductor of the Sydney Liedertafel. Later director of the NSW Conservatorium of Music. Wrote music for the comic operas *The Coquette; or, A Suicide Policy,* and *The Emperor.*

Orchid, The. 2-act musical comedy, text J.F.Tanner, music I.Caryll and L.Monckton, New Gaiety, London 26.10.1903; Her Majesty's, Melbourne 29.10.1904, initial 65 performances.

Orphée aux enfers (Orpheus in the Underworld). Four-act fairy opera, text H.Crémieux and L.Halévy, music J.Offenbach, Bouffes Parisiens, Paris 21.10.1858; Haymarket, London 26.12.1865; Princess's, Melbourne 30.3.1872, initial 1 performance.

O'Sullivan, Edward William. (See: Parliamentarians).

Otello. 4-act opera, text A.Boito after Shakespeare, music G.Verdi, Scala, Milan 5.2.1887; Lyceum, London 5.7.1889; Her Majesty's, Sydney 7.9.1901, initial 2 performances.

Othello. Tragedy by William Shakespeare, believed to have been first performed in London in 1602 or 1603; The Theatre, Launceston 22.7.1834.

Ould Erin. 4-act drama by Walter Reynolds, Queen's, Sydney 8.10.1881, initial 17 performances.

Our First Lieutenant. 2-act farce by David Burn, Caledonian,

Edinburgh, September 1829 under the title *Manias and Maniacs;* Royal, Hobart 5.7.1843. Subsequent performances Royal Victoria, Sydney 28.11.1844; Queen's, Melbourne 18.6.1846.

Our Girls. 3-act comedy by H.J.Byron, Vaudeville, London 20.11.1875; Bijou, Melbourne 1.6.1878, initial 54 performances.

Our Miss Gibbs. 2-act musical comedy, text J.Tanner, music I.Caryll and L.Monckton, Gaiety, London 29.1.1909; Her Majesty's, Sydney 24.9.1910, initial 110 performances.

Out on the Castlereagh. 4-act comedy-drama by J.C.Lee, Palace, Sydney 1.5.1909, a copyright performance. The play later had 5 performances at the same theatre, commencing 1.6.1909.

Poster for The Naked Truth *1883*

Virtue and Humor on the job. Uncle (W. Driscoll), Dave (Fred Macdonald), Dad (Bert Bailey) and Maloney (Edmund Duggan) denounce a villain in the backblocks.

The first production of On Our Selection *1912*

Scene from Othello *Sydney 1854*

Above: Pantomime transformation scene Melbourne Royal 1858
Below: 'A sketch from Life — children enjoying pantomime [but they left after the marching and the ballets.]' Melbourne 1884

P

Padlock, The. 2-act comic opera, text I.Bickerstaffe, music C.Dibdin, Drury Lane, London 3.10.1768; Emu Plains, 20.11.1830.

Pagliacci (The Strolling Players). 2-act opera, text and music R.Leoncavallo, Verme, Milan 25.5.1892; Covent Garden, London 19.5.1893; Princess's, Melbourne 9.9.1893, initial 13 performances.

Panorama, moving. A backscene on upright rollers at either side of the stage, which presented a moving scene or landscape to the audience as the rollers (out of sight) were turned. First used in England in 1820 in a pantomime, the moving panorama was soon adopted for all kinds of productions, from burlesque to Shakespeare. In 1823 the first aeronautic panorama was shown, depicting a balloon voyage from London to Paris. Another panorama, with a stationary though bobbing and dipping full-sailed ship in the foreground, 'moved' the audience through a sea voyage along a coast and past seaport towns. Yet others, with a gilded barge propelled by rowers, gave the effect of a trip through a fanciful, spectacular landscape. Some painted panoramas were up to 400ft in length, but most were like that used in a Sydney production of *Uncle Tom's Cabin* in 1856 — a panorama of New Orleans 100ft long; while for his burlesque of 1868 in Melbourne, *The Siege of Troy,* W.M.Akhurst managed to fit in a 'voyage' to Troy. One of the last appearances of the moving panorama on the Australian stage was that used in the early years of the present century for the chariot race in *Ben Hur.* The horses 'galloped' on a moving endless belt in the stage floor, while the moving panoramic background showed successive views of the crowded circus as the chariots raced to the finish. (See: Burlesque).

Pantomime. A form of what was once speechless, dramatic and balletic entertainment which developed through the harlequinade of the late

18th and early 19th centuries to the spectacular comedy-musical extravaganza known as the Victorian pantomime. The annual Christmas pantomime which was a feature of the Australian theatre up to the first 20 years of the present century, was originally an English institution. It began as a 2-part presentation: a dramatic, largely topical first part, followed by a harlequinade in which Harlequin, Columbine, Clown, and Pantaloon figured. Knockabout nonsense, tricks, gymnastics, and dancing were the main features of the Harlequinade, which was at first in dumb-show. In 1869 Garnet Walch wrote a new first part to the English pantomime, *Love's Silver Dream; or, The King, the Goddess, and the Fays of Fairyland; or, Harlequin Pygmalion and the Golden Demon of the Yawning Chasm*. As time progressed the opening or first part of the pantomime grew longer and longer, and eventually the Harlequinade was displaced altogether and the pantomime was given up entirely to a fantasy world, topical, imaginative, amusing, musical, and artistic. Stock figures in this were the Principal Boy (a girl), the Dame (a man), the Fairy Queen and the Demon King, plus children's and adults' ballets, with a military, Amazonian, or Brigands' marching scene for a noisy, rhythmic finale to an act or to the pantomime itself. In the early days Australian theatre managers produced English pantomimes. In time, some of these were localised for Australian consumption. Charles Young's *The Goblin of the Gold Coast, or, Harlequin and the Melbournites in California*, given at the Queens, Melbourne in May 1850, seems to have been the first by an Australian writer. Marcus Clarke and others also occasionally wrote the 'book' for an annual pantomime. A feature of all of them, from about 1850 onwards, was the highly artistic, ingenious, and elaborately mounted transformation scene, kept sometimes for the end or close of the pantomime, but sometimes provided as an ending to each act. In these, to the accompaniment of music, solo and concerted singing, and dancing of all kinds beautifully costumed women and girls danced, floated through the air, came down from the flies in all kinds of aerial carriages, or in ornate representations of flowers or fruit, or rose from the depths of the understage in anything from a conch shell to a gilded cage. (See: Coloured fire. Transformation scene).

Pardon de Ploërmel, Le (Dinorah). 3-act comic opera, text J.Barbier and M.Carré, music G.Meyerbeer, Opéra Comique, Paris 4.4.1859; Covent Garden, London 26.7.1859; Royal Victoria, Sydney 21.5.1875, initial 4 performances.

Paris the Prince and Helen the Fair; or, The Great Horse and the Siege of Troy. Burlesque extravaganza by W.M.Akhurst, Royal, Melbourne 11.4.1868, initial 13 performances. Later called *The Siege of Troy*.

Parker, Horatio Gilbert George (1862-1932). Known as Gilbert, later Sir Gilbert Parker. Canadian born poet, novelist, and playwright who started his adult life at seventeen as a schoolteacher. He was intended for holy orders, but after a short period as a curate he returned to teaching. Following an illness he came to Australia in 1885 in search of health. Here he became a member of the editorial staff of the *Sydney Morning Herald,* and in his spare time travelled, pursued his interest in oratory, and wrote plays and verse. In Australia he wrote, or rewrote, two plays. The first was a version of Goethe's *Faust,* or, more precisely, a version of a version of a version of *Faust,* for Parker seems to have done no more than rewrite the Dion Boucicault play of 1854 called *Faust and Margaret,* written for Charles Kean. As an advertisement in the *Herald* of 31.3.1888 put it: 'The poem has been dramatised upon the lines of the original play as adapted from the French by Mr Dion Boucicault . . .' But he and G.Rignold, who played Mephistopheles and produced the play, knew their public. *Faust* was lavishly mounted, scene changes were many, and there was truly 'something for everybody' in it. As a result the play had a run of 42 performances. Parker's next play was a dramatisation of A.C.Gunter's novel, *Mr Barnes of New York,* under the title *The Vendetta.* This had already been done by one or two other playwrights, G.Darrell among them. The play was a success, and no doubt it was the profits from these 2 productions which helped to pay his fare to London in 1889. He became a successful novelist and politician; was knighted in 1902; created a baronet in 1915, and 'sworn of the Privy Council' in 1916.

Parliamentarians. If the Australian political scene in the 19th century was remarkable for anything, it was surely remarkable for the fact that at least 10 Parliamentarians were dramatists.

The most notable was **James Alexander Kenneth Mackay** (1859-1935), who entered politics in 1895 as the member for Boorowa, in the Legislative Assembly. He resigned in 1899 to become a member of the Legislative Council and Vice President of the Executive Council from 15.9.1899 to 29.8.1904. On 18.10.1899 he took his seat as a life appointee, which he retained until 22.4.1934. By this time he had become Major-General James A.K.Mackay, CB, VD, OBE. Between 1887 and 1908 Kenneth Mackay, as he called himself, published three books of poetry and two novels. He also wrote an Australian drama in 5 acts in collaboration with the actor-dramatist, Alfred Dampier, *To the West* (1896).

Edward William O'Sullivan (1846-1910), entered the Legislative Assembly in 1885 as member for Queanbeyan. He was Secretary for Public Works 1899-1904, and Secretary for Lands for two or three weeks. In 1907, when he retired from politics, he was member for Belmore. In the 1890s O'Sullivan published a novel called *Esperanza,* and a non-fiction work dealing with political and other associations. In 1906 he published a collection of sketches, stories, and speeches called *Under the Southern Cross.* His plays included *The Eureka Stockade* (1898), rewritten as *The Eureka Rebellion* (1907); *Coo-ee; or, Wild Days in the Bush* (1906), *Keane of Kalgoorlie* (1908) and *A Quiet Little Dinner* (1908).

Jacob Levi Montefiore (1819-1885), member of the Legislative Council from 1856 to 1860, and from 1874 until he resigned in 1877. A Sydney and London merchant, he wrote one of the first books on economic theory published in Australia, *A Catechism of the Rudiments of Political Economy,* and wrote pamphlets on free trade. In 1843 he translated Lockroy and Baden's *Un Duel sous le Cardinal Richelieu* as *The Duchess of Chevreuse* (1843), and in 1847 he wrote the text of I.Nathan's opera, *Don John of Austria,* translated from the French of Delavigne.

Harold Wilberforce Hindmarsh Stephen (1841-1889), member for Monaro from 1885 to 1889, was a practising author and editor who also wrote a number of plays; *Buttons; or, Wives Exchanged* (1871); *Euchred* (1872); *The Golden Belt* (1875); *Drill: A Parade of Girls of the World* (1877).

Walter Hampson Cooper (1842-1880), briefly member for East Macquarie, wrote a number of plays. These are dealt with in the present work under his name.

George Ferrers Pickering (?-1876), journalist and poet, member for Goldfields North 1865-68. His early book of poems was published in Sydney in 1852. Wrote one play, *Lough Deargh's Shrine; or, The Cave of Penance* (1847).

Thomas Walker (1858-1932), member for Northumberland 1887-94, was the author of a book of poems (1855), a book of stories of the convict days, *Felony of N.S.W.* (1891), and a number of pamphlets. Later he became a member of the Legislative Assembly of Western Australia. Using the pen name Thomas Somers, and in collaboration with Alfred Dampier, he wrote *For the Term of His Natural Life* (1886). Next, still using his pen name but writing alone, came the drama *Voices of the Night* (1886), then, under his real name, *Marmondelle the Moor* (1893).

Randolph Bedford (1868-1941), member for Warrego 1923-1941 in the Legislative Assembly of Queensland. Author of 5 novels and various works of non-fiction. Also wrote plays, dealt with in the present work under his own name.

William Forster (1818-1882), member of Legislative Assembly of NSW 1856-76, when he was appointed Agent General in London. In that 20 years he held the offices of Premier and Colonial Secretary 1859-60, Secretary for Lands (1868-70), and Colonial Treasurer (1875-76). While in London he published two plays, *The Weirwolf: a Tragedy* (1876), and *The Brothers: a Drama* (1877). Another play, *Midas* was published posthumously in London in 1884. None of these was produced.

Alfred Deakin (1856-1919), entered politics in Victoria at the age of 23, gained Cabinet rank and represented Victoria in London in 1887 at the first Colonial Conference. A Federalist, he was second to the Prime Minister (Edmund Barton) in the first Commonwealth government. He became Prime Minister in 1903, resigned in 1910, and retired from politics in 1913. Author of a book of poetry, *A New Pilgrim's Progress* (1877), and a drama in 5 acts, *Quentin Massys,* published in Melbourne in 1875 but never produced. (See: Randolph Bedford, W.H.Cooper, G.Coppin).

Parramatta. The first city outside Sydney to enjoy professional theatricals. In 1833 a group of Barnett Levey's actors at the Royal decided at the end of that theatre's first season to open a theatre at Parramatta. The Royal was to be closed for some weeks, and during this 'resting' period the actors would receive no pay. Under the direction of John Meredith the group hired a room at Nash's Hotel, Parramatta, which even with the addition of a stage accommodated a large audience. Seating was in 2 sections, front seats 4s, back 2s and 6d. The opening programme of *Inkle and Yarico* (1787), and *The Spectre Bridegroom* (1821) was presented on 20.7.1833. Bad luck dogged the venture for a while with rain on each night of performance, and lack of an orchestra. Things eventually picked up, and Colonel Despard permitted the use of the band of the 17th Regiment, but in the long run the theatre was a financial failure, and the actors unwisely showed their disappointment on the last night of performance by getting uproariously drunk. The audience, '. . . finding they were defrauded, rushed on the stage and commenced the work of destruction. Mr Nash, who is highly respected by the townspeople, was forced to go on the stage and beg them to desist,' the *Sydney Monitor* reported. Six years later a group from Sydney's Royal Victoria, headed by the actor John Lazar, had more success. As time progressed, Army as well as civilian groups began to cater to the theatrical needs of the city, until finally the city had its own theatre, which was visited by travelling companies of all kinds.

Parsifal; or, The Redemption of Kundry. 4-act drama by T.H.Taylor, Her Majesty's, Sydney 22.12.1906, initial 51 performances. Published Angus and Robertson, Sydney 1906; Lothian, Melbourne 1907.

Passers By. 4-act drama by C.H.Chambers, Wyndham's, London 29.3.1911; Royal, Melbourne 27.1.1912, initial 17 performances.

Passing of the Third Floor Back, The. 4-act drama by J.K.Jerome, Opera House, Harrogate 13.8.1908; St James's, London 1.9.1908; Criterion, Sydney 18.6.1910, initial 28 performances.

Passion. 4-act comedy by W.Reeve, adapted from Mrs Campbell Praed's novel, *Policy and Passion,* (1881), Gaiety, Sydney 12.4.1884, initial 12 performances.

Paterson, Andrew Barton 'Banjo' (1864-1941). Known principally for his poems, *The Man From Snowy River, Saltbush Bill, J.P., Clancy of the Overflow,* and others. Was successively solicitor, journalist, editor, and soldier, and a novelist and short story writer as well as a poet. His only connection with the Australian theatre is in his collaboration with the composer E.P.Truman in the comic opera, *Club Life* (1895). On its first performance the *Sydney Morning Herald* described it as a clever sketch 'extended on the rack of an entire evening's entertainment.'

Patience; or, Bunthorne's Bride. 2-act aesthetic opera, text W.S.Gilbert, music A.Sullivan, Opera Comique, London 23.4.1881; Royal, Sydney 19.12.1881, initial 12 performances.

Paul and Virginia. 2-act musical drama, text J.Cobb after novel by B.Saint-Pierre, music J.Mazzinghi and W.Reeve, Covent Garden, London 1.5.1800; Royal Victoria, Sydney 18.4.1844, initially 1 performance.

Paul Clifford, the Highwayman of 1770; or, Crime and Ambition. 3-act drama by B.Webster, adapted from Bulwer Lytton's novel (1830), Coburg, London 12.3.1832; Royal Victoria, Sydney 15.9.1856.

Paul et Virginie. 3-act opera, text J.Barbier and M.Carré, music V.Massé, Opéra National Lyrique, Paris 15.11.1876; Covent Garden, London 1.6.1878; Gaiety, Sydney 28.1.1884, initial 6 performances.

Paul Jones. 3-act comic opera, text H.B.Farnie after H.Chivot and A.Duru's *Surcouf,* music R.Planquette, Prince of Wales, London 12.1.1889; Opera House, Melbourne 27.3.1890, initial 68 performances.

Peacock's Feathers. 2-act comedy by Marcus Clarke, adapted from Molière's *Le Bourgeois Gentilhomme,* (1671) Royal, Melbourne 23.9.1871, initial 5 performances.

Pearl Divers, The. 6-act drama by George Leitch, Royal, Sydney 31.7.1886, initial 12 performances.

Pepita. Three-act comic opera, text H.Chivot and A.Duru, adapted by M.Tedde from *Princesse des Canaries,* music C.Lecocq, Folies Dramatiques, Paris 9.2.1883; Court, Liverpool, 30.12.1886; Princess's, Melbourne 9.2.1889, initial 30 performances.

Périchole, La. 3-act comic opera, text H.Meilhac and L.Halévy, after the 1-act play *La Carosse du Saint Sacrement* by P.Merimée, music J.Offenbach, 2-act version Variétés, Paris 6.10.1868; 3-act version, Variétés 25.4.1874; Princess's, London 27.6.1870; Royalty, London 30.1.1875; Prince of Wales, Melbourne 1.5.1875, initial 13 performances.

Pericles and Aspasia. One-act play by W.L.Courtney, Elder Conservatorium, Adelaide 16.8.1909, initially 1 performance.

Perth, Theatres in.

1 Royal (1897). Perth's first real theatre, contained in a hotel building in Hay Street, and opened on 19.4.1897. The theatre had a well

Above: Exterior His Majesty's Perth 1904
Below: Auditorium His Majesty's Perth 1904

equipped stage, complete with flies and gridiron, adequate dressing rooms for actors and supers, and the requisite traps and understage facilities. The auditorium consisted of stalls, dress circle, and gallery. The colour scheme was principally in crimson and gold, with crimson plush front curtain and gilded picture-frame proscenium.

2 His Majesty's (1904). Incorporated in a hotel building on the corner of Hay and King Streets, this theatre was opened on 24.12.1904. The 4-storeyed building, 100ft high, had a 145ft frontage to Hay Street and 185ft to King Street. The entrance to the family circle and gallery was in King Street, that to the stalls and dress circle through the main entrance in Hay Street. This, with a tiled vestibule, led by a marble staircase to the dress circle foyer, an ornate chamber off which cloak and other service rooms opened. The auditorium measured 75ft by 70ft, the stage 65ft by 75ft. The stage had a painted asbestos fire curtain. The metal proscenium arch, 32ft by 30ft, was tinted in copper, blues, pinks, silver, and French white. Boxes on either side of the proscenium were similarly treated. The walls of the proscenium were panelled in gold, and on one side carried a large painting representing 'Night,' on the other side representing 'Morning.' The stalls could accommodate 974, the dress circle 540, and the combined family circle and gallery 1070 — a total 2584. The saucer-shaped ceiling had a central flat area divided to form a sliding roof. This dome was treated in alternate panels of gold and silver, embellished with scrollwork, and with heads in bas relief. The sliding roof was painted to represent an umbrella enriched with gold, silver, and bronze.

Peter Pan; or, The Boy Who Wouldn't Grow Up. 5-act drama by J.M.Barrie, Duke of York's, London 27.12.1904; Princess's, Melbourne 18.4.1908, initial 24 performances.

Petit Duc, Le (The Little Duke). 3-act comic opera, text H.Meilhac and L.Halevy, music A.Lecocq, Renaissance, Paris 25.1.1878; Philharmonic, London 27.4.1878; Academy of Music, Melbourne 9.8.1879, initial 6 performances.

Petit Faust, Le. 3-act comic opera, text H.Crémieux and A.Jaim, music Hervé (Florimond Ronger), Folies Dramatiques, Paris 29.4.1869; English text H.B.Farnie, Lyceum, London 18.4.1870; Opera House, Melbourne 15.2.1875, initial 11 performances.

Petite Mademoiselle, La. 3-act comic opera, text R.Reece and H.S.Leigh, music A.C.Lecocq, Alexandra, London 6.10.1879; Royal, Melbourne 4.4.1885, initial 24 performances.

Petite mariée, La. 3-act comic opera, text A.Vanloo and E.Letterier, adapted by H.Greenbank, music A.Lecocq, Renaissance, Paris 21.12.1875; Opéra Comique, London 6.5.1876; Prince of Wales, Melbourne 6.12.1876, initial 15 performances. An adaptation of this work by H.Greenbank was produced at the Shaftesbury, London 17.11.1897 under the title *The Scarlet Feather,* and at the Princess's, Melbourne 26.11.1900, initial 24 performances.

Philanderer, The. 4-act comedy by George Bernard Shaw, Cripplegate Institute, London 20.2.1905; Melbourne Repertory, Athenaeum Hall, 5.12.1914, initial 3 performances.

Phillips, Mrs Alfred (1822-1886). Character actress whose name is primarily associated with that of Frederick Robson and London's Olympic. While she and her husband were acting at the Olympic she wrote and produced 6 plays, *Caught in His Own Trap* (1851), *An Organic Affection* (1852), *The Master Passion* (1852), *Life in Australia, from our own Correspondent* (1853), and *My Husband's Will* (1853). *Life in Australia* was a drama of the gold discoveries, and may have been influenced by Charles Reade's *Gold* (1853). The play's tableaux included immigrants' tents, the gold diggings, and a distant view of Melbourne, with such properties as tents, crushing machines, and mining tools. In 1855 the Phillips came to Australia, where they lived for the rest of their lives. In Australia 2 of her plays had already been produced, *Caught in His Own Trap,* Royal Victoria, Sydney 17.12.1852, and *The Master Passion,* same theatre, 15.9.1853, so that when she and her husband made their first appearance they were not unknown. Many members of their audiences, drawn like them to Australia by the gold discoveries, would have seen them at the London Olympic. Over the years Mrs Phillips appeared in innumerable productions, including *Camille, Faust and Marguerite, Money, She Stoops to Conquer,* and *Twelfth Night.* In 1874 she appeared in Hobart in the last of her own plays, *Duty,* which was a failure. Her husband, Alfred, wrote a farce, *The Original Bloomers* (1851), and, some 20 years later, an adaptation of Charles Lever's novel, *Lord Kilgobbin,* called *Kilgobbin,* Academy of Music, Melbourne 25.5.1878. Their son, Hans Phillips, was for many years a well known actor in Australia, noted particularly for his ability as supporting actor in G.Darrell's plays, *Transported for Life, The Forlorn Hope, The Sunny South, The Four Fetes,* and *The Soggarth.*

Phormio. Comedy (161 BC) by the Roman dramatist, Terence (Publius Terentues Afer c.190-159 BC); performed by students, Great Hall, University of Sydney 24.1.1868.

Pierre, Adam. (See: Dampier, Alfred).

Pierrot in Australia. 1-act play by Arthur Adams, Standard, Sydney 19.8.1910. Published *Australian Soldier's Gift Book,* 1918.

Pigeon, The. 3-act fantasy by J.Galsworthy, Royalty, London 30.1.1912; Melbourne Repertory, Athenaeum Hall 26.9.1912, initially 1 performance.

**Pipelè; ossia, Il Portinaco di Parigi (Pipele; or, The Porter of

Paris). 3-act opera, text R.Berninzone after E.Sue's *Les Mystères de Paris,* music S.A. de Ferrari, San Benedetto, Venice 25.11.1855; Princess's, Melbourne 18.7.1871, initially 1 performance.

Pirates of Penzance, The; or, The Slave of Duty. 2-act comic opera, text W.S.Gilbert, music A.Sullivan, Opera Comique, London 3.4.1880. Copyright performances were given at the Royal Bijou, Paignton, Devon 30.12.1879, and in New York 31.12.1879. First Australian performance Royal, Sydney 19.3.1881, initial 42 performances.

Pit. Not, as so many have claimed, necessarily the cheapest area of the 18th and 19th-century theatre, but for a long time the most popular. The pit or ground floor of the theatre in the 18th century was occupied in the main by those who did not want to go to the boxes, where dress was necessary, and by the *hoi polloi*. At first it was occupied by men only, then, as time progressed, by women as well. Pitites were often the most experienced and critical of playgoers, as was acknowledged by J.R.Planche in an epilogue to a play in 1831:
  Ye critics who sit
  All so snug in the pit —
  An assemblage of clever and sly ones.
That the pit was not the poor man's area in the 18th century is evident from the admission charges to Drury Lane and Covent Garden in the middle of that century — boxes 5s, pit 3, lower gallery 2, upper gallery 1. At the beginning of the 19th century in Australia the pit drew the rowdiest section of the audience. As the number and size of theatres increased, former pitites were found in increasing numbers in the gallery, by now the cheapest part of the house. By mid-century the steady take-over of the pit area by what were called orchestra stalls, or just stalls, had begun. In the early days pit seats were plain wooden benches. Later, backs were added. Then the benches were covered with strips of carpet 'upholstery.' Finally, with the stalls came the introduction of single seats, usually upholstered. (See: Stalls).

Pizarro. 4-act tragedy by August von Kotzebue, *Die Spanier in Peru,* (1796), translated by R.B.Sheridan, Drury Lane, London 24.5.1799; Royal, Sydney 19.1.1835.

Playbill. In the days when there was very little newspaper or other advertising, theatre patrons were advised of the nightly programmes by an announcement made from the stage at the end of each performance, and by a small printed handbill. These bills were prepared each night by the prompter, and printed early the following day. Posters, a much larger form of playbill, often with an illustration from the play included in their design, were also distributed through a town or city. Typical 18th-century playbills, usually about 12 ins by 8 ins, are the 2 lone survivors from the Sydney Theatre held by the Mitchell Library. These detail the programmes at that theatre for 8 March and 8 April 1800. They were printed on a battered wooden hand press brought to Sydney by the First Fleet. The Mitchell Library also holds a copy of the larger and more detailed playbill printed for the opening of Barnett Levey's Royal of 1832. As the nineteenth century progressed, and advertising facilities and opportunities increased, the playbill was replaced by small 'newspapers,' or daily or weekly publications containing advertising matter, details of programmes, cast lists, and brief paragraphs of theatrical gossip. Typical of these are the *Lorgnette* and *L'Ent'r'acte*. The earliest English playbills date from the seventeenth century.

Plays about Australia. Australia itself, and the names of famous and infamous people associated with it, attracted the attention of English, French, and German dramatists from 1785, when John O'Keefe's *Omai; or, A Trip Around the World,* written to honour Captain Cook, was presented at Covent Garden. This was a pantomime, which in those days meant a spectacular play in dumb-show. O'Keefe took the title of his pantomime from the name of a Polynesian native brought to London by one of Cook's officers in 1775. In 1784 the native Omai was again mentioned in the description of Cook's third voyage, published that year. This was enough for O'Keefe's purpose. By 1788 it had inspired a French example in four acts, produced in October at the Theatre de l'Ambigu-Comique, *La Mort du Captaine Cook, à son Troisième Voyage au Noveau Monde.* This in turn gave rise to several English translation-imitations, including a ballet. Then it was Captain Bligh's turn to have dramatic status thrust upon him, with *The Pirate; or, The Calamities of Captain Bligh,* produced at London's Royalty on 3.5.1790. The following year interest turned to Botany Bay, with a play of that title being produced in Liverpool. Next came a product of the Utopian outlook inspired in the French by the Revolution, a play in which Australia was seen to be the ideal place for the new, classless society. *Les Emigrés aux Terres Australis; ou, Le Dernie Chaptre du'une Grand Revolution,* to give the play its full title, was produced at the Théâtre des Amis de la Patrie in Paris on 24.11.1792. Then came August Friedrich von Kotzebue's *La Peyrouse* in 1799, with its several English translations. The output by English playwrights of plays dealing wholly or in part with Australia was a large one, commencing with J.Amherst's *Michael Howe, the Terror of Van Dieman's* (sic) *Land,* Coburg' London 23.4.1831. A lighter view, this time of Botany Bay, was given in *Giovanni in Botany; or, The Libertine Transported,* by an unknown author, Olympic, London 12.3.1822. Then came W.T.Moncrieff's *Van Dieman's Land; or, Settlers and Natives,* Surrey 11.2.1830, and so on through the century until the infamous/heroic Ned Kelly's days. Several of the later English dramatists, in plays performed between 1844 and the gold rushes of the 1850s, adopted the practice of setting their plays in London for the first two or three acts, and adding a topical touch by placing one act in Australia. Typical are G.D.Pitt's

Cumberland Mary (1844), and E.Stirling's *Raby Rattler* (1847). The Kelly plays, of course, were set wholly in Australia, with sometimes surprising results.

Plot. 3-act drama by Marcus Clarke, adapted from the A.Dumas novel *Vicomte de Bragelonne* (1848), Princess's, Melbourne 12.8.1872, initial 11 performances.

Poetic drama. A species of play which, in its 19th-century Australian manifestation at least, was chiefly remarkable for its lack of stageworthiness. Usually written by literary enthusiasts, the majority of these had classical or Italian Renaissance settings and characters, and were usually tragedies. Few were acted, but many were published. They are to be found in Miller's *Australian Literature 1795-1938*. Typical are S.P.Hill's *Tarquin the Proud* (1843); E.Reeve's *Raymond, Lord of Milan* (1851); C.Harpur's *The Bushrangers* (1853); J.Finnamore's *Francesca Vasari* (1865) and *Carpio* (1875), and Alfred Deakin's *Quentin Massys* (1875).

Poliuto. 3-act opera, text S.Cammarano, after Corneille's *Polyeucte,* (1642), music G.Donizetti, San Carlo, Naples 30.11.1848 (posth). Revised version of *Les Martyrs,* text A.E.Scribe, Opera, Paris 10.4.1840; Covent Garden, London 20.4.1852; Royal Victoria, Sydney 22.10.1873, initially 1 performance.

Poor Jonathan. (See: *Arme Jonathan, Der*).

Poor Soldier, The. 1-act comic opera, text J.O'Keefe, music W.Shield, Covent Garden, London 4.11.1783; The Theatre, Sydney 23.7.1796.

Populaire. 3-act comic opera, text Thomas Moser, music H.R.McLean, Government House, Sydney 7.12.1886. Text published H.T.Dunn, Sydney, 1886.

Poses plastiques. (See: Living Statues).

Poulet and Poulette. (See: *La Belle Poule*).

Poupée, La. (The Doll). 4-act comic opera, text R.Sturgess after M.Ordonneaux, music E.Audran, Gaîté, Paris 21.10.1896; Prince of Wales, London 24.2.1897; Her Majesty's, Sydney 10.9.1898, initial 33 performances.

Practicable pieces. A term referring principally to doors and windows in stage settings that actually opened and shut rather than being painted. Even though in the early part of the century it was an accepted convention that the spaces between the stage wings could be used by actors for entry and exit, there were nevertheless some plays which called for the actor to enter a door and shut it after him, or to climb through a window. Such doors and windows were sometimes set in wings, sometimes in flats, and in stage directions in the play were always marked 'practicable.' Fireplaces, stoves, cupboards and so on were more often practicable than not, also bridges, porches, gates, steps, and verandahs.

Prairie King, The. (See: *The Scout*).

Predatoros; or, The Brigand's Bride. (See: *Handsome Ransom, The; or, The Brigand's Bride*).

Pres St Gervais, Les. 3-act comic opera, text R.Reece, music A.Lecocq, Criterion, London 28.11.1874; Prince of Wales, Melbourne 10.7.1876, initial 6 performances.

Prince of Pilsen, The. 2-act musical comedy, text F.Pixley, music G.Luders, Shaftesbury, London 14.5.1904; Royal, Sydney 30.5.1908, initial 36 performances.

Princess Caprice. (See: *Liebe Augustin, Der*).

Princess Ida; or, Castle Adamant. 2-act comic opera, text W.S.Gilbert, music Sir Arthur Sullivan, Savoy, London 5.1.1884; Princess's, Melbourne 16.7.1887, initial 29 performances.

Princess de Trebizonde, La. 2-act comic opera, text C.Nuitter and E.Tréfeu, music J.Offenbach, Baden Baden 31.7.1869; revised version, Bouffes Parisiens, Paris 7.12.1869; Gaiety, London 16.4.1870; Prince of Wales, Melbourne 22.6.1874, initial 29 performances.

Princess Toto. 3-act comic opera, text W.S.Gilbert, music F.Clay, Royal, Nottingham 1.7.1876; Strand, London 2.10.1876; Opera House, Melbourne 12.6.1886, initial 13 performances.

Prinz Methusalem. 3-act operetta, text K.Treumann after V.Wilder and A.Delacour, music J.Strauss, Carl, Vienna 3.1.1877; Folies Dramatiques, London 19.5.1883; Princess's, Melbourne 22.9.1883, initial 16 performances.

Prisoner of Zenda, The. 4-act drama by E.Rose, from A.Hope's novel (1894), St James's, London 7.1.1896; Princess's, Melbourne 13.2.1897, initial 24 performances.

Projected scenery. First used on the Australian stage at the Sydney Royal in 1835, during a production of the drama, *The Flying Dutchman*. When the author of this play, E.Fitzball, was faced with the news that the construction of a ship for the first performance of his play at London's Adelphi in 1827 would cost £200 for timber alone, he replied: 'Darken the scene by turning off the gas, then while your chorus, invisible in the darkness, sing, draw off the flats, and a gentleman I can recommend to you, will throw, with his magic lantern, on the invisible union a better phantom ship than all the ship carpenters in Woolwich Dockyard could build with Peter the Great to assist them.' This was done with the Sydney performance of the play. The 'invisible union' was a fine semi-transparent calico or gauze. By means of back-projection of a painted glass slide on to this sheet or drop a very convincing image of the dark shape of the storm-tossed phantom ship was not only presented, but could be made to move horizontally across the stage in a manner to cause gasps of astonishment from the audience.

Prologue. An introductory, expository verse, usually in rhymed couplets, spoken at the opening of a new theatre, play, or special performance. Some of the world's most notable theatrical prologues are remembered today by only one of their many rhymed couplets, as that from Dr Johnson's *Prologue at the opening of Drury Lane Theatre,* 20.9.1747:

   . . . The drama's laws the drama's patrons give,
   For we that live to please, must please to live . . .

There is also the couplet from the so-called Barrington Prologue, supposedly spoken at the opening of the Sydney Theatre, but in reality never spoken at any theatre. It was written and published by an English poetaster, Henry Carter, in the *Annual Register* for 1801. Apparently Carter used often to amuse himself writing imaginary opening prologues for all kinds of theatres. The Carter couplet is remembered not for its theatrical associations, but for its sardonic comment on the foundation of Australia:

   . . . True patriots all, for it be understood,
   We left our country for our country's good.

Australian newspapers throughout the nineteenth century published copies of prologues spoken at the opening of the various theatres, not one of which was in any way notable either as poetry or literature. Perhaps the prologue spoken at the opening of Levey's Sydney Royal on 5.10.1833 could be taken as typical of them all. (See: *Theatre Comes to Australia,* pp.107-109). The practice of reading or reciting prologues died out as the century began to draw to a close.

Promessi Sposi, I (The Betrothed). 4-act opera, text by unknown author, but based on Manzoni's novel, music A. Ponchielli, Cremona 30.8.1856; revised version Milan 1872; Alexandra, Melbourne 10.2.1887, initial 5 performances.

Prompt book. An interleaved copy of a printed or ms play in which the stage manager, actor, prompter, or producer marked movements and groupings, often supported by stage diagrams and sketches of the stage settings. The prompt book for a production was the manager's and prompter's *vade mecum*. In it were also marked cuts in the dialogue, additions or alterations, stage directions, light cues, and property lists. Today a well marked and illustrated 19th-century prompt book is extremely valuable, giving as it does all the 'mechanics' of a production. Most of the prompt books still in existence were the property of famous English and American actors such as William Macready, Charles Kean, and Edwin Booth. They are held today by the major university and public libraries in both countries.

Prompter, The. His primary task was to supply to the actor in audible tones the word or phrase needed when the actor 'dried up' or forgot his lines. He was one of the most important members of the company in a theatre which, for the first half of the century at least, had to provide programmes of extraordinary length and variety, with a different one almost every night. No doubt many plays had to be cut or shortened, but even so the demand made on the actors' memory was very heavy. Reviews of performances in Australian theatres in the first half of the century can be found many times over in which it was said that during a performance the prompter's voice was heard more often than the actors', or far too often. But the prompter had other duties as well. It was he who prepared the lengths or sides for each actor, or copied out whole plays; who wrote out the bills of the day for the printer; who had charge of stage properties, wrote 'puffs' for the newspapers, kept a record of fines imposed on actors for derelection of duties, and 'gave out', i.e. announced, the play for the next night at the end of each performance. Sometimes he was even called on to 'swell a procession' as a supernumerary. As theatrical programmes became shorter, and finally reached the one play a night production the work of the prompter diminished, and finally disappeared — except when an emergency arose. (See: Playbill).

PS and OP. (See: Stage directions).

Prophete, Le (The Prophet). 5-act opera, text A.E.Scribe, music G.Meyerbeer, Opéra, Paris 19.4.1849; Covent Garden, London 24.7.1849; Prince of Wales, Sydney 12.4.1864, initial 6 performances.

Protean. A term derived from Proteus, the Greek demi-god of the sea, who was able to change shape at will. In the 19th-century theatre the word was used to describe, and to advertise, quick-change music hall and vaudeville acts and artists. In a matter of seconds the actor would make quick changes in his appearance and character, sometimes in view of the audience, sometimes behind a screen, and then sing, dance or act in his new character.

Puritani di Scozia, I (The Puritans of Scotland). 3-act opera, text C.Pepoli, based on the play *Têtes rondes et Cavaliers* by J.Ancelot and X.B.Santine, and on Sir Walter Scott's novel *Old Mortality* (1816), music V.Bellini, Italian, Paris 25.1.1835; King's, London 21.5.1835; Prince of Wales, Sydney 6.7.1863, initial 3 performances.

Puritan's Daughter, The. 3-act comic opera, text J.Bridgeman, music M.Balfe, Covent Garden, London 30.11.1861; Varieties (a music hall), Melbourne 13.3.1869, initial 11 performances.

Purse, The; or, Benevolent Tar. Musical drama, text C. Cross, music W.Reeve, Haymarket, London 8.2.1794; Royal, Sydney 7.12.1833.

THEATRE ROYAL, SYDNEY.

The first Play Bill as Theatre Royal printed in this Colony

ON WEDNESDAY, DECEMBER the 26th, 1832,
THIS THEATRE
Will open for the first time, with New Scenery, Machinery, Dresses, and Decorations, under the management of

MR. MEREDITH.

The Pieces selected for the opening are first:
THAT MUCH ADMIRED

Nautical Melo-Drama,
IN THREE ACTS,
CALLED,

BLACK-EYED SUSAN;
OR,
ALL IN THE DOWNS.

ADMIRAL, by Mr. Vale.
CAPTAIN CROSSTREE, by Mr. Cooper.
LIEUTENANT PIKE, by Mr. Raymond.
BLUE PETER, by Mr. Richardson.
SEAWEED, by Mr. Taylor.
QUID, by Mr. Kirby.

DOGGRASS, by Mr. Buckingham.
JACOB TWIG, by Mr. L. C. Cook.
GNATBRAIN, by Mr. Vale.
PLOUGHSHARE, by Mr. Varley.
RAKER, by Mr. Hollingsworth.
HATCHET, by Mr. Hill.
YARN, by Mr. Sykes.

WILLIAM, BY MR. MEREDITH.
BLACK-EYED SUSAN, by Mrs. Love. DOLLY MAY-FLOWER, by Mrs. Weston.
Captains, Midshipman, Sailors, Villagers, &c. &c.

To conclude with that Far-famed Highly Comic Farce,
IN TWO ACTS,
FROM TAYLOR'S CELEBRATED POEM, ENTITLED,

MONSIEUR TONSON.

MORBLEU, by Mr. Meridith.
TOM KING, by Mr. Cooper.
JACK ARDOURLY, by Mr. Buckingham.
USEFUL, by Mr. Raymond.
WANTOM, by Mr. Taylor.
TRAP, by Mr. Kirby.

MR. THOMPSON, by Mr. Vale.
RUSTY, by Mr. Hill.
NAP, by Mr. Ryder.
FIP, by Mr. Hollingsworth.
WAITER, by Mr. Barnard.
SNAP, by Mr. Barns.

ADELPHINE DE COURCY, Mrs. Weston. MADAME BELLEGARDE, Mrs. Love.
MRS. THOMPSON, by Mrs Ward.

The Performance to be supported by the Band of His Majesty's 17th Regiment, kindly allowed by COLONEL DESPARD, and conducted by Mr. Lewis.

BOX SEATS, 5s. PIT SEATS, 3s.

Playbill for the first performance at Barnett Levey's 'saloon' Sydney 1832

Q

Quaker, The. 2-act comic opera, text and music C.Dibdin, Drury Lane, London 7.10.1777; Albert, Hobart 29.3.1842, initially 1 performance.

Quaker Courtship, A. 2-act comic opera, text and music G.Hindmarsh Jamieson, Repertory Theatre, Sydney 9.9.1914, initial 2 performances.

Quaker Girl, 3-act musical comedy, text J.Tanner, music L.Monckton, Adelphi, London 5.11.1910; Her Majesty's, Sydney 13.1.1912, initial 90 performances.

Quality Street. 4-act comedy by J.M.Barrie, Vaudeville, London 17.9.1902; Princess's, Melbourne 12.8.1905, initial 11 performances.

Queen of the Thames, The; or, The Anglers. 1-act operetta, text E.Fitzball, music J.L.Hatton, Drury Lane, London 25.2.1843; Royal Victoria, Sydney 2.10.1856.

Queen's Lace Handkerchief, The. (See: *Spitzentuch der Königin, Das*).

Queen's Love, The. 5-act tragedy by David Burn, Royal Victoria, Sydney 29.9.1845.

Queer Client, The; or, The Avenger. 3-act drama by C.A.Dibdin, from the story of the same title in Charles Dickens' *The Posthumous Papers of the Pickwick Club (1837),* Royal Victoria, Sydney 16.5.1842. Published W.Baker, Sydney, 1842.

Queen Venus. (See: *Moustique*).

Quiet Little Dinner, A. 1-act play by E.W.O'Sullivan, Royal Standard, Sydney 29.9.1908. (See: Parliamentarians).

Quite Colonial. Vaudeville by W.M.Akhurst, music S.Nelson, Mechanics' Institute, Melbourne 20.3.1854.

Quo Vadis? 5-act drama by W.Barrett, adapted from H.Sienkiewicz's novel (1895), Lyceum, Edinburgh 29.5.1900; Her Majesty's, Melbourne 10.9.1901, initial 4 performances.

Scene from Quite Colonial *1854*

R

Rainbow Revels. Entertainment written for the Stewart family by G.Walch, Mechanics' Institute, Launceston 26.12.1877, initial 4 performances. (See: Stewart, Nellie).

Raking piece. A cut-out painted to imitate rocks, mossy slopes, a flowering bank, etc., set at the back or sides of the stage. These were often practicable, being built for the actors to sit or lie on, or to make or hide a ramp, etc. (See: Set scene).

Raymond and Agnes. 2-act melodrama by M.G.Lewis, Norwich 22.11.1800; Emu Plains 11.6.1827.

Raymond, Lord of Milan. 3-act tragedy by Edward Reeve, Royal Victoria, Sydney 14.9.1863, initial 3 performances. Published Hawksley and Cunninghame, Sydney, 1851. Copy in Mitchell Library, Sydney.

Recruiting Officer, The. 5-act comedy by George Farquhar, Drury Lane, London 8.4.1706. First play to be performed in Australia, acted by convicts in Sydney in small hut converted to crude theatre, 4.6.1789.

Redgrave, George Ellsworthy (1872-1922). Better known as Roy Redgrave. Actor, playwright, and film star. Made his stage debut in the English provinces, and his first London appearance in the East End, at the Britannia, at the age of 22. A matinee-idol type of actor in his early years, he never got a chance to show his worth in the West End theatre. In 1904 he came to Australia under contract to J.C.Williamson, where he earned high praise for his acting in the character part of Flambeau in Rostand's *L'Aiglon,* (1900), which starred the young American-trained actress, Titell Brune. They toured Australia and New Zealand in this and other productions for more than a year, on their return appearing in

Camille. Redgrave established a following in Australia during these years, but like all other actors had his ups and downs. By 1908 he was back in London, playing lead in a production of the Walch-Dampier *Robbery Under Arms* at the Pavilion. Back in Australia again the following year, he played Dave Goulburn in the first production of *The Man From Outback* by Albert Edmunds. The *Argus* said he played in 'fine, manly, dashing fashion.' Following this he was given the role of Jack Macquarie in Randolph Bedford's *White Australia; or, The Empty North*. From then on he appeared in both Australian and English melodramas with success, usually as the dashing young hero. He was Jack Dunstan in *A Miner's Trust*, the French villain in *The Winning Ticket*, Jack Melton in *My Mate*, and Rodney Shannon in *England's Hope*. All of these were produced by W.Anderson, who on 7.10.1911 also produced Roy Redgrave's 4-act stage version of the Marie Corelli novel, *The Sorrows of Satan*. Redgrave had already had at least 6 plays produced in England. He remained in Australia, gravitating with the sudden growth of the industry to motion pictures. He starred in the following 'silents': *The Christian*, made in 1911; *The Crisis, Moondyne, The Remittance Man, The Reprieve, The Road to Ruin, The Sick Stockman* — all filmed in 1913; *Our Friends the Hayseeds* in 1917, and *Robbery Under Arms* in 1920. He died at St Vincent's Hospice, Darlinghurst, survived by his wife, Minnie.

Red Mill, The. Two-act musical comedy, text H.Blossom, music V.Herbert, Knickerbocker, New York 24.9.1906; Empire, London 26.12.1919; Royal, Sydney 11.7.1908, initial 39 performances.

Reeve, Wybert (1831-1906). English provincial actor and dramatist, born in London, who spent the second half of his life in Australia, principally in Adelaide. Apparently Reeve first visited Australia at the age of twenty-one, attracted by the gold rushes, for in 1880 the *Bulletin* reported that his first play, a farce called *An Australian Hoax*, was produced at Pyrmont, Sydney in 1852. The Adelaide publication, the *Lantern*, in 1889 gave the title of this as *An Australian Hoof*, and the year as 1850. By 1859 Reeve, now back in England, had produced the first of the 16 plays he wrote and produced before returning to Australia in 1878 — *A Match for a Mother-in-law* — produced at Manchester. Other centres in which his plays were first produced were Sheffield, Swansea, Scarborough, and Newcastle. Only two were produced in London, one at the Olympic and one at the Crystal Palace. He produced two of the 16 in Australia — *No Name* (1877), under the new title, *Great Temptation* in Melbourne in 1879, and *George Geith; or, A Romance of City Life* (1877) in Adelaide in 1880. While in Australia he wrote and produced seven plays, one of which was a dramatisation of Mrs Campbell Praed's novel, *Policy and Passion* (1881), which Reeve played under the title *Passion*. His most successful play, in terms of the number of performances it had, was *Only Dust*. In 1880 Reeve managed Garner's (the former White's

Rooms) in Adelaide; in 1889 he managed the Adelaide Royal for Williamson, Garner, and Musgrove, and in 1891 he became sole lessee of that theatre. He returned to England in 1900, being farewelled by the South Australian University Shakespearean Society, of which he was vice president. He was presented with a valedictory address by the Chief Justice of South Australia, Sir S.J.Way.

Revolte, La (The Revolt). 1-act play by V.Adam, translated by Lady Barclay, Bijou, Bayswater 5.4.1906; Melbourne Repertory, Turn Verein Hall 2.10.1911, initially 1 performance.

Repertory movement, The. Strictly speaking, what was called the repertory movement in Australia was misnamed. A true repertory theatre is one with several productions always in readiness so that a different one can be presented each night if necessary, and with a more or less permanent corps of actors. In Australia the term seems to have been largely used to denote the non-commercial, non-profit-making theatre, perhaps because the more appropriate word, 'amateur,' is sometimes used as a derogatory term associated with a lack of seriousness. These theatres were formed at the beginning of the present century by enthusiasts who believed that there was something more worthwhile than melodrama, and that the 'better class of play' could be written as well in Australia as overseas. Notable among the theatres or groups up to 1914 were Leon Brodzky's Playgoers' Society (originally called the Australian Theatre Society), founded in Melbourne in 1904 and disbanded in 1909. It seems to have concerned itself chiefly with play-readings. The next move came from Adelaide, where in 1909 Bryceson Treharne of the Adelaide Conservatorium formed a group which became the Adelaide Literary Theatre, and then the Adelaide Repertory Theatre. The most diverse and successful of the repertory theatres in Melbourne was that formed by Gregan McMahon in 1911, which successfully staged Australian and overseas 'serious' drama until the outbreak of war in 1914. Various dramatic groups were also formed in Sydney during the period, including the Sydney Repertory Theatre, the Players' Club, the Sydney Muffs, and the Playgoers' Club which produced work by Australian writers.

Resurrection. 4-act drama adapted by H.Bataille and M.Morton from the novel by Tolstoy, Vaudeville, London 23.10.1902; Her Majesty's, Melbourne 12.9.1903, initial 24 performances.

Return of the Prodigal, The. 4-act comedy by St John Hankin, Court, London 26.9.1905; Melbourne Repertory, Athenaeum Hall, 1.10.1912, initially 1 performance.

Revenge, The. 5-act tragedy by E.Young, Drury Lane, London April 1721; The Theatre, Sydney 16.1.1796.

Reynolds, Walter (1852-1941). Actor, dramatist, theatre proprietor who gained his experience in English provincial theatres. Arriving in Australia at the beginning of 1878, he made his debut at the Melbourne Academy of Music (Bijou), and from then until he left Australia in 1882 acted in the major Australian theatres. While in Australia he also tried his hand at playwriting, producing his *Gold and Alloy* (later retitled *Tried and True*), *The Sprissawneen,* and *Snow* in Melbourne, and his *Ould Erin* and *Vanity Fair* in Sydney. He also acted in a number of George Darrell's plays, and took over the lead in that actor-dramatist's *The Forlorn Hope* in 1880 when Darrell's wife died. Towards the end of 1882 he left for the USA, where he produced *Vanity Fair* and other plays. Back in England in 1885, between 1886 and 1899 he wrote a further 8 plays and became the proprietor of 2 provincial theatres. Persisting with his playwriting, in the new century he produced four more plays between 1901 and 1905, one of them, *The Sin of a Life,* being written for Charles Warner at London's Princess's. Then he apparently devoted himself to his managerial and other work for the next 25 years or so until, at the age of 82, he produced at London's Victoria Palace on 10.9.1934 what he believed to be his greatest play in a long lifetime of playwriting — *Young England.* It was both a triumph and a tragedy; a triumph in that it made him more than £3000, a tragedy in that the audiences which packed the theatre every night came merely to laugh at what they saw as an old-fashioned melodrama. The London *Times,* which said his attempt to restore virile melodrama to the London stage was bold enough to deserve success, was a lot kinder than these audiences, who howled and shrieked night after night and spoke the actors' lines for them. The author sat through many of these performances alone in one of the stage boxes, applauding each time an applause point was made, and entreating the audience to be quiet and listen. They continued to guy the play through each of its 282 performances, which were given first at the Victoria Palace, then at the Kingsway, Daly's, and the Piccadilly. It had a short revival at the Holborn Empire in 1939, where, with war a reality, its message was taken a little more seriously. Two years later its author died, aged 89.

Rheingold, Das. (See: *Ring des Nibelungen, Der*).

Richard III. Historical drama by William Shakespeare, believed to have been first performed in London in 1592 or 1593; Royal, Sydney 26.12.1833. Research has not yet established which of the many performances of this play in Australia were Shakespeare's, and which the Colley Cibber version. This was first performed in 1700, and up to at least the middle of the 19th century was regarded as a better acting version than the original.

Rickards, Harry (1845-1911). Stage name adopted by Benjamin Leete, an English music hall singer and comedian who established a chain of Tivoli theatres (variety or vaudeville houses) in Australia.

Above: George Rignold as Marc Antony 1889
Right: George Fawcett Rowe 1863

Trained as a civil engineer, he chose instead the life of a music hall singer and entertainer, being taken by the songs and mannerisms of the two most famous music hall singers of his day, G.Leybourne and H.Vance. They specialised in 'masher,' 'toff,' or 'swell' roles. In 1868 he was offered an engagement at Wilton's Musical Hall in London. His success there led to engagements at the larger Oxford, and Canterbury Halls, where he remained for the next 3 years. His most famous song was *Captain Jinks of the Horse Marines,* one of the army 'swell' songs popular at the time. (1870)

I'm Captain Jinks of the Horse Marines,
I feed my horse on corn and beans,
Which, of course, is a great deal beyond the means
Of a captain in the Army.

Other songs he made famous in his early years were *Oxford Joe,* and *Mugby Junction, My cabbage and my turnip tops,* and *I can do a double-shuffle with the thimble and the pea.* He brought a small company to Australia in 1871, and stayed until 1874. During this first visit he used material written for him by the Australian writers, Marcus Clarke and Garnet Walch. He then returned to England, moving between the 2 countries with varying degrees of success, but making his name well known throughout Australia and New Zealand. From 1892 he made Australia his home. Having proved that variety, a superior form of the earlier music hall turn (or vaudeville, as it was also known) was popular, he took a lease of the Sydney Garrick in 1893 and turned it into the first Tivoli, a theatre devoted entirely to vaudeville turns, bringing to Australia stars in the field from all over the world. He opened Tivolis in Melbourne and Adelaide, and had companies in Perth, Kalgoorlie, Brisbane, and New Zealand. The profits from his theatres for the 11 years before his death were estimated at about £250 000.

Rienzi; the last of the Tribunes. Drama by J.B.Buckstone, adapted from Bulwer-Lytton's novel (1835), Adelphi, London 3.2.1836; Royal Victoria, Sydney 2.3.1846.

Richelieu; or, The Conspiracy. 5-act drama by Bulwer-Lytton, Covent Garden, London 7.3.1839; Royal Victoria, Sydney 28.6.1853.

Rights of Woman, The. Vaudeville by W.M.Akhurst, music S.Nelson, Mechanics' Institute, Melbourne 24.7.1854.

Rignold, George (1838-1912). With his brother William (1836-1904), the children of actor parents, began his professional acting career in the theatres at Bristol and Bath in 1859, playing every part that came his way so as to gain experience. By 1862 he and his brother were the chief male supports at Bristol Royal. In 1863 a new Royal was opened at Bath with a production of *A Midsummer Night's Dream,* in which George played Theseus. The Titania was Ellen Terry. Soon after this, together with other members of the stock company who also achieved theatrical fame

— Marie Wilton, George Melville, Charles Dillon, W.H.Vernon, and others — he moved on to London. Here he played Caliban in *The Tempest* at the Queen's in 1871, and the following year launched a production of *Romeo and Juliet* in which he played Romeo to the Juliet of Adelaide Neilson. In this year (1872) Charles Calvert at Manchester put on a series of Shakespeare revivals at the Prince's, including an outstanding production of *Henry V*. This was sold outright — settings, costumes, properties, music, and 'book' — to Jarrett and Palmer of Booth's, New York. At Calvert's suggestion, George Rignold was chosen to play lead in the New York production, which opened on 8.2.1875 and is said to have run for more than 100 nights. From then on Rignold *was* Henry V. He played the role throughout the USA, in Australia, New Zealand, and in London up to as late as 1901, when he was in his sixty-third year. In 1876 he gave performances in San Francisco before leaving for Australia, where a Sydney season was given. He returned to the USA, but was back in Australia the following year, when performances were given in Melbourne, and throughout New Zealand. With the money he made from these productions he was able to lease Drury Lane in London, where he opened in *Henry V* towards the end of 1879. For the first time in English theatre history London thus received a Drury Lane production of *Henry V* via Manchester, New York, San Francisco, Australia, and New Zealand. London was not impressed. For the next few years Rignold alternated between London, New York, and Australia. In 1884 he made Australia his permanent home. From 1887 to 1889 he was part-owner and lessee of Her Majesty's, Sydney, and then lessee until 1895. Here he presented a series of artistically mounted melodramas. In 1888 he branched out as a dramatist, with a 5-act version of *Uncle Tom's Cabin*. In 1898 he made a final tour of New Zealand with *Henry V,* and the following year staged a sumptuous production of *Othello* at Sydney's Criterion. In 1899 he wrote *The Three Musketeers* with Bernard Espinasse; *Flesh and the Devil* on his own, and *Dreyfus; or, Vive la France* with Walter Bentley. He revived *Henry V* in 1900 and 1901, but from then on was rarely seen on the stage. He published the text of his versions of *Henry V* in Sydney in 1876 and 1887; of *Julius Caesar* and *A Midsummer Night's Dream* in 1889; *Macbeth* and *The Merry Wives of Windsor* in 1890, and of *Othello* in 1899. Copies are in the Mitchell Library, Sydney.

Rigoletto. 3-act opera, text F.M.Piave, based on Victor Hugo's play' *Le Roi s'amuse,* (1832), Fenice, Venice 11.3.1851; Covent Garden, London 14.5.1843; Royal, Melbourne 15.9.1860, initial 2 performances.

Ring des Nibelungen, Der (The Ring of the Nibelungs). Operatic tetraology by Richard Wagner, Bayreuth 13, 14, 16, 17.8.1876; Her Majesty's, London 5-9.5.1882; Her Majesty's, Melbourne *Das*

Left: Harry Rickards 1889
Below: G. H. Rogers 1854

Rheingold 19.8.1913; *Die Walküre* 22.8.1913; *Siegfried* 25.8.1913, *Götterdämmerung* 29.8.1913.

Rip Van Winkle. 3-act comic opera, text H.Meilhac and P.Gille, music R.Planquette, Comedy, London 14.10.1882; Opera House, Melbourne 1.1.1884, initial 27 performances.

Ristori, Adelaide (1822-1906). Italian actress, child of actor parents. Said to have made her first stage appearance at 14 in *Francesca da Rimini*. By the age of 18 she had developed into an actress of exceptional brilliance, outstanding as Juliet and in such plays as Goldoni's *La Locandiera*, Schiller's *Maria Stuart*, and in *Antigone*, and *Ottavia*, both by Alfieri. In 1847 she married the Marquis Capranica del Grillo, and retired temporarily from the stage. She made her debut in Paris in 1855, and in New York ten years later. Everywhere she was regarded as the outstanding tragedienne of her day. Madame Ristori visited Australia in 1875, where she appeared as Mary Stuart, Marie Antoinette, Medea, Phedre, Judith, and Lucrezia Borgia. Though all her plays were performed in her native tongue, her visit was as much a social as a theatrical occasion, and she never wanted for an audience. Everyone, critics included, found that her acting was so true to nature that she was able to make herself perfectly understood. General Bartolomeo Galletti, who accompanied Madame Ristori and her company to Australia, in 1877 wrote of their tour that it was not as financially or artistically successful as they had hoped it would be. 'In Sydney, Melbourne, Sandhurst (Bendigo), Ballarat, Geelong, and Adelaide, eighty five recitals were given, for which the company received £13 336,' he wrote. But they had expected more. They had heard that in Australia a pound was spent 'with the same indifference as five lira are in Italy. This we found to be quite the contrary.' He added that although there were plenty of wealthy people in Australia, 'yet a cultural class has not had time to form itself.'

Rivals, The. 5-act comedy by R.B.Sheridan, Covent Garden, London 17.1.1775; Royal, Sydney 14.11.1833.

Rob Roy MacGregor; or, Auld Lang Syne. 3-act drama by I.Pocock, Covent Garden, London 12.3.1818; Emu Plains, May 1830 (as *Rob Roy*).

Robert le Diable (Robert the Devil). 5-act opera, text A.E.Scribe and G.Delavigne, music G.Meyerbeer, Opéra, Paris 21.11.1831; Drury Lane, London 20.2.1832; Princess's, Melbourne 16.5.1857, initially 2 performances.

Roberto Devereux, Comte d'Essex. 3-act opera, text S.Cammarano after F.Ancelot's *Elizabeth d'Angleterre*, music G.Donizetti, San Carlo, Naples 29.10.1837; Her Majesty's, London 24.6.1841; Alexandra, Melbourne 17.1.1887, initial 5 performances.

Robin Hood. (See: *Maid Marian and Robin Hood*).

Robinson, Sir William Cleaver Francis (1834-1897). British civil administrator who held several posts as governor in the Australian colonies. He was at various times Governor of Prince Edward Island, Western Australia (three times), Victoria, and South Australia. An amateur musician and a patron of music in Australia, he was also a composer, with a number of popular ballads to his credit and the operetta *The Handsome Ransom; or The Brigand's Bride,* first produced at Government House, Perth in 1894. A revised version called *Predatoros; or, The Brigand's Bride* was given a public rehearsal before a selected audience in Melbourne's Vienna Cafe in July 1894, followed by a full performance at Melbourne's Princess's in November 1894. He also composed the opera *The Nut-Brown Maid* (1896) which was never performed.

Robbery Under Arms. 5-act drama by Alfred Dampier and Garnet Walch, founded on Rolf Boldrewood's novel (1888), Alexandra, Melbourne 1.3.1890, initial 42 performances. Produced at Princess's, London 22.10.1894, initial 17 performances. Later produced at Pavilion, London in 1908. Ms in British Library. Microfilm copy in Mitchell Library, Sydney.

Rogers, George Herbert (1812-1872). Born at Rochester, Kent, his stage training and experience were gained solely in the Australian theatre. Critics who had seen the leading actors of the English stage constantly compared his work to theirs, in his favour. A private soldier in an English regiment, he came to Hobart with the regiment, and soon became involved in amateur theatricals. It is said that he was seen to possess such a natural talent as an actor that a subscription was raised to buy his discharge. He acted first as a professional in Hobart, and then in Launceston, with George Coppin's company. He made his first appearance on the Australian mainland with the same company at Melbourne's Queen's, in 1845, when he played Colonel Dumas in *The Lady of Lyons*. Principally a comedian, it was said that 'his humour had a rich and unctuous character, which caused it to ooze out of him, as it were, at every pore.' His biggest successes were in such plays as *The School for Scandal, Romeo and Juliet, The Tempest, Camille,* and *A Midsummer Night's Dream*. He appeared in many plays by Australian dramatists, and played Mark Stornway in the first production of W.H.Cooper's *Sun and Shadow* in 1870.

Rolla of Ours; or, The Shameful Goings-on of the Spaniards in Peru. Burlesque of R.B.Sheridan's *Pizarro,* by W.M.Akhurst, Queen's, Melbourne 8.1.1855, initially 1 performance.

Romeo and Juliet. Tragedy by William Shakespeare, believed to have been first performed in London in 1595 or 1596; The Theatre, Hobart 31.3.1834. (See: *Capuletti ed i Montecchi, I*).

Roméo et Juliette. 5-act opera, text J.Barbier and A.Carré, based on Shakespeare's tragedy of the same title, music C.Gounod, Lyrique, Paris 27.4.1867; Covent Garden, London 11.7.1867; Princess's, Melbourne 2.4.1907, initially 1 performance.

Romeo and Juliet. 3-act opera, text and music G.W.L. Marshall Hall. Balcony scene only produced Her Majesty's, Melbourne 14.12.1912, initially 1 performance.

Rose of Auvergne, The. 1-act operetta, text H.B.Farnie (English version of *La Rose de Saint-Fleur*, Bouffes Parisiens 12.6.1856), music J.Offenbach, Gaiety, London 8.11.1869; Princess's, Melbourne 30.8.1871, initially 1 performance.

Rosencrantz and Guildenstern. Tragic episode in 3 tableaux by W.S.Gilbert, Vaudeville, London 3.6.1891; University of Melbourne Dramatic Club, Princess's 27.6.1910, initially 1 performance.

Rose of Castille (sic), The. 3-act opera, text A.G.Harris and E.Falconer, based on Auber's opera *Le Muletier de Toledo*, music M.Balfe, Lyceum, London 29.10.1857; Royal, Melbourne 14.6.1858, initial 3 performances.

Rose of Persia, The. 2-act comic opera, text B.Hood, music Sir Arthur Sullivan, Savoy, London 29.11.1899; Her Majesty's, Sydney 21.7.1900, initial 42 performances.

Rose of the Riviera, The. 2-act musical comedy, text R.Bacchus, music F.O.Carr, Eden, Brighton 25.5.1903; Lyceum, Sydney 28.5.1904, initial 29 performances.

Rosina. 2-act comic opera, text F.Brooke after Favart, music W.Shields, Covent Garden, London 31.12.1782; Royal, Sydney 15.9.1834.

Rosmersholm. 4-act drama by Henrik Ibsen, translated C.Archer, Vaudeville, London 23.2.1891; Melbourne Repertory, St Patrick's Hall, 5.12.1911, initial 3 performances.

Rowe, George Fawcett (1834-1889). One of three brothers, all born in Victoria and all of whom took to the stage. George Fawcett, the stage name he adopted, finished up as a dramatist whose work was performed in England and the USA, as well as in Australia and New Zealand. His father was an artist, and, inheriting some of his talent, George developed into a competent scenepainter. With the discovery of gold in the early 1850s, he joined in the rush to the goldfields, but, like the majority of the diggers, returned no richer than he had been when he left. So it was back to the theatre, but this time in the dual role of scenepainter and actor. Before long he was playing in such plays as *Camille* and *Faust*, and in Shakespeare's plays with G.V.Brooke. During all this he was also taking his first tentative steps as a playwright. In 1860 he earned high praise for his acting in R.H.Horne's *The Death of Marlowe*. The following year the first of his many plays, several of them adaptations of Charles Dickens's novels, was performed at the Melbourne Royal. In the mid-1860s he went to New Zealand, where in 1864 he opened a theatre in the Auckland Oddfellows' Hall. By 1866 he was in New York, and from then on alternated between that city and London. An 'Australian' occasion occurred at the Broadway, New York on 2.3.1878 when Rowe (as he called himself overseas) the Australian dramatist produced his drama from the French, *The Exiles,* with the Australian Alfred Dampier in the lead. It had an initial run of 43 performances. His plays, in nearly all of which he played lead, included: *Barnaby Rudge* (1861); *Dombey and Son* (1862); *David Copperfield* (1862); *The Woman in White* (1862); *North and South* (1863); *The Captain of the Vulture* (1863); *The Chamber of Horrors* (1863); *The Last of the Mohicans* (1863); *The Tower of London* (1863); *Nicholas Nickelby* (1864); *The Cricket on the Hearth* (1864); *Sampson's Wedding* (1870); *Found Drowned* (1870); *Sleigh Bells* (1872); *The Geneva Cross* (1874); *Brass* (1877); *The New Babylon* (1878); *Uncle Tom's Cabin* (1878); *Freedom* (1883); *The Donagh* (1884), and *Forward to the Front* (1888).

Royal Divorce, A. 5-act drama by W.G.Wills, Avenue, Sunderland 1.5.1891; Royal, Melbourne 1.8.1914, initial 30 performances.

Royal Middy, The. (See: *Seekadet, Der*).

Rudd, Steele. (See: Davis, Arthur Hoey).

Runaway Girl, A. 2-act musical comedy, text S.Hicks and H.Nicholls, music I.Caryll and L.Monckton, Gaiety, London 21.5.1898; Her Majesty's, Melbourne 15.2.1902, initial 54 performances.

Ruy Blas. 4-act opera, text D. d'Ormeville, after Victor Hugo, music F.Marchetti, Scala, Milan 3.4.1869; Her Majesty's, London 24.11.1877; Royal, Sydney 9.12.1876, initial 2 performances.

S

Sacred Flame, The. 1-act play by A.Buchanan, St Patrick's Hall, Melbourne 13.12.1911, initially 1 performance.

Sacred Place, The. 1-act play by Louis Esson, Turn Verein Hall, Melbourne 15.5.1912, initially 1 performance. Published with *The Woman Tamer* and *Dead Timber,* Fraser and Jenkinson, Melbourne 1912.

Saffo. 3-act opera, text S.Cammarano, music G.Pacini, San Carlo, Naples 29.11.1840; Princess's, Melbourne 12.7.1871, initial 2 performances.

Said Pasha. 2-act musical comedy, text S.Marble, music R.Stahl, Star, New York 25.2.1889; Criterion, Sydney 19.10.1901, initial 16 performances.

Saints and Sinners. 5-act drama by H.A.Jones, Prince of Wales, Greenwich 17.9.1884; Royal, Melbourne 7.12.1885, initial 15 performances.

Salathiel; or, The Jewish Chieftain. 3-act tragedy by Conrad Knowles, adapted from Bulwer-Lytton's novel *Leila: or, The Siege of Granada,* (1838), Royal Victoria, Sydney 4.8.1842, initially 1 performance. Published T.Trood, Sydney, 1842. Copy in Dixson Library, Sydney.

Samson et Dalila. 3-act opera, text F.Lemaire, music C.Saint-Saëns, Grand Ducal, Weimar 2.12.1877; Covent Garden, London 26.4.1909; Her Majesty's, Sydney 5.9.1911, initially 1 performance.

San Toy; or, The Emperor's Own. 2-act musical comedy, text E.Morton, music S.Jones, Daly's, London 21.10.1899; Her Majesty's, Melbourne 21.12.1901, initial 48 performances.

Above: The London production of Lord Byron's Sardanapalus *in 1834. The setting was copied for the 1857 Melbourne production at the Royal (below)*

Sardanapalus. 5-act tragedy by George Gordon, Lord Byron, Drury Lane, London 10.4.1834; Royal, Melbourne 19.10.1857, initial 12 performances.

Satanella; or, The Power of Love. 4-act romantic opera, text A.G.Harris and E.Falconer, based on Lesage's *Diable boiteux*, music M.Balfe, Covent Garden, London 20.12.1858; Royal, Melbourne 28.4.1862, initial 6 performances.

Scarlet Feather, The. (See: *Petite mariée, La*).

Scenepainting. Scenepainters and musicians, vitally important members of the 19th-century theatrical profession, have been unaccountably overlooked by historians. We know little about the orchestras or bands in the theatres of the period. The same is true of scenepainters, all of whom were, with few exceptions, remarkable artists. But their work, which involved an enormous outlay of time and physical labour, was ephemeral, and therefore their designs, maquettes, and the painted scenery itself have all been lost to us. All that remains are a few engravings and photographs of completed stage settings. Scenes for the 19th-century theatre were painted on flax canvas stretched on frames to make wings and flats; or attached to top and bottom wooden rollers to make an act drop, backscene, or cut cloth. The canvas was first primed with 'size', a liquid glue which had first to be brought to boiling point. When this was dry, the canvas was then primed with whiting mixed with size and water, painted on in the same way as the size. When this was dry the subject of the scene, or design for the wings or act drop, was drawn in with charcoal, and the work was then ready for painting. For his work the artist could draw on a palette of more than 30 colours (Lloyds), but sometimes only 25 (Benwell), plus the hundreds of tints to be derived from these. The medium was water-based distemper (dry colour) mixed with size, which always dried much lighter in colour than when it was wet. Besides having to juggle with this factor in choosing colour and density of colour, the scenepainter had also to take into consideration the change wrought in his colours at night by yellow gaslight and, subsequently, the glare of electric lighting. He had also to ensure that his scene 'carried' — that it presented an adequate and lifelike picture to each member of the audience. In the early days, when candles and oil lamps were the only lighting available, colour was much stronger than in the days of gas lighting. Under gas, for instance, ultramarine turned to muddy purple, yellow faded to white, light greens were darkened, and pinks lost their brilliance. Best books on the subject are Frederick Lloyds's *Practical Guide to Scene Painting and Painting in Distemper* (1875), and H.L.Benwell's series of articles in *Amateur Work*. (See: Bibliography. Also under Clint, Goatcher, Gordon, Habbe, Hennings, Wilson).

Schöne Galathee, Die. 1-act operettta, text P.Henrion, music F. von

Suppe, Meysel's, Berlin 30.6.1865; Gaiety, London (as *Ganymede and Galatea*) 20.1.1872; Queen's, Sydney 2.3.1878, initial 6 performances.

School for Scandal, The. 5-act comedy by R.B.Sheridan, Drury Lane, London 8.5.1777; Royal, Sydney 26.1.1835.

Scout, The. 3-act drama by Alfred Dampier and Garnet Walch, Alexandra, Melbourne 9.5.1891, initial 35 performances. Retitled *The Prairie King,* and produced Her Majesty's, Sydney 5.10.1895, initial 24 performances.

Seagull, The (Chaika). 4-act drama by Anton Chekhov, translated G.Calderon, Royal, Glasgow 2.11.1909; Little, London 31.3.1912; Melbourne Repertory, Athenaeum Hall 20.7.1912, initially 1 performance.

Searelle, Luscombe (1853-1907). Real name William Luscombe Searell. Author and composer. Born in Devon, he came to New Zealand with his parents in the early 1860s, where he completed his education at Christ's College, Christchurch. Intended for the law, but instead chose the theatre. His works for the stage, which were produced in Australia, New Zealand, England, the USA, and South Africa, include *The Wreck of the Pinafore* (1880); *The Fakir of Travencore* (1881); *Estrella* (1883); *Bobadil* (1884); *Isidora* (later retitled *The Black Rover*) (1885); *The Kisses of Circe* (1896), and *Mizpah* (1905).

Seating capacity. In 1907 interstate, previously intercolonial, rivalry between Sydney and Melbourne flared when a Melbourne newspaper claimed that that city was the 'theatrical headquarters of Australia.' The *Sydney Morning Herald* immediately rejected the claim, countering with the statement that J.C.Williamson had deliberately moved his offices from Melbourne to Sydney because he regarded Sydney as 'theatrically more important.' To rub it in, the *Herald* then quoted figures to show that in 1903, in 2 seasons, 121 grand opera performances had been given in Sydney, averaging all through £258 a week better receipts than Melbourne, where only eighty-four performances had been possible. This newspaper quoted what it said were capacity figures for Melbourne and Sydney theatres which showed that Melbourne theatres seated a total 15 600 people, but that Sydney theatres seated 20 300, without including such smaller theatres as the Royal Standard, New Masonic Hall, Protestant Hall, and Hippodrome. The figures quoted were: Melbourne, Her Majesty's, seating 2600; Princess's 2100; Royal 1900; Opera House 1600; Bijou (closed for a long period) 1500; gaiety 1500: Town Hall 2300; Temperance Hall 1200; Athenaeum Hall 900. The figures for Sydney were: Her Majesty's 2000; Royal 1900; Lyceum 1900; Criterion 1700; Palace 1300; Tivoli 1200; National Amphitheatre 2200; Oxford 700; Town Hall 3300; Centenary Hall 1500; YMCA Hall 700; Queen's Hall 700; St James's Hall 500; Victoria Hall 700. All these figures were for 'normal' nights. They ignored the illegal practices frequently indulged in by theatre managers when they had a 'winner' on their hands — selling 'standing room,' putting extra chairs down one side of each aisle, and sometimes putting a plank from arm-rest to arm-rest across an aisle to make extra seats, in their attempts to pack more people in.

Second Mrs Tanqueray, The. 4-act drama by A.W.Pinero, St James's, London 28.5.1893; Lyceum, Sydney 14.4.1894, initial 18 performances.

Second price. (See: Half-price).

Secret Service. 4-act drama by W.Gillette, Adelphi, London 15.5.1897; Her Majesty's, Sydney 26.8.1899, initial 18 performances.

Seekadet, Der (The Royal Middy). 3-act comic opera, text F.Zell, music R.Genée, Theater an der Wien, Vienna 24.10.1876; Daly's, New York (as *The Royal Middy*) 28.1.1880; Globe, London (as *The Naval Cadets*) 27.3.1880; Prince of Wales, Melbourne (as *The Royal Middy*) 1.10.1880; initial 20 performances.

Semiramide (Semiramis). 2-act opera, text G.Rossi, based on Voltaire's tragedy, music G.Rossini, Fenice, Venice 3.2.1823; His Majesty's, London 15.7.1824; Royal, Melbourne 22.1.1866, initial 6 performances.

Sensation scenes. 'Sensation is what the public wants,' the playwright Dion Boucicault is said to have told New York critic William Winter, 'and you can't give them too much of it.' Boucicault is said to have coined the term 'sensation scene,' and to have introduced the kind of scene it describes — one in which the sensation is a supreme example of the scenepainter's and machinist's as well as the dramatist's art; in which human beings are threatened or overwhelmed by natural or man-made disasters from which there appears to be no escape. Boucicault was, of course, simply restating or reintroducing something which had been a part of the drama since drama began. Nothing could have been more sensational than the scene in *Pizarro* (1799) in which Rolla crosses the wooden bridge over the cataract, pursued by soldiers who shoot at and hit him. Despite his wound, Rolla snatches the child whose rescue is the purpose of the pursuit, and 'tears from the rock the tile which supports the bridge, and retreats by the background, bearing off the child.' That collapsing bridge scene was to be used in many plays after *Pizarro*. Each generation called on the resources of the technology and engineering skills of its day, and as these advanced, so did the ingenuity of the sensation scene. When, in *The Cataract of the Ganges,* Moncrieff's drama of 1823, audiences saw a scene in a ravine in which a fierce fight is going on for the heights, and the trees in the ravine are set on fire, they also witnessed what was later to be called a sensation scene. 'The burning trees fall on all sides, and discover the terrific cataract of Gangotin, supposed to form the source of the Ganges — the Emperor and the Bramin's troops appear, pouring down the rocky heights around the cataract in every direction . . .' Another favourite sensation scene was the graphic representation of the sinking of a ship, popular from the days of *The Tempest* to those of *The Sins of Society* (1907). In Australia several dramatists followed Boucicault's lead, among them Cooper, Darrell, Dampier, and Holt. But it must not be assumed from all this that the sensation scene was the only worthwhile thing about these plays. Boucicault, particularly, wrote plays which to this day stand as models of characterisation and plotting. Seen in their correct context, they are also prime examples of successful stage dialogue. (See: Tank drama).

Serenade, The. 3-act comic opera, text R.Sprague, music V.Herbert, Knickerbocker, Boston 16.3.1897; Princess's, Melbourne 18.7.1903, initial 23 performances.

Sergeant Brue. 3-act musical comedy, text O.Hall, music L.Lehmann, Strand, London 14.6.1904; Criterion, Sydney 29.1.1910, initial 17 performances.

Set scene. As the century progressed stage settings became more elaborate, inasmuch as attempts were made to give them a third dimension. Landscapes were 'taken apart.' Instead of the whole scene being painted on one surface, such as a backdrop or the back flats, sometimes only the sky and clouds would be painted on the back scene. All other elements in the picture — a row of trees, a cottage front, a fence, a downward curving bank, a bridge, a rocky outcrop — would be made of separate, cut-out wood and canvas pieces and set one behind the other. Lights were sometimes placed behind these pieces, not only to provide added illumination but also to stop shadows being thrown from one to the other. The finished set scene was a huge advance on the backscene. Some of these scenes exhibited great ingenuity on the part of the designer. The pieces of which they were made were known as set pieces, raking pieces, ground pieces or ground rows, and set waters. (See under separate entries).

Set pieces. Separate, cut-out scenic pieces such as a cottage, the corner of a house, a porch, placed obliquely on one side of the stage. Set pieces also included paling and picket fences, low walls, the side of a ship, bridges, and so on, some being practicable. All were placed on stage in front of the backscene.

Set waters. Rows of painted waves, set at ground level like the ground rows.

Seven Little Australians. 3-act comedy by Beaumont Smith, based on Ethel Turner's stories, *Seven Little Australians* (1894), and *Miss Bobby* (1897), Palace, Sydney 26.12.1914, initial 39 performances. These, like

Above: One of the first built-up sets for the Merchant of Venice, *London 1853*
Below: Set scene for My Sweetheart, *London 1883*

the performances of the opera, *Hansel and Gretel*, were all afternoon performances. (See: *Wig, The; Wonder Child, The*).

Shakespeare, Plays by. Popular or not, Shakespeare's plays were always regarded as an essential ingredient in the theatrical menu. For the first three-quarters of the century at least, it was the practice for visiting actors to open in *Hamlet* or some other Shakespearian play to show their quality. But Shakespeare, except for a few productions which were Shakespeare sugar-coated, or Shakespeare as melodrama, did not pay. The first publicly voiced indication that *Hamlet* was a prestige rather than a paying production was given in 1861, when R.Tolano, then lessee of Sydney's Royal Victoria, was reported as saying that 'the legitimate would wentilate my theatre on the first night; and as for that dismal old guy 'Amlet, I wouldn't 'ave 'im at no price.' Ten years later the experienced George Coppin said in an address inaugurating his management of the Melbourne Royal, that, as a rule, Shakespeare without a star actor was not remunerative. He said he had been told that Shakespeare was attractive when presented by Brooke, but the truth was that the opposite was the case. Brooke was attractive in Shakespeare. Coppin then said that Brooke had drawn his largest audiences in such plays as *The Serious Family* (1849) and *His Last Legs* (1839), while the Keans had been most successful in *The Wife's Secret* (1848) and *The Jealous Wife* (1761). The same had applied to Sullivan and Montgomery on their visits, except that Montgomery's *Hamlet* had created a great deal of interest. Mrs Scott-Siddons echoed Coppin's remarks 8 years later, after acting in Shakespeare throughout Australia and New Zealand. Melodrama was the only thing that paid, she said. But an even more provocative claim was made by a reviewer in 1877: 'People go to see Shakespeare's plays as they go to hear Handel's music, not because they fully understand it, but partly because it is *de rigeur,* and partly because it is in the main tolerably familiar to them.' There were no dissentients. But this did not stop artists such as W.H.Hoskins and others mounting productions of Shakespeare's plays which would have been a credit to major English provincial cities. Significantly, they usually lost money on such productions. But not always. Montgomery had artistic and financial success with his production of *Antony and Cleopatra,* and Hoskins with his ornate production of *The Tempest.* George Rignold made such a success of his production of *Henry V* over a period of 20 years that to mention his name was to mention in the same breath *Henry V.*

Shakespericonglommorofunnidogammoniae. Burlesque by Charles Nagel, with songs set to popular airs of the day, Royal Victoria, Sydney 1.7.1844, initially 1 performance. Published W.A.Duncan, Sydney, 1843. Copy held in Archives Office of NSW.

Shamus O'Brien; or, The Rebel Chief of '98. 5-act drama by Alfred Dampier and Percy Kehoe, Gaiety, Sydney 1.10.1887, initial 12 performances.

Sharp, Cecil James (1859-1924). English folk music collector and editor, born in London and educated at Uppingham and at Clare College, Cambridge. After getting his degree he went to Australia, and at the age of 24 became an associate to the Chief Justice of South Australia. It was while he was in Adelaide (1889-92), where he established a music school and was cathedral organist, that he met Guy Boothby and they collaborated on the operetta *Dimple's Lovers* (1890), and the comic opera *Sylvia; or, The Marquis and the Maid* (1890). Soon after this Sharp returned to London. At the time of his death in 1924 he had 20 publications to his credit, most of them dealing with English folk music.

Shaughraun, The. 4-act drama by Dion Boucicault, Wallack's, New York 14.11.1874; Drury Lane, London 4.9.1875; Royal Victoria, Sydney 13.3.1875, initial 40 performances.

She Stoops to Conquer; or, The Mistakes of a Night. 3 act comedy by O. Goldsmith, Covent Garden, London 15.3.1773; Royal, Sydney 26.6.1833.

Sheridan, John F. (1848-1908). Popular Irish-born female impersonator who specialised in sophisticated 'widow' roles. The one for which he was known all over the world was Widow O'Brien in *Fun on the Bristol* (1882). When this was given its first London performance the *Theatre* described it as a 'wild, incomprehensible hotch-potch of a thing,' but admitted that it was nevertheless a romp from beginning to end. When performed at Melbourne Royal in 1884 it was advertised as 'now in the fifth year of its prosperous career throughout America, England, Scotland, and Ireland.' The Melbourne *Argus* said the play 'implies a somewhat contemptuous estimate of the average intelligence of the people of the Australian colonies on the part of those who have travelled so many thousands of miles in order to submit it to public criticism in our capital cities.' But it seems that Sheridan knew his public, for *Fun on the Bristol* ran for 30 performances, and was equally successful in Sydney and other centres. While he was in Australia, Sheridan and J.A.Meade, an actor in his company, collaborated on the writing of the comedy *Cuckoo*. He also collaborated with Alfred Dampier on a version of *Uncle Tom's Cabin* which Sheridan presented in London at the Princess's on 24.12.1887. Returning to Australia in 1902, Sheridan collaborated with P.Finn on a musical comedy called *Mrs Goldstein*, the title being changed in 1905 to *Mrs Dooley's Joke*. Sheridan died at Newcastle, NSW and, like his namesake, W.E.Sheridan, was buried in Waverley Cemetery.

Sheridan, William Edward (1839-1887). Born in Boston, USA, Sheridan gave up commercial pursuits in 1858 in favour of the stage, acting in theatres in Boston and Ohio in the period 1858-61. During the American Civil War he joined the Sixth Ohio Volunteer Infantry, and was subsequently promoted to captain. He was wounded in 1864, but by

1865 was acting again. Over the next few years he made a name for himself as a Shakespearian actor in most of the major American cities. He paid his first visit to Australia in 1882, and had a successful season in *King Lear, Othello, Louis XI,* and *Ingomar the Barbarian,* culminating in a benefit performance given him by members of the acting profession in Melbourne from which he received £200. He returned to Australia in 1886, but this time he was poorly supported and his visit was not successful. He died in Sydney, and was buried in Waverley Cemetery. A monument was erected above his grave by public subscription.

Shop Girl, The. 2-act musical farce, text H.Dam, music I.Caryll, A.Ross, and L.Monckton, Gaiety, London 24.11.1894; Princess's, Melbourne 25.5.1895, initial 6 performances.

Sicilian Vespers, The. (See: *Vêpres Siciliennes, Les*).

Sidaway, Robert. (See: Theatre, The Sydney).

Side. (See: Length).

Siege of Rochelle, The. 2-act opera, text E.Fitzball, music M.Balfe, Drury Lane, London 29.10.1835; Royal Victoria, Sydney 31.7.1848.

Siege of Troy, The. (See: *Paris the Prince and Helen the Fair*).

Sign of the Cross, The. 4-act drama by W.Barrett, Grand Opera House, St Louis 27.3.1895; Lyric, London 4.1.1896; Her Majesty's, Sydney 8.5.1897, initial 42 performances.

Silence of Dean Maitland, The. 3-act drama by E.Lewis Scott, adapted from M.Grey's novel, Bijou, Adelaide 2.2.1894, initial 2 performances. M.Grey was the pen-name of the English novelist, Mary E.Tuttiet.

Silver Box, The. 3-act comedy by J.Galsworthy, Court, London 25.9.1906; Princess's, Melbourne (University of Melbourne Dramatic Club) 27.6.1910, initially 1 performance.

Silver King, The. 5-act drama by H.A.Jones and H.Herman, Princess's, London 16.11.1882; Royal, Sydney 22.3.1883, initial 41 performances.

Simes, Thomas (1803-1846). One of the original members of Levey's Royal company, who in 1836 came to the fore as a costume and property designer. He was stage manager of the Royal in 1837, and the following year transferred to the Royal Victoria, where he became acting manager in 1841. He acted in many of the plays by Australian dramatists presented at this theatre, including *The Queer Client, Salathiel, Isabel of Valois, Contradiction,* and *The Duellist.* In the last year of his life he played the parts of Slender in *The Merry Wives of Windsor,* and Trinculo in *The Tempest.* (See: *Costume*).

Simmons, Joseph (1810-1893). Born in London, and said to have made his first stage appearance at the age of 12. Made 2 trips to Australia, where he had relatives, the first in 1830 when there was no theatre operating. On his way back to London in 1832 he pioneered stage entertainment for a night or two in Hobart and Launceston. He was back in Sydney at the end of 1833, and the following year partnered Levey in the running of the Sydney Royal. The partnership was notable for the disagreements between the two, but Simmons nevertheless put in some good performances in such varied works as *Othello, Hamlet, Venice Preserved, Macbeth,* and *Pizarro.* Simmons, a talented all-rounder, could also dance a satisfactory hornpipe and jig, sing comic and serious ballads, and do a convincing impersonation of the stage Irishman. In 1835 he leased the Royal and ran it himself as manager, actor, and general factotum. The following year he gave the theatre up and went back to commerce. At the same time he became a hotel-keeper, and spent his nights entertaining his customers with songs and recitations. Towards the end of 1838 he joined the Royal Victoria, playing Mark Antony in *Julius Caesar.* Again he finished up as stage manager. After a while he again gave up the theatre for commercial pursuits. Returning to the Royal Victoria in 1842, he created a sensation as the 'drag' lead in *The Mock Catalani, in Little Puddleton.* The following year he opened his own theatre, the Royal City, in Market Street. It was a period of financial depression, and the venture was ill-timed. He was once again penniless. He continued for the next few years to alternate between commercial and theatrical interests until, in 1879, in his 70th year, he was given a benefit during which he acted in *The Hypocrite* (1768) and *The Illustrious Stranger* (1827), apparently as exuberant, as boisterous, as talented as ever. But before long the fires began to dim, and he finished his working life teaching acting and production.

Skirt Dancer, The. 2-act musical comedy, text G.Ridgwell, E.Mansell, and F.Mackay, music H.Trotere, Artillery, Woolwich 28.3.1898; Princess's, Melbourne 27.8.1904, initial 12 performances.

Slaves of Sydney. (See: *Marvellous Melbourne*).

Sleeping Queen, The. One-act operetta, text H.B.Farnie, music M.Balfe, Gallery of Illustration, London 3.11.1864; Gaiety, Sydney 27.3.1884, initially 1 performance.

Smith, James (1820-1910). Born in Kent. Began his working life as a journalist. Came to Australia in 1854, where he practised as a journalist in Melbourne, first with the *Age* and the *Leader,* and then with the *Argus.* Was editor of the *Victorian Review,* and of Melbourne *Punch;* also edited the *Cyclopaedia of Victoria* (1903-5). Author of two or three novels, and published a great deal of occasional writing, including essays, articles, and lectures. Also author of three plays: *Garibaldi, the Hero of Palermo; A Broil at the Cafe,* and *The Duke's Motto.*

Snow. A Christmas Story. 3-act drama by Walter Reynolds, People's, Melbourne 7.2.1880, initial 6 performances.

Soggarth, The (The Priest). 4-act drama by George Darrell, Royal, Sydney 28.8.1886, initial 12 performances.

Somers, Thomas. Pen-name used by Thomas Walker. (See: Parliamentarians).

Sonnambula, La. 2-act opera, text F.Romani, music V.Bellini, Carcano, Milan 6.3.1831; Royal Victoria, Sydney 10.10.1842.

Sorcerer, The. 3-act comic opera, text W.S.Gilbert, music A.Sullivan, Opera Comique, London 17.11.1877; Academy of Music, Melbourne 28.7.1879, initial 6 performances.

South, William T.K. (See: *For the Term of His Natural Life*).

Southern Cross, The. 4-act drama by G.Walters and W.A.Cuneo, Lyceum, Sydney 24.9.1898, initial 6 performances.

Southern Cross, The. (See: *Democrat, The; or, Under the Southern Cross*).

Spec in China, A. 5-act comedy by R.H.Horne, Royal, Melbourne 24.7.1860, initial 2 performances.

Speed the Plough. 5-act comedy by T.Morton, Covent Garden, London 8.2.1800; Royal, Sydney 17.7.1834.

Spencer, Albert (1811-1854). Trained as a seaman, and no doubt given to reading Shakespeare to relieve the tedium of long voyages, Spencer left ship at Launceston in favour of the stage. He first appeared at Samson Cameron's newly-opened theatre in Launceston's British Hotel in 1834, as Bassanio in *The Merchant of Venice*. The *Independent*, summing up the company as a whole, said 'Mr Spencer appears to us generally to be the most perfect.' Tutored, no doubt, by Cameron, Spencer next played Othello, drawing from the same newspaper the extraordinary claim that his Othello 'will never be surpassed in this island . . . Mr Spencer was the Othello of Shakespeare.' From Launceston he moved to Hobart, gathering more laurels and the occasional brickbat. In 1836 he made his first appearance in Sydney, at Levey's Royal in *Richard III*. He had variety if little else in the reviews of this performance. The *Gazette* said he was a success, the *Australian* that he failed. When the Royal Victoria opened in 1838 he was chosen to read the opening address, and to play Iago. The *Commercial Journal* said he made a hit, the *Monitor* that he was not good, the *Herald* that it was his best part, and the *Gazette* that he had never played Iago so badly. But by this time he had 'arrived' as a tragedian, and was said to be 'one of the few up to Shakespeare.' Towards the end of 1838 he left Sydney for England, working his passage before the mast. He came back in 1841, presumably the same way, having been unsuccessful in England. From then until 1854 he was a permanent member of the Victoria company. He met his death when he and some friends left Sydney in the ketch *Peacock* for Brisbane Water. A few days earlier he had borrowed an old fowling piece from a Sydney gunsmith. When the boat was off Long Reach he was told there was a gull on the lee bow. Spencer, who had apparently overloaded the fowling piece, aimed at the bird and fired. The barrel burst and the right side of his face was shattered. He died in the Sydney Infirmary a few days later.

Spitzentuch der Königin, Des (The Queen's Lace Handkerchief). 3-act operetta, text H.Bohrmann-Riegin and R.Genée, music Johan Strauss, Theater an der Wien, Vienna 1.10.1880; Royal, Melbourne 12.8.1893, initial 7 performances.

Spring Chicken, The. 2-act musical comedy, text G.Grossmith Jr after A.Jaime and G.Duval's *Coquin de Printemps,* music I.Caryll and L.Monckton, Gaiety, London 30.5.1905; Her Majesty's, Melbourne 3.11.1906, initial 30 performances.

Sprissawneen, The. 4-act drama by Walter Reynolds, People's, Melbourne 4.10.1879, initial 6 performances.

Spurr, Mel.B.(1852-1904). Baptised Melancthon Burton Spurr, which he later changed to Mel. B.Spurr, his unusual name when he came to Australia gave the Sydney *Bulletin* the excuse it needed for one of its punning comments. This weekly claimed he had adopted the 'Mel.' as a compliment to Melbourne while he was in that state, and that as he visited each state of the new Commonwealth in turn he would change his name to Syd. N.Spurr, Ade. L.Spurr, Bris. B.Spurr, and so on. Very like the latter day Peter Lorre in appearance, Spurr was an actor, entertainer, comedian, and accomplished pianist. He was one of the first of a long line of piano-monologists. Known and liked the length and breadth of England, he began to look for new challenges and made a tour of South Africa in 1903. His success there was so great that his manager booked him for a tour of Australia, and he arrived in Melbourne on 27.10.1903. At first he had a poor reception, even though it was Melbourne Cup week, but before long business began to pick up. In May 1904 Spurr set out on a New Zealand tour, and was not back in Melbourne until the following August. In September he wrote to his family in England to say that he hoped to be home by the following April. He gave a performance on 19 September. The next day he took sick, and within a week he was dead. He was buried in the St Kilda cemetery.

Squatter's Daughter, The; or, The Land of the Wattle. 4-act drama by Albert Edmunds, Royal, Melbourne 9.2.1907, initial 36 performances.

Stage directions. Given from the point of view of the actor. Stage left, where the prompter stood or sat, was always known as PS (prompt side). Stage right was always known as OP (opposite prompt). Stage directions given in plays followed the layout of the stage, which was made up of a series of wings in grooves on either side of the stage opening, and of flats behind these, also in grooves. The flats were pushed or slid on-stage to meet in the middle and form the background to the scene. The wings and flats were numbered, starting with number one at the front of the stage. Entrances were made by the actors between the wings, so that the direction 'R.3 E.' meant that the actor made his entrance from the righthand side behind the third wing. The direction, 'A view of the country, 1st grooves,' meant that the flats in the first row of grooves were pushed on for a shallow scene close to the proscenium arch. The direction 'Cottage; door in flat (practicable) and lattice window in L. flat; another door R. 2 E.' meant wings and flats painted to represent the interior of a cottage, a door in the right flat which could be opened, a lattice window in the left flat, and another door (presumably also practicable) in the right-hand wing in the second grooves. 'The act closes' could mean not only the end of an act, but also that the last scene of that act was 'closed in' by the flats for the next scene being pushed on in front of it, while the old wings were withdrawn and the wings to match the new scene pushed on in their stead. 'Enter R. 3 E.' meant come in at the third entrance on the right (behind the wings in the third grooves). 'R.U.E.' meant right upper entrance, or enter on the right side up near the flats or backdrop. 'Upstage' meant up towards the backdrop or back flats; 'downstage,' towards the footlights. These last two directions developed from the fact that the stage was never level (except towards the end of the century) but had a slight slope upwards from the proscenium arch to the back wall. (See: Stage, raked).

Stage, Lighting the. In the earliest Australian theatres stage and auditorium were lighted by candles and oil lamps. The foot and orchestra lights in these early theatres were oil lamps — in Levey's Royal, of the most primitive kind — wicks floating in a container filled with oil, which not only smoked but also gave off an offensive odour. Later the Argand lamp, which had a central shaft for air, and a circular wick, came into general use. Levey's Royal also had candle chandeliers in front of the stage, and backstage lighting much the same as it had been in the 18th-century theatre — vertical strips of tin on either side of the stage, out of sight of the audience, on which lights were fastened with a reflector behind. It was not until the invention of the Argand lamp, followed by gas and then electric lighting, that the central chandelier was used, first as a light source, and then more as a decoration. Wooden posts or stands, with lamps or candles hung on them, were also used between the wings. With the arrival of gas lighting and the freedom it gave for the use of long pipes with light burners at regular intervals, the use not only of footlights but also of floodlights behind such things as groundrows became possible. Strip lights or gas battens were also used behind the borders above the stage. Much the same system as this was later used in the first few years of the changeover from gas to electricity — until it was learned that electricity was even more flexible and more easily manipulated than gas. (See: Footlights. Gas lighting).

Stage, Raked. Up to at least the end of the 19th century it was the practice to build stages with a rake or incline. Hence the terms 'up stage' and 'down stage' had a literal as well as other meanings, for the rake was upwards from the footlights to the back of the stage. The extent of the rake in overseas theatres varied (there seems to be no record of the rake used in Australia) from 5.6 per cent down to 1.5 per cent. The most common rake in England was said to be half an inch to the foot, or slightly more than four per cent. This rake was no doubt followed in Australian theatres. With the adoption towards the end of the century of built-up scenery the raked stage proved an embarrassment, and it was eventually abolished.

Stage, Working the. In the century under review there were several ways in which the stage was worked or 'set' for a play or other performance. One of the first consisted of 2 flats, or back scenes, stretched on wooden frames, and pushed on stage so that they met in the centre. To change the back scene, sceneshifters on either side of the stage pulled off the 2 halves of the used scene, and pushed on the 2 halves of the new scene. Wings, or side-scenes, were used with the flats, painted as a rule to match the back scene, so that each time a back scene was changed its matching wings had to be changed also. To facilitate the movement of back scenes and wings, each ran in a set of grooves — one at the bottom, fixed to the stage floor, and one at the top. The top set of grooves was hinged like the half of an opening bridge, and held by chains fixed to the fly gallery. These grooves were raised or lowered by the stagehands as required. Borders were also changed to match each scene. This system was sometimes used with backcloths instead of flats; cloths which could be rolled up on the same principle as the verandah blind, or pulled up instead into the flies. Used in conjunction with wings and borders, the backcloth needed only one man to change it, and was quick and less noisy in scene changes. Next there was the ladder or mechanical system of scene changing, as in the second Prince of Wales in Sydney (1863). Of this theatre it was said that 'the scenery moves with the regularity of a clock.' The stage, 100ft wide and 58ft deep, had a mezzanine floor 9ft below it, and a cellar whose floor was 8ft lower still. In these spaces were housed the revolving drums, winches, counter-weights, and ladders which reached up through the stage floor and on which were fixed the wings and back flats. All these, with the borders, were moved simultaneously by means of geared drums and windlasses. It was claimed of this system that it could present, in immediate succession, nine full-set scenes, including a 'working seashore' such as that used in the first scene in *The Tempest*. Then it was discovered that the free-standing flat — supported behind by a brace fixed to the stage floor — as well as the box set which the brace made possible, made grooves unnecessary. Braced flats also made possible the diagonal scene, or *scena per angolo,* in which braced and lashed flats were set diagonally across the stage, and painted in perspective to represent a large hall, state room, or the exterior of a building of considerable depth. A *scena per angolo* was used in the Melbourne production of *Sardanapalus* in 1857. Finally there was the built-up scene, the scene which attempted to provide a third dimension by presenting scenes built on the stage with the utmost realism, something like the much later movie set, including bridges, mountain paths, balconies on which any number of people could stand, and classic scenes with free-standing columns and arches. To speed up scene changes a wagon stage was sometimes used — a platform on wheels. The first scene would be set on a platform or wagon and placed before the proscenium opening. Alongside it, in the vacant 'dock' on the prompt or OP side of the stage, would be another wagon stage on which the next scene was set during the progress of the play. When the first scene ended the wagon stage containing it would be pushed into the vacant dock on the other side of the proscenium arch, and the newly-set wagon stage would be pushed on in its place. The first scene would then be dismantled, a new scene set, and then the initial process would be reversed. Wagon stages such as these were used in the 1887 Her Majesty's in Sydney, also scenes on rollers which first exhibited an interior, and were then reversed to show the exterior of the same building. (See: Box set. Flies, Scenepainting).

Stalls. From the 17th century onwards the ground floor of a theatre was known as the pit. Here audiences crowded in their hundreds on bare, backless benches. As time progressed, and boxes on the side and back walls of the auditorium were replaced by deep dress circle and gallery 'balconies,' it was realised that the front benches of the pit were in many respects the best seats in the theatre. Chairs, or separate seats, were then introduced into the first four or five rows of the pit, dubbed 'stalls' or 'orchestra' stalls, and an extra charge made for them. This is believed to have first happened in England in the 1820s. Before long, stalls became more popular than the dress circle, and so the pit benches, which by this time had had backs added to them, were pushed further and further back. Finally the ground floor was given over entirely to stalls — usually sold as front and back stalls. With the abolition of the pit the cheapest seats in the house were to be found in the gallery — sometimes called the amphitheatre, because it had no seats but was made up of a series of chair-high 'steps' on which the audience sat. (See: Pit. Seating capacity).

Star trap. A stage trap with a covering made of segmented pieces, like the sections of half an orange, so that when the fairy or demon, harlequin or clown shot through on to the stage the cover closed over again after them. One of the most effective traps invented, because of the element of surprise inherent in it, but also the most dangerous to use. The performer was shot through it from under the stage so that he literally flew through the air, and if, when he came down again, the trap had not shut, he stood a good chance of being hurt. (See: Traps).

Stark, James (1819-1875). Born in Windsor, Canada, Stark began his working life as a carpenter in Nova Scotia. But he was strongly attracted to the theatre, and before long he emigrated to Boston, where there were more opportunities for him to study acting. There he fell in with a fellow enthusiast who not only persuaded him to go to Europe, but financed him for 3 years of study in England on the Continent. Stark's teacher in England is said to have been the famous William Macready. Certainly he modelled himself on that actor. When he returned to America he was still a student of acting rather than an actor, but he had the good sense to travel to the mine boom-town of San Francisco, where he became the first actor to present *Hamlet, Macbeth, King Lear, Much Ado About Nothing, The Merchant of Venice,* and *The Taming of the Shrew* in that city. His partner was a Mrs Kirby, an actress 6 years older, and by all accounts no more experienced but more determined than he. She soon became Mrs Stark, making him her third husband. Together they opened the first Jenny Lind in San Francisco on 4.11.1850. A visit to Sacramento followed their San Francisco season, and then a return visit to that city. Their success in each season of plays emboldened Stark to try New York, but he was unable to make an impression there, and after further seasons in San Francisco he and his wife set out in 1853 on a tour of far away Australia. They left San Francisco in the paddle steamer *New Orleans* on 10.3.1853 and arrived in Sydney on 14.5.1853. They came on 'spec,' but were lucky enough to secure an engagement for 5 nights at Sydney's Royal Victoria. They arrived at a time when Australians needed just the kind of acting they presented — rabble-rousing, close to ranting, but exciting. So great was their success that their engagement was extended, after which they visited the other colonies, with equal success. While in Australia they appeared in *Hamlet, Othello, King Lear, The Stranger* (1798), *The Lady of Lyons* (1838), *The Iron Chest* (1796), *Richelieu* (1839), *Ingomar the Barbarian* (1851), *Damon and Pythias* (1831), *Virginius* (1820), and a version of Schiller's *The Robbers*. Towards the end of their visit they had the satisfaction of reading in the Sydney newspaper, the *People's Advocate* of 22.4.1854, that they had 'completely revolutionised the Australian stage.' And the tangible result of their success which they took home with them after a visit lasting about 11 months was put variously at £20 000 and £100 000. This tour was the peak of the couple's popularity, for their reception on their return to San Francisco was a sad let down. They had to woo their public anew, as though they were different people from the 2 who had left in March 1853. In 1856 he and his wife paid a return visit to Australia, and this time it was a repetition of their return to San Francisco. The magic had gone, never to return. In the flux and change of the gold-seeking 1850s popularity was swift but impermanent. Change was all. From then on Stark endured a decline which not even momentary success in San Francisco could halt. His wife divorced him in 1868, and a visit he made to Australia that year proved a failure. He was simply an old-fashioned actor. At the time of his death he was playing a very minor role in a New York production of *Hamlet* staged by the famous Edwin Booth.

Stark, Sarah (1813-1897?). Little is known of the early life of this actress. What is known is that she was married to an English actor named J.Hudson Kirby, who had a successful New York season and then went to London. He died there in 1848 aged 29. Soon afterwards she returned to America, where she married a man named Wingate. The two of them came to San Francisco in January 1850. A few weeks after she and James Stark opened at the Jenny Lind in 1850 (she still retaining Kirby as her stage name), Wingate died after a fall from a horse. In 1851 she married James Stark at Sacramento. When she and her husband came to Australia in 1853 she shared every bit of their tremendous success, despite the claim by one newspaper that the Starks did not 'come up to our standard of stars of the first magnitude,' and by another that they had a 'peculiar nasal Yankee twang,' and pronounced many words in a manner strange to English ears — 'pyou-er' for 'pure,' 'contumely' as 'con*choomly*,' and so on. Sarah herself became so much a favourite of Melbourne audiences that she was given a complimentary benefit at Rowe's American Circus in March 1854, when it was estimated that the amount of money taken at the door, and the cost of the diamond brooch with which she was presented, totalled £1000. After that, their return visit in 1856 was an anticlimax. She and her husband no longer 'drew.' From then on Sarah had a difficult time with James, who was moody, dissolute, and lost all their money. He sometimes gave up acting for long periods. But she never forsook the stage, acting wherever she could get an opening. In 1868 she divorced her husband and married a Dr Gray of New York. When he died she married a well-known actor-manager of the period who had also visited Australia in the 1850s, Charles R.Thorne. She also outlived him, her fifth husband. In 1897 she was said to be still living in San Francisco, 'a symbol of the city which survives catastrophe after catastrophe and yet continues its confident, indomitable course . . .'

Stella. 4-act opera, text and music G.W.L.Marshall Hall, Her Majesty's, Melbourne 4.5.1912, initially 1 performance. Shortened version given at Palladium, London 8.6.1914.

Stephen, H.W.H. (See: Parliamentarians).

Stevens, J.A. (See: *Convict 1240*).

Stewart, Nellie (1858-1931). Dubbed 'Australia's idol,' she was born in Sydney of English actor parents. Through her mother, Theodosia Yates, her theatrical pedigree stretched back to Mary Ann and Richard Yates, members of David Garrick's company at Drury Lane. Nellie made her first stage appearance at the Haymarket, Melbourne in 1864 as one of the two children in Kotzebue's *The Stranger* (1798). Early in the 1870s she began to make stage appearances in minor roles in Melbourne with her father and her 2 half-sisters, Docy and Maggie. Her real stage career began later in the same decade when the family, with the exception of her mother, began a tour with an entertainment written for them by Garnet Walch, *Rainbow Revels,* first presented at Launceston in 1877. In this each artist, including Nellie, played 6 different roles, singing, dancing, and acting. One of her first major roles — it is not necessarily so in the opera — was as the drummer boy in Offenbach's *Tambour Major,* a role offered her by George Musgrove, who was to play a vital part in her life. Her drummer boy captivated the audience wherever the opera was played, and put Nellie on the road to success. In 1882 'the Firm', J.C.Williamson, G.Musgrove, and A.Garner, was established and its bright particular star for some time was Nellie Stewart, in a succession of dramatic and operatic roles. In 1884 she married R.G.Row in Sydney, a marriage which did not last. In the meantime she had joined fortunes with G.Musgrove, with whom she lived until his death in 1916. It was he who advised her to leave J.C.Williamson, who was over-working and under-paying her, and to go with him to London. She spent a year there, studying music and dancing, and on her return to Australia in 1888 took up a round of engagements notable for their versatility. She made a not very successful London debut in 1892, and by the following year was back in Australia again. Tours of Australia and New Zealand followed, and a return visit to London, where Musgrove branched out as a successful manager and entrepreneur. In 1902, back in Australia, she played for the first time in what was to become her most famous role — Nell Gwynne in *Sweet Nell of Old Drury* (1900). It was that play which became associated with her name all over Australia and New Zealand. She played the role for the last time in Melbourne in 1929. In 1905 she tackled *Camille* (1853), but most critics agreed that she was not of the world of which Camilles are made. Early in 1931, the year of her death, she recorded scenes and songs from *Sweet Nell* for the Columbia Graphaphone Company at Homebush, records now held by the Mitchell Library, Sydney. (See: Yates, Theodosia).

Stewart, Mrs Richard. (See: Yates, Theodosia).

Stingaree the Bushranger. 4-act drama by E.W.Hornung, a dramatisation of his novel (1905), Queen's, London 1.2.1908, initial 24 performances.

Stirling, Mrs. (See: Yates, Theodosia).

Stock company. The resident or permanent theatre company from which normal nightly programmes were cast, and which played a supporting role when star actors were engaged. Most members of these companies could sing and dance as well as act, and with some their versatility extended to the playing of musical instruments, and scenepainting. For the first six or seven decades of the century the actors were hired, not for the run of a single play, but by the season. A season could last from 3 to 6 months. Between seasons the whole company 'rested' — were unemployed and unpaid. The stock company was an essential component of the 'standardised' nineteenth-century theatre, in which there was also stock scenery — 'Chamber,' 'Hall,' 'Prison,' etc., with wings to match — and more or less stock characters in drama and comedy alike. Ultimately the change from 3 and 4-part programmes to one play a night, and the rise of the actor-manager and the touring company brought an end to the stock company. The steady encroachment from the 1850s onwards by stall seats on pit space; the consequent movement of the noisier pit occupants to the cheaper gallery seats, and the withdrawal to musical halls and variety theatres of the vocal, musical, comic, and acrobatic turns which were once given between plays, also contributed to the end of the stock company.

Story of Waterloo, A. 1-act drama by A.C.Doyle, Prince's, Bristol 21.9.1894; Garrick, London 17.12.1894; Royal, Sydney 26.2.1910, initial 5 performances.

Stranger, The. 5-act drama by A.F. von Kotzebue, translated by B.Thompson, Drury Lane, London 24.3.1798; Freemason's Tavern, Hobart 24.12.1833.

Strife. 3-act drama by J.Galsworthy, Duke of York's, London 9.3.1909; Melbourne Repertory, Athenaeum Hall, 24.9.1913, initial 2 performances.

Strong as Death. Drama in prologue and four acts by Douglas M.Ford, adapted from Marcus Clarke's novel, *For the Term of His Natural Life*, Royal, Gloucester, 19.6.1899.

Struck Oil; or, The Pennsylvania Dutchman. 3-act comedy said to have been originally written by S.Smith as *The German Recruit*, rewritten by C.Greene as *The Deed; or, Five Years Away*, and then retitled *Struck Oil*, Salt Lake City, Salt Lake City, Utah 23.2.1874; Royal, Melbourne 1.8.1874, initial 43 performances.

Sullivan, Barry (1821-1891). Born in Birmingham, Sullivan was christened Thomas but adopted his mother's maiden name, Barry, for his first stage appearance. Educated in Bristol, he began to study for the law, but on seeing William Macready in the Bristol theatre he determined to become an actor. He joined a strolling company, and after a series of hardships he finally finished up as a member of the stock company in the Cork theatre in 1837. A year later he formed his own company and set out on a tour of the towns. By January 1840 he had had enough, and was back at the Cork theatre. Next he toured England and Scotland, and in 1850 he acted Othello in Liverpool to the Iago of William Macready, who later noted in his diary: 'The Othello, Mr Barry Sullivan, was really indifferent, and was vociferously applauded.' In 1852 Sullivan made his first London appearance at the Haymarket in *Hamlet*. According to H.Barton Barker he was 'a competent actor of the old bow-wow school; but though an enormous favourite in Ireland and the provinces, he never took any firm hold of the metropolitan public.' Following a tour of the USA, and an English provincial tour, Sullivan embarked on one of Australia. His first appearance in Melbourne in 1862 was an unqualified success, after which came an even more successful visit to Sydney lasting 7 weeks. Returning to Melbourne, he leased the Royal in 1863 and embarked on a season which lasted for 10 months, all of his productions earning praise for their high artistic standard. His lease expired early in 1866, and he made a visit to Sydney before returning to London towards the end of that year. In 1869 he managed the London Holborn, with the Australian-born Mrs Hermann Vezin as his leading lady, while in 1876-77 he had a successful season of 13 weeks at Drury Lane. Two years later he took part in the inaugural performance of *Much Ado About Nothing* for the opening of the Stratford Memorial Theatre. One critic said his Benedick was played 'in a manner that, no doubt, would have been highly acceptable to an East End London audience.' His following Hamlet was also adversely criticised. But the modern critic, J.C.Trewin, has placed against these unsympathetic remarks George Bernard Shaw's unequivocal 'I never saw great acting until I saw him.' Sullivan made his last stage appearance in 1887, ill-health forcing his retirement.

Sultan of Mocha, The. 3-act comic opera, text W.Lestocq, music A.Cellier, St James's, London 17.4.1876; Alexandra, Melbourne 9.11.1889, initial 27 performances.

Sun and Shadow; or, Mark Stornway's Nephews. 4-act drama by W.H.Cooper, Royal Victoria, Sydney 5.3.1870, initial 22 performances.

Sunlight, or sun-burner. Circular gas burner which abolished the need for the former central glass-drop chandelier in theatre auditoria. The sunlight was a circle of bat-wing gas burners grouped around a central conical cylinder which housed the gas supply pipe and a ventilator or draught pipe. It gave a light bright enough to illuminate the average theatre auditorium. This early type of sunlight was replaced in the late 1880s by improved models, used singly and in groups. In 1863 the

Prince of Wales in Sydney had a sunlight of 130 burners fitted with glass chandelier drops, thus enjoying the best of both worlds.

Sunny South, The. 5-act drama by George Darrell, Opera House, Melbourne 31.3.1883, initial 36 performances. Produced in London, Grand 27.10.1884; Survey 5.9.1898. Ms in the British Library. Published in National Theatre series by Currency Press Ltd, Sydney.

Sunshine Girl, The. 2-act musical comedy, text C.Raleigh, music P.Rubens, Gaiety, London 24.2.1912; Her Majesty's, Sydney 18.1.1913, initial 60 performances.

Supernumeraries. The 1s a night men who made up the armies, knights, bushrangers, rebels, citizens, and other 'crowds' in Shakespeare and melodrama productions. They were also known by the slang titles of spear-holders, banner-carriers, and carpet-layers. As many as 200 supers were used in an 1887 Sydney production of *Henry IV*. (See: Carpet, stage).

Sweet Nell of Old Drury. 4-act drama by P.Kester, Haymarket, London 30.8.1900; Princess's, Melbourne 15.2.1902, initial 32 performances.

Sweethearts and Wives. Comic opera, text J.Kenney, music J.Whittaker, I.Nathan, T.Cook, and G.Perry, Haymarket, London 7.7.1823; Royal Victoria, Sydney 23.12.1844.

Sydney, Theatres in.

1 Convict era. Australia's earliest audience and actors enjoyed their first Antipodean performance 17 days before they reached Australia, demonstrating how the human spirit can rise above the most degrading circumstances and surroundings. They were convicts, more than 200 of them, penned in the *Scarborough* (430 tons), with 30 seamen and 44 marines, for a voyage which lasted 36 weeks. Their quarters, in a ship built originally to transport soldiers from England to distant points of the British Empire, were bounded by 'very strong and thick bulkheads, filled with nails and run across from side to side 'tween decks abaft the mainmast, with loopholes to fire between decks in case of irregularities.' There was also a wooden barricade on the upper deck, about 3ft high and capped by iron prongs, to keep the convicts apart from marines and seamen. Yet on this particular night, 2.1.1788, 'the convicts made a play and sang many songs.' A year later, by which time convicted and free were more or less 'dug in' in the new British colony, a few of the convicts (no doubt some of those who had 'made a play' on the *Scarborough*) asked Governor Arthur Phillip if they could make a contribution to his celebration of the King's birthday, 4.6.1789. He gave permission for them to present a play at night to round off the birthday celebrations. They refurbished a crude hut, fitted it with roughly carpentered stage and benches, and were soon busy with paper, natural pigments, and

begged, borrowed and stolen cast-offs, preparing for the first play to be presented on the vast new continent which had not yet been named Australia — George Farquhar's *The Recruiting Officer* (1706). Convict theatres were also established, though only for brief periods, in 1796, 1825, and 1840. (See: Emu Plains. Norfolk Island).

2. Royal Assembly Rooms (1829). In 1826 the success of the Emu Plains convict theatricals caused such heartburnings in Sydney, which had no theatre, that there were frequent calls for something to be done about it. Two public-spirited citizens, James Underwood and Barnett Levey, each decided to supply Sydney's need. Underwood lost heart when, in digging the foundations for his theatre, workmen nearly undermined the offices of the Sydney *Gazette*. Levey, who was building his Royal Hotel in George Street, decided to incorporate a theatre in the building, at the back, with its main entrance in the back wall of his hotel saloon at the front of the building. Early in 1827 it was said this theatre would accommodate 900 in its pit, boxes, and gallery, but by June this figure had shrunk to 700 in pit and 2 tiers of boxes, the boxes being ranged around 3 walls of the auditorium. And then Levey fell foul of Governor Darling, who pushed through an Act making it impossible for anyone to give theatrical performances without first obtaining a government licence. Levey countered by naming his theatre the Royal Assembly Rooms, and holding a series of vocal and instrumental concerts. In 1830 his theatre was said to be 86ft long, 33ft wide, 19ft high, with 2 tiers of boxes and a pit. The stage would have occupied almost half of the length. The proscenium had stage doors on either side, painted with portraits of the Muses. These provided a colourful contrast to the green baize front curtain and the red baize lining of the boxes around the auditorium walls. Illumination was by candles and oil lamps. In 1832 Governor Darling was replaced by Governor Bourke, and Levey at last got his licence to present the drama in Sydney.

3 Saloon Royal (1832). By the time he got his licence Levey was bankrupt, and no longer owned his projected Royal. But he was able to make arrangements for its use, and in the meantime determined to convert the saloon of his Royal Hotel, 60ft long, 30ft wide, 17ft high, into a temporary theatre so that he could raise the money needed to complete the original Royal. A stage was installed, and a single tier of boxes around the room's 3 walls. Everything was necessarily on a small scale, particularly the stage, but seating was provided for 350 in the pit and 150 in the boxes, for which 5 and 3 shillings respectively was charged. This theatre was opened with a series of at homes or solo comedy performances by Levey. Later he was able to gather a group of actors, and the Royal, as it was called, was opened on 26.12.1832 with the melodrama *Black Eyed Susan* (1829), and the farce *Monsieur Tonson* (1821). For this, the first performance of drama in Sydney since the days of Sidaways theatre, no fewer than 650 people were packed hip to hip

and knee to back. This saloon Royal continued in use until the real theatre was opened.

4 Royal (1833). Levey's Royal, built into his hotel of the same name, was opened on 5.10.1833 with the melodrama *The Miller and His Men* (1813) and the farce *The Irishman in London* (1792). Early in the year it was said this theatre measured 45ft from the front curtain to the front boxes (which were on the back wall of the auditorium, facing the stage), was 30ft wide (the pit seats extended under the side boxes), and would seat 1200. The general colour scheme was green and gold, the boxes being lined with red baize studded with gold-headed nails, and the stage doors gilded. Lighting was by candles and oil lamps. The theatre had a pit, dress circle, second tier, and gallery, priced at 5, 4, 3 and 2s. In 1835 Levey let his theatre to 6 lessees, who made several improvements — a separate entrance to the boxes, a new proscenium, the dress circle ceiling raised, the upper circle enlarged, and the pit and gallery repaired. In 1836 Joseph Wyatt became sole lessee for 12 months. Levey died the following year, and his widow carried on for a while, but Wyatt persuaded her in 1838 to sell him the building, which he kept closed. The Royal was destroyed by fire 2 years later.

5 Royal Victoria (1838). In 1834 it was revealed that Sydney was to have a second theatre, to be built under the management of a 'gentleman of property.' This proved to be Joseph Wyatt, a retired haberdasher and property owner, and 1 of the 6 lessees who took over Levey's Royal in 1835. The theatre was to be built in Pitt Street, between King and Market Streets, and would be much larger than the Royal. The foundation stone was laid on 7.9.1836, but there were many delays before the theatre was finally opened on 26.3.1838. Early in 1838 the *Monitor* reported that the Royal Victoria was 111ft long, 50ft wide; the stage was 50ft square, the proscenium 21ft wide and 20ft high. The inclined benches of the pit were estimated to seat 800. The lower tier held 26 boxes, most of them intended to seat 9, but some more than 9. The centre tier was divided into 4 large boxes for families or individual patrons, and 2 side slips, the slips being for the 'women of the town'. The third tier contained the gallery. Box seats were cushioned and covered with crimson cloth. The tier ceilings were of zinc, against the danger of fire and the constant fall of dust from the wood and calico ceilings sometimes used. Each tier of boxes could hold 250, and the gallery from 400 to 500, making a total 1800 persons. On 17.3.1838 Wyatt let his almost completed theatre to Sydney's large Irish population for the annual St Patrick's Day Ball, the pit being boarded over level with the stage, making a ballroom which took in the floor space of the auditorium and the 50ft by 50ft stage. Nine days later the theatre was opened with a performance of *Othello* and the farce, *The Middy on Shore* (1836). There was praise for the new scenery, and the lighting, which was by the smokeless Argand lamp. The theatre was said

to be 'lofty' by comparison with the Royal, and was 'something of the horseshoe' in shape. The box fronts were coloured pale salmon, each with a pale blue panel, these being separated by circular medallions presenting, alternately, the rose, the shamrock, and the thistle, in gold on a crimson ground. Crimson cloth, probably baize, covered the seats and lined the dress boxes, while the stage boxes, one at each end of this tier, next to but not built into the proscenium, had 'elegant' chairs and were festooned with crimson drapery. Improvements were made to the stage in October 1838, and gas was installed in 1841. The theatre was subsequently renovated and redecorated about 20 times between 1841 and 1877. Major reconstruction took place in 1854, after the theatre, excluding the moveable interior fittings, was sold at auction for £24 000. Wyatt had to vacate the building by June. He decided to build his own theatre. Structural changes made by the new owners included moving the proscenium forward and widening it, and building in three boxes on either side. Further structural changes were made in 1865, when the plain curve of the box fronts was changed to ogee curves. From then on the Royal Victoria served Sydney as its major theatre until it was destroyed by fire in 1880.

6 Australian Olympic (1842). In August 1841 a small company consisting of Signor Luigi Dalle Case (gymnast, equestrian, specialist in 'living statues,' or 'poses plastique'), 2 young Brazilian girl gymnasts, and Signor Auguste, clown and dancer, had a successful season at the Royal Victoria. In October Dalle Case let it be known that he was about to build an amphitheatre on land at the corner of Hunter and George Streets 'for the exhibition of feats of horsemanship, and such theatrical representations in which that noble and segacious animal may be introduced.' This was the first Australian arena theatre, or theatre in which the whole or portion of the pit could be used, when required, as a circus or equestrian ring. The Olympic was opened on 26.1.1842, and for its first 3 months was immensely popular. The 'theatre' was really a marquee, but the interior was as attractive as ingenuity could make it. The canvas walls were hung with coloured drapery specially arranged by a Sydney upholsterer. The fronts of the boxes were painted with landscape medallions by the artist S.Prout, and between each was an 'elegant' gas bracket. The pit could be, and often was, enlarged by placing seats in the ring after the feats of horsemanship. The *Gazette* said the proscenium of the small stage was 'without exception the most beautiful we have seen; it is taken from the Judgement Hall of the Alhambra . . .' This, together with the stage scenery, was again the work of S.Prout. But Dalle Case became too ambitious. He decided to provide 'high class drama,' and to lure some of the leading actors from the Victoria with the bait of higher wages. Early in February the Signor advised the public that the stage was being extended to nearly 50ft. But towards the end of April his 'spirited liberality' showed itself to have

'Indian Temple' stage boxes Palace Sydney 1896

been a little too spirited. His name appeared in the list of insolvents, date of surrender 23.4.1842, and the insubstantial Olympic was auctioned to pay his debts.

7 Royal City (1843). Early in 1843 it was reported that the actor and former manager at Levey's Royal, Joseph Simmons, was about to apply for a theatre licence. On 9.2.1843 Sydney City Council dealt with 3 petitions — one from Simmons seeking approval of his plan to convert premises in Market Street, near George Street, into a theatre; one from a group of unemployed actors supporting the plan, and one from Joseph Wyatt, proprietor of the Royal Victoria, opposing it. Permission was granted and the Royal City, as it was named, was opened by the joint proprietors, J.Simmons and J.Belmore, on 20.5.1843. Contained in what had formerly been shop premises, its seating capacity was restricted, and its stage was not large enough to permit production of the 'big' melodramas which drew big audiences. Its actual seating capacity is unknown, but from advertisements it is learned that the theatre had a dress circle (five shillings), private boxes to seat eight (£2.0.0), and a pit (two shillings). The theatre was completed in a little under 3 months. Within the rectangle of the former shop were fitted a dress circle with boxes on 3 of the walls. A proscenium and stage filled the fourth wall, and the floor of the shop became the pit. The fronts of the boxes and the proscenium were painted in a *trompe l'oeil* effect, direct on wood or on canvas glued on wood, '. . . being white marble relieved with rich gilded mouldings and reliefs.' The ceiling was painted with a scene which represented a youthful choral band revelling amid festoons of flowers. From its centre hung a chandelier. Maroon drapery was used for the boxes, and a light blue velvet cushioned their front edges. There was the usual green baize front curtain, and a painted act drop which depicted Shakespeare and some of the characters from his plays as its central feature. Around the gilded frame of this painting were portraits of Queen Victoria, Prince Albert, Sir Richard Bourke, and Sir George Gipps. Three weeks after the opening another tier of boxes was constructed, and admission prices were reduced, but to no avail. The theatre was closed on 23.6.1843, and a week or so later Simmons, now sole proprietor, was declared insolvent. The theatre became in turn an auction room, bedding warehouse, furniture store, and tailor shop. In 1850 the theatre's fittings were offered for sale, including about 20 movable scenes, with grooves, together with wings, clouds (i.e. borders), drops, ornamental fittings, etc., a drop scene and a green curtain. The Royal City remained in existence until the early years of the present century, when it was demolished to allow for the extension of Farmer's department store.

8 Malcom's Amphitheatre (1850). It was usual for theatres, up to at least the end of the century, to have a hotel or grog shop attached. John Malcom, who held the licence for the Adelphi Hotel in York Street,

between King and Market Streets, reversed this order when he opened his circus in 1850 at the back of an already established hotel. The building had its first name-change 3 days after opening, to Circus Royal. By 1851 its owner had made enough money for him to make it a more permanent structure. Changes were made to the interior, and a proper roof was constructed. In June the circus was closed for a few days for further changes, while in August Malcom advertised that side boxes had been fitted up, with a saloon attached, and that the pit could seat 1000. By this time the building had received a third title, Malcom's Royal Australian Circus. By July 1852 renovations and rebuilding had given the circus a shingled roof, dress circle, side boxes, pit, and stage, and its name had been changed yet again, to Malcom's Royal Australian Amphitheatre. In April 1853 dress circle seats cost 3s, side box the same, pit 1s. Four months later these prices were increased by 1s for each section. Malcolm made an unsuccessful attempt in September to sell his amphitheatre, his advertisement including the following details. 'The interior of the theatre is handsomely fitted up with a net circle of dress and private boxes . . . In the front of the Adelphi Hotel is a spacious entrance to the private boxes — enclosed by a pair of gates. The interior of the house is arranged into three circles of boxes, with several private and family boxes — an extensive pit with raised seats . . . The size of the ampitheatre is 54ft by 30ft; the opening of the proscenium 28ft; the distance from front to front of the boxes 41ft; the height of the building 41ft.' There were also dressing rooms, a greenroom, and a gas chandelier in the centre of the roof. (See: Royal Lyceum).

9 Royal Albert (1854). Towards the end of 1851 a small circus was established in Castlereagh Street, near Market Street, named the Olympic. It served its purpose very quickly, for the public soon tired of it, and in May 1852 was converted into a theatre. For the next few years, like Malcom's Royal Australian Amphitheatre, it was called on to play a number of diverse roles. In July 1854 the stage was enlarged, the building was renamed the Royal Albert, and dramatic performances were given by some of the actors from the Royal Victoria, which was then undergoing alterations. These performances lasted little more than a month, after which the theatre had only intermittent use. It became in turn a dance hall, the Scandinavian Hall, Victoria Hall, and Academy of Music. (See: Gaiety below).

10 Royal Lyceum (1854). In October 1854 Malcom's Royal Australian Amphitheatre in York Street underwent further alterations, leading once again to a name-change for the building, this time to the Royal Lyceum. The amphitheatre boxes were brought forward 6ft, increasing accommodation; the arena was converted to a pit; a new proscenium was installed, with new act drop and scenery for the stage, and the theatre was reopened on 23.10.1854. It had a few weeks of good

Above: Interior Prince of Wales Sydney 1855
Below: Interior Royal Victoria Sydney 1874

houses, and then the novelty began to wear off and the company had to struggle for a living. The theatre reverted for a while to its equestrian beginnings. Then, in December 1855, the familiar 'extensive alterations and improvements' were again announced. (See: Our Lyceum below).

11 Prince of Wales (1855). When Wyatt was unable to renew his lease on the Royal Victoria he determined to build his own theatre, in Castlereagh Street, a few doors from King Street. He thus established a site for a theatre which remained in use for more than 100 years. His theatre, the Prince of Wales, was opened on 12.3.1855. It was larger and better equipped than the Victoria. The auditorium measured 70ft from the orchestra to the back of the pit, and 60ft across. The pit seated 1500, dress circle 500, upper boxes 750, and gallery 500 totalling 3250. The boxes each had 6 rows of benches, the era of comfortably upholstered individual chairs not yet having arrived. The distance across the body of the house, box front to box front, was 36ft. A somewhat sombre colour scheme was used, the box panels being a deep blue relieved only by the Prince's crest in gold against a marbled background. The ceiling was 58ft from the floor of the pit, had a central dome 15ft wide, and was painted to represent a bright summer sky. A large gas chandelier hung from the centre of the dome, and small ones from each wing of the dress circle. The stage, 87ft deep from the footlights and 60ft across, had a proscenium 36ft wide and 25ft high. The large pictorial act drop showed four female figures in the foreground, representing poetry, tragedy, music, and dancing, reclining in the shade of a bowered fountain. On the right was a grove of luxuriant foliage, overtopping which could be seen the classic temple of the muses; on the left was a tranquil lake stretching into the distance, dotted with tiny sails. The stage had about 100 pairs of flats, each 22ft high and 14ft wide, with wings to match. The height from the pit to the dress circle was 9ft. There were dressing rooms under the stage for the men (no natural light or ventilation) and above-stage for women. There was also a greenroom. It was said in 1855 that the Prince of Wales had cost £30 000 to build and equip. It was sold in 1858 for £10 600, and was destroyed by fire 2 years later.

12 Our Lyceum (1856). The Royal Lyceum continued in intermittent use as an equestrian amphitheatre until June 1856, when it was announced that 'an elegant *vaudeville* theatre is now in course of erection on the site of Malcom's Circus . . .' Early in July the first description of the new building, to be known as Our Lyceum was published. The theatre would have a single tier of dress and private boxes, above which would be the gallery. The pit would accommodate 1000, the space immediately in front of the orchestra being reserved for stalls. It was said the theatre would accommodate a total 2000. The completed building, which used only the 4 walls of the original Lyceum, stood on an area 82ft by 56ft. The box tier contained 19 boxes, 8 set apart for family or other groups. The new theatre was opened on 14.7.1856 for a series of Shakespearian

performances by the Irish tragedian, G.V.Brooke. In October the dress circle seats (benches) were backed, and the gallery was transformed into an upper circle with promenade. The following month the stage was deepened, and deepened yet again in December, when 9ft was also excavated from beneath it to provide for the installation of stage traps and under-stage machinery. A greenroom, property room, wardrobe, and dressing rooms were also built, and the stage was equipped with 25 pairs of flats with matching wings. But it transpired that Our Lyceum should have been called anybody's Lyceum. Over the next 20 years or so it suffered a bewildering number of changes, from dance hall to circus, from circus to theatre, and then the whole cycle again in reverse, while its name was changed to Adelphi, Cafe Chantant, and Royal. But that did not stop gamblers or optimists such as the actor W.B.Gill and a few others from coming forward to see if they could find the success which had eluded others. Gill took the theatre over in 1873, rebuilt and renovated it, and called it the Queen's — a name it retained for the rest of its life. (See: Queen's below).

13 Royal Albert (1860). Early in 1860 a small dance hall, the Assembly Rooms, on the corner of King and Sussex Streets, was converted to a theatre. Designed to cater to the waterfront trade, it had a brief life of about 6 weeks at admission prices of 1s 6d, and 3d. Its promoters were a small band of unsuccessful itinerant actors who, 2 years earlier, had launched a similarly unsuccessful venture in Parramatta.

14 Prince of Wales (1863). In 1861 R.Fitzgerald bought the Prince of Wales site and commissioned the architect, J.F.Hilly, to design a theatre. The second Prince of Wales was opened on 23.5.1863 with a performance of Flotow's opera, *Martha,* by the Lyster Opera Company. The new theatre could rightly be described as the first in Australia to be fully equipped mechanically. The building retained the street facade of the previous theatre, but all the rest was new. The seating capacity was said to be 2500, but when crowded the theatre could accommodate 3900. The pit measured 60ft from the footlights to the back wall, and each row of benches was backed. The height to the dress circle was 10ft 6ins in front and 14ft at the back. The dress circle front was of ornamental iron, and the front seats projected beyond the line of the upper circle and gallery tiers. All tiers were semicircular in shape, instead of the usual horseshoe. Seating in the dress circle was by means of 6 lines or rows of sofas, 70 in all, covered with amber satin tabaret, harmonising with the gold and white cornices and panels of the walls. Private boxes at each end of the dress circle measured 14ft by 12ft. The height between the dress circle and the upper tier was 10ft in front, 15ft at the back. The upper tier had 7 rows of covered seats, each 2ft 8ins wide. The height between this tier and the gallery was 10ft. Similar accommodation was provided in the gallery, the height between it and the roof or ceiling

being 12ft. The 'comfortable' seating capacity of each area was: pit 900, dress circle 400, upper tier 600, gallery 600. The auditorium was lighted by a central sunlight in the dome, which had 130 gas jets. The footlights had 36 burners, and the stage nearly 100. Around the central dome in the ceiling was a series of painted panels depicting classical figures. The proscenium was 29ft high and 30ft wide, and had a 6ft statue on either side in a niche, one of Thalia the other of Melpomene. Again the general colour scheme was green, white, and gold, with touches of amber and magenta. The proscenium was in delicate green with white and gold mouldings, while the front curtain was of magenta baize. The stage was the most complete and best equipped yet built in Australia. It was 58ft wide and 100ft deep from the footlights. There were 9 full-set scenes (wings, back flats, and borders), each of which could be changed mechanically by means of winches, drums, ropes and pulleys. A moving seashore with advancing and receding waves could be similarly 'worked.' There was a 58ft by 24ft scene room 22ft above the stage; and a painting room 30ft above the stage. The flies were fitted with shafts and purchase wheels capable of lifting an entire scene with its actors above the height of the proscenium. For understage working — traps and effects — there was a mezzanine floor 9ft below the stage, and a cellar 8ft beneath that. In 1863 it was estimated that with 1200 in the pit at 2s 6d, 500 in the dress circle at 5s, 600 in the upper circle at 2, and 600 in the gallery at 1, the takings for one night would be £365. But this theatre, despite its attraction as a piece of theatre architecture, and its efficiency as a 'machine for acting in,' had many vicissitudes, becoming at one time a skating rink, at another a circus. It was destroyed by fire in 1872.

15 Queen's (1873). The actor W.B.Gill, who had had a reasonably successful season at the Royal Victoria, took in hand the conversion of the former Our Lyceum into the Queen's in October 1873, and spent a great deal of money in having the former gallery dismantled and the auditorium ceiling raised. He turned the building into a theatre with stalls and circle only, prices 1s for the stalls, 2 for the circle, and 4 for seats in the centre box of the circle. As the Queen's the theatre had a brief popularity, but one of its many drawbacks as a workable theatre was its lack of understage space for traps, and flying space for scenery. In September 1874 another actor, Edmund Holloway, took the theatre over and tried to improve its appearance by installing a new proscenium and cleaning and redecorating the auditorium. But a gas explosion backstage one night, and the consequent cancellation of that night's performance just after it had started, so annoyed some members of the audience that a near riot ensued in which the gas fittings were torn from the walls, seats were smashed, and the paper-covered proscenium badly damaged. Early in 1875 the whole of the interior fittings were dismantled, a new dress circle installed with seats upholstered in crimson

and gold damask, and with boxes on either side. A new proscenium with an arched top was supported by two white and gold fluted columns on either side. Pit and stalls were reseated, the stall seats having upholstered sloping backs; those in the pit, behind the stalls, being raised to improve the view of the stage. The *Herald* said it was difficult to reconcile the new interior with one which had been 'the abode of dirt and dinginess, the refuge of acrobats and buffoons, the receptacle of audiences that consumed refreshments and indulged in the weed during the performance.' The changes were made to house the first Sydney performance of J.C.Williamson and Maggie Moore in *Struck Oil*. But, their successful season over, the theatre reverted to its previous history of decay and refurbishment — a surface rehabilitation — until it was finally condemned as unsafe by the Royal Commission into Sydney theatres in 1882, and closed. Its seating capacity was then put at 818.

16 Haymarket (1874). The haymarket at Brickfield Hill was converted to a theatre in 1874, apparently as a single-floor building divided into pit and stalls. The stage was adequately equipped, and had a proscenium painted by the scenepainter, W.J.Wilson. But the threatre had a brief life of only a few months before it succumbed to the competition provided by a nearby circus. The stage equipment, scenery, and grooves were auctioned early in 1875.

17 Royal (1875). The second Sydney Royal was built on the site of the first and second Prince of Wales, in Castlereagh Street, and incorporated the street facade of the two earlier buildings. Planned as early as 1872 as a third Prince of Wales, work did not start on the site until 1875. The building was 136ft long, 60ft wide, and 40ft high. The auditorium took up 70ft of the length the stage the remaining 66ft. The dress circle was said to seat 200, the stalls 400, pit 1200, and the family circle or gallery 500, totalling 2300. But these figures, quoted from the *Herald,* disagree with those published in the *Illustrated Sydney News,* which gave 360 for the stalls, 1000 for the pit, dress circle 220, family circle 500. This weekly said the theatre would seat 2080 under normal conditions, but up to 2600 when crowded. The theatre was opened on 11.12.1875. The audience saw a house lighted by a central chandelier and sunlight with 376 burners, the footlights having argand burners, glasses, and plated reflectors. The general colour scheme was in white, gold, and grey relieved by light blue wallpaper and the crimson baize front curtain. The blue ceiling to the dress circle was powdered with gold stars. Dress circle seats were individual white oval-backed arm chairs, upholstered in crimson velvet. Around the walls was a row of oval ormolu and gilt mirrors, each having girandoles or small gasaliers. Similar seats were in the stalls, but upholstered in crimson morocco. Pit seats were wooden benches. The proscenium was painted and gilded, and when the front curtain was raised an act drop depicting a scene on the Nile was revealed. The stage had the usual complement of grooves,

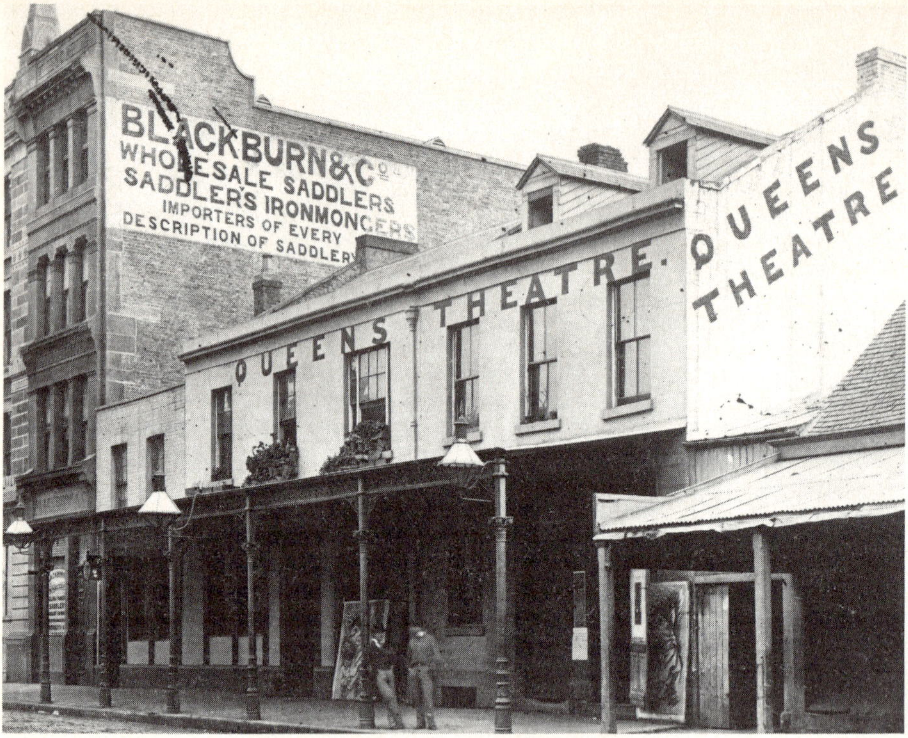

Government Printing Office NSW

Above: Exterior Queen's Theatre Sydney 1882
Below: Exterior Sydney Royal 1875

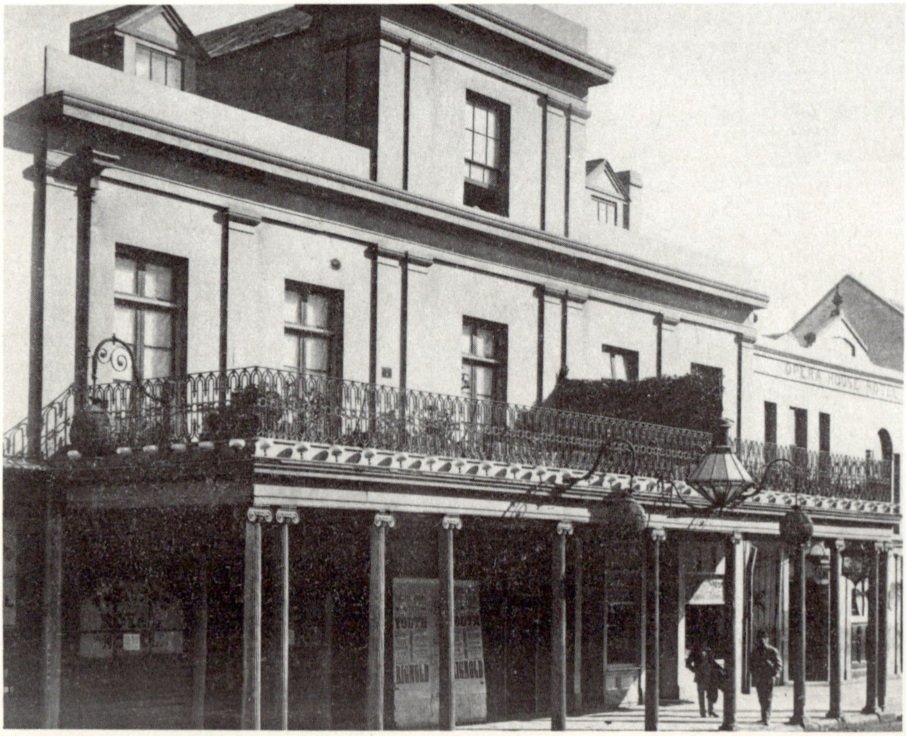

wings, flats, and borders, the flats and wings being 20ft high. The flies were high enough to allow a drop being lifted out of sight by folding (i.e. the bottom bar of the drop or 'blind' being pulled up to meet the top bar, the whole being then lifted above the proscenium opening), but not to the full extent of its depth. This theatre was cleaned, renovated, and redecorated in 1882, the year in which it was taken over by Williamson, Garner, and Musgrove. In the same year the Royal Commission of Inquiry into the Construction of Theatres reported that the Royal still had only a wood and canvas wall separating the auditorium from the stage. The auditorium by this time was said to seat only 1445. The dressing rooms, scene dock, wardrobe, and carpenter's shop were in temporary buildings behind the stage. Ceilings throughout the building were of wood covered with canvas and painted or papered. The boxes on either side of the proscenium and the proscenium itself were of the same materials. There were 60 gas jets around the walls of the dress circle, 6 in the stalls, 8 in the family circle, and 4 in the pit. At the time of this report the theatre was being wired throughout for electric lighting. In 1892 fire damaged the proscenium and boxes, and destroyed the ceiling of the auditorium, revealing that the wood and canvas structures reported by the 1882 Commission had not been replaced. Constant pressure over the years resulted in a brick proscenium wall being built, metal ceilings being installed, and changes of all kinds being introduced to reduce fire risks. This theatre, many times redecorated, renovated, rebuilt, remained in constant use until demolished in 1972, the site having been occupied by a theatre for 117 years.

18 Academy of Music (1879). In 1875 Sydney's Catholic Guild built a Guild Hall in Castlereagh Street, alongside St George's Church. This incorporated a meeting room or hall 100ft long, 40ft wide, and 32ft high, with a gallery at the entrance end. In July 1879 the hall's small stage was brought forward, a proscenium installed, the gallery raised and converted into a dress circle, and the floor divided into stalls and pit. The hall was then opened for dramatic and other uses as the Academy of Music. The venture was not a success, and by the end of August the building was again being called the Guild Hall. This it remained until it underwent another conversion, this time to the Gaiety.

19 Opera House (1879). Another wood, paper, and canvas auditorium, this time located on the first floor of a warehouse on the corner of King and York Streets. Built originally to house comic opera and vaudeville performances, which demanded little more in the way of scenery than backdrops and wings, this theatre was outwardly as attractive and comfortable as paint, gilt, cut glass, satin, silk, and velvet could make it. And, like its predecessors, it had a series of renovations, rebuildings, and redecorations over the years until it was finally condemned in 1900. This theatre was contained in an area 92ft long and 55ft 6ins wide. It seated 900 in stalls and pit, 300 in the dress circle,

which had its entrance in York Street. Pit and stalls were entered from King Street. The proscenium wall was of brick, and was said by the *Daily Telegraph* to be the only one in Australia apart from that at the Princess's in Melbourne. But in fact this 'wall' was no more than two wings reaching to the ceiling, the proscenium arch itself being of the usual wood and canvas painted. The stage, 32ft deep and 52½ft wide, had a proscenium arch 26ft wide. On either side of this were three stage boxes. The Royal Commission in 1882 reported that this theatre seated 806. In 1886 it was said that the theatre was contained in a space 90ft long, 53ft wide, and 25ft high, and that the maximum number it could contain was 1100.

20 Gaiety (1880). The former Guild Hall-Academy of Music was opened on 26.12.1880 as the Gaiety. Converted to seat up to 1500, it had 2 stage boxes on either side of the proscenium. The original gallery was extended along the side walls to meet the boxes. The stage was 40ft deep and 42ft wide, the proscenium being 24ft wide and 18ft high. Flies above the stage enabled scenery to be flown to a height of 18ft. By 1882, because of various changes, the seating capacity of this theatre was put at: orchestra chairs 135, stalls 250, balcony 320 totalling 705, with a maximum of 800. Again this was a theatre with a painted wood and canvas proscenium wall. The general colour scheme was in blue and gold, with crimson curtains and carpets, the boxes being hung with amber and azure satin and white lace curtains. This theatre had many changes to its interior before, towards the end of the century, it was abandoned as no longer theatrically viable.

21 Academy of Music (1882). This small theatre was opened in Castlereagh Street, near Market Street, on 23.9.1882, on the site previously occupied by the Olympic Circus, Albert Theatre, Scandinavian Hall, and Victoria Hall — in that order. As the Academy of Music it at first seated only 436 on one floor and a gallery. By 1886 various alterations made to the original had resulted in a building 84ft long, 28ft wide and 22ft high capable of seating 750. The following year it was closed for alterations, and 3 years later was demolished to make way for the Garrick.

22 Academy of Music (1884). Opened at the Haymarket on 28.7.1884 as a concert hall to seat 600. A year later it became the long-lived Alhambra. (See: Music hall).

23 Royal Standard (1886). Built in Castlereagh Street as a hall for the Foresters' Lodge, this theatre was opened on 8.5.1886. The building had a dress circle and a ground floor divided into stalls and pit — total seating capacity 960 to 1000. The hall, 99ft long, 86ft 6ins wide, and 32ft high, had a stage 36ft wide, 25ft deep. The proscenium, with an arch 20ft wide, was of the usual wood and canvas construction. A central chandelier had 40 gas jets. This theatre, which underwent many conversions in its life of about 30 years, served in turn for melodrama, vaudeville, and repertory performances.

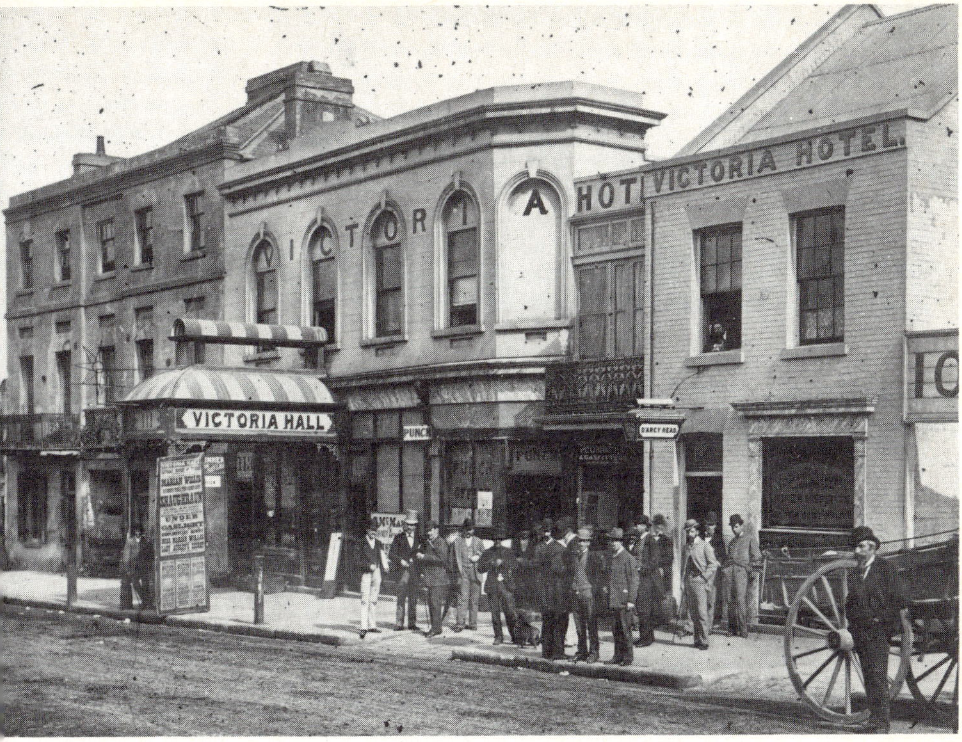

Government Printing Office NSW

Above: Exterior Victoria Hall Sydney 1881
Below: Warehouse which housed Sydney Opera House 1882

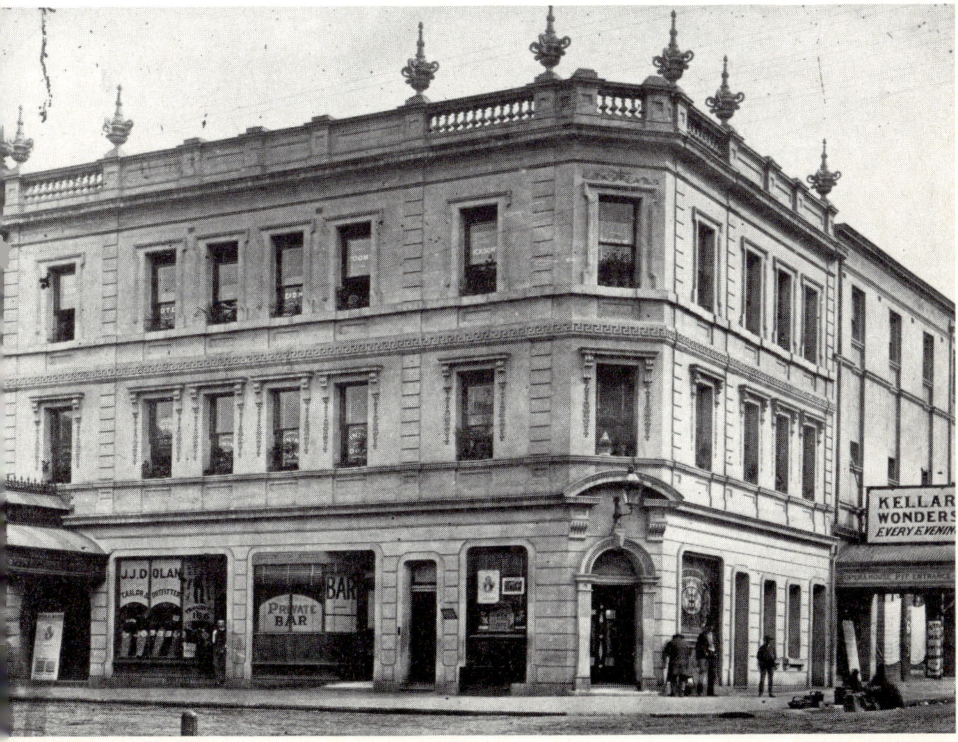

Government Printing Office NSW

24 Criterion (1886). Situated on the corner of Park and Pitt Streets, the Criterion was opened on 27.12.1886. There was apparently little of note about the interior of this theatre, for not even the size of its auditorium was mentioned in newspaper reports, and there were disparities in the accounts of its seating capacity. The *Herald* said in December 1886 that the theatre could seat 200 in the stalls, 150 in the back stalls, 250 in the dress circle, 450 in the upper or family circle, and 650 in the gallery, totalling 1700; but the Colonial Architect's report towards the end of 1887 put the figures at 314, 138, 210, 329 i.e. 991. The orchestra was located under the stage, while the actors' dressing rooms were in the basement under the auditorium, with no natural light and insufficient ventilation to overcome the fumes from the gas meters nearby. All that was said about the auditorium was that it was lighted by a central chandelier; that the general colour scheme was in light blue and gold; that the stage boxes were hung with blue and gold brocades, bordered with ruby-coloured plush and gold fringe, and that the stall and dress circle seats were of gold-coloured iron upholstered in ruby plush. The stage, whose dimensions were not given, had a gold-fringed ruby plush curtain instead of the usual green baize, while its act drop represented a framed painting of the landing of Captain Cook and the reading of the proclamation. Major alterations were made to this theatre in 1892, when the roof was raised 12ft and the flat ceiling had a dome and sliding roof installed. The stage boxes were abolished, except for one at each end of the dress circle. The proscenium arch was lowered and widened, and the stage itself increased from its previous size (not specified) to 36ft deep and 58ft wide. Behind the stage was a 22ft by 40ft scene dock, with a painting room above. A suite of 10 dressing rooms was built on the floor above the stage. The auditorium colour scheme was in pale blue, duck-egg green, fawn, cream, and old gold. The proscenium, 2 feet wider and 3 feet lower than before, was framed in terracotta, crimson, and gold. Above it was painted a series of figure studies depicting the 7 ages of man. The Captain Cook act drop was replaced by a more conventional one depicting the interior of a Moorish palace, to fit in with the Moorish style of the theatre's new decor. The Criterion was remodelled again in 1905, and the seating capacity increased. Most of the other changes were to fit in with the new fire laws — more exits, and the fireproofing of ceilings and timberwork.

25 Her Majesty's (1887). This theatre, opened on 10.9.1887, was the largest and best equipped in the Sydney of its day. Although first mooted in 1882, with tenders being called the following year, work on the building was not started until December 1884. It continued until May 1886, when there was a delay of 6 months. Work then continued until the theatre was completed. Early in 1885 the *Sydney Mail* said the theatre was the centre of a seven-storey building which also housed a 100-room hotel and offices. The stage was to be 84ft wide and 50ft deep. There

would be 18 dressing rooms. The auditorium would consist of stalls, dress circle, family circle, gallery, and 18 private boxes. Two years later, when the theatre was almost completed, the usual confused information was provided in contemporary newspaper reports. The *Echo* said the theatre seated 2500; the *Daily Telegraph* said 1680, but that 2500 to 3000 could be crammed in, while the *Builder and Contractors' News* said seating was provided for 1650, but a total 2200 could be seated. The stage was said by the *Echo* to be 90ft wide and 56ft deep, while the *Daily Telegraph* gave the figures as 84ft by 50ft. The proscenium arch, 38ft square, was decorated with the rose, shamrock, and thistle in gold against a crimson background. It was surmounted by an elaborate bronzed and gilt trophy 'encircling a full achievement of the royal arms in heraldic blazonry.' (*Society* 1887). The cream satin tableau curtains came from London's Lyceum, where Henry Irving had first used them for his production of *Romeo and Juliet*. The old fashioned groove system of stage setting was discarded in favour of a German system using wagons for the horizontal shifting of entire sets on and off stage. It was also possible to turn scenes 'inside out' by means of rollers working on pivots attached to the scenery. The stage was lighted principally by five borders of 35 electric lamps each, and 40 electric footlights. There were also 60 bunch and hanging lights. All electric lighting was duplicated with gas. Electricity was provided by 2 dynamos for the incandescent or glow lamps, and a 7-light arc machine for the 2000 candlepower lamps used to light the exterior of the building. Power was generated by a steam engine. All these, together with the gas meters, were housed in the basement of the building. The auditorium, 74ft square, had 3 tiers — dress circle, family circle, and gallery. There were also 3 stage boxes on either side of the proscenium. Dress and family circle walls were covered with tapestry. The fronts of the 3 tiers had a ground of primrose with gilded bas-relief wreaths of flowers. Carpet was on the floor of the dress and family circles, and their bronze-coloured seats were upholstered in crimson plush. The roof of the auditorium was supported by circular arcading springing from bronzed columns, 'the spandrels being panelled, and the panels ornamented with gilt devices upon fields of turquoise blue, while the stiles are coloured a delicate buff brightened with vermilion lines,' (*Society* 1887). Radiating 'tablets' with gold bas-relief decorations surrounded the central dome. Between the points of these were 12 medallions, from the centre of each depending a gilded tube or rod with a 5-leafed electric lamp at the end. These surrounded, but were below, the gas chandelier, like 12 stars around a sun. The interior of this theatre was totally destroyed by fire in March 1902.

26 Garrick (1890). This small theatre, opened on 22.12.1890, on the site of the Academy of Music, had an auditorium 45ft by 55ft. The building, adjoining the Imperial Arcade, had a frontage to Castlereagh Street of 66ft and depth of 180ft. About 1000 could be seated in the

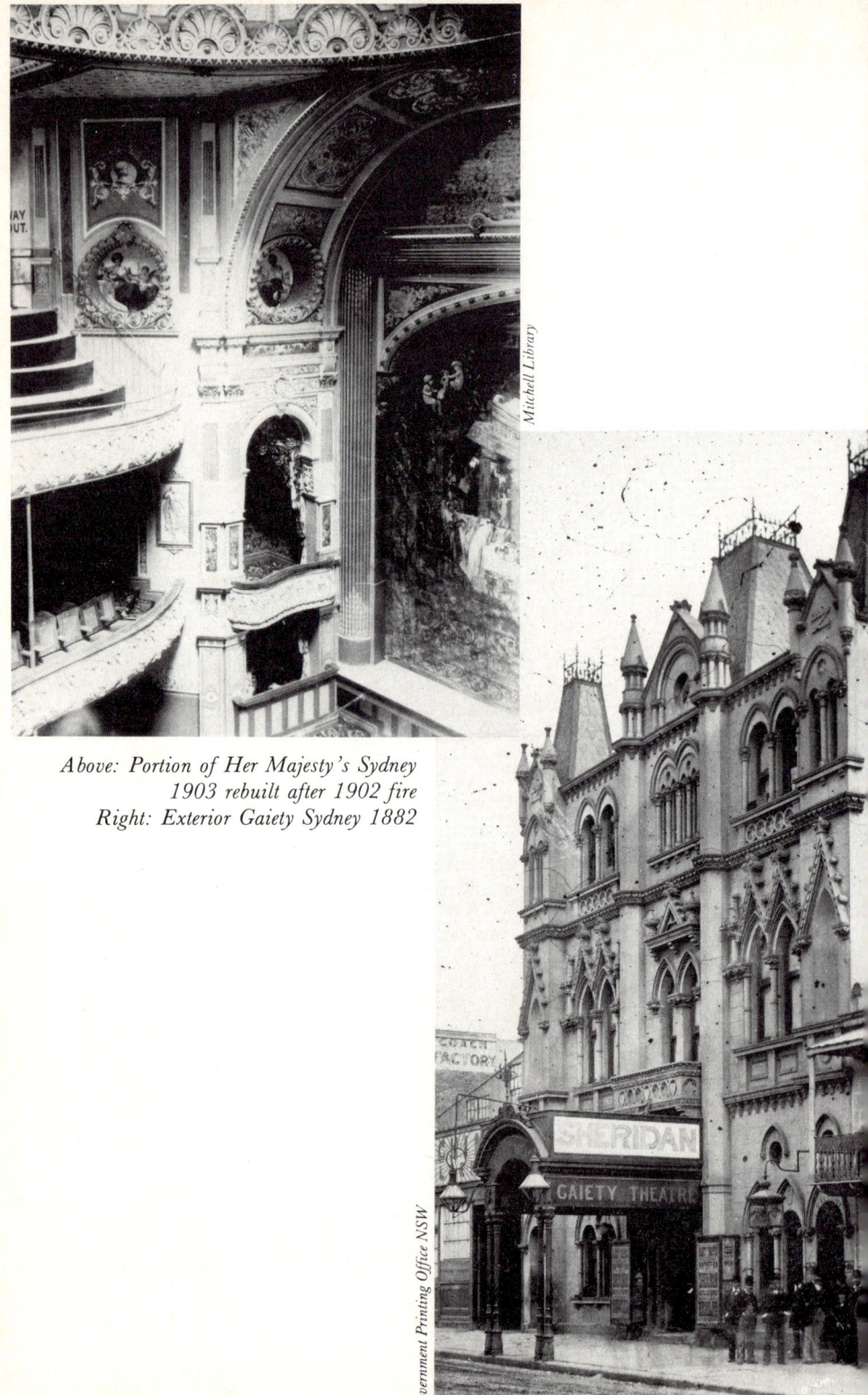

*Above: Portion of Her Majesty's Sydney
1903 rebuilt after 1902 fire
Right: Exterior Gaiety Sydney 1882*

auditorium — 450 in the stalls, 165 in the dress circle, 350 in the family circle. There were also 4 boxes. The stage, 45ft by 50ft, had a proscenium 25ft square. The orchestra was placed below the level of the stalls. The domed ceiling of the auditorium had a sliding roof 10ft in diameter. The general colour scheme of gold, orange, and blue was complemented by deep red upholstery and a brighter red front curtain. Electric lighting was used throughout, duplicated, as usual at this time, with gas. But the Garrick proved too small for a drama theatre and in 1893 it became the first Tivoli.

27 Lyceum (1892). Plans for this theatre, opened in Pitt Street on 26.12.1892, were announced early in 1891. Incorporated in a 5-storey office building, it was designed to seat 1700, but when opened was said to be capable of seating 2250. The stage was 63ft wide, 60ft deep, with a height of 51ft to the gridiron. There was a 'sink' or cellar 21ft under the stage. Fly galleries 10ft wide were 30ft above the stage. The picture frame proscenium in gold and silver was 29ft wide, 38ft high. An act drop by Phil Goatcher in *trompe l'oeil* effect depicted a yellow satin banneret painted with classical figures and surrounded by perfectly modelled silver-grey curtains. Boxes on either side of the proscenium were staggered at different levels. There were only 2 tiers, a dress circle, and a family circle with a gallery behind. The general colour scheme was in peacock blue and gold, the fronts of the tiers being decorated with shells of gold and silver in which nestled 'pearls' of electric light. The domed ceiling, with its glass chandelier, had a sliding roof. Steel boilers, engines, and dynamos to supply power for 500 electric lights were installed in the basement.

28 Tivoli (1893). This, the former Garrick, was taken over by Harry Rickards as a vaudeville theatre on 18.2.1893. Among minor changes were the abolition of the footlights, 'lifting' of the orchestra so that it could be seen as well as heard, and the installation of a new sliding roof. The floors were carpeted. In 1897 the auditorium was redecorated and refurnished in the gold and crimson plush style of the period. The theatre was destroyed by fire in 1899.

29 Palace (1896). 'Gorgeous as an Indian temple,' was the general opinion of this visually exciting little theatre when it was opened on 19.12.1896. Designed as a variety house to seat 1000, it had a frontage of 56ft to Pitt Street and a depth of 125ft. As usual at this time the basement housed the greenroom, dressing rooms, music and property rooms, and, beneath the theatre's entrance vestibule, the engine room with its three boilers and three engines. These were capable of providing power for 4000 electric lights. This theatre was the first in Australia to have all its lights behind stained glass screens or panels. Even the dome in the auditorium was lighted without a lamp being in sight. The *Daily Telegraph* said of the Indian design adopted for the auditorium that 'in no other theatre in the world has an auditorium of this kind been at-

tempted,' but in fact it had, in America at the Broadway, Denver, Colorado. The ceiling of the Palace was of groined arches springing from the tops of slender columns. The proscenium arch, also in the Indian style, had a golden figure of Buddah at its peak. Four stage boxes on either side of this were like miniature Indian temples, with arched fronts, each topmost box surmounted by a cupola. The interior of the boxes was treated in tufted satin, some in blue, some in gold. The upholstery of the dress circle, which seated 200, was in old gold and peacock blue. The stage, though small, was fitted with the most modern mechanism available. It had a front curtain designed by the artist who designed and carried out the decoration of the auditorium, Phil Goatcher, and was a patchwork or mosaic design of 3500 pieces of hand-painted satin, made at a cost of £1000. In 1899 it was said that the depth of the palace stage was to be increased from 30ft to 46ft, and the proscenium opening widened by 2ft 6ins. In 1905 the owners, following the report of a government committee appointed to 'consider what steps should be taken to minimise the risk of fire and the danger of panic,' had to move the boilers and engines from the basement to a nearby building.

30 Tivoli (1900). The second Tivoli, opened on 12.4.1900, was able to use the facade of the previous Garrick. The other walls, stage, and auditorium were entirely new. Built in the short space of 7 months, this theatre's auditorium was 60ft deep and 40ft wide, compared with the previous 55ft by 45ft. The tier fronts were brought closer to the stage than before, to provide more seats in the dress circle and gallery. From the floor of the stalls to the underside of the dome the new building measured 42ft, with another 16ft to the sliding roof. The dome, 26ft in diameter, was divided into 24 decorated panels, each again divided into 3 smaller panels, the patrea or circular ornament in each holding an electric light. The proscenium arch, 22ft by 23ft, with 2 stage boxes on either side, was supported by ornamental scrolls with an entablature. The stalls seated 480, dress circle 201, family circle, with gallery at back, 500 totalling 1181. Circle fronts were decorated with acanthus leaves and clusters of fruit and ribbons in the prevailing colours of cream, gold, silver, light greys, and turquoise blue, relieved with terracotta tints. The stage, 40ft wide and 45ft deep, had a scene dock and paint room at the back. A separate 4-storey building at the rear of the theatre housed dressing rooms and offices.

31 Her Majesty's (1903). Opened on 1.8.1903, the new auditorium of this theatre was in many ways different from the original. Starting with the vestibule in Pitt Street, instead of the narrow, winding staircase on the right which led to the dress circle, there was now a broad central white marble staircase. On either side of this were wide entrances to the stalls, leading down seven steps instead of by 14 steps up as before. All the levels of the new theatre were a floor lower than the old. There were 2 tiers instead of the former 3, the seating being: stalls 670; dress circle

236; gallery or amphitheatre 1000. As usual, this amphitheatre was divided into family circle and gallery. The stage, 74ft by 46ft, had a proscenium 32ft wide and 28ft high. A backstage switchboard with dimmers had about 300 switches. Electric buttons were connected with all the dressing rooms to warn the artists. The gridiron, 62ft above the stage floor, was 'dressed' with about two tons of the best ropes, and 300 blocks. Above the stage was a paint room with 2 46ft by 30ft paint frames. An act drop depicting 'The Eighth Olympiad' was backed by an asbestos fire curtain. On the Market Street side of the stage was a 4-storey building containing dressing rooms and offices. The auditorium was decorated in colour scheme of cream, biscuit, warm brick red, and light robin's egg to turquoise blue. The large arch over the proscenium had panels treated to represent tapestry, while the wall over it was in a rich brocade pattern. The frame of the proscenium was treated to represent chased metal. Two boxes on either side of the proscenium were in harmony with the surrounding colour scheme, and had blue silk plush and gold satin curtains. Figure and flower paintings were placed at strategic points throughout the auditorium, in keeping with the general colour scheme. The front curtain was of azure blue silk plush finished with a heavy gold fringe. Stalls and dress circle chairs were of natural oak upholstered in velvet of the same colour as the curtain. Wilton carpets were laid in the dress circle and stalls, linoleum on stairs and in the corridors, and carpet in the star dressing rooms and the ballet rooms.

32 National Amphitheatre (1906). Formerly the premises of the National Sporting Club in Castlereagh Street, near King Street, this variety house was opened on 22.12.1906. Stalls were located where the boxing ring had been, and a stage and proscenium constructed. Stall seats were padded, but the remainder of the house was a bare but backed amphitheatre of wooden benches rising tier on tier from the stalls to the back wall of the auditorium. This primitive arrangement seated, when the house was full, 4000 people; provided an unimpeded view of the stage, and made the usual gallery and dress circle unnecessary. The theatre provided vaudeville and variety turns of a slightly lower standard than those provided by the Tivoli.

33 Adelphi (1911). A large theatre built on the corner of Castlereagh and Campbell Streets at the Haymarket end of Sydney, the Adelphi was opened on 5.4.1911. Designed primarily as a melodrama house, it was nevertheless equipped to handle anything from the most extravagantly mounted pantomime to grand opera. It thus fulfilled many functions before it was demolished in the second half of the present century being renamed first the Grand Opera House, and then the Tivoli. The Adelphi was notable for three things not shared with its predecessors. It was the first theatre to be built in accordance with the provisions of the State Act regulating the construction of theatres and public halls; it was the first to have its tiers or galleries constructed on the cantilever

principle, doing away with most of the iron columns hitherto necessary to support the front of each tier, and it was the last theatre to be built in Sydney in the period under review. Licensed to seat 2400, the theatre had a stage 60ft square, with a suite of 15 dressing rooms on one side of it and the scene dock and paint room on the other. Its three sliding roofs included one over the stage. (See: Seating capacity. Theatre, The, Sydney).

Sylvia; or, The Marquis and the Maid. 2-act comic opera, text Guy Boothby, music Cecil Sharp, Royal, Adelaide 4.1.1890, initial 2 performances.

Exterior Criterion Sydney c. 1913

Tableaux. The use of the tableau — 'all the characters are arranged in a picturesque manner, and stand in fixed attitudes, like images on pedestals, when the curtain drops' — can be dated back to at least the early years of the 19th century. Its use in the English, French, and American theatre was widespread. The tableau was also often used in the Australian theatre, at the end of each act, or sometimes only at the end of the play so as to send the audience home with a striking or happy 'picture' in mind. As Nicoll notes; 'Those "Pictures" were loved by the spectators almost as much as the dialogue and dramatic action, and the more successful efforts were loudly applauded.' One of the earliest notices of tableaux in connection with an Australian production occurs in the *Sydney Monitor* of 17.3.1837. This was a complaint that the Royal practised a stage effect 'which appears to us to violate nature, theatrical custom, and the good taste of our Sydney audience.' He referred, the writer said, to the practice of placing the actors 'in striking attitudes, at the end of an act or play, when a catastrophe takes place.' He said he had never seen this sort of thing practised in either the London or provincial theatres. Twenty years later G.V.Brooke appeared in Sydney in his version of *The Corsican Brothers,* called *La Vendetta,* which had no fewer than five acts and nine tableaux. In Melbourne in the same year W.M.Akhurst's *The Fall of Sebastopol* presented striking examples of the effectiveness of the properly stage-managed tableau. The first act closed with the destruction by an avalanche of the exiles' hut in Siberia; the second with some picturesque groupings of the dead and wounded on the heights of Alma, and the third with the storming of the Redan, 'where the discharge of artillery, the glare of conflagration, the judicious disposition of men and horses, and the clashing accompaniment of the orchestra combined to excite the audience to a pitch of enthusiasm . . .'

Later again George Darrell and Alfred Dampier were exciting audiences with the carefully staged tableaux with which they embellished their melodramas. At one period the use of these became so widespread that plays were described as in tableaux rather than acts. (See: Living statues).

Tag. The last few lines of a play, which resolved the story and pointed the moral it advanced; the kind of sentiment which in the 18th and 19th centuries was deemed the proper end to a story. The tag dates from the early 18th century, and was in use for the better part of the 19th. One of the earliest examples is to be found in the rhymed couplets with which *The Roman Father* (1750) ends:

> Grief may to grief in endless round succeed,
> And nature suffer when our children bleed;
> But still superior must that hero prove
> Whose first, best passion is his country's love.

A typical early 19th century example is to be found in *The Ocean of Life* (1836); '. . . is there lady or lowly lass, seaman or landsman, alow or aloft, here, that can blame my pretty Bella for marrying one, whose only boast is, that his commander is pleased to think him . . .' At this moment his commander steps forward and says '. . . every inch a sailor.' In *Camille*, or *The Lady of the Camellias* (1852)' the tag is a famous and, to many Victorians, a shocking one; 'Sleep in peace, Marguerite! Much will be forgiven you, because you greatly loved.' A final example, this time from Australia, is found in the ending to W.H.Cooper's *Colonial Experience* (1868): '. . . money itself is of far less value than Colonial Experience. And even this is only a slight part of the moral to be drawn from our lives from day to day. The world's experience ever teaches us that in the great game of life, Honest Hearts are always trumps.'

Tales of Hoffman, The. (See; *Contes d'Hoffmann, Les*).

Tame Cat, The. 4-act comedy by Arthur H.Adams, Criterion, Sydney 11.7.1908, initially 1 performance. Adams wrote the first version of this play in England, and rewrote it in New Zealand. It was revised again for a performance at the Criterion on 16.10.1909.

Taming of the Shrew, The. Comedy by William Shakespeare, believed to have been first performed in London in 1593 or 1594. (See; *Catharine and Petruchio*).

Tank drama. Real water was sometimes used in a large on-stage tank to represent a river, lake, pool, or stream in which a character in the play was 'drowned,' or rescued from drowning. *The Scout* and *The Trapper* by Alfred Dampier and Garnet Walch, in which horse and rider fall from a great height into the 'river,' were typical tank dramas of the Australian theatre, as was F.Scudamore's *First Class*, in which George Darrell rescued the heroine from the 'Thames' each night by diving from a bridge.

Tannhäuser und der Sängerkrieg auf der Wartburg (Tannhäuser and the Singing Contest at the Wartburg). 3-act opera, text and music Richard Wagner, Dresden 19.10.1845; Covent Garden, London 6.5.1876; Royal, Sydney 14.1.1901, initially 1 performance.

Tapfere Soldat, Der (The Chocolate Soldier). 3-act operetta, text R.Bernauer and L.Jacobson after George Bernard Shaw's *Arms and the Man* (1894), music O.Straus, Theater an der Wien, Vienna 14.11.1908; English version H.S.Strange, Lyceum, London 10.10.1910; Royal, Melbourne 26.8.1911, initial 52 performances.

Tapu; or, A Tale of a Maori Pah. 2-act comic opera, text Arthur H.Adams, music Alfred Hill, Opera House, Wellington, New Zealand 16.2.1903, initial 6 performances; Her Majesty's, Sydney 9.7.1904, initial 19 performances.

Tea-Room Girl, The. 1-act play by William Moore, Turn Verein Hall, Melbourne 5.10.1910, initially 1 performance.

Tempest, The. Romance by William Shakespeare, believed to have been first performed in London in 1611 or 1612; Royal Victoria, Sydney 15.7.1839.

Tenderfoot, The. 2-act musical comedy, text R.Carle, music H.Heartz, Daly's, New York 22.2.1904; Adelphi, Sydney 11.4.1914, initial 18 performances.

Ten Nights in a Bar Room. 5-act temperance drama by W.W.Pratt, from T.S.Arthur's novel (1858), Victoria, London 26.11.1867; Princess's, Melbourne 22.2.1879, initial 53 performances.

Tess of the D'Urbervilles, 4-act drama by L.Stoddard, from Thomas Hardy's novel (1891), St James's, London 2.3.1897; Royal, Sydney 13.1.1900, initial 30 performances.

Theatre on the goldfields. (See: Goldfields, Theatre on the).

Theatre, The Sydney. Robert Sidaway, an emancipated convict, holds the distinction of being the first to open a public theatre in Australia. This was the building known simply as The Theatre, opened on 16.1.1796 with the play *The Revenge* (1721) and the afterpiece *The Hotel* (1776). Its location is thought to have been in or near Bligh Street, though this is still a matter of conjecture. Sidaway was transported for housebreaking, but he was emancipated before long and soon became one of the earliest 'empire builders.' According to *Saunders's News-Letter* of 12.9.1797 he had by then achieved 'a contract for serving the colony with bread . . . a perpetual grant from government of several hundred acres of land, which he cultivates . . . the best house of public entertainment in the place, and lately has erected a theatre, of which he is the manager.' This theatre closely followed the provincial Georgian theatre design, with boxes around the three walls of the auditorium, pit,

Interior of the Royal Sydney after the 1892 fire. Ten years earlier a Royal Commission into theatre construction had reported that the theatre still had the original 1875 wood and wallpaper construction.

and gallery. Morgan McMahon gives what is purported to be a first hand description of the interior of this theatre, derived from a letter written from Sydney by one of the 'Scottish Martyrs.' McMahon gives no provenance for this letter. 'They entered the building,' he writes, 'and saw what one of them described in a letter to a friend in the old country as a miniature resemblance of a country [county?] theatre at home. There was a stage, there were scenes fitted to it, there were footlights, there was a pit and a gallery, and there were side boxes in which the Sydney "quality" might take their ease.' Admission charges to The Theatre, Sydney were; boxes 5s, side boxes 3s 6d, pit 2s 6d, gallery 1s. Those who could not pay cash were allowed to pay in kind — flour, meat, spirits. Records of this first public theatre are scant, consisting chiefly of a few newspaper reports, and 2 playbills held by the Mitchell Library, Sydney. It is believed it was closed by the Governor in 1800 because of riots.

Theatre Fires. The 19th century theatre had 2 unremitting enemies — fire, and dirt. Until well into the 1880s, and even later in some instances, few theatre interiors remained attractive for longer than 3 years without renovation and redecoration. Inadequate cleaning and fumigating, and the use of oil lamps, candles, and gas soon tarnished the brightest colours and smudged and muted canvas, cloth, and paper. What they did not damage or destroy, the dust which at times drifted or was blown in clouds from untarred streets, soon did. Fire hazards also existed in the flimsy construction of theatre interiors, and in the backstage, understage, and passageway clutter of old scenery, costumes, furniture, and properties. Although electric light was first used in the 1880s, gas had to be used with it for many years afterwards, and as late as 1900 it was still accepted that the stage should be lighted by borders of open gas jets. Theatres destroyed by fire included: Royal, Sydney 1840; Prince of Wales, Sydney 1860; Olympic, Melbourne 1866; Varieties, Melbourne 1870; Haymarket, Melbourne 1871; Royal, Melbourne 1872; Prince of Wales, Sydney 1872; Royal Victoria, Sydney 1880; Bijou, Melbourne 1889; Royal, Sydney 1892; Tivoli, Sydney 1900; Her Majesty's, Sydney 1902.

Theatre, Opposition to the. In the 1820s, when B. Levey was trying to establish a professional theatre in Sydney, he had not only the governor against him but also a large body of the church-going population, all of whom were convinced that the theatre was the invention and abode of the devil. Even when theatres were well established this opposition died hard. In the early years it was compounded by the official or legal view that actors were little better than vagabonds or thieves, and that the theatre encouraged idleness, drunkenness, and licentiousness among the lower orders. As late as 1859 George Coppin felt it necessary to have republished in Melbourne a pamphlet in support of the theatre first published in the USA, and then in England, and written by an American clergyman. There is no way of discovering if or to what extent this influenced those still opposed to the theatre, but such opposition did lessen as the years passed. It was not until the 1880s that public reaction against the often hypocritical 'religious' attitude to plays and the theatre began to manifest itself in newspapers, a campaign led if not initiated by the facetious and irreverent Sydney *Bulletin* in its relentless fight against what it called 'wowserism.' (See; Moral attitudes).

Theatre research. Charles Lamb's Elia, sighing nostalgically, gives in his essay 'On Some of the Old Actors,' a list of names of which the very mention conjures up for him mental pictures of what those actors had been like in this, that, and the other play. To today's reader they will remain little more than a list of names unless he takes the trouble to seek out the work of some theatre historian which will tell him what he wants to know. Writing in the *Australasian* some 50 years after Elia's essay, 'old Stager' remembered with comparable nostalgia a group of actors who had enlivened the theatrical scene in Victoria in 1858-1868. 'Nothing, nobody can compare with them today,' he wrote. Precisely. Today's, any day's theatregoer can make his own list, indulge in his own remembrances, make his own value-judgments. Only the theatre historian, with his discovery of the relevant facts through research, and his interpretation and reconstruction of those facts according to his knowledge and understanding, can bring those lists nearer to actuality for us. Theatre research has a great deal of academic value, but it also has its practical value. Its fruits should prevent actors and producers from substituting 'art' for history — from hiding their ignorance of the one behind a burlesque or 'mod' interpretation of the other. Its fruits should also prevent those solecisms so often committed with a self-conscious giggle in the production of 19th century plays. It might even prompt theatre people to ask themselves why an 18th century play is always presented with a real attempt at 'period,' while the approach to 19th century plays is too often that of burlesque, ham, or — even worse — 'interpretation.' It was not without reason that M.Willson Disher, in *Theatre Notebook,* Vol. 6, wrote; 'There can be no doubting the value of theatrical research. Without it Sadler's Wells would not have been rebuilt; *The Beggar's Opera* would have been forgotten. Years of persistent propaganda by antiquarians produced results. The Phoenix Society proved what scholarship can do. Its revivals of Jonson and Dryden were finer than any staged by professional managements. Actors, left to themselves, still regard Jonson as 'unactable.' C.Walter Hodges, artist, author, and theatre historian, 20 years later added his *credo* when he wrote that 'one may say that the theatre as an institution is the pre-eminent arrangement whereby human beings work out the models of their own conduct, their morality and aspiration, their ideas of good and evil, and in general those fantasies about themselves and their fellows which, if persisted in, tend eventually to become facts in real life. If this is so, and it would be hard to deny, then the theatre must be seen as a most powerful instrument in the social history of mankind, and its own history must therefore be allowed a corresponding importance.'

Theatre Royal. Originally the use of this title meant that the theatre proprietor/s had a Royal Patent. In 18th century London, Drury Lane and Covent garden Theatres had a Royal Patent, and were truly Theatres Royal. A few provincial theatres were also patented. Theatres with this patent were restricted to seasons of 60 days, the longest period for which, under the act of 1788, magistrates were empowered to issue a licence. The Act of 1843 removed all these limitations. In Australia in 1832, when Barnett Levey called his theatre 'Theatre Royal,' and he used the Royal coat of arms at the top of his advertisements, he did both without any legal entitlement. But anybody and everybody seems to have used the word 'Royal' at will. Ambiguity also attaches to another widely-used 19th century theatre title, Academy of Music, though this has nothing to do with real or imaginary royalty. It seems to have been an American 'front' for a music, variety, or burlesque house, and may have been adopted in an attempt to avoid the use of 'Royal.'

Theatres. (See under names of individual capital cities).

Thérèse. (See: *Belle Thérèse, La*).

Thérèse. 4-act drama translated by A.T. de Mattos from Emile Zola's *Thérèse Raquin* (1867), Royalty, London 9.10.1891; Lyceum, Sydney 12.12.1896, initial 3 performances.

Thirty Thieves, The. (See: *Mariana; or, The Thirty Thieves*).

Thomas, Julian. (See: James, John Stanley).

Thou Fool. 4-act drama by George Walters, Palace, Sydney 1.11.1900, initial 2 performances.

Three Little Maids. 3-act musical comedy, text and music P.Rubens, Apollo, London 10.5.1902; Princess's, Melbourne 14.5.1904, initial 18 performances.

Three Musketeers, The; or, The Queen, The Cardinal, and the Adventurer. 3-act drama by C.Rice, from Alexander Dumas' novel (1844), Manchester 2.8.1850; Grecian, London 20.10.1851; Royal Victoria, Sydney 10.11.1856.

——. 5-act drama by Alfred Dampier, after Dumas, Royal, Adelaide 6.5.1899, initial 10 performances.

——. 3-act drama by Bernard Espinasse and George Rignold, after Dumas, Criterion, Sydney 18.5.1899, initial 26 performances.

Thunderbolt. 4-act drama by Ambrose Pratt and A.S.Joseph, founded on *Three Years With Thunderbolt*, by W.Monckton, published serially in the *Argus*, 1905, Royal, Sydney 14.10.1905, initial 18 performances.

Time Is Not Yet Ripe, The. 4-act comedy by Louis Esson, Melbourne Repertory, Athenaeum Hall 23.7.1912, initially 1 performance. Published Currency Press Ltd, Sydney, 1973.

Tom Jones. 3-act comic opera, text R.Courtneidge and A.Thompson, music E.German, Prince's, Manchester 30.3.1907; Apollo, London 17.4.1907; Royal, Melbourne 1.10.1910, initial 36 performances.

Tomorrow. 1-act play by J.Le Gay Brereton, St James's Hall, Sydney 18.5.1912, initially 1 performance. Published Angus and Robertson, Sydney, 1910.

Toreador, The. 2-act musical comedy, text J.T.Tanner and H.Nicholls, music I.Caryll and L.Monckton, Gaiety, London 17.6.1901; Her Majesty's, Melbourne 11.10.1902, initial 36 performances.

Torning, Andrew (1814-1900). One of many talented and versatile men of the 19th century theatre who seemed to be able to turn their hand to almost anything. In his long and eventful life he was a ballet dancer, pantomimist, gymnast, actor, scenepainter, interior decorator, artist, theatre lessee, founder of a fire brigade and its first captain, and Deacon of the Pitt Street Congregational Church, Sydney. He painted the scenery for many of the productions at Sydney's Royal Victoria, Prince of Wales, and Queen's. He also redecorated the interior of the Royal Victoria in 1843 and 1872, and the Queen's in 1875. In 1854 he became lessee of the Victoria. The following year he was lessee of the Victoria and the Prince of Wales. Notable among the productions for which he designed and painted the scenery were W.H.Cooper's three plays, *Sun and Shadow, Foiled,* and *Kodadad.* At the time of his death few were living who could remember anything of his lively interest in and control of theatrical affairs in Sydney in the 1840s and 1850s. As one newspaper report put it, he was a stranger to thousands in the city where he had laboured for more than half a century. He was survived by a married daughter, 6 grandchildren, and 19 great-grandchildren.

Tosca, La. 3-act opera, text L.Illica and G.Giacosa, after V.Sardou, music G.Puccini, Constanzi, Rome 14.1.1900; Covent Garden, London 12.7.1900; Her Majesty's, Sydney 11.10.1911, initially 1 performance.

To the West. 5-act drama by K.Mackay and Alfred Dampier, Her Majesty's, Sydney 8.2.1896, initial 18 performances, (See: Parliamentarians).

Tragedy of Donohoe, The. 5-act tragedy by Charles Harpur. Though it was never produced, extracts from this play were published in the *Sydney Monitor* in 7 of its issues between 7.2.1835 and 28.2.1835. Harpur worked on the play over the ensuing years, and it was published as *The*

Bushrangers, a play in Five Acts, and other poems, W.R.Piddington, Sydney, 1853.

Transformation scene. This evolved from, or was the direct outcome of the transformation of the characters in the first half of a pantomime into the figures of the harlequinade. At a touch of the Fairy Queen's wand these characters would be transformed into Harlequin, Columbine, Clown, and Pantaloon. Then similar transformations were tried with stage scenes, changing one scene into another before the eyes of the audience in a way that seemed to be sheer magic. Rocky grottoes and ice caves were favourite early subjects, which were changed into leafy dells or realms of bliss. As time progressed these transformations became increasingly elaborate and ornate, calling on all the art, imagination, and ingenuity scenepainters and machinists could muster. Percy Fitzgerald gives a perfect pen-picture of a transformation scene in action in the 1870s or early 1880s. 'First the "gauzes" lift slowly one behind the other — perhaps the most pleasing of all scenic effects — giving glimpses of "the Realm of Bliss", seen beyond in a tantalising fashion. Then is revealed a kind of half glorified country, clouds and banks, evidently concealing much. Always a sort of pathetic and at the same time exultant strain rises, and is repeated as the change goes on . . . Now some of the banks begin to part slowly, showing realms of light, with a few divine beings — fairies — rising slowly here and there. More breaks beyond and fairies rising, with a pyramid of these ladies beginning to mount slowly in the centre. Thus it goes on, the lights streaming on full, in every colour and from every quarter, in the richest effulgence. In some of the more daring efforts, the "femmes suspendus" seem to float in the air or rest on the frail support of sprays or branches of trees. While finally, perhaps, at the back of all, the most glorious paradise of all will open, revealing the pure empyrean itself, and some fair spirit aloft in a cloud among the stars, the apex of all . . .' Michael Booth's reprint of *Theatrical Trades* reveals that for the Drury Lane pantomime of 1883 no fewer than 20 limelights were used in a transformation scene, with 20 pans of coloured fires. H.L.Benwell says that 'Transformation scenes, as a rule, should commence with almost utter darkness, the lights gently rising before the first change is made, so that the first cloth may be seen distinctly by the audience; the stage continues to get lighter and lighter, and the scene ends with the greatest possible lightness which can be produced by the painter, added to which are Dutch metals, foil paper, spangles, and logies, all displayed under the illumination of the limelight and coloured fires.' This can be matched with a description of a transformation scene in a Melbourne Pantomime in the early 1870s. 'But here we are on the transformation scene, a remarkable combination of garish tinsel, Dutch metal, paint, unfolding and developing ferns, and raising of beaded net fringes to the final home of the Prince and Princess, who stand on a revolving wheel in the centre, while members of the

Left: Stage trap
Below: A parallèle *used in transformation scene*

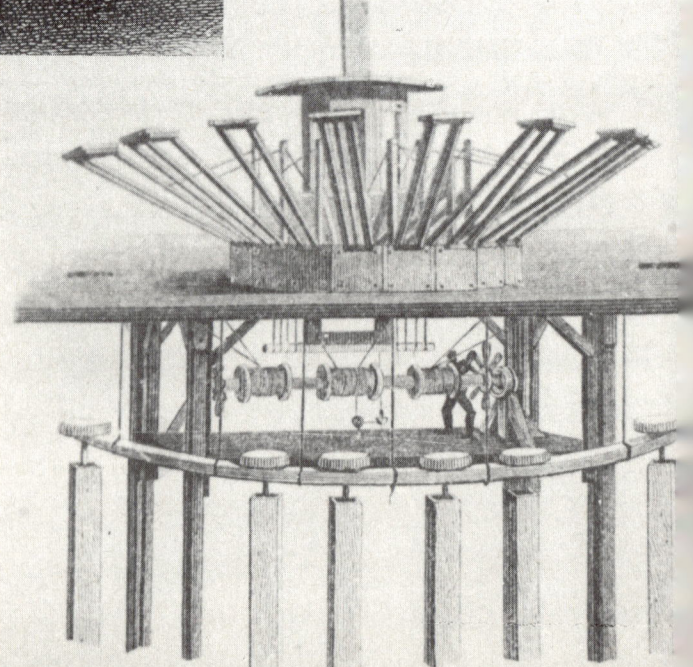

corps de ballet lie on the edge of clouds, or float by means of wires in rows along the wings. A blaze of red and blue fire almost shuts the scene off from view as Clown, Pantaloon, Harlequin and Columbine dash down the stage and begin their antics.' A final quotation from Fitzgerald provides some idea of the mechanical background to these transformation scenes. 'But large platforms, or "equipments" as the French call them, are the essential of every transformation, consisting of a vast stage rising slowly from below, and suspended by ropes and counterpoises, and so nicely balanced that a couple of carpenters can raise them, although burdened by a score of *figurantes,* each strapped to her iron. This is the principle which underlies all these effects, but it is infinitely varied, and there are even platforms upon platforms which rise in their turn after the first has risen. Thus allusion has been made to the "crowning of the edifice," at the close of the transformation, when, perhaps, a semicircular group of fairies will rise, and from out this group a central figure will mount slowly, becoming the apex, as it were, of the whole. Then it will be noted that the semicircle begins to open, the group to separate, and the figures to glide down and forward by some mysterious agency. It is contrived by ingenious machinery called by the French a "parallèle." This consists of a number of light pedestals, about 12ft in height, which are ranged closely around a centre pedestal, the tops being drawn close to it by cords brought down and secured to a windlass worked by a man who ascends with the machine. At the proper moment he "lets go," and the weight of the figures, checked by the counterpoises, allows the pedestals to open out, exactly as the ribs of an umbrella would do . . .' (See: Coloured fires. Pantomime).

Transported for Life. 4-act drama by George Darrell, Queen's, Dunedin, New Zealand 21.8.1876, initial 6 performances. Royal, Sydney 23.6.1877, initial 24 performances.

Transvaal Heroine, A. (See: *Jess*).

Traps. Apertures in the stage floor, put to various uses in the movement of actors on and off stage. At the beginning of the 19th century a well equipped stage had 2 to 4 side traps, one each in the front and back corners of the acting area, and 2 larger traps in the centre, one behind the other. The first of these central traps was used for the grave scene in *Hamlet,* and was oblong in shape. The second, a square trap, was primarily used for the sinking of the cauldron in *Macbeth,* and for the arrival and departure of the Ghost in *Hamlet.* By the end of the century these traps had been reduced in number to a central grave-trap, with 2 smaller square traps slightly forward of it. Traps had their most frequent use during the pantomime season, and in burlesques and extravaganzas, when demons and fairies were shot up on to the stage from the depths by a system of counterweights; or slowly descended to their respective areas to the accompaniment of suitable music and coloured fires. Traps were also used as companionways to the lower decks of a ship in nautical scenes. As such they sometimes constituted a danger to unwary actors, if one of the stagehands forgot to cover the trap after use, or to warn the actors that a trap was open (See: Star traps).

Travelling companies. The claim that J.C.Williamson introduced the travelling company to Australia is not correct. Companies of actors were travelling about Australia, New Zealand, and even India and the East in the 1850s, 1860s, and 1870s, long before Williamson came to Australia. In the 1870s and 1880s George Darrell and Alfred Dampier led the way with the self-contained company equipped to present plays in anything from a theatre to a large tent. They, and similar but smaller companies, travelled as far north as Gladstone, as far west as Perth and Fremantle, and in between to every centre in which an audience could be found. Several opera companies did the same. They had to travel to get to Australia, and once in Australia they had to keep on travelling so that they could stay together. Later, the popularity of the Gilbert and Sullivan and other comic and light operas, and the occasional melodrama led to the large travelling company of the J.C.Williamson kind, in which everything, from orchestra to ballet and sceneshifters, was included. Because of cost, and transport difficulties, these visited only the capital cities, where a reasonable 'run' would ensure a profit. In the early years of the present century, with the growth of interest in the cinema, travelling companies dwindled to a mere handful. A writer in Melbourne *Punch* in 1925 noted that whereas 20 years before there had been 31 travelling companies (including the major circus companies), in 1925 there were only two.

Traviata, La (The Lady Gone Astray). 3-act opera, text F.M.Piave after *La Dame aux camélias* by Dumas fils, music G.Verdi, Fenice, Venice 6.3.1853; Her Majesty's, London 24.5.1856; Royal, Melbourne 13.4.1859, initially 1 performance.

Trelawney of the 'Wells.' 4-act comedy by A.W.Pinero, Court, London 20.1.1898; Her Majesty's, Sydney 17.6.1899, initial 7 performances.

Trial Before Herod, The. York Mystery play of the 14th century, performed at St James's Hall, Sydney at a single matinee performance 6.6.1913.

Trial by Jury. 1-act comic opera, text W.S.Gilbert, music A.Sullivan, Royalty, London 25.3.1875; Prince of Wales, Melbourne 24.6.1876, initial 12 performances.

Triboulet the King's Jester. Probably title adopted for C.A.Barnett's drama, *The Bell Ringer; or, The Hunchback of Notre Dame,* music Isaac Nathan, Sadler's Wells, London 31.3.1834; Royal Victoria, Sydney 21.4.1846.

Tried and True. (See: *Gold and Alloy*).

Trilby. 4-act drama by P.Potter, from George Du Maurier's novel (1894), Haymarket, London 30.10.1895; Princess's, Melbourne 6.4.1896, initial 35 performances.

Tristan und Isolde. 3-act Opera, text and music Richard Wagner, Munich 10.6.1865; Drury Lane, London 20.6.1882; His Majesty's, Melbourne 14.6.1912, initially 1 performance.

Trovatore, Il (The Troubador). 4-act opera, text S.Cammarano, music G.Verdi, Apollo, Rome 19.1.1853; Covent Garden, London 10.5.1855; Princess's, Melbourne 21.10.1858, initial 5 performances.

Truman, Ernest E.P. (1870-1948). Australian composer, noted for his string quartet, *The Australian Seasons*, his cantata, *The Pied Piper*, and a Magnificat dedicated to Cardinal Moran. He also wrote the music to the comic opera, *Club Life*.

Turf dramas. Several plays by Australian dramatists featured a horse race as one of its 'sensations,' but only a few were really turf dramas — plays in which the whole story is concerned with horse racing and its followers. Notable among these was R.P.Whitworth's *Flying Jib; or, The Derby Day* (1868), which may have owed a debt of some kind to Dion Boucicault's highly successful *The Flying Scud* (1866). The play (Whitworth's) included a ballet in jockey costume, and a scene at Epsom Downs on race day. There was also George Darrell's *The Double Event; or, A Tale of the Melbourne Cup* (1893), and *The Winning Ticket* (1910), by W.Anderson and T.Harrison, which was also built around the running of the Melbourne Cup.

Turner, Ethel Sybil (1872-1958). Born at Doncaster in England, Ethel Turner came to Australia with her parents in 1881. Educated at Sydney Girls' High School, her first published writings appeared in school magazines. Ultimately she wrote more than 40 novels, mostly about children, her first and most popular, *Seven Little Australians*, being published in 1894. Two years later she married Herbert R.Curlewis, a judge of the District Court of NSW. Ethel Turner also wrote short stories and poems, and, like other Australian writers of her day, wrote plays which the commercial managements of the time would not risk staging. They preferred the safety of the imported success. In the same year that her *Seven Little Australians* was published her 1-act farce, *The Wig*, was produced by Sydney University Dramatic Society. A dramatic version of *Seven Little Australians* written by Beaumont Smith was staged with considerable success in Sydney in 1914. Under the pseudonym 'Private Boxer,' a writer in the *Bulletin* in 1915 said Ethel Turner had submitted a play, *The Sundowner*, to J.C.Williamson, only to be told 'Australians do not care for Australian plays.' (See: *Seven Little Australians; Wig, The; Wonder Child, The*).

Tutti in maschera. 3-act opera, text M.Marcello after Goldoni's *L'Impressario Delle Smirne,* Music C.Pedrotti, Verona 4.11.1856; Royal, Melbourne 14.3.1877, initial 2 performances.

Twelfth Night. Comedy by William Shakespeare, believed to have been first performed in London 1599 or 1600; Royal, Melbourne 6.4.1866.

Two Gentlemen of Verona. Lyrical comedy by William Shakespeare, believed to have been first performed in London in 1594 or 1595; Royal, Melbourne 6.6.1859.

Two Lovers, The; or, The Ghosts in the Churchyard. Farce by J.G.Marwick, Royal Adelphi, Sydney 11.6.1870, initially 1 performance. Published in J.G.Marwick's *Spare Moments in Australia,* John Sands, Sydney, 1877. Copy in Mitchell Library, Sydney.

Tyrrell, Inigo. Real name Inigo Tyrrell Weekes. (See; *His Natural Life*).

Tyranny of Tears, The. 4-act comedy by Charles Haddon Chambers, Criterion, London 6.4.1899; Royal, Sydney 12.5.1900, initial 9 performances.

The cartoonist 'Hop' (Livingston Hopkins) attends a performance of Thunderbolt *at the Theatre Royal Sydney, 1905*

U

Uncle Tom's Cabin. Drama in 3 acts by unknown author, Royal, Geelong 4.4.1853, initially 1 performance. Founded on Mrs Harriet Beecher Stowe's novel about slave life in America, plays with this title held the world's stages in hundreds of different versions up to the 1930s. It was undoubtedly the world's greatest hit. The novel was first serialised in the *National Era* in 1851-52. It was first published as a novel on 20.3.1852. Three thousand copies were sold on the first day, 10 000 in the first week. It was first published in London in May 1852, and by the following May had appeared in 23 different editions and sold more than a million copies. The first of the hundreds of stage versions (all of them pirated) of the novel was given at the Baltimore Museum on 5.1.1852 as *The Southern Uncle Tom*, 3 months before serialisation of the novel had been completed. The first version to appear on the New York stage was C.W.Taylors' 23.8.1852, but the most popular and long-lived American stage version was G.L.Aikens's, Troy Museum 27.9.1852. The first German version, *Negersleben in Nord-Amerika*, was staged in Berlin in November 1852, and the first French version, *La Case de l'Oncle Tom*, in Paris in 1853. In London there were 10 versions produced between September and December 1852, E.Fitzball writing versions for 3 different theatres. There were also some homegrown versions in Australia, the first being Frank Fowler's *Eva; or, Leaves From Uncle Tom's Cabin*, written for the child actress, Anna Maria Quinn, who as Little Eva died most heartbreakingly for four nights to the accompaniment of tears and sobs from the audience. Alfred Dampier wrote the next two, *Uncle Tom's Cabin* in five acts, Victoria, Newcastle 3.7.1879, initial 2 performances; and a new version seven years later, Gaiety, Sydney 13.2.1886. In this Dampier played the slave, George Harris, while John F.Sheridan, who usually played 'drag' roles, took the part of the lawyer,

Mr Jurisprudence Marks. When this version was produced the following year at London's Princess's it was advertised as being by Alfred Dampier and John F.Sheridan. On 8.9.1888 George Rignold produced his 'happy ending' version, in 5 acts, at Sydney's Her Majesty's.

Under The Gaslight; or, Life and Love in These Times. 5-act drama by A.Daly, New York, New York 12.8.1867; Duke of Edinburgh, Melbourne 25.4.1868, initial 12 performances. Produced three months before the first London performance.

Unseen Eye, The. 4-act drama by Randolph Bedford, Palace, Sydney 26.10.1912, initial 18 performances.

Utopia Limited; or, The Flowers of Progress. 2-act comic opera, text W.S.Gilbert, music Sir Arthur Sullivan, Savoy, London 7.10.1893; Princess's, Melbourne 20.1.1906, initial 18 performances.

V

Vagabond, The. (See: James, John Stanley).

Valkyrie, The. (See; *Walküre, Die*).

Vanity Fair. Drama in 11 tableaux by Walter Reynolds, Gaiety, Sydney 24.7.1882, initial 11 performances.

Vaudeville. Originally, in 16th century France, these were comic and satirical songs set to popular tunes, and used in comedies with music. In time the term was used to describe a light musical-dramatic entertainment, somewhat similar to the English ballad opera. When Sydney Nelson came to Melbourne with his family in 1852 he employed several local writers, including W.M.Akhurst, to write such entertainments, which he set to music he composed, or to popular airs of the day, and called 'Vaudevilles.' In the USA the term was taken over to describe a variety performance with no 'book' or story, such as the music hall performances in England. This hybrid music hall-vaudeville kind of entertainment was first established in Australia with music halls, and later it developed into the vaudeville-variety entertainment of the kind provided in his Tivoli theatres by the 19th century music hall-vaudeville star and entrepreneur, Harry Rickards.

Vendetta, The. 5-act drama by G.Parker, after A.C.Gunter's novel, *Mrs Barnes of New York,* Her Majesty's, Sydney 23.2.1889; initial 24 performances.

Venice Preserved; or, A Plot Discovered. 5-act tragedy by T.Otway, Dorset Garden, London, February 1681/2; Royal, Sydney 18.10.1834.

Vêpres Siciliennes, Les (The Sicilian Vespers). 5-act opera, text A.E.Scribe and C.Duveyrier, music G.Verdi, Opéra House, Paris

13.6.1855; Drury Lane, London 27.7.1859; Prince of Wales, Sydney 12.5.1870, initial 5 performances.

Vercingetorix; or, Love and Patriotism. 3-act lyric drama, text M.Mainiel, music Henri Kowalski, Garden Palace, Sydney 1.4.1881, initial 2 performances. A subsequent performance, this time with an English text by J.Lake, was given at the Town Hall, Melbourne 24.9.1881. Text published by W.H.Williams, Melbourne, 1881.

Vernon, Howard (1845-1921). Real name John Lett. The first to play the Gilbert and Sullivan roles of Koko *(The Mikado),* Shadbolt *(The Yeomen of the Guard),* Grand Inquisitor *(The Gondoliers),* and Bunthorne *(Patience)* in Australia, with J.C.Williamson's Royal Comic Opera company. He also sang in such operas as *Faust, Il Trovatore, Maritana, The Bohemian Girl, Fra Diavolo,* and *Der Freischutz,* with the W.S.Lyster and J.C.Williamson companies, and in the 'legitimate' appeared in *Hamlet, Othello, Richard III, The Merchant of Venice, Romeo and Juliet, Macbeth,* and other plays. Born in Collins Street, Melbourne, Vernon first earned a living as a clerk at 15 years of age. At 16 he became a tea-taster and blender. Not long after this he took to the stage, singing and acting, making his first appearances with Walter Montgomery and George Coppin. Later he worked with and was instructed by Barry Sullivan, Charles Kean, W.H.Hoskins, James Anderson and other notables of the 1860s. He varied his dramatic experiences with seasons as a member of a minstrel company. Until he worked for W.S.Lyster in the 1870s he travelled throughout Australia, New Zealand, and the East with various companies, and one or two of his own, gaining valuable experience. Peter Downes writes of him: 'His first visit to New Zealand . . . had been as early as 1874 when he was touring a small group of singers he had organised and given the name Royal English Opera Company. They sang in Australia, New Zealand, India, China, and other Eastern countries, and in 1877 they were given the honour of being the first Europeans allowed to perform in Japan.' Vernon's first experience with a Gilbert and Sullivan production came in 1876, when he and Alfred Plumpton were touring the East. They put on a performance of *Trial by Jury* at Singapore, with the assistance of the band and members of the 74th Highlanders, then stationed in that city. The following year he was in London, where he met up again with the conductor and composer, G.B.Allen, with whom he had earlier worked in Australia, India, China, and the East. At this time Allen was musical director for Gilbert and Sullivan productions at the Opera Comique, London. Vernon next returned to India, where Alfred Plumpton was then stationed, and they produced *Trial by Jury* and *The Sorcerer,* with which they opened a new theatre in Bombay. He returned to Australia, then went to San Francisco as a member of Emilie Melville's Opera Company, and finally returned for good to Australia. Here he made a name for himself as producer, actor, singer, and dancer in light, comic, and grand opera productions. Until well into the twentieth century he continued to produce and act in J.C.Williamson and his own company productions in Australia and New Zealand.

Veronique. 3-act comic opera, text A.Vanloo and G.Duval, adapted by H.Hamilton, music A.Messager, Coronet, Notting Hill 5.5.1903; His Majesty's, Melbourne 11.11.1905, initial 24 performances.

Vestale, La. 3-act opera, text S.Cammarano, music S.Mercandante, San Carlo, Naples 10.3.1840; Royal, Sydney 23.6.1877, initial 2 performances.

Vezin, Mrs Hermann (1827-1902). Born in Bath, a daughter of the English actress, Martha Mary Thomson, Jane Eliza Thomson (at first Mrs Charles Young, and then Mrs Hermann Vezin) came to Tasmania in 1837 with her parents and elder sister. Trained largely by her mother as a dancer as well as an actress, she developed into a remarkably talented and versatile artist. In the early, formative years she gained her practical experience in the Australian theatre, first in Launceston, then in Melbourne, where she and her first husband became members of G.V.Brooke's Shakespearian company. Here at the Queen's in 1855 she first played Emilia to the Desdemona of Fanny Cathcart (later Mrs G.Darrell) and Brooke's Othello. She had married the colonial actor, Charles Young, in Tasmania in 1845, and in 1857, at her mother's insistence, she and her husband left for England, where it was felt her talents would be better appreciated. But her first role overseas was in the USA, in Philadelphia, where, at the Walnut Street Theatre, she first appeared on 7.9.1857 as Mariana in *The Wife* (1833). Making his American debut at the same time and in the same production was Hermann Vezin (1829-1910), an American who had trained and first acted in England. The following month Mr and Mrs Charles Young were at Sadler's Wells in London, where they became prized members of the company formed at that theatre by Samuel Phelps, especially Jane. All the critics, even the difficult to please Henry Morley, agreed that Mrs Charles Young, the actress from Australia, had won her first laurels at Sadler's Wells, 'and is provided there with the best opportunities of triumph.' Morley said of her in *The Provoked Husband* (1728) '. . . she is as truly the high-bred lady as her husband is the high-bred lord, but she is the lady who floats lightly on the surface of society, while her sedate lord is one of its foundations . . . Lady Townly is, perhaps, the part in which Mrs Charles Young has found herself most free to exercise her skill.' For his part, Charles earned himself at Sadler's Wells a place in theatrical history as 'the first Australian actor to take a leading position on the London boards.' They appeared in *Love's Labor's Lost, The Provoked Husband,* and *The Hypocrite,* among other plays. Jane's future in London was now assured, and her next season was at the

Surrey, where she first appeared as Lady Macbeth in June 1859. The following year she was back with Phelps. Hermann Vezin had by now been added to the company, and together they took part in a long and arduous season of Shakespeare's plays, and other tragedies and comedies. After this she moved on to the Haymarket, where she played Portia to the Shylock of the American tragedian, Edwin Booth. In 1862 she divorced Charles Young, who returned to Australia, and the following year she married Hermann Vezin. By 1878 it was said of her performance in *The Winter's Tale* at Drury Lane that the main personages of the drama were 'completely overshadowed by Mrs Hermann Vezin.' (*The Theatre* 1.11.1878). The following month it was asked in the same journal, 'when shall we see a Shylock worthy of appearing in the trial scene by the side of a Portia like Mrs Vezin's, or Miss Ellen Terry's?' For Jane the question, though flattering, was academic. In 19th century terms she was by this time an old woman, while Ellen Terry was not only 20 years younger, but had also found Henry Irving.

Vicar of Bray, The. 2-act comic opera, text S.Grundy, music E.Solomon, Globe, London 22.7.1882; Princess's, Melbourne 20.5.1893, initial 24 performances.

Virgin Unmasked, The. Ballad opera by Henry Fielding, correct title *An Old Man Taught Wisdom; or, The Virgin Unmasked,* Drury Lane, London 1734; The Theatre, Sydney 8.3.1800.

Voices of the Night. Drama in 5 tableaux by Thomas Somers (T.Walker), Royal Standard, Sydney 24.7.1886, initial 18 performances. (See: Parliamentarians).

Voysey Inheritance, The. 5-act drama by G.Barker, Court, London 7.11.1905; Melbourne Repertory, Turn Verein Hall 9.10.1911, initially 1 performance.

W

Walch, Garnet (1843-1913). Australian-born journalist, newspaper proprietor, magazine editor, poet, short story writer, biographer, anthologist, and dramatist. His first work for the stage, a pantomime called *Love's Silver Dream; or, The King, the Goddess, and the Fays of Fairyland*, was performed at Sydney's Adelphi on 24.12.1869. From then on he wrote a number of pantomimes, burlesques, and extravaganzas for Sydney and Melbourne theatres. He was also expert at writing dramatic sketches and short comedies designed to give actors the opportunity to appear in a number of different characters. Typical of these are *Shy, Dreadfully Shy* (1872), *The Great Hibernicon* (1874), *Rainbow Revels* (1877), *If; or, An Old Gem Rest* (1879). A comedietta he wrote for the actor Alfred Dampier and his 2 little daughters, *Helen's Babies* (1877) was played by Dampier and his children in England, the USA, Canada, and Australia. His first full length play, a comedy called *Humble Pie* (1877), was not a success, nor was his first drama, *Her Evil Star* (1881). His real success as a dramatist began when he joined Alfred Dampier to write a dramatisation of the Dumas novel, *The Count of Monte Cristo* (1890). This was followed by their most successful work as collaborators, the dramatisation of Rolf Boldrewood's *Robbery Under Arms* (1890). Between 1890 and 1892 Walch and Dampier collaborated on six other works for the stage. Walch's last play was his alone, *Silver Chimes; or, The Message of the Bells* (1892). He did not write for the theatre again after that.

Walker, George Ralph. (See: Leitch, George).

Walker, Thomas. (See: Parliamentarians).

Walküre, Die (The Valkyrie). 3-act opera, text and music Richard Wagner, Court Opera, Munich 26.6.1870; Her Majesty's, London 6.5.1882, Princess's, Melbourne 4.5.1907, initial 2 performances.

Waller, Emma (1820-1899). English born actress who married an American actor, Daniel W.Waller. Apart from a brief visit to Australia in 1854, she lived the rest of her life in the USA, where she became famous as an exponent of Marina in R.H.Horne's version of *The Duchess of Malfi*. Her husband had played Antonio in the premiere of this version at Sadler's Wells, London in 1850. Emma gained her early stage experience in English provincial theatres. She married Waller in 1849. In 1854 she and her husband came to Australia from San Francisco, and enjoyed successful, prolonged seasons in Sydney, Melbourne, Hobart, and Launceston 1854-55. Ophelia, Juliet, Desdemona, and Marina were her most successful roles. In 1855 she played Lady Macbeth in Melbourne to the Macbeth of G.V.Brooke. Her first London appearance was at Drury Lane in 1856 as Pauline in *The Lady of Lyons*. In 1857 she made her first appearance in Philadelphia as Ophelia, and the following year made her New York debut in *The Duchess of Malfi*. As with so many 19th century husband and wife theatrical partnerships, Emmas was the more talented and resourceful of the two.

Walter Brand; or, The Duel in the Mist. Comedy by E.Fitzball, Surrey, London 30.12.1833; Royal Victoria, Sydney 7.12.1840. (See: Multiple setting).

Walters, George (1853-?). Progressive Unitarian minister who was also a successful playwright. Born in Liverpool, England, he was educated at Rawdon Baptist College, and then at the Unitarian College, Manchester. In 1884, after a long pastorate in Scotland, he accepted the pastorate of the Unitarian Church at Eastern Hill, Melbourne. He stayed there for four years before accepting a Sydney pastorate. His three produced plays are: *Joseph of Canaan* (1895), *The Southern Cross*, with W.A.Cuneo, and *Thou Fool* (1900).

Waltz Dream, A. 3-act operetta, text F.Doerman and L.Jacobson, music O.Straus, Carl, Vienna as *Ein Waltzertraum*, 2.3.1907; Hick's, London 7.3.1908; Her Majesty's, Sydney 12.2.1910, initial 28 performances.

Wanda. 5-act drama by George Leitch, from Ouida's novel (1883), Bijou, Melbourne 28.5.1887, initial 18 performances.

Wang. Comic opera, text J.Goodwin, music W.Morse, Broadway, New York 4.5.1891; Criterion, Sydney 9.11.1901, initial 12 performances.

Wasters, The. 3-act comedy by Arthur H.Adams, Unley City Hall, Adelaide 27.8.1910, initially 1 performance.

Waterman, The; or, The First of August. 2-act ballad opera, text and music Charles Dibdin, Little Haymarket, London 8.8.1774; Royal, Sydney 24.5.1834.

Wattle Tree Farm. 1-act play by Alfred Hill, Repertory Theatre, Sydney 28.7.1914, initially 1 performance.

Weekes, Inigo Tyrrell. (See: Tyrrell, Inigo).

Werner. 5-act tragedy by George Gordon, Lord Byron, Royal, Bristol 25.1.1830; Our Lyceum, Sydney 26.9.1856, also at Royal, Melbourne on same date.

What Next? Farce by T.J.Dibdin, Drury Lane, London 29.2.1816; Royal, Sydney 23.3.1833.

What the Public Wants. 4-act drama by Arnold Bennett, Aldwych, London 2.5.1909; Melbourne Repertory, Athenaeum Hall 16.3.1912, initially 1 performance.

Whitworth, Robert Percy (1831-1901). Born in Devonshire and trained for the law, Whitworth came to Australia in 1855 and began a varied life partly dedicated to journalism, partly to the stage, and to the writing of novels, short stories, poems, and plays. He acted for a while in G.V.Brooke's company in Melbourne, then moved from the stage to the land, going in for horse-breaking in the Hunter River district of NSW. In the early 1860s he returned to Sydney and took up journalism. It was here that he wrote his first 3 plays, all of them designed to incorporate the dances, war games, and songs of a band of Maoris from New Zealand — *Whakeau the Pakeha Chief* (1862), *Rangatira Wahena; or, The Maori Queen* (1862), and *Haie Waikonaitai* (1862). In 1865 Whitworth's novel, *Mary Summers. A Romance of the Australian Bush,* was serialised in the *Australian Journal.* He was said by this journal to be the author of *Uncle John, The White Woman of Mundarrah, The Regent's Vengeance, Whakau, the Pakeha Maori,* and *Matutira, the Maori Queen.* Again he tired of journalism, and this time took a job as riding master. A serious fall put an end to that, and he moved on to Melbourne, where he worked at various times on the *Argus, Age,* and other newspapers, as well as running, unsuccessfully, one or two journals of his own. While in Melbourne he had three plays produced, *Catching a Conspirator* (1867), *Maximilian; or, The Empress and the Traitor* (1867), and *The Duke's Arrival* (1867). He spent the next few years in New Zealand, where he acted for a while in Auckland and Dunedin theatres, and had two more plays produced, *Flying Jib; or, The Derby Day* (1868), and *The True Heart* (1868). He then travelled from centre to centre, sometimes acting, sometimes working on one of the local newspapers. In 1870 he was in Dunedin, working on the *Otago Daily Times.* In this year he went with a party to explore Martins Bay, on the West Coast, to find a site for a settlement. The report he wrote and published under the title 'Overland from Martin's Bay, New Zealand,' was so well done that the Otago Provincial Council voted him a bonus of £50. The following year he was back in Melbourne, in time to play Joseph Grudge in W.H.Cooper's *Colonial Experience.* Returning to journalism, he also compiled a *Handbook of the Land Acts of Victoria, New South Wales, South Australia, and Queensland* (1872), and published four collections of his short stories. In 1873 his

Left: William John Wilson 1883
Below: Garnet Walch

novel, *Lost and Found,* was published. Another, *Cobb's Box,* was published in 1875, together with a Christmas annual called *Crushed.* Then followed other novels, short story collections, Christmas annuals, official guides, a volume of the 2-volume *Victoria and Its Metropolis Past and Present,* and *A Short History of the Eureka Stockade* (1891). His last plays were *The Red Cross* (1876), *Puck; or, Gladys Geraint* (1878), *The Three Ambassadors* (1879), and *Rum and Bitters* (1881).

White Australia; or, The Empty North. 4-act drama by Randolph Bedford, King's, Melbourne 26.6.1909, initial 18 performances.

Whither? 3-act drama by Mary Wilkinson, Melbourne Repertory, St Peter's Hall 18.7.1914, initial 3 performances.

Wig, The. 1-act farce by Ethel Turner, University Dramatic Society, Royal Standard, Sydney 24.7.1894, initially 1 performance. (See: *Seven Little Australians; Wonder Child, The*).

William Tell. (See: *Guillaume Tell*).

Williamson, James Cassius (1845-1913). Born in Pennsylvania, a doctor's son, Williamson displayed an interest in the theatre at an early age. As soon as he reached 16 he entered on the life of the travelling actor, sometimes employed, sometimes not. Perseverance and hard work brought him in a few years to New York, where he became a member of J.W.Wallack's famous company. He concentrated on dialect roles, the more bizarre the better. At the same time he was busy learning the arts of production and management. In 1871 he went to San Francisco, where he first met and acted with his future wife, Maggie Moore. They married in 1873, and the following year they first appeared in the play that ultimately made them world famous — *Struck Oil* — he playing a sentimental old Dutch shoemaker, described as a wonderful piece of character acting, and she his daughter. He had bought the play from an old amateur dramatist named Sam Smith for £100. He paid another playwright to rewrite and expand it, made a few changes of his own, and from then on never looked back, once he and Maggie had reached Australia. They had been engaged for this tour by George Coppin. Against all advice, Williamson opened his Australian tour in Melbourne with *Struck Oil* on 1.8.1874, and was rewarded with a run of 43 consecutive nights. In Sydney the play ran for 50 nights. The same success greeted them everywhere they played it including India, England, Scotland, Ireland, and the USA. The immense success of the play, plus the undoubted talent he and his wife displayed in whatever other play they acted in, laid the foundations of his fortunes in his adopted country. The pair returned to Australia in 1879 with the rights to the Gilbert and Sullivan *HMS Pinafore*. A year later he took his first plunge into management with the formation of his own comic opera company. In between their appearances with this company he and his wife continued to give dramatic performances — chiefly of *Struck Oil,* and the plays of Dion Boucicault, all of them sure-fire successes but by now becoming a little overfamiliar. He tried desperately to find a play which would repeat the success of *Struck Oil*, and for a while thought he had found it in a play called *Eureka*, written for him by the American playwright Fred Marsden (real name W.A.Silver). He first produced this at the Melbourne Royal on 23.10.1880, but it was a failure. In 1882 he went into partnership with Arthur Garner and George Musgrove, and J.C.Williamson's, known as 'the Firm,' was born; a firm which, despite many changes in partnership and control over the years, held a strong hold on the Australian popular theatre until well into the present century. With his success in the USA and England, Williamson could be said to have had a foot in both camps, and there is no doubt that in his view all good things theatrical came only from those 2 countries. Throughout his managerial life he relied almost exclusively on the imported play, comic opera, and musical comedy, and rarely produced an Australian example of these genres. He was in the entertainment business, and he knew his business very well. In one sense he could be said to have created a taste for the frothy and ephemeral, in another he could be said to have done no more than feed an existing hunger. He was thus able to build up a monopoly which controlled the major Australian and New Zealand theatres as well as most of the stage successes from England and America. Just how much his monopoly stifled the growth of a purely Australian theatre can only be conjectured. He did, in a sense, 'support' Australian actors (he had to, they were his bread and butter), but he always drove a hard wage bargain. With Australian playwrights he had no sympathy whatever, as the testimony of Arthur H.Adams, Alfred Hill, Steele Rudd, Ethel Turner, and others has shown. He did put on one or two such plays during his more than 30 years as actor, producer, and manager, but he usually greeted each offer of a play by an Australian author with the stock response: 'Australians do not care for Australian plays.' This despite the success of plays by George Darrell, Garnet Walch, Alfred Dampier, Steele Rudd, Albert Edmunds, and others. Perhaps it was not the Australian play he distrusted so much as his own judgment. Years of buying works which had proved successful overseas probably diminished whatever ability he may have had to judge the worth of a play fresh from the author's hands. It is difficult today to understand how a man who had made his greatest success in a play called *Struck Oil* could have overlooked the possibilities in a play such as *On Our Selection*. Soon after Williamson's death in 1913 (he died in Paris, but was buried in his native America) his 'Firm' launched a plan for a J.C.Williamson Memorial Theatre to seat 1500 at a cost of £40 000. This was to have been built on the Melbourne site first occupied by Coppin's Olympic. The architect, W.Pitt, designed a building of which the Melbourne people would have been proud, but it was never built. No doubt one of the things which militated against fulfilment of this tribute to Williamson's memory was the outbreak the following year of World War I.

Wilson, William John (1833-1909). Artist and scenepainter, Wilson was born in London, the son and grandson of artists. His grandfather, John Wilson, was a Scottish marine and theatrical painter. His two sons, William and John, were also talented artists. W.A.Wilson, W.J.'s father, was an architectural painter, and scenic artist at Drury Lane, Covent Garden, Her Majesty's, and other London theatres. W.J.Wilson did his first scenepainting at Edinburgh at the age of 12, helping his father with a production of *Macbeth*. Returning to London, the 2 of them worked for some time in the painting room at Drury Lane. In his spare time W.J.Wilson concentrated on his easel paintings, exhibiting with the Society of British Artists (of which his grandfather was one of the founders), and the Royal Academy. Towards the end of 1854, looking for bigger opportunities, he embarked for Australia, arriving in Melbourne on 6.3.1855. Here he was employed almost immediately at the only theatre, the Queen's. Actively employed for the next 5 years at the Queen's, Olympic, and Royal, he also helped to launch Melbourne's Garrick Club, whose members included R.H.Horne, G.H.Rogers, W.Akhurst, G.Ireland, J.Smith, and Dr Nield. In 1861 Wilson moved to Sydney, where (apart from brief visits to New Zealand) he spent the rest of his life as scenepainter, theatre lessee and manager, artist, and theatre decorator. He painted many scenes for the various opera companies, for pantomimes, and for Shakespeare's plays — all of which demanded work more colourful and grandiose than the average melodrama. For some years he was associated with the actors and playwrights W.H.Cooper, G.Darrell, Mrs Scott Siddons, and the Majeronis. A year before his death he held an exhibition of his small land and seascapes at his home in Dowling Street — scenes on the Thames, on the Australian coast, in Venice, and in rural England.

Windmill, The. 2-act operetta, text by C.H.Smith from the French of Melesville, music M.Heuzenroeder, Albert Hall, Adelaide 18.6.1891, initially 2 performances.

Wings. Side scenes placed obliquely or horizontally one behind the other, each side of the stage, to hide the view of the backstage area from the audience. The spaces between the wings were also used by the actors as entrances and exits. Until, towards the end of the century, free-standing wings were used these were always moved in grooves set in or on the stage floor, and in an extension arm at the top of the wing.

Winning Ticket, The. 4-act drama by William Anderson and Temple Harrison, King's, Melbourne 10.9.1910, initial 36 performances.

Winstanley, Eliza (1818-1882). The first Australian-trained actress to achieve success overseas, Eliza played her first stage part in a production of *Clari; or, The Maid of Milan* at Sydney Royal in 1834. She arrived in Sydney from England with her family in 1833, and as her father was almost immediately employed as scenepainter at the Royal, it is not surprising that she should show an interest in the theatre, or that she should be put through her paces by the leading actors of that theatre. She proved to be a 'quick study,' i.e. she quickly read and memorised a part. After her debut she moved into the donkey-work of the average stock company, playing every conceivable role from the distressed heroine of melodrama to Ophelia, transferring to the Royal Victoria when it opened in 1838, and then in turn to the Olympic and the Royal City. In 1841 she married H.C.O'Flaherty, a violinist in the Royal Victoria orchestra, and 5 years later, after constant slogging in the theatres of Sydney, Hobart, and Melbourne she left Australia to try her luck overseas. Despite her marriage, her stage name continued to be Winstanley, sometimes Mrs, sometimes Miss. She made her first appearance in England at the Manchester Royal in 1847, subsequently making a total 17 appearances. From Manchester she moved to other provincial theatres, finally finishing up at the Princess's in London. Then she crossed over to the USA, appearing in New York at Wallack's in *The School for Scandal* on 27.9.1847. Here she stayed until, on 4.9.1848, she transferred to the Park, New York. Then followed a season in Philadelphia, after which she was back in New York for the opening of Burton's on 19.11.1849. Then, at the invitation of James Anderson, who had leased Drury Lane, she returned to London. His season there was not a success, and there is a blank in her story until November 1851, when she joined Charles Kean's company at the Princess's, playing Mistress Quickly in *The Merry Wives of Windsor*. Here she remained for some three or four years, playing with Kean in the command performances at Windsor Castle as well as those at the theatre. When Kean completed his season at the Princess's she transferred to the Lyceum. In the meantime, as a second string to her bow, she began a career as a writer, publishing her first novel, *Shifting Scenes in Theatrical Life,* in 1859. From then on she seems to have made her living as a novelist and short story writer, and as editor of the women's magazine, *Bow Bells*. In her novels, published in *Bow Bells* in the main, she drew a great deal on her first hand knowledge of the Sydney of 1833-1846. She is known to have published at least 18 novels, though she may well have published more, and seven of these found their way to the English stage as melodramas. She died in Australia, having returned in the late 1870s or early 1880s.

Winter's Tale, The. Romance by William Shakespeare, believed to have been first performed in London in 1610 or 1611; Royal Victoria, Sydney 3.2.1845.

Woman of No Importance, A. 4-act drama by Oscar Wilde,

Nellie Stewart as Prince Charming 1901

Haymarket, London 19.4.1893; Criterion, Sydney 9.1.1897, initial 12 performances.

Woman Tamer, The. 1-act play by Louis Esson, Turn Verein Hall, Melbourne 5.10.1910, initially 1 performance.

Women as men. In his *Music in London* (1890), George Bernard Shaw writes of the sex inversion roles in burlesques and opera bouffe that the rule was 'women should appear as men and the men be hidden as much as possible behind the women.' He says that in these productions 'every regiment of soldiers was a row of mincing, plump, self-conscious young women in satin uniforms, pinched at the waist and toes, and bulbous in the unpinched regions.' Women and men have, of course, represented their opposite ever since the theatre began. Not even such characters as Hamlet, Romeo, or Macbeth have been considered sacrosanct by women, while they have also delighted in playing the more risque and daring characters such as highwaymen, burglars, and 'mashers' or 'swells.' But the 4 principal venues for the female transvestite on the stage have always been the pantomime (where the principal 'boy' was always a girl), the burlesque, and the comic opera. The first woman to play a man on the Australian stage was the actress Maria Taylor, who in 1834 played the leading role in W.T.Moncrieff's *Giovanni in London* (1817). (See: Men as women).

Wonder Child, The. 3-act musical drama by J.J.Utting, adapted from Ethel Turner's novel (1901), Royal, Hobart 25.11.1903, initially 1 performance. (See: *Seven Little Australians; Wig, The*).

Wreck of the Pinafore, The. 2-act comic opera, text Horace Lingard, music Luscombe Searelle, Prince of Wales, Dunedin, New Zealand 29.11.1880; initially 2 performances.

Wyatt, Joseph (1788?-1860). Said at the time of his death to have spent 47 years in the colony of NSW, Wyatt's age was given on his death certificate as 72. He was born in England, place and date unknown, and died at his home, Castlereagh Street, Sydney on 20.7.1860. For many years he was a hotel or tavern keeper, and then he conducted a highly successful haberdashery business in Pitt Street, acquiring in the process various city properties of considerable value. In 1833 he retired from shop-keeping. One of many businessmen who saw that while Levey's Royal was badly or uneconomically conducted it was nevertheless making a great deal of money, Wyatt was one of 6 Sydney businessmen who persuaded Levey to lease his theatre to them for 2 years. They took over at the beginning of 1835. Early in 1836 Wyatt became sole lessee, having apparently bought out the other lessees, and towards the end of the same year he was named as proprietor of another theatre being built in Pitt Street. This, the Royal Victoria, was opened in 1838. Knowing that Sydney at this time could not support two theatres, he bought the

Royal from Levey's widow (Levey had died in 1837) and closed it. In 1854 Wyatt's lease of the land on which the Royal Victoria stood expired, and he was unable to renew it. He decided to build another and better theatre, the Prince of Wales. But at this time most of Sydney's best tradesmen were still on the goldfields, and those left were not only slow and inadequate, but also costly. By the time the new theatre opened it had cost him more than £30 000. To make matters worse, it was not a success, for Sydney was still not ready for 2 theatres, and certainly not 2 theatres the size of the Royal Victoria and Prince of Wales. Finally, Wyatt struck financial difficulties. He had over-extended himself and could not meet his commitments. His properties and his theatre were all sold in an attempt to fill what seemed to be a bottomless well of debt. In 1858 he had to let his Prince of Wales go for a third of its value. When he died, a lonely and embittered man, it was said that at one time he had owned 6 houses with stores behind in George Street, between King and Market Streets; 3 other houses in George Street; several houses in Pitt Street, and houses in Castlereagh Street, Brougham Place, and opposite his theatre in Castlereagh Street.

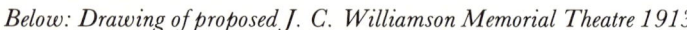

Above: Emma and Daniel Willmarth Waller (right) in The Hunchback, *Sydney 1854*
Below: Drawing of proposed J. C. Williamson Memorial Theatre 1913

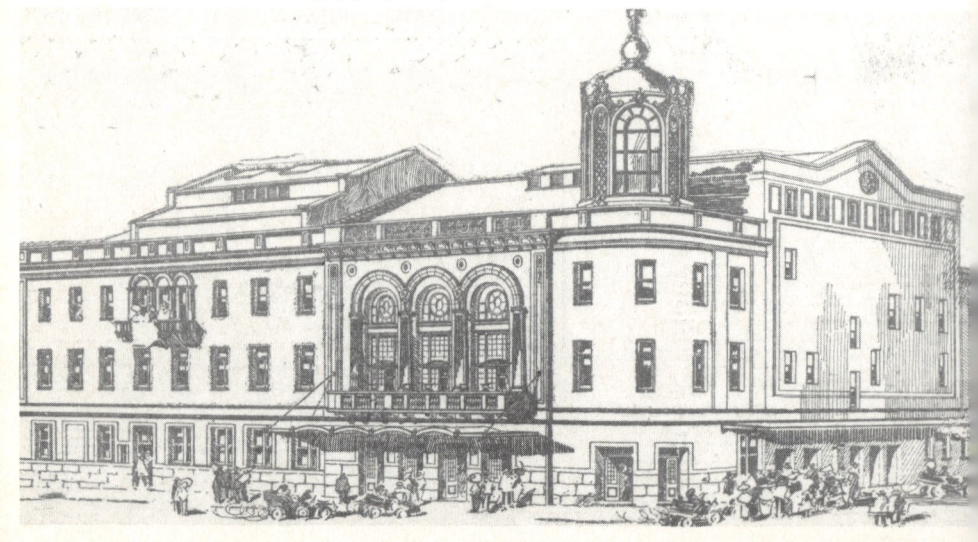

Y

Yates, Theodosia (1815-1904). Great grandchild of Mary Ann Yates, who was a member of David Garrick's company at Drury Lane, London. Theodosia, the mother of the actress Nellie Stewart, was herself a member of the Drury Lane company when, in 1841, Mrs Clarke from Hobart asked her if she would join a company she was forming to go back to Tasmania with her. Theodosia thus joined the talented Howsons and one or two others in a small group which arrived in Tasmania in 1842. She made her first appearance in Hobart at a concert in the Argyle Rooms, and from that time onwards was not only intimately connected with the development of the Australian theatre, in opera as well as drama, but was also one of the most popular stage personalities of her period. When she arrived in Hobart in 1842 she adopted the name Mrs Stirling, which she used until she married a theatre musician named James Guerin. He died in the early 1850s, leaving her a widow with 2 young girls, Docy and Maggie. In 1857 she married a young English emigrant named Richard Towzey, who became an actor and changed his name to Stewart. Their first child, Eleanor Stewart Towzey, grew up to become 'Australia's idol,' Nellie Stewart. Their second child, Richard, was also an actor. Theodosia was yet another of those remarkable Victorian women of the stage who managed everything and everybody, and yet remained essentially feminine and lovable. She acted night after night, 6 nights a week; sang in operas (she was Australia's first Maritana) or frolicked in knockabout comedies; played Lady Macbeth one night, Lady Teazle the next; looked after a husband and 4 children; travelled immense distances by the most primitive modes of transport, and yet survived it all to become a public favourite and grand lady of the Australian theatre.

Yeoman of the Guard, The. 2-act comic opera, text W.S.Gilbert, music A.Sullivan, Savoy, London 3.10.1888; Princess's, Melbourne 20.4.1889, initial 42 performances.

You Never Can Tell. 3-act drama by George Bernard Shaw, Bijou, London 23.3.1898; Royal, Melbourne 27.7.1912, initial 13 performances.

Young, Charles Horace Frisbee (1819-1874). Born in Doncaster, England, the child of actor parents, Young received a thorough training in all aspects of stage work from his earliest years. In early manhood he gave up the stage for a few years and joined first the navy and then the merchant marine. In 1843 he arrived in Australia as ship's second officer, and was reunited in Hobart with his sister, who was married to the actor G.H.Rogers. He decided to return to the stage making his first appearance in Hobart. In 1845, as a member of George Coppin's company in Launceston, he signed an agreement to travel to Melbourne with the company for a season at the Queen's. Coppin at this time described him as a versatile actor, equally at home in tragedy, comedy, or burlesque, and a good singer and dancer. Before leaving for Melbourne he married the young actress and dancer in the company, Jane Thomson. In 1857 he and his wife returned to England, where the pair acted in a number of productions at the St James's and Sadler's Wells. Returning alone to Australia in 1861, he acted as support to Walter Montgomery and Barry Sullivan during their Melbourne seasons, and then in all the principal Australian and New Zealand theatres until his death in 1874. His wife divorced him in 1862.

Young, Mrs Charles. (See: Vezin, Mrs Hermann).

Youth. Drama in 8 tableaux by P.Meritt and A.Harris, Drury Lane, London 6.8.1881; Royal, Sydney 8.7.1882, initial 47 performances. George Rignold, who played the lead in this, mounted his own production at Her Majesty's, Sydney 22.12.1888, where it had an initial run of 54 performances.

Z

Zar und Zimmermann (Tsar and Carpenter). 3-act opera, text and music G. Lortzing, Leipzig 22.12.1837; Gaiety, London 15.4.1871; Alexandra, Melbourne 16.5.1887, initially 1 performance.

Zigeunerliebe (Gipsy Love). 3-act comic opera, text A.Willner and R.Bodanzky, music Franz Lehar, Carl, Vienna 8.1.1910; English version B.Hood, Daly's, London 1.6.1912; Her Majesty's, Sydney 13.6.1914, initial 48 performances.

Bibliography

Allen, Shirley S., *Samuel Phelps and Sadler's Wells Theatre,* Wesleyan University Press, Connecticut, 1971.
Altick, Richard D., *The Shows of London,* Harvard University Press, Massachusetts, 1978.
Anderson, James R., *An Actor's Life,* Walter Scott Publishing Co. Ltd, London, 1902.
Archer, William, *Play-Making,* Chapman & Hall Ltd, London, 1913.
Baker, H. Barton, *History of the London Stage and its Famous Players (1576-1903),* George Routledge & Son Ltd, London, 2nd ed., 1904.
Baker, Michael, *The Rise of the Victorian Actor,* Croom Helm, London, 1978.
Barker, Kathleen, *The Theatre Royal Bristol 1766-1966,* Society for Theatre Research, London, 1974.
Bedford, Randolph, *Naught to Thirty-Three,* first published 1944, reprinted Melbourne University Press, Melbourne, 1976.
Bergman, Gösta, *Lighting in the Theatre,* Almquist and Wicksell International, Stockholm, 1977.
Blainey, Ann, *The Farthing Poet,* Longmans, London, 1968.
Blom, Eric (ed.), *Everyman's Dictionary of Music,* J. M. Dent & Sons Ltd, London, revised edition, 1954.
Booth, Michael, *English Melodrama,* Herbert Jenkins, London, 1965.
——, *English Plays of the Nineteenth Century.* Vols 1-4, Oxford University Press, London, 1969 (vols 1 and 2) and 1973 (vols 3 and 4).
—— (ed.), *Victorian Theatrical Trades,* Society for Theatre Research, London, 1981.
Bordman, Gerald, *American Musical Theatre,* Oxford University Press, New York, 1978.
Brewer, F. C., *The Drama and Music in New South Wales,* Government Printer, Sydney, 1892.
Brown, T. Allston, *History of the American Stage,* reprint 1870 edition, Benjamin Blom Inc., New York, 1969.

Ceram, C. W., *Archaeology of the Cinema,* Thames & Hudson, London, 1965.
Clinton-Baddeley, V. C., *All Right on the Night,* Putnam, London, 1954.
———, *The Burlesque Tradition,* Methuen & Co. Ltd, London, 1952.
Davidge, William, *Footlight Flashes,* The American News Company, New York, 1866.
Disher, M. Willson, *Melodrama Plots that Thrilled,* Rockliff, London, 1954.
Downes, Peter, *Shadows on the Stage,* John McIndoe, Dunedin, 1975.
Fitzgerald, Percy, *The World Behind the Scenes,* Chatto & Windus, London, 1881.
Fleetwood, Francis, *Conquest. The Story of a Theatre Family,* W. H. Allen, London, 1953.
Forbes-Winslow, D., *Daly's — The Biography of a Theatre,* W. H. Allen, London, 1944.
Fowler, Frank, *Southern Lights and Shadows,* Sampson, Low, London, 1859.
Gascoigne, Bamber, *World Theatre,* Ebury Press, London, 1968.
Hardwick, J. M. D. (ed.), *Emigrant in Motley,* Rockliff, London, 1954.
Heaton, J. H., *Australian Dictionary of Dates,* George Robertson, Sydney, 1879.
Hodges, C. Walter, *Shakespeare's Second Globe,* Oxford University Press, London, 1973.
Holloway, David, *Playing the Empire,* Harrap, London, 1979.
Hughes, Alan, *Henry Irving, Shakespearean,* Cambridge University Press, Cambridge, 1981.
Irvin, Eric, *Theatre Comes to Australia,* University of Queensland Press, Brisbane, 1971.
———, *Gentleman George. King of Melodrama,* University of Queensland Press, Brisbane, 1980.
———, *Australian Melodrama,* Hale & Iremonger, Sydney, 1981.
Jefferson, J., *Autobiography,* T. Fisher Unwin, London, 1890.
Lawrence, W. J., *The Life of Gustavus Vaughan Brooke,* W. & G. Baird, Belfast, 1892.
Leech, C. and Craik, C. W. (eds), *The Revels History of Drama in English,* vol. 6, 1750-1880, Methuen & Co. Ltd, London, 1975.
Levi, J. S. and G. F. J. Bergman, *Australian Genesis. Jewish Convicts and Settlers 1788-1850,* Rigby, Adelaide, 1974.
Lloyds, Frederick, *Practical Guide to Scene-Painting,* George Rowney & Co., London, n.d. (1875).
Loewenberg, Alfred, *Annals of Opera 1597-1940,* John Calder, London, 3rd ed., 1978.
Love, Harold, *The Golden Age of Australian Opera,* Currency Press, Sydney, 1981.
Lubbock, Mark, *The Complete Book of Light Opera,* Putnam & Co. Ltd, London, 1962.
McLaren, Ian F., 'Marcus Clarke: Books and Drama in North America,' *Margin,* vol. 8, 1982, Monash University, Clayton, Victoria.
Mayer, David and Richards, Kenneth (eds), *Western Popular Theatre,* Methuen & Co. Ltd, London, 1977.
Miller, E. Morris, *Australian Literature 1795-1938,* Melbourne University Press, Melbourne 1940, reprinted with corrections and additions, Sydney University Press, Sydney, 1975.

Moody, Richard (ed.), *Dramas From the American Theatre 1762-1909*, World Publishing Company, Cleveland, 1966.
Morley, Henry, *The Journal of a London Playgoer*, George Routledge & Sons Ltd, London, 2nd edition, 1891, reprinted Leicester University Press, Leicester, 1974.
Moses, Montrose J., *The American Dramatist*, Little Brown & Co., Boston, 1925, reprinted Benjamin Blom Inc., New York, 1964.
Newton, H. Chance, *Crime and the Drama*, Stanley Paul & Co. Ltd, London, 1927.
Nicoll, Allardyce, *The Development of the Theatre*, George G. Harrap & Co. Ltd, London, 3rd edition, 1948.
——, *A History of English Drama 1660-1900*, 6 vols, Cambridge University Press, Cambridge, 1965-1973.
Odell, George C. D., *Annals of the New York Stage*, 15 vols, Columbia University Press, New York, 1925-1949.
Orrey, Leslie (ed.), *The Encyclopaedia of Opera*, Pitman Publishing Ltd, London, 1976.
Pask, Edward H., *Enter the Colonies Dancing*, Oxford University Press, Melbourne, 1979.
Pearson, Hesketh, *The Last Actor-Managers*, Methuen & Co. Ltd, London, 1950.
Reade, Eric, *Australian Silent Films*, Lansdowne Press, Melbourne, 1970.
Rees, Abraham, *Cyclopaedia; or, Universal Dictionary of Arts, Sciences, and Literature*, London, 1803-19.
Rees, Terence, *Theatre Lighting in the Age of Gas*, Society for Theatre Research, London, 1978.
Reynolds, Ernest, *Early Victorian Drama 1830-1870*, W. Heffer & Sons Ltd, Cambridge, 1936.
Richards, Kenneth and Thomson, Peter (eds), *Nineteenth-Century British Theatre*, Methuen & Co. Ltd, London, 1971.
Rosenfeld, Sibyl, *A Short History of Scene Design in Great Britain*, Basil Blackwell, Oxford, 1973.
Rowell, George, *The Victorian Theatre*, Oxford University Press, London, 1967.
Sands, Mollie, *Robson of the Olympic*, Society for Theatre Research, London, 1979.
Saxon, A. H., *The Life and Art of Andrew Ducrow*, Archon Books, Connecticut, 1978.
Skill, Marjorie, *Sweet Nell of Old Sydney*, Urania Publishing Company, Sydney, 1973.
Smith, James L. (ed.), *Victorian Melodramas*, Dent, London, 1976.
Southern, Richard, *Changeable Scenery*, Faber & Faber Ltd, London, 1952.
Stewart, Nellie, *My Life's Story*, John Sands Limited, Sydney, 1923.
Tait, Viola, *A Family of Brothers*, Heinemann, Melbourne, 1971.
Thomson, John Mansfield, *A Distant Music*, Oxford University Press, Auckland, 1980.
Trewin, J. C. (ed.), *The Journal of William Charles Macready 1832-1851*, Longmans, London, 1967.
——, *The Pomping Folk in the Nineteenth-Century Theatre*, J. M. Dent, London, 1968.

Tucker, James, *Ralph Rashleigh,* Angus & Robertson, Sydney, 1952.
——, *Jemmy Green in Australia,* Colin Roderick (ed.), Angus & Robertson, Sydney, 1955.
Wearing, J. P., *The London Stage 1890-1899,* The Scarecrow Press, Inc., New Jersey, 1976.
——, *The London Stage 1900-1909,* The Scarecrow Press, Inc., New Jersey, 1981.
White, Eric Walter, *The Rise of English Opera,* John Lehmann, London, 1951.
Winter, Marian Hannah, *The Pre-Romantic Ballet,* Pitman Publishing, London, 1974.
Wischhusen, Stephen (ed.), *The Hour of One. Six Gothic Melodramas,* Gordon Fraser, London, 1975.
Young, William C., *Famous Actors and Actresses On the American Stage,* R. R. Bowker Company, New York, 1975.

Articles

Benwell, Henry L., 'Practical Scene Painting for Amateurs,' *Amateur Work, Illustrated,* series of 31 articles published vols 4-7, Ward, Lock & Co., London, 1884-1888.
Duerdoth, A. G., 'The Early Development of the Carbon Arc,' *Tabs* 13:1 (1955) 24-32.
Esmond, George, 'Theatre Cavalcade. The Stage through the Century,' *South Australian Homes and Gardens,* 1.6.1936.
Fischer, Gerald, 'The Professional Theatre in Adelaide 1838-1922,' *Australian Letters* 2:4 (1960) 79-97.
Goodman, Lawrence P., 'More Light on the Limelight,' *Theatre Survey* 10:2 (1969) 114-120.
Hamilton, Winifred, 'Steele Rudd. His Life and Letters,' ms held by Mitchell Library, Sydney.
Haugher, George. 'Offenbach in English: A Checklist,' *Theatre Notebook* 34:1 (1980) 9-14.
Kennedy, G. A.,'Musical Memoirs,' series of 17 articles on musical activities in Wellington from 1870s, published in the *Dominion* 1936, bound copy in Alexander Turnbull Library, Wellington, New Zealand.
Larson, Orvill K., 'New Evidence on the Origins of the Box Set,' *Theatre Survey* 22:2 (1980) 79-91.
McCredie, A. D., 'Alfred Hill (1870-1960). Some Backgrounds and Perspectives for an Historical Edition,' *Miscellanea Musicologica* 3 (1968) 181-257.
McDermott, Douglas, 'McKean Buchanan: The Actor as Character,' *Theatre Studies* 24-25 (1977-79) 95-106.
McMahon, Morgan, 'Australia's First Players,' *The Lone Hand* 8:44 (1910) 89-96.
Musgrove, Harry, 'Stage Secrets,' series of 16 semi-autobiographical articles, *Table Talk,* August-November 1926.

Oppenheim, Helen, 'The Author of the Hibernian Father: An Early Colonial Playwright,' *Australian Literary Studies* 2:4 (1966) 278-288.
——, 'Coppin — How Great?', *Australian Literary Studies* 3:2 (1967) 126-137.
Starks, The, Monograph 6, Theatre Research W.P.A. Project 8386, L. Estavan (ed.), San Francisco, 1938 (roneoed).
T.G.R., 'Music and the Drama,' *The Queenslander,* Jubilee Number, 7.8.1900, pp.50-52.
Telbin, William, 'Art in the Theatre: Act Drops,' *Magazine of Art,* 1895, pp.335-340.
White, Eric Walter, 'The Usual Banditti,' *Opera* 3:12 (1952) 726-732.
——, 'English Opera in Australia,' *Opera Canada* 15:2 (1973) 14.15.
Wingfield, Lewis, 'The Drama in the Antipodes,' *New Review,* 7 (1892) 217-226.